I0761882

northern lights

northern lights

Leo Solstrom

Northern Lights

For more information contact the author at
www.leosolstrom.com

ISBN: 978-1-7358508-2-5

Solstrom, Leo
Northern Lights / Leo Solstrom - 1st ed.

Summary: A young man named Leo lands a summer job, working at a wilderness canoe camp in the Boundary Waters of Northern Minnesota, where he makes two new friends: Aria and Esther, who join him for a three-day canoe trip surrounded by the lakes, trees, and stars of the North Woods. Their surprising adventures lead to a deeper understanding of true friendship, young love, and the more important things in life.

[1. Identity - Fiction. 2. Adventure - Fiction.
3. Young adult - Fiction. 4. Contemporary romance - Fiction.
5. Friendship - Fiction.] I. Title.

To my beloved and our daughters
for sharing many wonderful trips to
the Boundary Waters with me.

prologue

gods and goddesses

"Anything is possible."

They say the gods and goddesses used to walk the earth long ago before being cast up into the heavens. I wonder . . . what if it were true? What if some of them actually did return to visit us from time to time in the moments that we needed them most? I think it's possible. No, actually, I think they have.

I'm convinced I have been visited by them: gods and goddesses, angels, and spirits in the wilderness at critical times in my life, in times of great joy, and in times of terrible sadness too. In those moments, they have mysteriously shown up and appeared as magnificent human beings clearly out of place, but daring to walk among us and freely share their wisdom with us for a time.

Then, when their time is over, they leave us again. They disappear or are reborn and rise back up to their places in the night sky high above, leaving us with memories, with experiences, and with all the life lessons we've struggled so hard to learn.

They say, "Anything is possible if you just believe." Ever since childhood, I've heard dreamy words like those—from my parents, from teachers and counselors, even from a couple of profs in college. I used to think it was just another slick phrase I'd been led to believe. I figured I'd outgrown words like those, that I didn't believe them anymore, but now I'm not so sure.

It's not easy to explain, but I'm certain that I've been visited by the divine, and I'll never be the same again. I'm not who I used to be. Everything is changed. I see everything and everyone with new eyes.

Now, life is more vibrant and colorful in all sorts of hopeful ways. It's more meaningful and more purposeful. It's deeper, richer, wider, and stronger. Now, life is more thought-provoking, more disconcerting, and more spiritual too.

As to how or why, those questions remain a mystery to me. Still, I can't help but think that there is something greater going on in this world, in our lives, and all around us. Yes, the gods and goddesses are up there somewhere, looking down on us. They're watching with keen interest to see what we will become, to see what we will do with our time on this earth, to see if we will overcome ourselves and rise one day to join them in the sky.

I think it's possible, but for now, I think it's up to us. I believe it's in us, hidden somewhere deep down inside. We just have to find it. We just have to open our hearts and accept it freely. We have to learn to love each other, take care of each other, and talk to each other on a deeper, more meaningful, more powerful level. When we are able to do that, anything is possible.

Anything, absolutely anything, is possible.

chapter 1

On my Way

"There's more water up there than land," they said, "and the only way to see it is by canoe."

I was speeding north on Highway 61, going as fast as possible, zooming past slowpokes who stared at me, bewildered or perhaps amused as I shot around them like an out-of-control bottle rocket, pushing the gas pedal of my old '79 Volkswagen Beetle down hard to the floor. I raced along the narrow pothole-infested highway that hugged every curve and cranny of Lake Superior's North Shore like a worn-out zipper. The cheap VW radio was spewing noise from a classic rock station out of Duluth as my little air-cooled engine happily whistled along, roaring through tunnels cut into huge cliffs of granite, the old tires squealing around hair raising turns where the edge of the road dropped straight down to the rocky shoreline below.

It was Monday, Memorial Day, the 29th of May as I recall. The place I was heading for in such a hurry was up ahead somewhere. I was having a blast weaving around the locals—in and out, back and forth—threading the needle of the North Shore: a place foreign and exotic to me, a place I had never been before. A few leftover blisters from my temp job still tingled in my hands as I hightailed it away from where I'd grown up, the flat fields of Iowa, heading for the North Woods of Minnesota.

It was an exciting day for me: a kid born in North Dakota and then raised, for the most part, in Story City, Iowa. I'd grown up surrounded by a patchwork of family farms, each with muddy pens full of cows and pigs and far-reaching fields of corn and beans. As a boy, I'd spent a fair amount of time in those fields, walking beans and detasseling corn out under the hot sun. It was grueling work but good money for a junior high kid who just wanted to get his first car and a girlfriend to go along with it. In high school, I had gotten used to hard sweaty summer jobs—shingling roofs, milking cows, pitching hay, and hauling fifty-pound bags of feed around on my back.

When I graduated, I chose Concordia College: a liberal arts school in Moorhead, Minnesota. It was a small private college full of friendly people and down-to-earth professors. It was academically challenging, but I loved it. Besides, it was far enough away from Iowa to let me feel as if I were really on my own.

That's not to say that I didn't like my family. They were all right. My dad had always been fairly hands-off, but my mom was another story. She was so affectionate, bubbly, and loving, it almost made me uncomfortable, but I knew she cared deeply for me. I missed my big sister, though, who was going to grad school out west.

After my junior year when school let out in May, I had some time to kill before starting my real job, so I picked up a temp job on the north side of Ames, working in a metal shop for a few weeks. The job was pretty simple. All I had to do was shove long bars of steel re-rod through a giant metal cutting machine—piece after piece, hour after hour, day after day. That was it. For two weeks, that wicked machine twisted my wrists and tore at my hands, sending sharp needles of pain straight through the thick leather gloves that the boss had so graciously given to me.

On the first day, huge blisters bubbled up on the palms of my hands and turned me, overnight, into an aspirin addict. It took a solid week for the blisters to harden up, but the searing pain wouldn't go away. So after two weeks, I quit that wretched job and waited for my real one to begin. For a few days, I loafed around the house and slept in, giving my poor hands a much-needed break from the hell I'd just put them through, all for a few extra bucks. It would be okay. I had a better job waiting for me up north. I relaxed and soaked up the sun in my folks' backyard, dreaming of cool water, clear blue skies, and beautiful golden sunsets.

A few months earlier, I had applied for a couple of jobs at some outdoor adventure camps in Minnesota. I knew the pay wouldn't be as good as a factory or farm job. I was simply looking for one that didn't involve carrying heavy bags of animal feed or shoving steel bars of re-rod through a noisy metal chopper all day. The job that intrigued me the most was the one I ended up getting and where I was heading in such an awful hurry.

It was a canoe camp called Northern Lights Adventure Center, tucked away in the northeast corner of Minnesota, just this side of the Canadian border. I had applied to be a canoe guide at the camp, which was located on the eastern edge of the Boundary Waters Canoe Area. The BWCA encompassed about one million acres of undisturbed wilderness in the Superior National Forest, which had been set aside years ago to preserve its natural beauty. "There's more water up there than land," they said, "and the only way to see it is by canoe." All that was required was that I was twenty-one and lifeguard certified. That was easy. The rest they would teach me.

I was eager to get there. I had been driving north since daybreak, gassing it straight up I-35 into the Twin Cities, where I suddenly found myself caught in a traffic jam surrounded by hundreds of other vehicles going in the same direction. We were all crammed together tightly on the huge four-lane freeway that clearly wasn't wide enough for all the noisy cars and trucks that gradually slowed down to a crawl and then a complete standstill, hopelessly stuck in the morning rush hour traffic. Everyone sat paralyzed in their cars, bumper to bumper, moving forward a few feet, then braking hard, then moving forward again, revving their engines and staring blankly ahead. The traffic slowly inched its way forward like a herd of trapped turtles, crawling ever closer to the tall skyscrapers that gleamed like heavenly crystals in the early morning light.

Surrounded by so many city slickers in nice new automobiles, I felt a little out of place in my bright yellow VW convertible, inching my way through the big city with the soft top down. I got a few stares, but I was used to it. After all, my car was a bit unusual. It wasn't just a plain old Volkswagen Beetle. I was driving in style.

A few years earlier at a party right after my high school graduation, a couple of girlfriends and I got a little tipsy and decided to decorate my old wreck of a car. We, meaning mostly they, painted flowers, butterflies, and peace signs all over it, turning it overnight into a flaming hippie-mobile. The next morning when I sobered up, it was a bit of a shock to see what they had done, but the cute makeover gradually won me over. So, I decided to keep it that way on into college. It was a little weird, but I took a certain degree of pride in having the coolest car on campus, and besides, I never had trouble finding it in a crowded parking lot again.

The congested mess through the Twin Cities seemed as if it would last for eternity, but then like the parting of the Red Sea, we were clear again. As the freeway opened up ahead, everyone blasted off like Indy racecars. I tore off in my little yellow Bug too, leaving a smoky haze in my wake, curving east around some old run-down buildings, roaring side by side with a sweet blue Mustang through a couple of dark, dingy tunnels, and then flying over the Mississippi River like a rusty tin can shot out of a homemade potato gun.

The smog and congestion of Minneapolis gradually gave way to a wide-open stretch of four-lane freeway that wound northeast out of the big city. All of us in the northbound lanes raced away to freedom as we laughed at all the suckers on the other side who were slowing down to a crawl, preparing to inch their way down into the belly of the beast. From there on out for me, it was a straight shot north to where I knew my dream job was waiting.

The long straight stretch of freeway north of the Twin Cities seemed to remind me of what I was leaving behind: my home, my family, my friends, my girlfriend . . . everything it seemed. My life was going nowhere, which was kind of ironic because it was an exciting day for me. After all, I *was* going somewhere. I didn't know exactly where, but I was in an awful hurry to get there.

To be completely honest, I was probably just trying to escape something, or a lot of things: my past, my childhood, my fears, my failures, my . . . I don't know . . . something, but there was plenty to choose from in my life. Go ahead, pick one. You'd be right!

I had just broken up with my girlfriend, Bess, and I was single again. It was a phone breakup, and it sucked.

"All right, you're a free man now," she said bitterly. "That's what you want. Go ahead, have it your way. I'll see you around."

That was her parting shot, and it was a lot nicer than it could've been. So, I took it and hung up the phone. I couldn't face her like a decent human being . . . so I ran.

It was my fault. I was afraid to commit. At least that's what Bess said. She was right, of course. Maybe that's why I pulled out so soon. I could see the handwriting on the wall. We were in one of those death spirals, falling tragically straight down out of the sky. Actually, it had been out of control for months. I'd been getting ready for it to crash and burn, and sure enough, it did.

I felt bad for hurting her like that. It was just so damned unsettling to realize how quick and easy it was to do, but I knew in my heart that I didn't love her. So, I made up a lot of lame excuses for my poor behavior, and I told myself I wasn't about to be tied down again anytime soon. Still, I was a free man, and it felt good.

But my hands still hurt. My head hurt too, and doggone it . . . my heart hurt too. I think it made me reckless. Maybe that's why I was racing north like a maniac. I was running away from everything: my family, my hometown, my past life, my personal failures, my fears of intimacy and commitment . . . even myself.

As I zipped along north of Minneapolis, the landscape gradually changed from familiar oaks and maples to stands of aspen, pine, and spruce. I didn't get too excited about it—the green of it all—but as the freeway made a long slow curve down into the bustling city of Duluth, I could tell something was different. It felt a lot like coming in for a landing in a crop duster plane back in Iowa.

As I descended from the bluff, I could see the old city's tall buildings tucked up close against the steep hillside to the west. Huge loading docks, enormous piles of iron ore, and massive processing plants were scattered everywhere along the lakefront, as if tossed randomly about in a rush to get the old logging city up and running a long time ago.

But what struck me the most was the beautiful big blue waters of Lake Superior. After an entire day of seeing nothing except green everywhere, I decided that blue was my new favorite color—deep luminescent sapphire blue—just like the glistening waters of that enormous lake.

Large ships moved at a snail's pace far out on the lake, while others chugged carefully around the bay. One big brown barge was passing slowly under a huge steel frame bridge that had been raised to let it pass through, supposedly on its way to a shipyard in Superior, Wisconsin, which looked like a sleepy little village compared to the bustling city of Duluth.

As I descended from the bluff, the city gradually swallowed me whole. I raced along, swerving right, then left, ducking under overpasses, rushing ahead with all the other traffic, wondering where everyone was going in such a hurry. But of course, I was in a rush too, anxious to get through the city and up north to the summer job that awaited me. As I raced ahead, I got lost again in dreamy thoughts of quiet lakes and sunsets, when suddenly, the freeway curved sharply up to the left and abruptly ended at a red stoplight.

I slammed on the brakes and came to a sudden stop along with everyone else, and waited for the light to turn green. I studied the road signs—a bit confused—but by the time everyone started rolling again, I had it figured out. I followed the two lanes that turned right and continued north on Highway 61, this time at a more relaxed pace, cutting through a scenic part of town, where old houses, each one unique and well kept, lined the road that eventually narrowed down to just two lanes. Soon I was free of the big city and zooming off again, going as fast as I possibly could.

Just like everyone else, I was in a hurry too.

chapter 2
the edge of a knife

"It was simply impossible to comprehend the fierce, raw wildness of it all."

At a certain point along the highway, it dawned on me that I was entering a strange new world. In fact, it felt as if I were caught in the middle of two strange new worlds, not just one. On my left was the thick boreal forest of the North Woods, and on my right were the rugged cliffs that dropped away to the choppy waters of Lake Superior. The cliffs rose and fell and plummeted steeply down, sometimes straight down to the rocky shoreline below.

I had a sudden sense of how massive and unforgiving that great body of water actually was. After driving for an hour, it had become so vast and wide, I could no longer see the other side of it. I wondered how far down it went and how many millions of gallons of water it held. Aside from its breathtaking beauty, there was no way to fully appreciate the immense power and ferocity of that mighty lake. From my vantage point high above, it looked like a pretty postcard with tiny whitecaps rolling gently into the stony beaches along the shoreline. On that bright, sunny spring day, it was simply impossible to comprehend the fierce, raw wildness of it all.

As I raced northeast, it felt as if I were traveling on the edge of a long sharp knife, with the lake on my right and the forest on my left. As I moved along, it became apparent that the forest on the left was just as wild and foreign and fierce as the lake on the right. The hills and bluffs rose steeply, sometimes precariously straight up from the road, which made me feel as if I were driving along an ancient scar cut into the wilderness long ago. The road was nothing more than a thin slice of narrow pavement that barely scratched the surface of the dense foreboding forest next to the enormous lake. It was true wilderness, thick with pine and spruce, aspen and birch, and the underbrush so dense in some places, you'd need a machete to work your way through.

The winding red road seemed to be the last sanctuary of human civilization, except for the occasional cabins or lodges tucked up close to the highway on tiny plots of land cut into the woods here and there. Behind the cabins and up above them, however, lay that thick, impenetrable wilderness that hemmed everything in and kept me hugging the thin spindly highway along the shoreline.

"How had people survived up here all these years?" I wondered. "It must have been a rough life, scratching a living in this cold unforgiving forest on the edge of Lake Superior, which stretched for hundreds of miles to the north far into Canada."

I continued on, zooming northeast as fast as my little car could carry me, fascinated by the allure of the wilderness, which was calling to me and drawing me ever closer. Ever since I'd first heard my college friends talk about the beauty and splendor of Northern Minnesota, I had an intense desire to go and see it for myself. I'd listened intently to some of them rave about working up there too, and when I had the opportunity to make a break from the familiar surroundings of Iowa, I jumped at the chance. It was that untamed wildness and mystery of the North Woods that drove me to apply for the job as a wilderness canoe guide. And there I was, finally, heading straight into it for an entire summer.

After two-plus hours, I coasted down a long hill into Grand Marais: the last town I would see for three months. I stopped to fill up on gas and have a quick look around. It was a cute little tourist town nestled up next to the lake, complete with a cozy harbor, a handful of sailboats tied up in the bay, and a tiny lighthouse set out on a rocky pier.

It had a warm, friendly feel that made me want to linger just a bit. I took a few minutes to stroll around town and people-watch for a while. The main street was lined with a few art galleries, some quaint cafés, and several novelty shops that specialized in handmade crafts and candy. You could get the best donuts in the world there and all kinds of odd Scandinavian souvenirs of varying appropriateness. The camping supply stores in town had just about everything needed for a wilderness adventure. You could also get all sorts of cheesy custom-made T-shirts, for cheap, in several shops scattered around town. It was definitely a tourist trap, but a lovely one.

After about an hour, I walked back to my VW Beetle and put the top back up. Then, I slid into the front seat and hit the road again. I backtracked a bit and found the sign for Highway 12, which was referred to by the locals as the Gunflint Trail. I turned right and gunned my car up the steep city street that climbed straight up the hill and deposited the vehicles onto the trail, which was another narrow highway lined with tall evergreens, aspen, and birch. The road continued up the steep slope that rose above the little town, heading into the thick forest that would have been utterly impassable, except for that rusty red road that seemed to swerve and slice daringly straight into the thick of it.

The road was narrow and dangerous to follow—curving sharply around massive hills, cutting across thick ravines, swerving close to drop-offs and lakes below, and at times, shooting straight north like a patriotic shotgun aimed directly at the southern border of Canada. I continued on, driving slower than before, heading for the end of the trail at the eastern entrance to the Boundary Waters.

I followed the road, reading the peculiar wooden signs that marked all the resorts, lakes, camps, and getaways nestled all along the way. I kept an eye out for moose and bear that I'd been told roamed freely across the entire region. As I neared the end of the trail, the curves in the road became sharper and tighter. One curve nearly sent me off into a swampy ditch next to the road, so I finally slowed down and took it easy the rest of the way.

At long last, I spotted the sign for Northern Lights Adventure Center: the place I'd call home for the next ten weeks. I hung a left and slowly coasted down a steep gravel road that ended in a parking lot half full of cars and vans next to a beautiful blue lake. The only other building I could see was a brown cabin built along the shoreline just a little way down from a long wooden dock. Out on the lake, a large yellow canoe was heading straight for the dock where two other people were waiting with their luggage.

"Okay, I made it," I mumbled as I stretched my arms and legs from the long day's ride. "I'm actually doing this."

As I threw my heavy duffel bag over my shoulder, my hands flinched with one final shot of pain. I tucked my sleeping bag and a pillow under my left arm and grabbed my guitar out of the back seat. I glanced briefly at my green John Deere farmer's cap resting on the dashboard. After a brief hesitation, I snatched it up and flipped it on top of my head.

"Who cares if I'm from Iowa," I thought to myself. "This place is probably full of hicks just like me."

I heaved a long nervous sigh and walked casually down to the big wooden dock as the yellow canoe gently coasted in off the lake. I didn't have a clue what I was getting myself into, but at that point, there was no turning back.

My dream job was about to begin.

chapter 3

first impressions

"Welcome to Northern Lights!"

"Greetings!" the woman in the front of the big canoe called out to the three of us waiting on the dock. There were four high school boys, who looked like little Viking sailors, doing all the paddling. One was in the back, steering the enormous boat while the other three were in the middle, working up quite a sweat.

"Welcome to Northern Lights!" the woman in the front called again. She looked like the captain of a ship, who was just along for the ride. "Would someone be so kind as to grab on to the bow of the boat as we pull up to the landing!"

I dropped my gear and grabbed on to the front of the canoe before it hit the dock. The other two helped out as well, and together we pulled the big boat in safely. The paddlers held on to the side of the dock as the woman stepped out onto the landing. She had successfully gotten everyone else to do all the work for her, and it looked like she was used to getting her way most of the time.

I recognized her from the recruiting fair at Concordia College. She was the camp program director. She was probably about thirty years old, fairly tall, with gray eyes, high cheekbones, and blond shoulder-length hair that appeared to have been bleached in the sun. Her arms and face were sunburned as well. She spoke with a slight Scandinavian accent, with thick R's and extra-long O's, like many others I knew who'd grown up in Northern Minnesota. She looked stern and carried herself in a way that seemed to command attention.

"Thanks for helping us out there!" she exclaimed loudly and with slightly exaggerated hand gestures, similar to many of my professors in college. Immediately, I knew who was in charge and where I stood in the pecking order.

"I'm Cassie, the summer program director at Northern Lights," she announced. "I'm in charge of all the programs this summer, including base camp and out-trips. If you're a canoe guide or a base camp counselor, you belong to me."

I listened attentively to her welcome speech, but her style was a bit over the top. I remembered interviewing with Cassie a few months earlier back at school. She seemed slightly different from before, not as easygoing and relaxed as I'd been expecting. It was as if she had switched gears somehow since then. She appeared to be in command and control mode for the summer.

She recognized all three of us, though, and greeted us by name. There was a girl named Anika, who was a first-year canoe guide like me, and a big guy named Jim, who would be working in base camp as a program assistant. Cassie greeted each of us with a firm handshake and an intense staredown. I got the feeling she was trying to size us up and intentionally put on a show of force to let us know who would be in charge that summer.

Her big broad over-the-top mannerisms made me step back and shut down a bit. As the three of us politely listened and nodded along to her wordy opening monologue, it seemed to please her just fine. Eventually, we joined the little Vikings in the yellow Voyageur canoe, as she called it, and shoved off.

"All right, team!" Cassie barked out. "Everyone, grab yourself a paddle! Let's get this beast moving across the lake!"

Over the years, I'd canoed down a few rivers in Iowa, but never on a lake that big. The water was choppy, and the canoe was enormous, clearly designed to hold about forty people. It was a chore to keep it moving, but with the help of the young sailors, we managed all right. I noticed that Cassie kept standing in the front of the canoe, watching as the rest of us got to work. As we pulled our paddles through the water, she seemed to be sizing all of us up like a fat cat or a spoiled queen who always got her own way.

As the canoe cut through the choppy waters of the big blue lake, Cassie resumed her monologue: a well-rehearsed and informative speech about the camp. It sounded as if she had given the same address several times already that day.

"Northern Lights Adventure Center has been in existence since 1963," she began. "It started as a retreat center for troubled youth in the Twin Cities, but over the years, it has become a destination for many people, attracting youth of all ages, some church groups, as well as community organizations and service agencies. The camp consists of two islands here on the east end of Diamond Lake. Turtle Island to the south is the larger of the two, and from above, it looks like a giant reptile with a curly tail. Eagle Island is the smaller one, but it rises up higher off the water's surface, as you can see from the bluffs coming into view. The islands are connected by a red cable suspension bridge that spans nearly two hundred feet of open water between them. We typically refer to the channel between the islands as the narrows. That's where we will be docking shortly. We're so glad you've chosen to be with us at Northern Lights this summer. I'm looking forward to getting to know each and every one of you."

As we paddled into the channel between the two islands, the water on the lake became gentle and calm. Cassie continued to chatter on about the camp, but I sort of tuned her out. I was struck by the extraordinary beauty that surrounded us on every side. Three simple things made up everything in my field of vision: the blue sky above, the blue lake below, and the green pine trees in between. There were evergreens virtually everywhere, along with a smattering of birch and aspen. It was an incredible sight—bright blue above, deep blue below, and a thick forest of green in between—so simple, yet absolutely breathtaking and stunningly beautiful.

As the afternoon sun glistened on the calm surface of the lake, a few fluffy clouds drifted across the blue sky in the west. It was like paddling into a picturesque scene that I had only viewed in National Geographic magazines. The trees and clouds captured my gaze as they displayed their simple beauty above and were perfectly reflected in the lake below. As we drew closer to the islands, I couldn't believe I was going to spend an entire summer in such an incredible place. I had an overwhelming feeling that my time at Northern Lights was going to change my life forever.

As we approached the islands, what immediately stood out was the red suspension bridge that spanned the narrow channel between them. People were standing on it, watching us as we drew near in the canoe. Cassie pointed out the dining hall, called Starlight Lodge, which jutted out from a bluff about fifty feet up on the southern island. To the north, five or six massive wooden rafters shot up through the trees on Eagle Island. Cassie told us they were the peaks of an open-air cathedral where the entire camp gathered each day before breakfast for something called "Morning Light," a time to hear readings, sing songs, and reflect on the beauty of creation.

As we passed under the bridge, more of the camp came into view. I could see two brown lodges and a few cabins scattered in random places on each side of the narrows. Most of the camp was on the larger Turtle Island to the south, where a long wooden dock was located next to a sandy beach. Tall stacks of canoes—dozens of them—were piled up high on wooden racks next to the forest.

A few people were hanging out on the dock waiting to pull us in. About fifteen people were playing an intense game of volleyball on the beach nearby. It was exciting to realize that they were the ones I would be rubbing shoulders with for the rest of the summer. As the Voyageur canoe bumped up against the dock and people swung into action, a chill of excitement shot through me. The place looked exactly as I thought it would.

It was going to be a great summer!

chapter 4
rough beginnings

"There's no turning back now."

As I waited to get out, I half expected Cassie to thank us for flying Voyageur Airlines and announce that she'd be happy to assist as we got our carry-on luggage down from the overhead compartments. When the canoe came to a stop, however, she just stepped out onto the boat landing and let the little Vikings tie it down.

"Well, this is it," I thought. "There's no turning back now."

"Jim, Anika, Leo," Cassie called out to us commandingly. "Grab your gear and come with me. Let's get you three settled in."

We climbed out of the canoe and followed her as ordered. When we reached the end of the dock, two dogs ran up to us, wagging their tails. I knelt to greet them as they sniffed me and my duffel bag.

"Any place that would let a couple of dogs run around freely has to be a great place," I thought. They were both mutts, but I could tell they were friendly, and that's all that mattered to me.

"That's Siri," Cassie said, pointing to the bigger dog. "The little one is Star. He's just a pup. We got him a few weeks ago. Cute, huh?"

"Do they belong to you?" I asked.

"No, they're the camp dogs," Cassie said. "They just run around wherever they want to."

I kept scratching little Star behind the ears and waited for Cassie to give us further instructions. She looked in the direction of the group playing volleyball on the beach nearby.

"Percy!" she yelled. "Hey, Percy! Get over here and welcome these new staff members to Northern Lights!"

We watched as a tall young man broke away from the game and jogged across the sand toward us. With a solid thump, he jumped up on the dock and smiled broadly, focusing his immediate attention on Anika, who grinned shyly back at him.

"Welcome to Northern Lights, you guys . . . and girl," he said, throwing a wink in Anika's direction. "My name is Percy, and I'm a third-year canoe guide this summer. You're standing in the heart of Northern Lights. As you can see, this is where we hang out a lot. If you look to the west, you'll see the racks of canoes, which will be something you'll become well acquainted with soon enough. The paddles and life jackets are stored in the shed over here by the dock. The trail behind you leads up to the bridge you just paddled under, and then it goes farther on up to Starlight Lodge. That's where we'll be having dinner in a little while. You can't see the lodge from here, but it's up in the trees just past the bridge."

I listened to Percy's smooth introduction about the camp and was impressed with how much he knew. He seemed like the ultimate canoe guide: tall, good-looking, confident, and somewhat entertaining. It was easy to see that he was a bit of a flirt, but Anika didn't seem to mind the individual attention he gave her one bit. I wondered how she really felt about it as she grinned and giggled nervously as Percy kept jabbing her with subtle comments, extra eye contact, and attention that was clearly meant for her alone.

I started to feel a bit left out of the flashy one-man show, and I had a hunch he wasn't just a one-woman man. There were too many good-looking girls around. In fact, they were all good-looking. As Percy chattered away, I gazed over at the group playing volleyball in their shorts and swimsuits, jumping around, shouting, and having fun.

"This is going to be so much better than working on a farm all summer long," I thought, straightening the John Deere cap on top of my head. "Yeah, I've come to the right place."

I watched anonymously as Percy continued his flirty introduction with Anika. I respected him for who and what he was, even though I despised him for the same reasons. He was the top dog, the alpha male, at least with the women, or so he thought.

"Okay, Anika . . . lovely Anika," Percy teased. "You can go with Janice, here, who will show you to your cabin. I hope to see you later, though." His eyes followed her as she grinned uncomfortably and walked off with Janice, who gave Percy a knowing glare.

"He's even making me uncomfortable," I thought to myself. "I wonder what the girls really think of him?"

"Now, let's see," Percy said, rotating back to Jim and me. "Who do we have here? Oh yeah, Jim Hansen. I'll show you to your cabin. Then, I have to get back to the volleyball game. Grab your gear and follow me." The two of them took off across the beach toward a trail that led up into the woods.

Halfway there, Percy turned back and yelled, "And you, um . . . you just wait there. I think your cabinmate will be coming for you soon. See you later . . . bud!"

He turned and took off up the trail with Jim. It was obvious he hadn't remembered my name. I stood there alone, not knowing what to do or where to go. Cassie had long since walked away to the other end of the dock to talk to someone else. A sudden rush of frustration and embarrassment shot through me. I stood on the edge of the dock, like a lost kid waiting to be picked up at an empty baseball field because his parents forgot him there by mistake. I started to wonder if it was going to be as great of a summer as I'd first thought.

Thankfully, Siri and Star returned to check on me every once in a while. They repeatedly scampered off to the beach, then down to the lake, and then back to me again. I could tell they were just looking for attention and food, but even so, I was happy for their company.

After about ten minutes, I saw Percy emerge from the woods and walk back onto the beach. It had been a long wait, and I wanted to get settled. I wanted to meet the other people too, even though Siri and Star seemed to think they'd already become my best buds.

"Hey, Percy!" I shouted. "What should I do? I'm still waiting for someone to show me where to go."

Percy glanced in my direction, but he just ignored me and kept walking toward the volleyball court. I looked around and noticed Cassie glaring at him as she pointed to me. Her outstretched arm stopped him dead in his tracks. He let out a long pitiful sigh. Then, he shrugged his shoulders and walked back over to me.

"I guess Baby Bear ain't gonna show," Percy said. "I suppose I'll have to get you to your cabin." He pulled out a piece of paper from his back pocket that listed everyone working at Northern Lights that summer. "So, what was your name again?"

"Who's Baby Bear?" I asked.

"Baby Bear?" Percy looked up, confused at first; then he chuckled. "Oh, Baby Bear, that's what we call your cabinmate. He's kind of, well, he's kind of . . . hairy, you know, like a bear."

"What did you say?" I questioned him, not fully appreciating what I was hearing.

"You'll get it when you see it," he said with a chuckle. "His name's actually Chuck, but he's got kind of a Grizzly Adams sort of thing going on, if you get what I'm saying."

I got it and decided to move on. "Leo," I said, "Leo Solstrom."

Percy stared at me for a second, confused again, and then the light clicked back on. "Oh, yeah, your name."

I waited as he ran his middle finger slowly down the list of names. "Solstrom, Leo," he mumbled. "Okay, here it is. So, it looks like you'll be staying in Pleiades Village up on the hill. It's on the other side of the beach over there."

He used the same finger to point me off in the direction of the big stacks of canoes past the volleyball court. I didn't know if he realized what he was doing with his finger or not, but I did know how I was being treated—like he didn't care enough to give me the time of day. I'd been treated that way before, and I didn't like it one bit.

"I'm sure you can find it by yourself," he said, scratching his nose with his finger. "It's the third cabin on the left or maybe the fourth. Just look around for Baby Bear. He's probably wandering around in the woods up there, picking blueberries or something."

Percy grinned with satisfaction at the series of insults he'd pulled off right in front of me. I just wondered why. I hadn't done anything to set him off. I was as tall as him and as good looking too, but I couldn't figure out where the attitude was coming from.

I stared at him angrily and let him feel it. "Thanks for nothing," I said. "See you around, Percy. That's your middle name, isn't it?"

"Hey man, chill out," he whined; then instantly, he regained his cocky attitude. "I'll take you if that's what you need, Solstrom. I just didn't think I'd have to hold your hand, that's all."

"I'll find it by myself," I replied as I smoothed back my hair and shoved my hat down on top. Then, I picked up my gear and walked past him close enough to brush him firmly with my bag.

"Hey, man," he said. "Take it easy, hairball." Immediately, he took the bait I'd offered and jumped right in behind me.

"Good," I thought, "I ticked him off." I walked ahead of him, satisfied, but by then, he was riled up and had a good excuse to do some more finger-pointing. Siri and Star sensed something was up, I guess, because they jumped right in alongside me as well. They kept wagging their tails happily as they followed along.

"You don't have to get all huffy about it," Percy said. "You don't even know me." He followed on my tail, along with Siri and Star, as I walked by the noisy volleyball court where the others were jumping around and scrambling after the ball.

"You can go now, Percy," I replied without looking back. "I don't need your help anymore."

"Fine, big man!" he exclaimed as he hopped back away from me. I kept right on walking around the court toward the canoes and the trail that was somewhere over there in the trees.

Suddenly, a volleyball careened past my head and hit the sand in front of me with a thud. Simultaneously, from out of nowhere, a tall dark-skinned girl came screaming after it. I tried to move, but she slammed into me so hard, I flew clean off my feet and landed, spread eagle, on my back in the sand next to the ball. The girl, however, came down squarely on her two feet, directly in front of me.

I was stunned by the sudden blow, but I couldn't help but admire her powerful presence. She stood over me, looking fierce and strong and as solid as a brick. She had dark brown eyes and tight curly hair that sprayed out every which way around her pretty face and down over her broad shoulders.

Everyone, including Percy, looked on as the girl shook her fist at me and shouted, "Watch it, farm boy! You got in my way!"

Then, she snatched up the volleyball and jogged back into the game, shouting more orders. "Hey, Percy! Stop daydreaming and get your butt back in here!"

Percy grinned. "Yeah, all right! You need me, babe!" he announced proudly. "Hold your horses, I'm coming!" Then, he sauntered back onto the court and stood by the net.

The girl let out an angry groan as she spun the volleyball in her hands and prepared to serve. "Call me babe one more time, *Perky*, and I swear I'll break your face!"

Percy threw his arms out to his side and reverted to his old whine-and-forgive-me mode. "All right, Aria, I'm back in ba—." He checked himself. Then, he said, "Go ahead and serve the ball, darling."

The girl huffed scornfully and spun the ball again. Then, she tossed it in the air, jumped up, and slammed it hard with the palm of her hand. The ball flew like a flaming rocket straight at Percy's smiling face, making him yelp like a wounded puppy as it ricocheted off his forehead and shot sky-high. He stumbled backward into the net and crumpled down into the sand in the center of the court. Several girls ran to his aid as he held his head and moaned in pain. As everyone gathered around to check on Percy, the girl stood tall and strong in the back of the court. At that moment, she was the most amazing and magnificent creature I'd ever seen in my entire life.

As I picked myself up off the sand, the girl glanced over at me. She grinned and threw me a little wink. Then, she walked over to the others and said, "Oh, Perky, I'm so sorry. Are you okay?"

I felt the pain in my chest, where the girl had slammed into me a few seconds earlier. It still kind of hurt, but it felt good too. I'd gladly take a chest-thumping any day, if it meant knocking Percy on his big behind every once in a while.

"Aria," I said to myself. "I think I'm going to like her."

chapter 5

baby bear

"The guy was hairy, really, seriously hairy."

As I turned to look for the trail to my cabin somewhere over the hill and through the woods, I noticed what appeared to be an enormous woodchuck emerging from the forest. I looked again and realized it was a fairly short, stout young man with a full beard and mustache and a head of hair that fell down in messy clusters around his dark beady eyes. He was wearing blue jean cutoffs and a plain white T-shirt that seemed to fit his rugged appearance. He also had on a pair of big brown hiking boots that made him look somewhat chubby and small and friendly . . . like a fuzzy little . . . bear. I couldn't help but acknowledge Percy's apt description of him, and no matter how hard I tried, I couldn't get the image or the nickname out of my mind. This was Baby Bear.

The hairy young man started walking across the beach in my direction, kind of swaying back and forth, almost as if he were drunk or at least a little bit tipsy. His arms, which were also extremely hairy, swayed back and forth as he lumbered forward. His legs, which also followed the familiar furry theme, seemed to be a bit bowed, as if he'd grown up riding horses on a ranch out west somewhere. But it was definitely the hair that made the man. I mean, the guy was hairy, really, seriously hairy.

Even from a distance, I knew the bearded lumberjack was my new cabinmate, Chuck. I hoped we would get along, or at least that he wouldn't kill me one night in the woods and eat me for dinner. In those regards, a good sign came from my new buddies, Siri and Star, who raced off ahead of me to greet him. He ignored the dogs, though, and kept trudging across the sandy beach in my direction.

When Chuck got closer, he noticed me standing there with all my gear, probably looking more than a little lost and confused. He smiled and waved and then starting jogging across the sand toward me. I felt like dropping my stuff and running back to the safety of the boat landing, but he was smiling, so I made the snap decision to stay put and not make any sudden moves.

"Hey, dude!" he exclaimed cheerfully as he hobbled up to me, slightly out of breath. "You must be Leo. I'm your cabinmate for the summer. My name's Chuck Boots."

He thrust out his hairy arm and held it there. I dropped my sleeping bag and shook it. He had a firm grip, and he shook my hand enthusiastically, almost furiously.

"Sorry I was late," he said as he scratched his thick beard and wiped his nose with the back of his hand. "I sort of overslept."

"No problem," I replied.

"So, I'm here to escort you to Pleiades Village," he said, grinning like a happy bellhop waiting for a tip.

"What's that?" I asked.

"The staff cabins up on the bluff," he replied, throwing his arm back toward the trail. "There's seven of 'em, two guides each. A bit drab at first glance, but they're pretty cozy."

"Okay, let's go," I said.

"Here," he said. "Let me get your stuff." He grabbed my sleeping bag and the duffel bag too. With a bewildered stare, he eyed my pillow as I clutched it like a baby blanket. Then, he shrugged his shoulders and took off ahead of me back toward the trail.

"So, Leo," he said, leading us into the woods and up the windy trail. "I bet you're excited to finally get here. Did you get a chance to meet some of the other camp staff?"

"Yeah," I replied, trying to keep up. "I met Cassie and Percy and a couple of other new people."

"Percy!" Chuck exclaimed. "Now there's a character! You probably saw him put on quite a show for the ladies, am I right?"

"Um, yeah," I replied.

"Hey, don't let it get to you," he said, swinging his hairy arms back and forth. "Percy's okay. He's just a spoiled prince, that's all."

I wondered about his use of the word prince. It seemed to fit Percy perfectly. As I listened to Chuck chatter on and on, he seemed keenly aware of everyone and everything going on at the camp. His friendly banter was interesting, valuable, and comforting. I took an immediate liking to my new cabinmate. Clearly, there was a lot more to the guy than all that hair. I figured that I could probably learn a lot from him about being a canoe guide.

"Yeah, it was a late one last night," Chuck continued. "I got a bit swamped with my new job and all.

"What's your job?" I asked.

"I've been a guide for two years now," he replied. "I wanted to keep doing that, but it didn't work out this summer." He reached around and scratched his bottom with his hairy hand.

"Man!" I thought. "This guy has hair everywhere."

"Yeah, they really needed a trail shack hand," he continued happily. "But the gal they thought was coming, suddenly backed out. So, guess who got the phone call?"

"You?" I offered.

"Yup!" he exclaimed as he jumped sideways around a big rock in the trail and swaggered forward. "I'm fine with it, though. It's probably for the best, actually."

"Why's that?" I asked as we passed the first cabin on our left.

"Well, I ain't exactly the best canoe guide out there," he said as he lumbered ahead past a mossy log and a few more rocks in the trail. "Cassie knows what I'm like, and she's in charge, you know."

I wondered what he was hinting at, but I didn't want to pry. I just kept following along behind him, enjoying his friendly way of talking and carrying on.

"It's kind of hard for me to relate to people," he explained as we passed another cabin. "Kids especially, they don't get me. I'm happy in the trail shack, I guess. I like food, as you can tell. Actually, I'm pretty organized, even if it don't look that way to most people."

"Well, thanks for finding me," I offered as we approached the third cabin on the left. "There's no way I could've found this place up here on my own."

"Oh, you'll be all right," he replied as he huffed sturdily onward. "This place is great and all, but the real deal is out there." He motioned to the water down the hillside on our right. It wasn't far away, just through a cluster of small evergreens that served as a barrier between the cabins and the narrow channel of the lake below. "That's why you came here I'm betting, and that's why I can't seem to leave."

I understood and appreciated his read of me. Chuck suddenly stopped with a jerk and turned to face the third cabin. "Well, Leo, my man, this is it." He thrust his arm out to the side and stepped back slightly, as if to let me pass. "This is our castle for the next three months. It ain't much, but you should have the first honor."

He clearly intended for me to go in first. I climbed up the three narrow wooden steps to the cabin, the third in a line of seven of them on the ridge overlooking the narrows below. The little shack had been erected on cutoff telephone poles a couple of feet off the ground and stained light brown on the outside. It had open-air windows on all four sides, covered with wire screen mesh that started at about four feet up and extended to the exposed rafters. The rickety old door had the same style of screen stapled to the top half of it, but it had no handle, so I pulled the side of the door back and peeked inside.

"Go on in!" Chuck prompted me with a wave of his hairy hand. "Make yourself at home."

I stepped into the rustic wooden cabin. It was tiny but inviting. There was a small table built into the side of the stud frame wall on the right and a few narrow shelves built into the walls on each side below the screens. In the back, if you could call it that, there were two wooden bunks, also attached to the walls. Chuck had already claimed the lower bunk, so the top one was mine.

"Hope you don't mind me being on the bottom," he said. "I need to be. So, if you had your heart set on it, I apologize."

"No problem," I said as I climbed up the wooden ladder and sat on the top bunk. It was so close to the ceiling, I almost hit my head, but the little space had a nice screen window that stretched across the rear gable end of the cabin to see outside. It felt good. It was a cozy little space, and it was all mine for the summer.

"Hey, this bunk has a nice view outside," I said cheerfully, trying to reassure Chuck that the top bunk was fine. "Yours doesn't have a window like this one."

"Yeah, no biggie," he said. "You won't be here much. It's just a place to crash when you're off the lakes—a couple days at a stretch. You'll probably be out on the water most of the time."

"Oh, yeah," I mumbled as I listened and learned. I could sense his great love for the Boundary Waters and his wish to be a canoe guide for the summer. I didn't entirely know what a trail shack hand was, but I was sure he'd be a good one.

"So," Chuck said, motioning to the shelves on the left, "I got my stuff over here on this side of the cabin. You can have the other side. I don't need the desk. I don't have that much anyway."

He was right. All I could see of his things were a few short stacks of clothes and a sleeping bag on his bunk. He didn't even have a pillow. I wondered if it had been a mistake for me to lug mine all the way up there and let everyone see me carrying it across the beach. Life there was starting to look pretty stark. I wouldn't be bringing a pillow on any canoe trips, that's for sure, but I rolled my sleeping bag out and fluffed my pillow at the top anyway.

"So, Leo," Chuck said from the bunk below, "I've got sort of a condition."

"Yeah?" I responded, then waited for him to continue, unsure if I wanted to know his condition so soon in our relationship or not.

"So, a couple of months ago, I got diagnosed with . . ." He stopped and sighed softly, then just sat there silent and still.

"It's okay, Chuck. What is it?" I replied, trying to reassure him as I waited patiently up above.

"Epilepsy," he said firmly with a certain degree of disgust. "It's not so bad, really . . . just happens every once in a while, is all."

"So, isn't that kind of dangerous in a canoe?" I asked, getting straight to the point.

"Oh, no, not really," he replied. "When I feel it coming, I just slide down into the bottom of the boat, and after it passes, I'm fine."

"Oh, okay, that's not so bad," I said.

I wondered about his easy explanation and dismissal of his condition. I wondered, too, if anyone else knew. They had to know. It was probably the real reason Chuck had been asked to take the trail shack job for the summer. I felt sorry for him, sitting down there in silence. It was obvious he wanted to be out on the lakes, not stuck in some building packing food or whatever it was.

"I'm okay, though," he said, coming back to life. "So, if you ever see me slip down into a canoe, just hold on and let me do my thing. Just stay away from me, though, if it happens. I can't control what my arms and legs do when I have an episode."

"Okay, Chuck," I replied.

"It'll be fine," he said, drifting away into silent thought again.

I hopped down off my bunk and started unpacking my gear. I wondered how he was dealing with his newly discovered condition. I couldn't imagine what I'd do if something like that ever happened to me. It would probably really mess me up.

"Yeah, it'll be fine," he said. "You'll love it here."

chapter 6
big bear

"Is he nice?"

We didn't stay in the cabin very long. There wasn't that much to do there anyway, so Chuck led the way back down to the beach. When he stopped at the edge of the woods, I came up and stood beside him. His dark beady eyes scanned the people from one end of the clearing all the way across to the dock by the lake. He took it all in, carefully, every person moving around or standing still, every detail that lay out there in the open before him.

"See that guy over there?" Chuck said in a hushed tone.

"Where?" I asked. I looked around the beach, but I couldn't tell who he was talking about.

He pointed subtly with his finger toward the edge of the clearing, up where a trail came out of the woods next to an old shed. A man was standing in the shadows of the tall pines, almost completely hidden behind the understory of bushes and smaller trees. The man seemed to be eyeing the beach too, precisely as Chuck had done. He was older, forty, or maybe fifty-something. From a distance, I could tell that he had white hair, pure white, and even though he was in the shade, it stood out from far away. He was holding a bucket in one hand and a fishing pole in the other.

"That's Finn," Chuck said respectfully. "He's the camp's executive director."

"Does he like to fish?" I asked.

"Yeah, I suppose so," Chuck replied. "We don't see him much, though. Cassie pretty much runs things during the summer."

"Who's in charge?" I asked. "Finn or Cassie?"

"Finn is," Chuck said, "but Cassie usually gets her way when it comes to the summer program. I don't think this place would survive without Finn around, though."

"Why not?" I asked.

"A lot of reasons," Chuck replied, speaking with discernable reverence and admiration. "He's seen the camp through some tough times, and if anything happens, it's always Finn who takes care of it. There are a lot of different stories about him. He goes way back, as long as anyone can remember. He's sort of become a living legend here at Northern Lights."

I stood silent and still, but uneasy. Even at a distance, I had a strange feeling that Finn knew we were looking at him, maybe even knew we were talking about him. I finally turned my gaze back to Chuck, who was still eyeing Finn at the edge of the forest.

"You'll hear most people refer to him as Big Bear," Chuck said. "But I just call him Finn or Mister Kriger. I don't think he'd appreciate the Big Bear title, even though it fits him."

I understood his comment and wondered if Chuck knew the name Percy had bestowed on him.

"What do you like to be called?" I asked.

"Chuck," he said plainly, "just Chuck."

I glanced back over at Finn, still standing motionless on the edge of the forest. "What's he like? Is he nice?"

"Who, Finn?" Chuck answered. "Oh, yeah! Kind of hard to get to know at first, but he's a great guy with a big heart. He really knows his stuff. He loves it up here, but you won't see much of him. He's busy with office work and probably lots of off-site stuff too. He's super friendly, though. He's a big old-fashioned Swede with a sweet wife and two little boys."

I listened to Chuck ramble on as I looked back at Finn, standing at the edge of the forest. He didn't look like a bear at all. He looked like an old gray wolf to me, eyeing the people on the beach as if he were hunting prey. He seemed out of place, standing there with the bucket and fishing pole at his side . . . or maybe, it was the other way around.

Perhaps he was the one who belonged, and all the others were out of their element. He watched, silent and still, from the edge of the woods as the rest of the camp staff laughed and played volleyball out in the open on the bright sandy beach.

Chuck said that Finn knew the area around there so well, he could do ten miles or more in the dark of night, and he could find just about anyone out on the lakes if necessary. It was both fascinating and a bit unsettling at the same time. I took solace in Chuck's initial words about him, though, that he was friendly for the most part. From that time on, I had a feeling of both safety and danger whenever Finn was around. Maybe it was his quiet way of suddenly appearing and disappearing around camp, or perhaps it was his tall thin frame and his ever-watchful eyes that seemed to scan a room from corner to corner, or maybe it was the big fishing knife he always carried strapped to his thick leather belt.

I looked at the people laughing and jumping around down on the volleyball court. I wondered what Finn thought about them, goofing off like that. I glanced back toward him at the edge of the forest, but he wasn't there anymore. He had disappeared back into the woods someplace. A sudden chill ran down my spine. Here was a true woodsman of the north, a big white Swede who could find his way through a blizzard in the dark of night. I was totally impressed, fascinated, and terrified all at once.

Later that summer, I came to be friends with Finn, but it took a long time. I always regarded him with the highest respect. Northern Lights needed someone exactly like him, not the most enthusiastic or flashy person in the world, but a man who cared for people and had a heart for what was going on at the camp. It was reassuring to know that if something bad happened—an emergency or something else—Finn would be there to rescue us.

I was just hoping he wouldn't have to do that.

chapter 7
crown of victory

"I had a feeling about it."

The camp staff at Northern Lights was made up of about forty-five people in all. There was a handful of program coordinators and specialty positions that included a family camp director, a volunteer coordinator, and a naturalist. There were also about ten staff members assigned to base camp, which was primarily located around the cabins and lodges scattered all over Turtle Island. It was their job to host visitors, families, and volunteers who would be coming and going throughout the summer.

There were about twenty canoe guides on staff. Our main job was to lead groups out on the lakes, usually five to six days at a stretch. Cassie told us we would probably get to do about eight or nine trips that summer.

There were also about a dozen high school students hired on as junior guides. They were called "swampers" apparently due to their inexperience and thus their tendency to swamp canoes. The swampers served as helpers in various capacities around camp. They did daily chores, worked in the kitchen, and went out on canoe trips when necessary. All in all, it looked like an awesome group of people, and the gorgeous setting wasn't that bad either.

Staff training at Northern Lights was a full two weeks long. It included a series of intense training sessions that covered all sorts of things we needed to know for the summer. I had come to camp already lifeguard certified, but in those first two weeks, we covered a lot more. We were certified in CPR and wilderness first aid. We learned how to use a map and compass to find our way across open water in the dark. We learned how to use a WhisperLite stove and to cook over an open fire. We learned how to read the weather and find portage heads and campsites from a distance. There wasn't a lot of free time to relax and have fun, but when we got it, we took full advantage of our freedom to enjoy and explore the camp.

A couple of days before heading out on the lakes for our first guide training trip, everyone had a half-day off to relax. The annual canoe race around Eagle Island was set for that afternoon. It was open to any pair of camp staff willing to give it a shot. Percy had won it the past two years in a row, and I could tell he was excited to go for the glorious three-peat. The award was simply a leafy crown given to the winners of the race, but everyone knew that it was more about the glory and status that came along with it.

On the morning of the race, I wandered up to Starlight Lodge with Chuck for breakfast. He was going to be my partner for the race, but he wasn't too excited about it.

As I got behind Cassie in the breakfast line, Percy quickly slipped in between us and pushed me out of the way. Cassie gave us both a stern look, as if to say, "I'm watching you two."

Percy glanced back at me and bellowed, "Hey, Leo, are you learning everything there is to know about being an awesome canoe guide in the Boundary Waters, or what?"

I just stared back at him in disgust as he grabbed a plate and moved on up the line behind Cassie.

"Awesome!" Percy exclaimed. "That's great! Me too!"

"He doesn't need me," I thought. "He's got himself, and that's all that matters in his small world."

Of course, his world also revolved around women. Well, actually, it revolved around the women who revolved around him. In either case, he was both fascinating and repulsive to watch.

That morning, one of the servers behind the counter was a high school girl named Andie. She had been hired as a swamper, but the kitchen staff was so shorthanded, Andie ended up getting stuck in there for the entire summer.

Percy started right in flirting with her. "Hey there, Andie, my girl, my beautiful dining service maiden."

"Hey, Percy!" she replied as she smiled happily and ate up the attention from the older attractive male.

"So, my beautiful Andie," he continued. "How's it going on this wonderful spring morning?"

"Oh, you know. I'm still chained to the floor back here in the kitchen," she replied as she dumped a pile of eggs on his plate. "I gotta keep all of you buff canoe guides fed and watered."

Percy leaned over and motioned with his finger for her to come in close. "I'm gonna break you out of this dungeon one of these days," he whispered loudly.

"Well, that would be nice, Percy, but you already tried that once." She dropped a heap of greasy hash browns onto his plate, then topped it off with a few sausages.

"I'll cut you loose one of these days," he whispered loudly again. "You just wait and see!"

"Sure, you will," Andie said sarcastically as she dumped a pile of eggs on my plate next. "You know where to find me."

Percy swept up the line, close to Cassie, and bragged, "You know, Cassie, I'm gonna win the race today."

"Oh, really?" Cassie replied calmly. "As a matter of fact, I've got my money on Leo and Chuck."

Percy glanced back at me, then insisted, "I'm winning the race."

"Oh, you think so?" Cassie said skeptically. "Want to make it interesting and put your money where your mouth is?"

"Okay," Percy replied instantly. "If I don't win the race, I'll volunteer for an entire week in the galley." He snapped a flirtatious wink back at Andie, standing behind the serving counter. "But Cassie, if I win, you have to let Andie go out with me as a swamper on a canoe trip this summer."

Cassie eyed the tall cocky canoe guide as if he were stepping directly into a bear trap. "Okay, hot stuff, it's a deal."

As Cassie turned to go, Percy grinned at Andie and whispered, "I'm breaking you out of this snake pit. You just wait and see."

Cassie stopped suddenly and whispered loudly back at him, "You know, Percy, I'm entering the race myself this year, and I'm gonna kick your sorry little behind back to preschool."

Percy backed off in shock and dismay. Everyone knew Cassie was an experienced veteran, and she was strong too. I could tell that he wasn't so sure of the wisdom of his hastily-made bet.

"Good luck, loser," I said, flashing him a big grin as I took my plate and sat down with Chuck for breakfast.

Chuck didn't look too optimistic about the whole episode that had transpired at the serving counter. He just kept his eyes down and focused on his breakfast.

"Do you think we can beat him?" I asked.

"Don't count on it," Chuck said. "Percy's a big weasel. I'm bettin' he finds a way to win."

I wondered about our chances of winning. I had a feeling we could take him or anyone else in the race. Chuck was tough, and I was pretty confident in my own abilities as well. To be perfectly honest, I wanted that leafy crown so badly I could taste it.

After a picnic lunch on the south side of the island, everyone gathered down at the beach for the big race. During the day, Percy had been wheeling and dealing to increase his chances of winning. He'd somehow convinced Jim to be his partner. Jim was tall and strong, and together, they looked like two guys trying out for the Russian hockey team. Chuck and I were ready to go, but compared to them, we looked more like Rocky and Bullwinkle. Cassie's partner was a veteran guide named Carly: a tough Norwegian rowing champion from the U.P. who looked really intense and really hungry.

Andie and the high school swampers weren't allowed to enter the race, so most of them had gathered up on the bridge to watch. I noticed Aria standing up there as well. It was only then that I realized she was a swamper too.

Finn stood on the dock holding a huge shotgun. When the teams had lined up at the water's edge, he shouted, "On your marks, get set!" The shotgun went off with a deafening "Boom!" Immediately, total pandemonium broke loose on the shoreline.

There was a mad dash as everyone, about fifteen teams in all, scrambled out into the water and frantically leaped into their canoes. Everyone was screaming and shouting as the chaotic race got underway. Chuck and I were entangled in the midst of the watery fray as Percy and Jim raced off ahead of everyone.

As the canoes jostled and rammed into each other, water and foam splashed everywhere. People were yelling and shouting from the dock and up on the bridge. All I could hear were frantic voices yelling, "Hey! Get out of the way! We're coming through! Paddle! Paddle! Move it, you guys! Come on! Go! Go!" I looked ahead at Percy and Jim, racing off with Cassie and Carly close behind. I knew from the very start that we had no chance of beating either of them.

The rest of us struggled on, desperately trying to keep up, but at each stroke of our paddles, the two lead canoes pulled farther and farther away. Everyone raced northeast around the edge of Eagle Island, then out into the lake, heading for the point off the north side. But then, out of the blue, Percy cut sharply to the left as the rest of us kept paddling toward the point.

Immediately, I could see what he was up to, but it was too late to do anything about it. Percy steered his canoe into a rocky shoal between the island and the point to the north. The shoal was blocked with big jagged rocks sticking out of the water everywhere, but that didn't stop Percy. He and Jim scrambled out of their canoe and carried it over the rocks. Then, they hopped back in and raced off on the other side. By the time the rest of us rounded the point, they were already entering the home stretch. Chuck and I paddled like mad to catch up, but the race was already over. Percy won by a long shot. He cruised easily across the finish line to the excited cheers of Andie and the rest of the camp staff.

Cassie, however, was furious. She ran her canoe aground; then she jumped out and marched straight up to Percy.

"Cheater!" she yelled, shaking her finger in his face. "You didn't win! You cheated!"

"Easy, darling," Percy whined. "We won fair and square. We were just faster than everyone else."

"You took a short cut, you weasel!" Cassie yelled. "You knew you couldn't beat us, so you cheated!"

"We paddled around Eagle Island just like everyone else," he cried. "You're just a sore loser."

The insult infuriated Cassie. She seemed ready to boil over and lose it at any minute, as if she hadn't already. There was no getting through to Percy, though, who contentedly grinned as she railed him up one side and down the other. Finn walked up to them, and for a while, he watched the big catfight as if slightly amused. In his presence, the two of them simmered back down to a low boil, but the argument wasn't over by a long shot.

After listening to both sides and weighing the evidence, Finn finally settled it once and for all. He allowed Percy's victory to stand, but he backed off regarding the bet they had going about Andie.

Finn simply said, "Cassie's in charge of the summer staff. That's her decision to make."

After the race, everyone was treated to a huge pile of watermelon, chocolate chip cookies, and lemonade. Then, it was time for the awards ceremony on the beach. We were forced to watch as Percy was presented with the crown of victory: a leafy laurel made of pine branches interwoven with clumps of moss and wildflowers. I noticed that it was Aria who did the official crowning of the victors, and she did it with exceptional grace and dignity. For the rest of the day, Percy strutted around the camp, showing off the crown to everyone as he bragged about his victory in the race.

Later that evening, however, the news quickly spread that Percy had come down with a bad case of poison ivy. How he'd gotten into the stuff, nobody knew. It had started on his forehead, then trickled down the front of his face onto his shoulders and arms. His hands and fingers ended up being covered with it as well, including his legs, belly, and even his groin. Apparently, it was pretty painful. He just couldn't stop itching himself, so the camp nurse smeared calamine lotion over his entire body. For the next few days, Percy didn't look like the mighty victor at all. Instead, he looked more like the Energizer bunny with a severe case of acne.

After the race, Cassie was so upset that she refused to let Andie go on a canoe trip with him or anyone else. Percy had won the race, but in the end, he couldn't free Andie from the deep dark dungeon of the camp kitchen. Andie sank back into utter despair when she realized that her fate had been sealed once and for all.

For the rest of the summer, Andie always looked so pitiful and depressed, standing behind that serving counter as if tied to a heavy ball and chain, condemned to serve everyone else as they came and went on their great adventures out on the lakes. Percy never forgave Cassie for going back on her word, but she insisted he hadn't won fair and square. She was the one in charge, however, so he paid the price for it in more ways than one.

No one could figure out how Percy acquired that case of poison ivy, but I found out later from Aria that whoever made the victor's crown "accidentally" wove poison ivy in with the pine branches. Aria wouldn't say who the guilty party was, not until the summer was almost over. Only then, did she finally admit to it.

Everyone suspected Aria was the culprit, but no one could say for sure. It was just another reason why I grew to like that girl. Later in the summer, we would become good friends, but at that point, I merely admired her from afar.

I had a feeling about it, though.

chapter 8

stay the course

"It's coming! I promise!"

I knew Chuck loved to canoe. What I didn't realize was that he loved to surf too. One windy afternoon during a break in the schedule, Chuck dragged me out on a long trek across Diamond Lake. I went along because he asked, not because I wanted to. He said he wanted to go surfing and that it was the perfect weather for it. I didn't know what he was talking about, and he wouldn't tell me any more than that. So, off we went.

I was in the back of the canoe, and Chuck was in the front. The wind was blowing straight into our faces and whipping across the lake like a typhoon. I'd never seen it so windy, and I was baffled as to why he had chosen that exact time to go surfing. As soon as we paddled out into the open water, I wanted to give up and head back to camp, but Chuck kept shouting to me from up in front.

"Keep her pointed into the wind, Leo!" he yelled. "Don't give up, dude! Stay the course! It's coming! I promise!"

It seemed pointless to me. I didn't know what was going on, and I openly complained the entire way across the lake. The pain in my arms and shoulders became so bad, it felt as if they were on fire. We worked our way across an open stretch of the lake. Then, we took a break behind an island, only to paddle out into the wind again and wrestle our way across more open water to another island. The lake was so big, and we just kept paddling like idiots straight into that relentless and unforgiving wind.

"Isn't this far enough?" I kept asking him, but he refused to quit until we got all the way across. When we finally reached the calm water on the far shore, I said, "All right, Chuck, we're here. We made it. Now let's go back."

Chuck quietly sat up in front, not saying a word. He let me simmer down for a while, and then he explained a few things to me.

"Leo, thanks for doing this," he said. "It means a lot to me. I'm gonna show you how to surf here in a few minutes, but what we're doing today is so much more than that."

"What do you mean by that?" I asked, still frustrated.

"This is what life is like out here in the Boundary Waters," he said. "Sometimes it won't make any sense. Sometimes it won't always go the way you want it to. Sometimes it'll get pretty rough, and you'll have to work your way through some really tough stretches. But if you persevere, you'll get to where you're supposed to be. But that's not even the main point, actually."

"What's the main point?" I asked.

"It's like this," he said. "It's not so much about the destination, Leo; it's about how you handle the journey. You have to keep pressing forward. You have to stay the course. And if you do that, the end will be all the more sweet because of it."

Immediately, I understood what he was saying. All my complaining across the lake suddenly made me ashamed to be sitting in the same boat with him. I should have kept my mouth shut and trusted that he knew what he was doing. All I could think about was giving up, and if we had, well . . . there'd be no surfing, that's for sure.

I felt the same way about my journaling. Sometimes, at the end of a long day, I would be so tired that I'd have no desire to stay up and write. If I just rolled over and went to sleep, by the next morning I'd have forgotten all the little details that happened, the deeper things that people said, and the lessons I'd learned the day before.

Chuck was saying that sometimes it's tempting to give up or take the easy way out. It's like heading out into the wind on a big lake. Early on, it seems like nothing is happening. It looks like you're not getting anywhere, but you are—slowly, inch by inch. And actually, it's in those tough stretches that you find out what you're made of inside. You have to push through and persevere to grow stronger.

It's like a book you might be reading. At first, it seems to be going nowhere, and you're tempted to give up. It would be so easy to jump ahead and skip past the initial work of the opening chapters. But if you did that, you'd be sure to miss out on some significant parts of the story, elements that are crucial to the understanding of its entirety. It's essential to stick with it—all of it, the easy parts and the difficult ones, and as you do, the end result will be all that more meaningful and rewarding.

Chuck started to rig up a sail in the front of the canoe. He wrapped an old tent fly around two wooden paddles and then jammed them in between the sides of the front seat. They formed a sort of V shape, all tied down with some spare rope and a few carabiners.

"Paddle us back out into the wind," he said, moving to the center of the canoe. "You'll just need to steer the canoe and keep it going with the wind, so we don't tip over."

"Which way do I go?" I asked.

"Those two islands," he said, pointing straight east. "The wind will be out of the northwest, so be ready for it when it takes us."

We moved back out into the open water. Then all of a sudden, a gust of wind blew over and started pushing us forward. Gradually, the canoe began to pick up speed until we were racing over the top of the water, shooting straight east like a catamaran on the open sea.

"All right, Leo!" Chuck shouted with an excited glance back at me. "Hang on! I'm gonna go for it!"

Carefully, he stood up with his feet spread out wide and his arms flapping wildly at each side. I knew he shouldn't have been standing up in the canoe, but I was just hanging on for dear life as we shot out of control across the lake. Chuck began to bounce up and down in the middle of the canoe as it sped along with the waves that were crashing all around us.

"Awesome!" he shouted into the wind. "This is awesome!"

Then, ever so carefully, he stepped up higher, putting one foot on the front seat and the other on the yoke. He balanced up there with his arms flung out wide and the wind whipping through his hair as we were carried across the lake like a dry leaf blowing in the breeze. As I hung on, he glanced back at me with a big smile on his face.

"Whoo-eee!" he shouted out loud and long. "Leo! Dude! Don't give up! Keep the faith, man! Persevere! If you do that, you can accomplish anything! Stay the course, and you'll learn to fly!"

It was the best sermon I'd ever heard in my entire life, and at that moment, I totally believed him. He was standing up there, balancing like a trapeze artist on a high wire—his arms stretched out wide, his hands feeling the wind, soaring like an eagle across the sky. He was flying with the angels in heaven.

As I watched him from the back of the canoe, I had an epiphany, if you could call it that. I had a peculiar feeling that he was going to be with the angels sooner than later, and I think he knew it too. I could tell that Chuck loved life, so he was making the most of it while he still had the time.

When the wind let up behind a little island, Chuck launched himself off to the side and dove into the lake. He swam around for a while, and then, he came back over to me, grinning from ear to ear. He was having the time of his life in his favorite place in all the world: the Boundary Waters of Northern Minnesota.

"Leo, let's switch," he said. "You give it a shot, dude!"

Chuck climbed in, and we switched places for the second half of the lake. I tried my best, that's for sure, but I wasn't as daring and carefree as he had been. When I hopped up onto the seat and threw my arms out wide, it felt as if I was going to tumble right over into the water, but somehow, I managed to stay up there for a couple of minutes as the wind carried us back across the lake. It was only then that I realized all the work we'd done to get to the far side of that big lake had been worth it.

"Oh, yeah! This is awesome!" I shouted back to Chuck as the wind whipped around my body.

Later that night, I stayed up late and wrote down everything that happened that afternoon. I wrote down what Chuck said too. "Stay the course, Leo! Don't give up! Persevere! Keep the faith. It'll be totally worth it in the end!"

That night, I wrote a few other things to myself too. Actually, I did a lot of writing and talking to myself that summer—every single day, in fact, no matter if I was out on the lakes or back at base camp. I wanted a record of everything that happened that summer at Northern Lights. I didn't want to forget anything.

I've gone back to my journal several times and reread the account of Chuck and me out on Diamond Lake. It didn't seem like much at the time, but it has come to mean so much more. I'm so glad I wrote it down. It's helped me think through and process everything that happened to me over the summer. It's been a source of inspiration and guidance through some difficult and confusing times since then. It's compelled me to rethink my life and to put some of my more personal thoughts down on paper. It's what I do, actually. I write and talk to myself all the time. If, by chance, a person could read a part of my journal, it might go something like this.

"Leo, I bet you're wondering where your life is going and why nothing seems to be happening. When is it going to start making some sense? I know it's tempting to skip ahead and write about the main thing that happened last summer. I know you'd love to do that right now, but you simply can't. You've got a little more work to do first. Stay the course, Leo. Keep the faith!"

"I suppose, later, after it's all written down, you could skip ahead a couple of chapters—three or maybe even four if you wanted to. But don't do that now. It'll be so much sweeter if you just stay the course. I know you wish you could jumpstart the story of your life right in the middle of it—in a place where everything is happening and it all seems to be coming together, where everything makes sense and all of your problems seem to fade away. But if you did that, you'd miss out on so many "Aha!" moments. You'd miss out on what's really important: all those life lessons and intense struggles that are integral to who you are becoming as a person."

"The same goes for this story you've got cooking. If you skip too much at the beginning of the summer, the rest of it won't make any sense. You'd forget what life was actually like at Northern Lights. You've got a few more tall tales to tell before you get to the main one.

I know it doesn't make for the perfect novel to beat around the bush like this, but you've got to do it anyway. These short stories are important to you, and they really do need to be told to bring the main one into focus. So, bear with me here; the main act will be coming along soon enough."

"Remember, you can't always rush into things, especially when it comes to the most important things in life. You're getting there, and in this case, it's the journey that counts, more than the destination. Don't forget, the best things in life take time. Sometimes they take heaps of commitment, dedication, and sacrifice too. Sometimes you have to work for it, and then, when it finally comes, the end is all the more sweet. So, this is just something to keep you from giving up on me and then losing out on the best part of the story. Be patient, friend. We'll get there soon enough."

"Stay the course. It's coming. I promise."

chapter 5

maiden voyage

"You can do this."

Two of the most memorable trips I had all summer were the guide trips we did during staff training. For the first one, I was in a group led by none other than Percy himself. At first, I thought that would spell trouble, but it didn't.

The day before we left, Cassie pulled the two of us aside. She said we were being put in the same training group, and then she sternly told us to basically "work it out" and set our differences aside. Then, she said if we couldn't work it out by ourselves, she could, and we wouldn't like her way of doing things one bit.

I wanted to explain to her why Percy and I weren't getting along, but I kept quiet. Percy did too. After the little chat with Cassie, I never had any more real trouble with Percy. He still acted like an arrogant jerk sometimes, but not in an in-your-face kind of way. I just found myself cringing every once in a while when I was around him. Actually, I learned a lot from Percy that summer, mostly about how not to do things and what not to say.

Our trip started on a cold and drizzly morning. Percy led the way with three other canoes trailing behind, trying desperately to catch up. Percy was strong, and he could really move in the water. He led us through a maze of islands near Northern Lights, then out west across the big open waters of Diamond Lake. By the time we pulled into the first portage, he was already out of the water and hoisting a canoe onto his shoulders all by himself.

As he took off up the trail, we were left to figure it out on our own.

It took us a while. We hopped out and began assisting each other with the big Duluth packs and heavy canoes. As I was helping a first-year guide named Anne with a pack, Percy reappeared out of the woods. He gave me a look of superiority. Then, he grabbed another canoe and took off again. As Anne followed after him up the trail, I realized that I was the only one left there with the last canoe.

I waded out into the water and grabbed it like I'd seen Percy do so easily. Then, I swung it up over my head, but it kept on going and crashed down in the water on my other side. I cursed under my breath and tried it again from the opposite side, but for some reason, I couldn't even lift it above my waist. So, I did the next best thing. I pulled the canoe up onto the rocky shore and flipped the front end upside down. I carefully backed my way underneath until the harness pads rested squarely on my shoulders. Then, I pulled the front of the canoe down and leveled it off. It was beastly heavy.

"You can do this," I mumbled as I took off up the trail.

At first, I thought I was far behind the rest of the group, but halfway along the portage trail, I caught up to Anne lugging her pack. Then, I passed two other guides who were swapping out a canoe beside the path. As I kept going, the weight of the canoe started to really dig into my shoulders. I didn't want to stop, though; I desperately wanted to catch up to Percy.

I didn't know precisely how long the portage was. The map said it was 105 rods, and Percy had informed us that one rod was about the length of a canoe. As I stumbled along, I tried to figure it out in my head. About seventeen feet for a canoe multiplied by 105 rods equaled about 1,800 feet, which was almost a third of a mile, or six football field lengths. As I trudged along, I tried to estimate how many steps it took to make one rod, how many football fields I had covered, and how much farther I had to carry that nasty canoe.

When I finally reached the other side, Jim came rushing up to help. He pushed the front of the canoe up above his head as I lowered the back end down to the ground and stepped out. Together we flipped it over and carried it into the water. As the others arrived, we helped load the packs back in the canoes and shoved off. Meanwhile, Percy waited for us offshore, looking irritated and impatient. When everyone was back on the water, he swung his canoe around and raced off ahead of us again. My shoulders ached, but I was glad to have the first portage, a big one, under my belt.

We traveled like that through a chain of pretty lakes heading southwest. Throughout the rest of the summer, I would become familiar with the route we were taking: Diamond Lake to Alpine Lake, then around to Jasper Falls and a rocky uphill portage into Jasper Lake, then west to a small lake called Kingfisher, then on to Ogishkemuncie, which was a long lake with several big bays and peninsulas. At the portage into Ogish, Percy tossed the map into my canoe and told me to guide the group to the next portage. Then, he hopped in his canoe and raced off ahead again.

I lagged behind, reading the map as I paddled, trying to figure out the twists and turns of the big long lake. From a distance, certain islands didn't look like islands, and the different sizes and shapes of the bays were tricky to read. I would head one direction, thinking it was the right way to go, then realize the shape of the lake had somehow changed and have to adjust course. Finding the right way proved to be more difficult than I had first anticipated.

As I moved at a snail's pace in the back of the group, Percy would paddle ahead and then turn his canoe to the side and peer back to see what was taking me so long. Then, he would race on ahead again. When I struggled to find my way through a narrow channel that seemed to be hiding in the middle of the lake, I learned a valuable lesson. It suddenly dawned on me that no matter what I did in the back of the pack, Percy was always paddling directly toward where I was supposed to be heading. Suddenly, my job became extremely easy. For the rest of the way across the lake, I simply followed him. It must have been torturous for him to have to keep turning around to see us all moving so slowly, but I knew exactly where we were going. And sure enough, as we approached the end of the lake, there it was, the portage, right in front of the nose of Percy's canoe.

As he waited for me to find it, I cruised by him and called out, "This is easy! It's a piece of cake!"

We kept moving steadily westward, through a string of smaller lakes. Ogishkemuncie led to a pretty little lake called Annie, which for some reason was surrounded by dozens of dead spruce trees. Then, it was on to Jenny Lake, a beautiful body of water that branched out into four separate bays. It looked like a glistening jewel to me, one worth exploring for an entire day or two, but Percy kept pressing on. We portaged into Eddy Lake and kept going west.

By that time, it was late in the afternoon. We were exhausted, so we took a break at the next portage. We could hear the sound of waterfalls in the forest near the trail. We left our canoes in a clearing on the far side of the portage and hiked over to see the falls. They were loud and large, with several pools scattered at different levels, extending up over a hundred feet into the woods. Some of the falls looked big enough to stand under. On a hot day, it would be an ideal spot to cool off and get a free shower in the middle of the wilderness. The water was ice-cold, and it was still drizzly out, so going in was really not an option. Besides, Percy insisted that we keep moving, so we shoved off again. We started looking for a campsite on Knife Lake: a long wide stretch of water that extended for several miles to the southwest.

I could tell that Percy was pushing us hard on purpose. At first, I thought it was purely out of meanness, but eventually, I understood that he was just following Cassie's orders to harden us up and prepare the guides for an entire summer of living out on the lakes. I gained some respect for Percy on the trip as well, mostly for his natural ability to find his way across a lake and to do it in a hurry. That could be useful in a pinch, I thought, but I didn't learn much more from him. He seemed only interested in moving as fast as possible and getting to the next lake. He didn't seem to be able to slow down and appreciate the incredible beauty and natural wonder of the lake he was currently on. For Percy, it was always and forever about the next lake, and then the one after that, and so on, and so on.

Thankfully, the others on the trip weren't taking anything too seriously. Jim, especially, helped to bring some joy and laughter to our travels. His job for the summer was not as a canoe guide but as a program specialist in base camp. He was in charge of organizing camp activities, leading games with kids, and planning the evening campfire programs. He chattered away cheerfully as we paddled along. He taught us fun songs too. He called them "paddling songs," and we sang along with him, keeping time with each stroke of our paddles. Jim was the guy who was always ready to help. At each portage, he hovered around like a busy bee getting packs unloaded, helping to hoist them onto our backs, lifting canoes for people, and offering to take things the rest of the way on the trail.

Jim was quite the chatterbox as well. He seemed to talk constantly about what he was doing, what our next goal was, and what our group had accomplished. He was always cheering us on, talking to each person by name, and offering words of encouragement and support. I learned a lot from Jim, not only about how to lead a tired and weary group of paddlers, but also how to build them up and make each day more enjoyable.

Jim would talk incessantly with the person who happened to be in his canoe. He'd ask question after question, clearly more interested in hearing from the other person than talking about himself. I found that if I kept my canoe close to his, I could find out everything I ever wanted to know about a person and more. It was invaluable to me since I was an outsider and more than a bit of an introvert.

As the trip went along, I realized that Jim turned out to be our group's true leader. Percy kept quiet and aloof for the most part. I wondered if Cassie had said something else to him after giving us the "work it out or else" speech. As the trip went along, he seemed to become more and more withdrawn from the rest of the group, but that was perfectly fine with me.

Percy still had his moments, though. He took pride in explaining how to set up the tents, get clean water from the lake, gather dry firewood, and hang a bear rope properly. He showed us how to work the WhisperLite stoves we used to cook all our meals. He also showed us how to flip over a canoe and use it as a tabletop at a campsite. It was an ideal place to work on meal prep, set up the stove, and do dishes too, especially since there were no tables or chairs anywhere.

If you were lucky, there might be a couple of logs set around the fireplace by previous visitors to the site.

Each campsite had two essential things placed there by the U.S. Forest Service. The first was an iron fire grate that was anchored to the ground and lined with rocks to protect it from the wind. The fire grate was always the first thing we looked for when we were searching for a campsite.

The other important structure placed at each campsite was called the throne. As the word implied, the throne was a place of extreme importance, a place to sit and do important things, great and mighty things, but usually, it was not visible from the main part of the site. The magnificent throne was so important, one had to go and search for it back in the woods.

It was usually hidden deep in the forest behind the campfire ring at the end of a well-worn path. Inevitably, upon arriving at a vacant campsite, the throne was the second thing most people looked for because what happened there was critical to their survival in the wilderness. Usually, the person who found the trail had the privilege of being the first to get to sit on it.

The throne was simply a wooden or fiberglass box placed on top of a mound of dirt. It sat up higher than the rest of the ground, as if to signify the vital role it played in the middle of the woods. On top of the box was a lid that looked like a toilet seat. Actually, it was a toilet seat, and upon lifting it up, one could immediately discern why it was so important. From inside the deep recesses of the black hole beneath the throne rose the unmistakable fumes of all the important duties that had been executed while sitting on top of it. And if you've ever needed to go in the woods, the sight of that smelly box with a toilet seat on top of it could look pretty good.

It was always a welcome relief to find such a structure placed there so kindly by the U.S. Forest Service. That's why, when anyone made a trip to the throne, they would proudly announce the glorious news to everyone else in the campground. Then, they'd grab the bag of toilet paper and scurry off down that well-worn path deep into the forest to have a sit on the high and mighty throne.

As we moved along on our trip, I admired Jim for his gift of gab and his friendly style of leadership. I found that I could do it too, but it really wasn't my style. Actually, it wore me out. The activities that were quieter seemed to be what gave me energy. I enjoyed going out on the lake by myself to collect water or skirt the shoreline to look for firewood. It was during those alone times that I would renew my spirit and feel the most alive.

On the trip, I found myself turning to what I knew best: people watching. Ever since I was a kid, I'd always done a lot more listening than talking, especially in larger groups. It always amazed me how some people could talk about anything and everything, most of which seemed so trivial and meaningless. I wondered why most people didn't talk about more important things, deeper things, on a more intimate and personal level. I found that I longed for times to share openly and freely, to be heard and understood, to be known by others without being judged or shut down.

In spite of my shyness, I wished it were easier for people to open up about their personal beliefs, what they wanted to be in life, and why. I longed for opportunities to talk about what was right and wrong in the world and how to make it better and more beautiful for everyone. I wanted to hear people's life stories, the events that shaped who they were, the lessons they'd learned, the joys and sorrows they'd known in life, and their hopes and dreams for the future.

I had a feeling other people felt the same way, but they opted for the easy way out—the silly jokes, the casual conversations, the weather—content to merely scratch the surface of each other's lives, never really discovering what was going on inside. I did it too. In fact, I was so bad at communicating, I found it difficult to simply talk to people, let alone get them to talk to me.

I noticed that Jim was really good at getting people to open up around the campfire. Usually, it was just shallow surface chatter, but every once in a while, he would draw something deeper out of a person, and that's when everyone's ears perked up. All of a sudden, everyone would become silent and still and just listen, as if we had suddenly discovered gold or something, as if the secrets to some buried treasure were being whispered to us right then and there. As the fire burned and crackled, we would listen along in the darkness as someone shared something deep and personal with the rest of the group. Then, the intimate moment would quietly vanish, like the smoke rising up into the night sky, as everyone returned to the safety of their casual conversations once again.

On that first trip, I noticed how the wilderness had a way of drawing out the hidden truths in all of us. The North Woods seemed to provide the perfect amount of time and space for us to tune into our spirits and reconnect with what was important in life. It was a safe place set apart from the cares and worries of our normal lives, a place where we were free to simply be ourselves and share our deeper, more meaningful thoughts with each other. It wasn't always easy to open up like that, but when we did, it made me wonder if everyone, including our friends, our families, our communities, and the whole world would be better off because of it.

I wanted to live like that for the rest of my life.

chapter 10

anne's tragedy

"There was only one word for it."

On that first of many trips into the Boundary Waters, I noticed something else. It wasn't the quiet sunsets or the gentle moonrises or the misty mornings on the lakes. It wasn't about learning the different kinds of loon calls or hearing the cries of wolves in the distance. It was something quietly happening right before my eyes.

I have to admit that after all these months, I can't remember exactly everything about it, so I might be stretching this one a bit. But it is what it is, another tall tale from the North Woods with a bit of Greek tragedy tossed in there for good measure. You can believe all of it if you like, or just some of it . . . or none of it. Whatever you decide is fine with me. I'll leave it up to you.

One evening around the campfire, as Percy told a story of a bear encounter, I noticed Anne: a first-year guide who was quiet and shy. She was seated next to Percy on the ground, listening to his tall tale about the crazy bear. She hung on his words and reacted to his gestures and jokes. She intently watched as he dramatized the story. She laughed at the goofy way he portrayed the bear. She was fascinated, not with the story, but with Percy.

During the week, Anne tried to get Percy's attention in her own quiet way, but he simply didn't know she was even there. I could see the disappointment in her eyes as Percy would overlook her, walk away, or brush her off in his determination to move on to the next lake. He was such a flirt with most of the girls, so I wondered why he didn't notice her.

Anne was nice, and pretty too, but she was hiding inside herself somewhere, and she couldn't seem to make any sort of impression with Percy. The tender way in which she talked was so attractive to me, but she didn't seem to know I existed, except for the fact that I was physically present. Aside from being kind and polite, she hardly said a word to me.

No, Anne only had eyes for Percy. She knew he didn't have a girlfriend. Not one, at least; he had many, and they were more of the temporary and convenient kind for him, not the deep and lasting kind. I wondered what kind of girl Anne was willing to be for Percy. Was she attracted to his looks or his flamboyant personality? Did she see some familiar traits of her father in him? I couldn't figure it out, so all week long, I watched them both with curious fascination.

Percy was quite watchable himself, just in a painful sort of way. Another thing I never learned from Percy, but saw him do a lot, was fish. It was hard not to notice because he talked about it all the time, yet he wasn't very good at it. At every campsite, once everyone settled down, Percy would go out in a canoe with his fishing pole and a little tub of bait. He usually stayed out for an hour or so, sometimes even after dark, but he wasn't having any luck.

One evening, I noticed him slipping away from shore again. He paddled across the lake and set up shop under a big rocky cliff. From a distance, it looked as if he were sitting in a dark cave under the rocks, and he sort of disappeared into the shadows of the cliff. Not long after he left, we began to hear thunder in the west. Percy knew he shouldn't have been out there, but he couldn't resist another chance to go fishing. With storm clouds rolling in and Percy far away across the lake, there was nothing we could do but wait.

Anne went down and perched herself on some rocks by the water. She called for Percy to return, but he wouldn't budge. As he kept at it, the storm rolled over us, and it began to rain. Then, the lightning came along with a torrential downpour. Everyone scattered to the tents to stay dry. The thunder and lightning boomed and flashed, but Anne simply would not abandon her spot on the rocks. We called for her to join us, but she just kept gazing out across the water.

There was good reason to be concerned. A canoe is the last place you want to be in a lightning storm. Every time there was a flash of lightning, Percy would light up like a Roman candle across the lake. At each strike, his silhouette flashed against the blackness of the cave, showing him sitting in that aluminum canoe with the fishing pole still in his hands. I thought he'd get fried to a crisp for sure, and all my troubles would be over, but thankfully, it didn't turn out that way.

The storm gradually passed, leaving it cold, dark, and miserable outside. We got the fire going again and waited for Percy to show up, hoping that he actually would. Anne kept waiting down on the rocks. About an hour later, sure enough, we heard his canoe pull up, and out of the darkness they came. Percy looked like a miserable wreck. His shirt was covered in blood, but he was grinning from ear to ear. He had his fishing pole in one hand and a bloody mass of something in the other. Anne stood behind him, sopping wet and shivering, but she was smiling as well. It was nice to see them together.

Percy held up the gory mass and said, "I caught me a mess of fish!" He beamed with pride as we stared at the blood everywhere.

"What happened to you?" I asked. "You look like you were in a life and death battle with a monster or something."

"Yeah, that was some storm, wasn't it!" He replied, bubbling over with excitement. "I wasn't catching anything at first, but when that storm hit, they started biting like mad! I stayed dry under the cliff and just kept reeling 'em in one after another."

"But what about all the blood?" I said, still confused.

"I decided to clean 'em in the canoe while I was waiting for the storm to pass," Percy said with a smile. "I chopped their heads off and gutted 'em over there. Then, I threw 'em in the lake!"

Still confused, I stared at the bloody fish parts hanging from his hand. "So, you brought us the heads?" I asked.

"No, you idiot!" he exclaimed in frustration. "These are the fish! So, who wants to fry 'em up?"

We looked at the bloody mass of fish parts in his hand, then at each other, wondering who would be dumb enough to volunteer for the awful task.

"I will," Anne quietly said as she stepped out from behind Percy and smiled up at him.

"Great!" he said, carefully handing his trophies off to Anne. "While you get 'em ready, I'm gonna go get cleaned up."

Anne took the fish down to the lake and rinsed them off. Then, she returned and sprinkled some pepper and spices on them. We watched as she settled down by the fire and began to fry them up.

Percy returned in a new shirt, excited about his big catch. To me, it looked like only a few small scraps—two, or at most, three fish—but he insisted it was a great haul—nine or ten at least, maybe more.

For the first time, Percy watched Anne with keen interest. I'm sure she could feel his gaze as she slid the precious morsels around in the frying pan, carefully flipping them over as they sizzled and popped. It was clearly a momentous occasion for Percy, which validated all the fishing he'd done that week. It was a momentous occasion for Anne too. It was as if she'd been suddenly freed from her chains and freed from her anonymity in Percy's eyes too.

As she fried up the fish, she began to talk. "My folks like to fish at our lake cabin near Bemidji," she said. "Both of 'em do, but my mom never let me fry 'em up before. I've watched her do it a hundred times, though. It's nice to get to do it for the first time."

"They look great!" Percy said, eyeing the pan of fish that, to me, seemed to be visibly shrinking by the second. His comment went for miles with Anne, though. She gazed happily up at him, moving to the side so he could watch as she nudged the fish around, flipped them over, and swished them back and forth.

"I'd be happy to fry up your fish the next time you catch some more," she said. The rest of us quietly laughed as she tried to butter, flip, and fry up Percy right there in front of us.

"Yeah, okay," he said with his eyes glued on the fish.

I had to hand it to him. It was the only time I actually saw Anne happy, and Percy made it happen with that little pile of bloody fish. Everyone got a taste, which went well with the hot cocoa we broke out for the special occasion. We let Percy have most of it since there wasn't very much to go around.

"That was mighty tasty!" Percy exclaimed as he patted his full belly. "Okay, I'm heading for the throne now."

"Thanks for the fish, Percy," Jim said. "They were good."

"No problem!" he exclaimed, heading off into the woods with his flashlight and the bag of toilet paper.

Anne watched him as he lumbered away into the darkness. She had been waiting for him to thank her for all the work she'd done, but he said nothing.

"Thanks, Anne, for cooking up the fish," Jim finally offered from a corner of the fire ring. She sighed sadly as Percy disappeared like a bumbling bear into the deep, dark woods.

A few minutes later, he returned and stretched out by the campfire. He snoozed there as Anne scrubbed the pan clean. He'd noticed her for a split second, but just as quickly, his heart had drifted away again. Anne went back to being unnoticed, anonymous, and sad. Actually, there was only one word for it . . . just sad.

Anne continued to find ways to be near Percy, to help him set up a tent, or casually offer to be his canoeing partner. She was so quiet, and he was so preoccupied with himself. I waited for something to happen, but nothing ever did. For the entire trip, Anne remained helplessly lovestruck. Percy remained self-absorbed and oblivious to it all. And I remained the silent observer.

For the rest of the summer, every time I passed through Annie Lake on the main route to Eddy Falls, I thought of Anne. The dead trees that surrounded that pretty lake reminded me of her. I hoped that someday she would find someone who would notice her, someone who would truly love her.

I was hoping the same thing for myself too.

chapter 11

the chuck and nancy show

"I know what I need, Charles, and I know how to get it."

As staff training rolled on into the second week, there was much to learn and do. We were taught how to lead activities and games in the woods, how to identify a variety of wildflowers and edible berries, how to swamp a canoe and get it back to shore, and how to help someone suffering from hypothermia. The time in camp was nice, but I just wanted to be back on the lakes exploring the wilderness, which was right there at my fingertips.

A few days later, we were out again on another trip. It started out cold and drizzly like the first one, but thanks to Chuck, it was a completely different experience. He was the leader of our group. At first, I worried about it, but my fears were soon put to rest.

Chuck's leadership style was the exact opposite of Percy's. He didn't tear off ahead of everyone else. Instead, he insisted that we stay together, especially on the bigger lakes and in windy weather. He never paddled straight to the next portage, but instead, he led us back and forth, going out of the way to explore a quiet cove, or skirt slowly by a tiny island, or stop to watch a pair of loons in the distance.

It was downright irritating at first, but I grew to appreciate his carefree style. It wasn't about steaming straight ahead as quickly as possible. Instead, it was about taking the time to explore the rocky cliffs, the tiny islands, and the hidden gems along the way. It was about slowing down to see the secret delights, like the delicate water lilies floating in a shallow cove or a majestic moose grazing peacefully by itself in a swampy bog.

Under Chuck's wise but wandering eyes, we finally learned how to be proficient canoe guides. As he trailed along behind, soaking up everything about the place he so dearly loved, we were forced to find our own way to the next lake. He simply handed the map off to someone, who then had to get the group to wherever it was we were going. Chuck just sat back and watched us work it out. He was in no hurry to get anywhere—in fact, the slower, the better.

At one point, I got a bit frustrated with his lollygagging around all the time. I was trying to navigate the group across a confusing lake to a hidden portage somewhere in the distance, and he was off in the back staring up at the clouds in the sky.

"Chuck," I called back to him. "Can you help me out here? Where exactly am I supposed to go?"

"What do mean?" he replied with a carefree grin. "You're already there, Leo. Just enjoy it, dude."

With Chuck wandering around all the time, we eventually realized he wasn't going to find the next portage for us. If someone was having trouble navigating across a lake, we'd all chip in ideas. Together we'd point out campsites and portage heads on a lake. Chuck would just watch and listen, that is, if he wasn't already paddling off to look at a beaver's hut or a turtle sunbathing on a log.

On our second day out, the weather turned absolutely gorgeous, but that wasn't the only thing that caught my attention. I had become friends with a girl named Nancy. She was a second-year guide from St. Olaf College in Northfield, Minnesota. She was friendly, charming, and cute as a button. She could portage a canoe as far as anyone else. She could even lift one on her own if she needed to, but what I found so attractive was her enthusiasm for life and the cheerful way she approached everything. She talked with such emotion and energy. Sometimes it would wear me out just to be around her. It didn't take long to notice that she had her eye on someone in our group. To my surprise, it was none other than Chuck.

When I figured it out, I happily laid back and watched the show. I'm sure Chuck knew what was going on, but he seemed content to just play along with the whole idea like a toy he was tossing around just for the fun of it. Strangely enough, Nancy didn't seem to mind. She'd innocently laugh and toss the toy right back in his face.

I learned a lot by watching the Chuck and Nancy show. We all did. It was fun to see the two of them carry on like an old rooster and a mother hen. I especially enjoyed how Nancy refused to call Chuck by his common name. She preferred to call him by his proper name, Charles. It didn't fit his personality, but it suited her just fine. Each night, everyone gathered on the logs around the fire and waited for the show to start. It was like sitting down in the living room back home waiting for reruns of *I Love Lucy* to come on at six o'clock.

One episode that week featured Chuck and Nancy attempting to show us the proper way to start a campfire. Of course, Chuck refused to use the WhisperLite stoves, ever. I don't know why we even brought them along—just extra weight in the gear bag, I guess.

"No, the only way to cook is on the fire grate," he insisted. "The U.S. Forest Service took the time to put it there, so we're gonna use it. So, you guys go find some firewood because we'll need it for our spaghetti supper, then a campfire later, and breakfast too."

As we scattered into the forest to look for wood, Nancy stubbornly stood her ground. "No, no, Charles, someone has to stay here with you and get supper ready, and it may as well be me."

"Sure, Nancy," he agreed like a whipped mule. "Why don't you go ahead and start on the noodles."

Once we had collected enough wood, everyone gathered back at the fire ring, and Chuck resumed the training.

"Okay, here's how to get a good cooking fire going," he patiently explained, breaking up some small cedar twigs. "Start small at first. Then, add a bit of birch bark and pine needles. Then, light it and blow softly. Once it catches, just add a few bigger branches and viólà! You've got yourself a fire!"

"No, no, Charles!" Nancy objected, as she gently pushed him aside and cleared her throat. "You've got to build a little teepee of sticks over the pine needles first. You know that, silly!" She nudged her way into his space and began stacking branches on the already burning fire. "See, Charles, like this."

"Yeah, well," he mumbled, enjoying the attention. "I guess that works too, but if you don't blow on it, Nancy, it's gonna go out."

"Well, silly," she chattered back. "That's your job, Charles. I'm the one who built the fire, for Pete's sake."

He scratched his beard and calmly said, "I don't think you can't just light a fire and walk away. You gotta keep at it for a while."

"Sure, you can," she replied. "You can walk away from it. Just watch and see. It won't go out."

Nancy got up and sat on a big rock overlooking the fire, leaving him there, still leaning over it, scratching his beard. As the fire began to die, Chuck leaned in and blew on it gently.

"Ha!" she chirped triumphantly, talking over Chuck to the rest of us glued to the TV set. "See, there's proof you can walk away from a fire, and it won't go out!"

"Oh well, c'est la vie," Chuck mumbled.

"That's right!" she replied cheerfully. "What would you ever do without me? I'm right, and now you know it too, you big lug!"

Chuck grinned sheepishly. "Yup, I suppose I do," he said as he threw on a big piece of birch bark just for kicks.

"Blow harder, Charles!" Nancy shouted. "And for goodness sake, don't catch your beard on fire!"

As the birch bark took off, Chuck blew furiously into the fire. It sent a massive puff of smoke billowing up into the air, which engulfed poor Nancy, who was sitting right there next to it.

She jumped up and shouted, "I hate rabbits! I hate rabbits!" She batted her arms frantically at the smoke and pranced around the fire. When the smoke eventually shifted away, she sat back down and proudly declared, "Works every time!"

Chuck just sat back on the ground and laughed as the fire took hold and the flames shot up through the fire grate.

Immediately, Nancy proceeded to the next step in their funny courtship dance. "Charles, it's time to put a pot of water on the fire."

"Yup," Chuck said. "You're right again, Nancy."

"I sure am!" she joyfully announced. "I know what I need, Charles, and I know how to get it."

Chuck laughed. "Yup, Nancy, you sure do."

"I'll get the pot, Charles," she said. "You just take care of the fire like a good boy, and I'll be back in a jiffy!"

"I'm sure you will, Nancy," he replied. "I'm sure you will."

We watched the Chuck and Nancy show go on like that night after night. They could have sold popcorn and soda pop. I would have paid money to see it, but that wasn't necessary because they performed a brand new episode every night around the campfire for free.

During that week, I developed my own secret crush on Nancy, but I wasn't about to spoil the adorable relationship that was blooming right before my eyes. Nancy didn't act that way around anyone else, just Chuck. She was nice to me, and I appreciated it, but she saved her silly pestering ways for Charles: the big hairy bearded man of her happy-go-lucky dreams.

Back at camp, Chuck always seemed like a fish out of water, but out on the lakes, he was right at home. It seemed as if he'd been made for that kind of lifestyle. To me, it felt as if he'd been born a hundred years too late. He would have made a great French fur trapper back in the day, but I couldn't imagine him ever killing anything. He was hairy as all get-out, but he was more like an actual beaver, rather than a trapper who hunts them.

Chuck was a nature lover for sure, a genuine tree hugger, and proud of it, but he was also weirdly domesticated too. Rather than merely boiling water and mixing in dry ingredients, Chuck taught us how to actually use our cook kits the way they were meant to be used.

One morning, I awoke to the sound of Chuck fiddling away in front of the fire grate. He already had a perfect cooking fire going with plenty of hot coals all spread out. Nancy and a couple of others were sitting around looking on and learning from the master. He had a floury batter mixed up in a pot sitting on a rock nearby.

"Pancakes," I thought as I sat down to watch, but there was no frying pan on the fire, just the large cooking pot, which was about one-third full of water, nestled in a heap of coals.

"Gotta wait 'til it's boiling," Chuck said, leaning over the pot. "Then, you pour the batter in the cake pan."

"The cake pan?" I wondered. I'd never seen anyone use the round cake pan in the cook kit before. In fact, most people didn't even bring it along. No one knew how to use it, but Chuck did. When the time was right, he poured the batter into the cake pan and set it down on top of another little pot in the boiling water.

"Then, you add some sugar and cinnamon, and let 'er bake," he said, sprinkling a generous handful over the batter. "Then, you cover it with the fry pan, add a few hot coals to the top, and wait."

We watched and waited as Chuck babied the fire and kept tabs on the Dutch oven he'd just made. After a few minutes, we could smell it: the delicious scent of sugar, cinnamon, and cake. Even the curious chipmunks and a few neighborly birds gathered around to see what Chuck was cooking up for breakfast.

"Okay, then you lift the lid off and check on it," he said, as a big poof of steam wafted into the air. "Looks done to me," he said, poking at the crusty top with a fork. "So, let's lift it out and let 'er cool down."

It looked perfect and smelled so good.

"Viólà," he announced happily. "Homemade coffee cake."

I couldn't believe my eyes. It was so tasty, moist, and sugary sweet. I swore my own mother couldn't make coffee cake that good in her own kitchen oven. And there we were in the middle of nowhere, sitting around an open fire, eating like kings and queens.

"Oh, Charles," Nancy swooned. "This is some mighty delicious coffee cake."

"Thanks," he replied with a grin.

"No, really, Charles, it's scrumptious," she said, nudging him with her elbow. "I love a man who can cook. Guess what, Charles, I'm gonna get you a birthday present when we get back to camp."

"My birthday ain't 'til December," he said.

"Oh, that don't matter," she replied with a wave of her hand. "I'll send it to you as a Christmas present then."

"What?" he asked.

"A chef's hat and a cooking apron," she chirped. "You'd make a handsome chef in a fancy restaurant someplace."

"Thanks," he replied.

"You could cook this up at my place anytime you like," Nancy said, gushing uncontrollably over her big hairy man.

"Yeah," Chuck replied. "Maybe someday."

We watched as the two of them kept at it. I was happy for Chuck. Nancy was quite a catch, but it didn't seem like he was too interested in catching her. Still, I had a feeling she was the one who'd be doing the catching, and he was already hooked.

The next day, we paddled north on Knife Lake and got stuck behind a slow group of fishermen at the portage into Hanson Lake. Chuck grabbed the map and started studying it as we waited.

"How about we take a more scenic route when we get up into Hanson," he suggested. "I'd like to show you guys a lake or two that most people never see around here."

"Sounds good to me," I replied. Everyone else agreed too. We'd follow Chuck anywhere, as long as he kept feeding us coffee cake.

We waited behind the fishermen, and then we portaged into Hanson Lake. About halfway up, we pulled off the water near a campsite on the western shoreline.

Chuck jumped out of the canoe with renewed life. "C'mon, let's go!" he shouted as he lifted a canoe onto his shoulders and took off.

We grabbed our gear and followed after him. It was the steepest portage I'd ever seen. It went straight up, climbing at least a hundred feet before leveling off and going even higher. It was a hundred and ten rods of pure sweat, toil, and agony that led deep into the heart of the Boundary Waters. An hour or so later, we came out of the woods and onto the shores of Cherry Lake, which stretched to the west and was surrounded by beautiful aspen, pine, and birch trees.

We lingered there for a while and rested at the edge of the lake. Then, we portaged almost immediately again, going higher and deeper into the forest through Lunar Lake, Rivalry, and Lake of the Clouds. Each time, we seemed to climb higher until it felt as if we were hiking in the Rocky Mountains. The portages were difficult and hard to find, but the feeling of trekking off into such a remote area filled us with renewed energy. When we drifted out onto Lake of the Clouds, the sun was sinking low in the west just above a long ridge of dark pine trees. We floated there at the top of the world and listened to the loons calling as the day slowly came to a close.

As we paddled north, we didn't say much. We portaged into the last lake for the day, where we camped on an island out in the middle. It was called Gijikiki, which Chuck informed us meant "Cedar Lake" in the Ojibwe language. When I went out later to collect water, sure enough, the entire shoreline was covered with cedar trees.

It had been a long day, but it felt great to be so far away from everything, just a mile or so south of the Canadian border. That night, we sat around the campfire and talked about deeper things. The scent of the burning cedar logs filled the air all around us like sweet perfume. A pair of loons were calling to each other out on the lake. The stars were shining overhead, and the moon was on the rise. We knew we were utterly alone in the heart of the wilderness.

But then, in the darkness, we heard something scraping on the rocks down by the shoreline, followed by heavy footsteps coming up from the lake. Out of the darkness, a figure appeared. No one could believe their eyes as Finn calmly stepped over a log and sat down next to Chuck. What was he doing there? Why had he come? At first, I thought something must have happened, but Finn flashed a reassuring smile at everyone around the campfire ring.

"I thought I'd pay you guys a visit tonight," he said quietly.

"What? Pay us a visit?" I thought. I couldn't believe the old tracker had found us that far out in the middle of nowhere. We were at least ten miles from base camp. There were dozens of lakes and all sorts of different places we could have been. But there he was, Finn, the Big Bear, sitting across from us in the fire ring.

"Oh, Finn, you look exhausted," Nancy said. "You just sit still while I make you some hot tea."

"Sure, darling, that'd be fine," he replied graciously. "You know, you guys are hard to track down."

Finn didn't look exhausted to me. He looked like he could go another ten miles if he wanted to. He was out there paddling around the North Woods, tracking us down, simply because he knew he could, and he was having fun doing it too.

"Nice to see you, Finn," Chuck finally said. "Is everything all right back at camp?"

"Oh, yeah, Chuck, everything's fine." Finn accepted the drink from Nancy. "Thanks, darling," he said, taking a long, slow sip. "I'm just out visiting the guide parties this week," he explained. "I ran into Percy's group back on Pickle Lake earlier today. Carly is out with another party too, you know. I saw them two days ago down on Thomas Lake. Too bad, though, they got a bear on their first night out and lost almost half their food. So, I gave 'em what I had, but it wasn't much. They'll be heading back early tomorrow."

I still couldn't believe Finn was there in the flesh, telling us where all the other parties were and what they were up to. He must have taken off from base camp at least two days after the groups left, and he was sitting there, giving us an update on all of them.

We sat around the fire for another hour or so before heading off to the tents. We gave each other backrubs that night. It felt wonderful on our sore muscles. Nancy made sure to be the one to give Chuck a backrub, and to her delight, he graciously returned the favor. As I fell asleep, I could hear Nancy in the other tent.

"Oh, Charles, you give such heavenly backrubs. I'd drive halfway across the country for one of your backrubs."

"I'm sure you would, Nancy," he replied. "I'm sure you would." I had a feeling he was blushing up something fierce in that tent.

Finn didn't join us in the tents that night. Instead, he politely excused himself and said he'd bed down outside somewhere. We never knew where he slept or when he left, but by morning, the old tracker was nowhere to be found.

The next day, we portaged north into Ottertrack Lake, which was a long narrow passageway along the Canadian border. We followed it northeast to Lake Saganaga and camped on another island there.

The next day was especially windy, but it was in our favor. So instead of paddling, we sailed. Chuck gathered our four canoes together and told us to hang on to the sides as he pulled out one of the tarps. Then, he instructed the people sitting in the front of the two outside canoes to stick their paddles straight up and wrap the tarp around them. What resulted was a giant blue sail that spanned the entire front of the four canoes.

At first, the wind almost blew the tarp away into the lake, but once it was secured correctly, it caught the wind and pushed us forward. Except for the two holding the tarp, everyone could simply lie back, relax, and enjoy the ride. Chuck did a fair amount of work in the stern too. He leaned back with his paddle and steered us between two large islands and on into another big section of the giant lake.

"Leo, you steer for a bit!" he called across to me in the wind. "I'm gonna take a shower!"

"You're what?" I cried back as I grabbed my paddle and plunged it into the water. We were really cruising by then, and it was quite a chore to keep the canoes moving in the right direction.

Chuck whipped off his shirt and spun around in his seat. "Hold on to my boat!" he shouted to the girl next to him.

Then, he leaned over and dipped his entire head completely under the surface of the rushing water. A second later, he popped back up, grinning from ear to ear.

"Oh yeah! That feels great!" he shouted with delight as he shook his head and sprayed everyone in the canoes. Screams ensued, but he seemed completely unaware of everyone's disgust.

Chuck plopped back down in his seat, smiled happily, and asked, "Anyone else want to take a shower?"

"Charles!" Nancy shouted from up in front. "If I were back there, I'd kick you in the lake!"

"I'm sure you would, Nancy!" he replied with a contented laugh. "I'm sure you would!"

The wind carried us almost the entire way across Saganaga. We didn't have to start paddling until we were nearly to the narrow boat channel on the east side of the lake. From there, it was only an hour or so more until we found ourselves rounding the islands back at camp. It had been a great trip.

I was finally beginning to feel at home. I enjoyed the quiet conversations around the campfires, the long paddles across the lakes, and the hard work of camping in the woods. There were so many people at Northern Lights who had a peaceful, rustic, earthy feel to them. They shared a deep sense of responsibility and a sincere love for the earth. They carried themselves with quiet dignity and spoke with careful respect for everyone and everything. I was beginning to feel like one of them.

There was a sense of kinship among us, especially the canoe guides, but with the others at camp as well. It felt as if I'd somehow become a member of a secret wilderness cult without my ever perceiving it. It just happened gradually over those first two weeks. I even felt a kinship with Percy and began to accept him for who he was. But it was the people like Chuck and Nancy, Jim, Anne, and Finn, whom I was most drawn to in the early weeks of that summer.

There was a richness and a depth of character in the people I had come to know. It was seeping into the way I acted, how I thought, and even how I spoke. It was seeping into my heart and soul as well. What had started pretty rough at first was becoming a part of me, and I was beginning to see the impact it would have on my entire life.

I never could have anticipated how those early experiences would change me. I still had eight more weeks of camp to look forward to, and I never could have imagined what was about to take place then either. I felt at peace inside as I prepared to serve as a canoe guide for the rest of the summer.

I had come to the right place after all.

chapter 12
chicago style pizza

"That's it! You two are dead meat!"

My first trip as a canoe guide was completely different from the ones during staff training. It was a rude awakening for me, especially since I was on track in college to become a high school science teacher. Despite the difficulties, I would have to admit that I'd remember it for the rest of my life simply because of one person—someone who was sent along at the last minute, someone who would become a very special friend of mine.

The trip was with a high school youth group from a church in Milwaukee. As I was introduced to them, I had an uncomfortable feeling that it was going to be a rough week. They were young, giggly, and excited, but I got a sense that they were holding themselves back. For some reason, they seemed to remind me of a herd of wild billy goats. I wasn't exactly sure why, but the feeling wouldn't go away. At first, I was amused by their constant giggling, but that feeling would change soon enough.

The leader who brought them made up some excuse and said she couldn't go on the trip after all, so Cassie had to scramble to find a swamper to go along. Thankfully, the one she found was Aria Hunter: the girl who leveled me in the sand on the first day of camp. I didn't know her at all, but when she showed up, I had a feeling that together we would somehow manage things.

As we went through the trip orientation with the group, I realized that the kids had no idea what they were getting into. Most of them were decent paddlers, but they looked shocked when they learned that they'd be cooking, doing dishes, and paddling several miles each and every day. It wasn't at all what they had been expecting. They got a lot more than just sunshine, blue skies, sandy beaches, and s'mores around a cozy campfire.

Aria and I got a lot more too. As we paddled away from camp in the rain, their giggly excitement went through a gradual transformation from quiet and friendly to loud and obnoxious. Their conversations, if they could even be called that, were crude and offensive, usually having to do with dirty jokes, sexual innuendos, random gossip, who's hot, and who's not.

At the first portage, I explained how we'd work together and help each other until everything was across to the next lake. When I was done with my little lecture, however, the students just watched as Aria and I got to work. Aria noticed it immediately. She began to call the students by name, recruiting each one to do a specific task. She divided them into pairs to help lift the packs onto each other's shoulders. Then, she sent them on their way down the trail.

As I trudged off with a canoe, I saw Aria and the last remaining girl lifting the front end of a canoe above their heads. As I hiked away, I could hear Aria encouraging her to give it a shot.

"You can do this!" she yelled. "Come on, Jackie! I believe in you! You can do it, girl!"

On the other side, I dropped my canoe into the water and turned around. To my surprise, there was Jackie hauling that big canoe down to the lake all by herself, followed by Aria, who was beaming with pride. Jackie looked like she was ready to pass out, so I grabbed the canoe and lifted it off her shoulders.

Aria ran over to Jackie and shouted, "Good job, girlfriend! I knew you could do it! You were awesome!"

Jackie nodded and smiled as the boys looked on, amazed.

"Come on, guys!" I yelled. "Let's go get the last two canoes! Who wants to carry one?"

"I do!" came a loud chorus of replies. The guys weren't about to be outdone by a girl, but it was already too late. Jackie had beaten them to the punch.

We paddled north through a long channel that ultimately opened up into Lake Saganaga and the Canadian border. It took us over two hours to make it to the lake. When we got there, I quickly realized that the gusty wind on the big lake was going to be too much for the group. After trying to help them navigate the wind and the waves, we pulled behind an island to rest.

"This is bad," Aria said to me from the front of our canoe.

"Yeah, I don't think they can handle it," I replied, looking at my map for guidance. "It's gonna be dangerous out there in the big part of the lake too."

The weather had grown progressively worse throughout the day. At that point, the clouds overhead were visibly churning and spitting sheets of rain down upon us. As we sat in the canoes wondering what to do, I heard a loud clap of thunder in the west. That was the last straw for me.

"Come on, guys!" I called. "We're going ashore!"

We made a bee-line for the island nearby where everyone hastily scurried up onto the rocky shore. I yanked the canoes up halfway out of the water as Aria dug a tarp out of the equipment pack. As the storm opened up overhead, we all huddled together in a clearing back in the woods. The kids looked miserable standing there like wet rats in their multicolored rain ponchos. Aria ran up with a blue tarp and threw it over everyone. Then, she ducked underneath and joined the huddle. She was grinning from ear to ear.

"This is a nasty one, isn't it!" she cried excitedly. "Come on! Everyone grab the edge of the tarp and sit down!"

The kids obeyed, and soon we were talking and laughing inside our cozy blue bubble. We played games, told stories, and got to know each other as we sat out the storm. Aria taught the group a goofy camp song called "Singing in the Rain," which perked up everyone's spirits. The storm eventually passed over, but the wind didn't. It had become even more blustery, and it appeared as if another wave of storm clouds would be heading our way soon.

I located a couple of campsites nearby, so we set off into the choppy water and headed straight for them to see if one was open.

Thankfully, they both were. We pulled up to the first one and took it. We all worked to unload the canoes and get off the lake. As we raced to set up our tents before the storm hit, the kids pitched in, but they looked a bit shell-shocked from the rough start to the trip.

After the second wave of showers passed through, we talked about how we would divvy up meal chores. The girls seemed to be on board with Aria as their leader, but the boys were still wrestling with the fact that they were being called on to do more work. The girls ended up cooking supper that night, which meant the boys were up for dish duty. The spaghetti meal was not the best, but it was warm and filling. Afterward, everyone sat around the struggling campfire in the growing darkness, enjoying a moment of rest.

I finally got up and began prepping for dish duty in the dark. When I asked the boys to come over and help, I just got blank stares and a few chuckles of laughter. I asked again, but none of the boys moved a muscle. Finally, I walked over to the fire ring and repeated my request, but still, I only got blank stares and lame excuses as the boys tried to avoid eye contact with me. They clearly didn't like the idea of having to wash the dishes in the middle of the woods in the dark.

I was at my wit's end. I had no idea how I was going to get those boys to get up off that log and pitch in. Then, I heard Aria mumble something under her breath as she stood up and stepped into the middle of the fire ring. She faced the four boys and carefully sized up the pathetic situation.

"Okay, you guys," she said coldly. "The girls did the cooking, so now it's your turn. If we're going to survive this trip, you're gonna have to do some work around here."

The boys stared defiantly at her in the dark. Two of them giggled and whispered something to each other.

"All right," Aria said, pointing at the culprits. "You two characters get up and help Leo with the dishes . . . now!"

"Who's gonna make me?" a kid named Morty shot back.

Before Aria could reply, I blurted out, "No one's gonna make you, but if you don't want to get your butt whooped by Aria, you better get up and do as your told."

"Get my butt whooped?" the cocky kid exclaimed with a defiant smirk. "Yeah, right!"

"That's it!" Aria snapped. "You two are dead meat!"

She spun around and stomped down to the lake to cool off. At least, that's what I hoped she was going to do. It was evident that we had a situation brewing, but still, I had absolutely no idea how to handle it. I was disappointed in the guys, who were clearly testing me to see what they could get away with. I didn't know what to do, so I simply tried to smooth things over.

"So, Morty, I'm sorry," I said. "I shouldn't have used those words to get you to help out, but we all need to pitch in."

"I thought this was going to be a vacation," Morty complained. "You guys are making us do all the work."

"Everyone has to help out," I repeated. "If you don't, Aria isn't going to be too happy about it."

"She doesn't scare me," he said stubbornly. "She can't do anything to me and neither can you."

"So, Morty," I said calmly. "Do you remember that big guy, Percy, back at camp when you arrived?"

"Yeah, he was awesome," replied Morty, still digging away at me. "Why couldn't we have him as our guide?"

"Well, you know, Aria . . ." I said slowly, beginning to grin. "She kind of took care of him."

"What do you mean?" he asked, suddenly curious.

"Well, let's just say that…" I spoke slowly and quietly. "Percy said something not so nice to Aria, and that's the last time he ever did that."

"Something not so nice?" Morty echoed, assuming the worst thing imaginable. "What did she do?"

"Oh," I replied with a sly grin. "Let's just say that Aria knocked him flat on his butt right in front of everyone."

"No way!" he shot back in disbelief.

"Oh, yeah," I said calmly. "All it took was one big smack from Aria, and he was crying like a baby who just got spanked. You can ask anyone back at camp. They all saw it."

"What did she do?" he asked again.

"Yeah, good old Percy was seeing stars for the rest of the night," I said, ignoring his question. "I'm just saying that I wouldn't want to be in your shoes right now."

"What do you mean?" he asked.

"It's your butt, Morty," I replied. "I like you and all, but if you don't want to end up like Percy, you better get up off that log and do what Aria said, or else…"

"Or else what?" he replied nervously.

"I don't know. We'll see, won't we?" I said, growing more irritated with him by the second.

To my dismay, Morty sat there unmoved, still mulling over his options. He was a stubborn kid. I thought the battle had been lost, until I saw Aria coming back up from the lake. I grinned with delight as she walked right into the middle of the fire ring, carrying one of the canoes on her shoulders. She marched straight up to Morty and stood directly in front of him.

"Okay, hot stuff," she said firmly. "You can keep acting like a freak if you want to! But I swear, this train is coming through whether you like it or not!"

"What?" I heard him mutter in confusion as Aria walked straight at him. As she approached, he tumbled backward behind the log, landing with a thud on his butt in the dirt. He had no choice but to helplessly lie all the way back in the mud as Aria stepped over the log and put her foot down onto his chest. I lunged forward to catch the canoe as it teetered overhead, but it was unnecessary. Aria somehow managed to maintain her balance. I heard Morty gasp as she stepped onto his chest and kept right on walking forward with the canoe. The other boys sitting beside him had to duck down to keep from getting whacked by the end of the canoe as it passed overhead.

Aria walked behind the fire ring and flipped the canoe back over. Then, she lowered it down onto another log to make a table for the dish crew. She didn't say another word. She simply went to work, setting up the pots of water for the cleanup process. I gave Morty and the boys a wide-eyed look of terror and waited to see what they would do next.

Needless to say, Morty and his troublemaking sidekick got up and went to work on the dishes. Aria didn't look at either of them again. She just snapped orders as they did whatever she said. Their rotten attitudes didn't immediately change, but at least they stopped being lazy good-for-nothings. They huddled together, mumbled complaints, and scrubbed away on the pots and pans for the next hour or so as the rest of us sat around the fire.

After the dishes were done, the boys and I had fun hanging the food pack, but actually, it was more like a game of chicken to them. I attached a rope to a rock. Then, I showed them how to launch it up into the air in an attempt to swing the rope over a branch big enough to hold the pack. The boys saw the danger in the game and immediately took to it. They all wanted a turn at tossing the projectile straight up into the air. Each time the rock went up, they would yell and scramble off in every direction to keep from getting hit by it on its way back down. After several near misses, the rope finally made it over a suitable branch. Fortunately, no one got beaned in the head, and the pack got hung in the end.

We sat around the campfire for a little while longer; then it was off to bed. Once they were in the tents, I checked the campsite over; then I took a big breath and joined the boys. The lame jokes and hot air continued inside the tent for another hour. I suffered in silence as their immature minds spewed out whatever they could think of to get someone to laugh. O, the joys of being a canoe guide in the beautiful, pristine, wild woods of Northern Minnesota!

- - -

The next day was just as windy and rainy as the first one. Sadly, we had to give up our hopes of continuing north to Canada, so we turned south instead. All day long, it was wind and rain, rain and wind, and more wind and rain. We portaged into Red Rock Lake along a muddy mess of a trail. As I carried the last canoe over and dropped it into the water, the kids stood by shivering like miserable wet rats. Aria threw the last pack into the canoe and hopped in.

"Hey, Farm Boy!" she shouted. "Are you having fun yet?"

"Yeah, Hunter! This is a blast!" I replied.

I hopped in with her and called back to the others to follow. They slowly trudged out into the cold water, where the canoes were all nicely prepared and waiting for them. I could hear the canoes scraping on the rocks as they pushed off into the lake. Aria and I looked back and had to laugh just a little bit.

"You know," Aria said with a devious grin, "I'm starting to really enjoy this trip. It's kind of fun torturing a bunch of spoiled high school kids out here in the middle of nowhere."

"You're pretty good at it!" I replied. "Thanks for your help with Morty and the guys last night."

"No problem, Farm Boy!" she said. "I'm just glad you approve of my disciplinary tactics."

"Sure thing," I said. "It's great having you along on this trip. I don't think I could have done this without you."

"We make a pretty good team," she replied. "You're the good cop, you know, and I'm the bad cop."

"Yeah," I agreed. "It's working out pretty well."

"Totally," she said, swinging her paddle into the water. "I'm happy to kick a little butt every now and then."

As we paddled ahead, the rest of the group slowly followed behind through the rain. For the rest of the day, we inched our way slowly across Red Rock Lake until we found a campsite on the south end that was out of the driving wind.

The rain finally let up later that evening. Aria and the girls went to bed early. The boys went off to their tent soon after. I wasn't tired, so I sat and babied the fire for a while. I could just barely hear the boys and girls talking in their tents back in the woods. It was nice to be alone for a while and get a break from their constant chatter. A little later, Aria came back out to the campfire ring. We sat around and talked as the kids drifted off to sleep.

"Hey, Leo," Aria said quietly. "I don't know if I can take three more days of this."

"Why not? You're doing great!" I replied.

"Ugh, I don't think so," Aria grumbled. "I hate to say it, but I don't have much in common with those girls."

"Yeah, that's for sure," I agreed. "But you're doing an awesome job with them anyway."

"Thanks," she replied. "But all they want to do is talk about the latest gossip, who they're dating, and how cute they look. They don't care about anyone else, not even each other."

"Yeah," I agreed. "I see it too, but you're showing them that there's more to life than that. You're setting such a great example for those kids to follow."

"They don't follow me," Aria said as she tossed a stick into the fire. "They don't respect me at all."

"Well, I do," I said. "I think those girls, and the guys too, for that matter, really look up to you. They might not say it, but I think they admire you for being who you are."

"Thanks, Leo," she replied. "I'm really glad I got to come along on this trip. I just didn't expect it to be like this."

"I'm glad too," I said. "It's been great getting to know you."

"You too," she replied. Aria grinned and gave me a little wink. I could see the same fire in her eyes that I'd seen on the beach when she took out Percy with the volleyball.

I meant what I said to Aria, every word of it. I'm not sure if the Milwaukee girls ever grew to respect her or not. I noticed that they watched her quite a bit, but they never changed much. They whispered and giggled among themselves a lot, but they never really included Aria in anything. In their tent at night, I could hear them talking incessantly about their personal lives. Not once did they ask Aria about herself, her life in Chicago, or why she was working at Northern Lights. They simply couldn't break free from their own little lives to notice that there was someone else there too.

I wondered if it was because Aria was only a year or two older than them. I think she could have made a huge impact on the girls if they had been younger, but it seemed like it was just too late. They had already decided who they were going to be, and we wouldn't get to see any real changes in just one week.

Clearly, it was a difficult situation for Aria to be thrown into. It made me realize how tough she was both physically and mentally. There was no question about it; she was great with the students and way more effective than I was. The kids never really cozied up to Aria, but I could see they were watching her. It took a while, but they slowly grew to respect, admire, and fear her.

Through it all—the nasty weather, the tough work, and the difficult kids—Aria really shined. She saved that trip from completely falling apart. She lifted everyone's spirits and kept us on track, including me. When the clouds finally lifted after two days of wind and rain, I realized what an amazing person Aria was: tough, adventurous, enthusiastic, assertive, energetic, spunky, helpful, caring, and creative. The list of outstanding qualities could go on and on.

The weather turned clear and sunny for the rest of the trip. We continued to wrestle with the students over simple chores, like helping to prepare meals, getting water, doing dishes, setting up tents, loading canoes, portaging packs, and even merely paddling. They wanted to sit around everywhere—at portages, in the canoes, at campsites—always trying to get out of doing anything helpful. It was a never-ending game to them. It felt as if Aria and I were physically pulling the entire group through the wilderness all by ourselves. As a matter of fact, that's exactly what we were doing. C'est la vie!

- - -

The next day, we paddled south into Alpine Lake and explored the islands scattered around everywhere. Two of the boys, Morty and a big kid named Oliver, kept paddling ahead of the group for some reason. No matter what I said, they simply wouldn't stay with us. Late in the afternoon, as we approached a big bare rock in the middle of the lake, the boys spotted a pair of white gulls sitting on a large nest on top of the rock. They looked back at me as if to ask for permission to go on ahead and explore the nest. Regardless of what I might have said, they were too far ahead for me to do anything about it. All I could do was watch as they paddled straight for it.

"I wouldn't do that if I were you," I mumbled softly to myself, but it was already too late.

As Morty and Oliver drew near the rock, the gulls stood up and began to squawk nervously. When the boys got within fifty yards of the rock, both of the birds lifted off and began to circle overhead. I tried to call to the boys, but they were too far ahead to hear me. As they paddled stubbornly forward, the two gulls began to swoop down right over the top of them in their canoe. I couldn't figure out why the boys weren't getting the message.

For some reason, they just kept paddling forward, straight into the danger zone. As they drew up to the rock, the two angry gulls finally had enough. They began to swoop straight down over the boys in their canoe just like dive-bombers strafing an enemy ship. The boys raised their paddles up to fend off the angry birds, but it only seemed to make matters worse.

We watched in shock and awe as the two frantic gulls swooped right over the top of the boys' canoe, laying down long streams of white poop, some twenty yards long, that splattered across the surface of the water and came down all over them and their canoe. They screamed in horror and waved their paddles in the air, but that only made the birds more agitated. They squawked incessantly and kept right on bombarding the boys and their canoe in a wild frenzy. The rest of us stopped paddling and had a good laugh as the wild poop fight carried on in the distance.

Finally, the boys turned and paddled away as quickly as possible, chased by the two angry birds that kept on swooping and pooping all over the place as they retreated. When the rest of us caught up to them, we enjoyed hearing their wide-eyed tale of the battle with the crazy seagulls with a bad case of diarrhea. The two boys and their canoe were plastered with the stuff everywhere.

"There's only one way to wash all that crap off," Aria said, pulling up next to their canoe.

"How's that?" Morty asked.

"Like this!" Aria said, giving the side of their canoe a big shove down in the water.

Both of the boys screamed as they tumbled headfirst into the lake. Aria tried to tip their canoe over too, but it wouldn't go. For the next few minutes, Morty and Oliver swam around in the lake and got cleaned off as they recovered from the fierce battle with the angry birds. We left them there to figure out how to get back into their boat as we paddled on ahead for a while.

After a lazy day of exploring Alpine Lake, we meandered south, thanks to a slight tailwind that pushed us gently across the lake. We portaged up into Jasper Lake and stopped to take pictures of the waterfalls there. We made camp shortly after that on the east side of Jasper in the narrow channel not far from the falls.

- - -

After supper, Aria gathered everyone in a grassy clearing down by the lake to play a game she called Star Tipping. One person stood in the middle of a circle made up of everyone else. The person in the middle looked up at a star in the night sky and spun around as everyone else slowly recited the words of an old English poem. "Starlight, star bright, the first star I see tonight. I wish I may; I wish I might have the wish I wish tonight."

After that, Aria shined her flashlight in the person's eyes for a split second. Then, everyone held their hands up to catch the person who tried to remain upright for as long as possible. It was never very long before the person would tumble off to one side or the other and fall over into the arms of someone in the circle. The kids absolutely loved the game.

Aria was the last one to go. When she stepped into the middle, the kids got really excited. They spun her around faster and longer than anyone else, and then they let her go. She stood still for a split second and then started to hobble sideways, trying not to tip over. She drifted left toward Morty, who should have caught her, but instead, he stepped back and let her keep going.

"Whoops, my bad," he mumbled as Aria tumbled helplessly off-balance past him in the direction of the lake.

As she desperately tried to keep her balance, Aria started running in a sort of off-kilter way, faster and faster, straight into the lake. With a scream, she finally flopped over into the water and went completely under. The kids erupted with screams of delight at the grand finale to Aria's fun game. She came back up, however, gasping for air and roaring like a fire-breathing dragon.

"Morty!" she screamed. "You're gonna pay for that!"

Aria came stampeding out of the water after Morty, who yelped like a scared puppy and took off at a sprint toward the fire ring. Aria chased him all around the campsite, shouting at the top of her lungs. Over the logs, around the tents, and down the trail to the throne, they both went. Then, they came back past us again, where out of sheer terror, Morty bolted straight into the lake at a dead sprint.

"Stay out there, freak!" Aria yelled from the edge of the lake. "If you know what's good for you, you won't get out of the water until I've gone to bed!"

We all gathered around the campfire and hung out for a while. Morty eventually got out of the water and tiptoed by us, shivering with cold on his way to the tent. Aria threw him a threatening glance as he shuffled by shaking in fright. She definitely made an impression on the ornery kid, that's for sure.

- - -

The next day, we backtracked into Alpine Lake again and turned for home. I led the wandering flotilla of lazy paddlers north around a point and down some rapids that fed into Diamond Lake. We had to jump out of the canoes and hold on to the sides as we bounced around rocks and hopped over slippery logs in the rushing water. There were a few scrapes, and a few kids got dunked, but it was worth it.

Thanks to a nice tailwind on Diamond Lake, we strapped the canoes together and sailed east. It was still early in the afternoon when Aria spotted a sandy beach on the north shore tucked nicely underneath a few enormous cedar trees. We pulled in closer and discovered that it was an open campsite, so we stopped for lunch.

We ended up staying there for the rest of the afternoon. As the kids played and lazed around on the beach, Aria and I set up camp and tried to do as little as possible.

Later, as we were making homemade pizza for supper, Aria surprised us all. She pulled out a whole extra slab of mozzarella cheese she had smuggled out of the trail shack before we left. She had an extra summer sausage and more pasta sauce to go with it too.

"How did you get away with that?" I asked.

"Where is Chuck in the middle of the night?" she hinted.

"Sleeping," I replied.

"Exactly," she said with a sly grin.

The kids were thrilled with the thick doughy pizza we made over the open fire. They couldn't believe how good it tasted. I figured they were starving by then, so just about anything would taste good. I had to hand it to Aria, though; she had really come through for us.

"That's Chicago-style pizza!" Aria announced proudly. "That's the kind they make in the Windy City."

"It's awesome!" Morty replied. "It's the best pizza I've ever had!"

That evening, the kids were exhausted and went to bed early again. I stoked the fire as they laughed and joked inside the tents. I had no desire to sleep with a bunch of billy goats, even for one more night, so I rolled out my sleeping bag by the fire. It was the most peaceful time of the entire trip for me.

After the girls fell asleep, Aria snuck out and joined me. We sat around the fire and talked quietly as the kids in the tents gradually drifted off to sleep.

"Well, Leo, this has been a pretty fun trip," she said.

"It sure has," I replied. "These kids have really been something, though, haven't they?"

"They've been all right," she said softly. "You know, they sort of remind me of myself."

"How so?" I asked.

"I used to be a lot like them when I was younger," she replied. "I think they just need a heavy hand, but it doesn't sound like they're getting it back where they come from."

"Yeah, they're pretty stubborn," I said. "Don't you wonder what they're going to be like when they grow up?"

"If they grow up," she added.

"Yeah," I replied. "It seems impossible, but miracles can happen."

"If you say so," Aria said, looking somewhat skeptical.

"We did what we could," I replied, wondering if it were actually true or not.

"Well, I'm cashing it in," Aria said with a sigh. "I'm wiped out from this trip . . . mentally wiped, that is."

"I am too," I said. "I'm so glad you're here, though."

"Right back at you, Leo," she replied.

We sat around staring into the fire for a long time as the flames danced and swayed back and forth. The small pine branches popped like tiny firecrackers. The sparks shot swiftly upwards and disappeared into the darkness above.

"Come on, Leo," Aria said suddenly. "Come with me."

"Where to?" I asked.

"Out on the lake," she said. "Let's go out for just a little while."

"Okay, that sounds good to me," I replied.

Without making any noise, we tiptoed down to the beach and carefully hopped into one of the canoes. I climbed up into the front and let Aria steer in the back. We paddled quietly through the water away from the shore. After just a few minutes, we were a hundred yards away from the campsite. It looked tiny and peaceful so far away on the shoreline. All our struggles with the rebellious teens suddenly seemed to disappear.

I stopped paddling and just sat back as Aria kept moving us forward. She quietly steered the canoe farther and farther away from the shore. I didn't say anything to stop her. I just let her take us wherever she wanted to go. In that quiet moment, I felt a bond forming between the two of us. It was as if she and I had suddenly found each other, by surprise, and realized how much alike we actually were. Aria finally stopped paddling and let the canoe float aimlessly on the glassy lake.

"You love it up here, don't you, Hunter?" I said.

"Yeah, this is the best place in the whole world," she replied. "It really makes me feel at peace inside."

"What are you going to remember from this trip?" I asked.

"Oh, I don't know," she said. "I'm not very good at answering questions like that. I'll probably remember Morty the most. He's been a pretty hard case this whole trip."

"He's gonna remember you, that's for sure," I said. "I wouldn't be surprised if he ended up as a canoe guide someday."

"Oh, I don't know about that," she replied.

"You know what I'm gonna remember from this trip?" I asked quietly from the front of the canoe.

"What?" she asked.

"You, Aria, I'm gonna remember this trip because of you."

I felt like saying a few other things, but I checked myself. I still hardly knew anything about Aria Hunter, but I had a feeling the trip was something that both of us would look back on with fondness. At the time, I didn't know what it meant to her, but she would tell me more about it later that summer.

"Cool," she said quietly from the back of the canoe. "That's cool, Leo. Thanks."

She didn't say anything else, but I could tell she was thinking about my words. I was thinking about them too. I wondered how much more we would get to be together over the next few weeks. I was hoping for more, and I hoped she was too.

We floated around on the glassy lake for a little while longer. It was a cloudy night, but we could still see a few stars in different patches of the sky. It felt good to be out there with Aria, floating on the water together. We drifted around in silence for over an hour, enjoying the quiet stillness of the night.

It was tempting to paddle away and leave the students there, but we had a responsibility to keep. We hadn't hung our food pack either. So, reluctantly, we paddled back to shore. It was quite the reality check to return to the messy campsite just to guard the food and a bunch of snoring teenagers as they slept, oblivious to everything good and decent and beautiful in the world.

"Goodnight, Aria," I said, settling back down in my sleeping bag by the campfire. "See you in the morning."

"Yeah, Leo, goodnight," she said as she walked slowly away to the girls' tent. "Thanks for everything."

Aria crept back to her tent and joined the girls who were fast asleep inside. I curled up by the fire for the night, happy to sleep by myself in the open air. The ground was hard as a rock, but that didn't matter. I was out like a light in just a few seconds.

- - -

In the middle of the night, I felt something kicking me in the side. I thought it was just part of a dream, so I ignored it at first. Then, it kicked me again, and a low voice came from directly above.

"Hey, Leo," it mumbled. It was a deep voice, Oliver's, the big blond kid in the group.

I half-opened my eyes and stared up into the darkness. Oliver's big frame stood over me, completely black, silhouetted against the starry sky above. He was leaning over me, lying there on the ground next to the smoldering remains of the fire. As I slowly drifted out of my foggy dream somewhere, the kid reminded me of a big fuzzy rabbit in a world full of billy goats. He kicked me again. It took a few seconds for his words to actually make any sense to me.

"Hey, Leo, dude, are you okay?" His words tumbled down on me like boulders. He sounded strangely worried.

"Yeah, Oliver, I'm fine," I grumbled with dismay. I rolled over in my sleeping bag and tried to go back to sleep, unimpressed at his sudden concern for my personal well-being.

Oliver, however, didn't go away. Instead, he loomed over me and repeated his desperate plea, "Dude, dude, Leo, dude."

His deep voice was like a drum pounding away at my sleepy peace of mind. I realized the big kid wasn't going to let me off the hook until he got what he wanted, whatever it was. I cracked an eyelid open again and squinted up into the darkness.

"What is it?" I asked, more than a bit irritated.

I only half remember what exactly he said, but clearly, it was an emergency. Standing over me there in the dark, Oliver rambled on about how he needed to go to the throne. I struggled to regain consciousness as his words tumbled down around me. Like a hammer and chisel, they continued to pound away on my aching skull. Where was something? A trail? A rabbit hole? And what about the toilet paper? Where was it?

"You're a big boy, Oliver," I said harshly. "You can find it on your own. I'm sure of it."

But the big kid apparently couldn't. So, painfully, I rolled over and felt around for a flashlight somewhere on the ground. Then, for the longest time, and with that big helpless kid following close behind, I stumbled and fumbled around the campsite shooting the light back and forth in the dark. It was a royal mess. Packs, paddles, life jackets, and clothes were strewn everywhere.

Oliver hobbled along after me, hopping up and down like a crazed jackrabbit, growing ever more frantic as the seconds ticked by. He really had to go something fierce! Finally, I spotted it: the equipment pack, which had been shoved under a canoe a few hours earlier. It was jammed so far underneath that only a witless billy goat could have done it. With a muffled curse, I yanked it out. Then, with reckless abandon, I dug through the pack and found the bag of toilet paper.

I handed it off to him like a prized carrot and mumbled, "There you go, Oliver, have at it."

But the big kid just stood there, still desperately hopping up and down and scratching his thick mop of ratty blond hair. He was a good-looking teen, just not at four o'clock in the morning. Why he didn't just find a tree, or a hole, and let it fly was beyond me. I just wanted him to do it somewhere far, far away.

"Where's the trail?" he asked. He looked around helplessly in the dark, peering back into the woods. I let out another muffled groan under my breath. There was no way in hell I was going to hold his hand all the way back to the throne, stand there while he did his duty, and then walk him back and tuck him into bed again. The stubborn kid was on his own!

"If you really gotta go, Oliver, you'll find it, believe me," I said as I handed him the beloved flashlight and pointed aimlessly to the entire woods behind him.

"Oh, okay," he said, tumbling to the side on one wobbly leg. He hopped, skipped, and jumped his way back into the woods with the bag of toilet paper flipping and flapping back and forth in his hand. It was such a relief to hear the crinkly sound of that plastic bag as it drifted farther and farther away into the darkness.

I don't know if he ever found the throne. I didn't care one way or the other. I dropped back down onto my sleeping bag and slowly closed my sleepy eyes again. He could have gone to Canada for all I cared. I was sure that whatever it was would run its course, and all would come out okay in the end.

But then, as I lay drifting off to sleep, wouldn't you have guessed it, I had to go too! With one last muffled groan, I got up again and found a tree nearby. Fortunately, the entire forest is a throne when you're alone at night in the woods.

"Sleep," I mumbled to myself as I slowly drifted off to sleep again. "Wonderful sleep."

About an hour or so later, I woke up again as it started to get light out. Unfortunately, I could never keep my eyes shut when the sun was up. Still sore and groggy from sleeping on the bare ground, I rose and started getting ready for the day. I paddled out and got water from the lake, built a fire, and made a heaping pile of pancakes for the group before even one of them rolled out of bed.

We lazed around the campsite and down at the beach all morning. After breakfast, we loaded up the canoes and headed for home. It was only a hop, skip, and a jump back to base camp. For some reason, the kids broke into joyful song as we paddled through the labyrinth of islands along the way.

Morty and Oliver paddled on ahead as usual and disappeared around a small island. Nobody noticed until the two of them snuck up behind us and started a splash fight with the girls. We took a break to play bumper boats and get each other completely soaked. Then, it was off again for Northern Lights.

On the way back, I soaked up the morning sunshine like medicine. The beauty all around was breathtaking—the light reflecting off the sleepy lake, the swirling ripples from the canoes, the lichen-covered rocks that stuck out of the water, the subtle shades of green trees, and the silvery dead tree trunks along the shoreline. I tuned out the rest of the group and breathed in the misty morning air. I listened to the sound of my paddle gurgling through the water. I watched a family of nervous mergansers swim hurriedly along the edge of the lake. A bald eagle soared high overhead. I slowly hypnotized myself as I paddled steadily, my eyes half-closed—stroke, stroke, stroke—through the calm, clear water.

It was only when we rounded the point near base camp and then drove our canoes up onto the sandy beach by the boat landing that I finally awoke again. It was good to be back.

I looked around at my helpless group of kids. The beach was littered with their stuff: canoes, life jackets, paddles, Duluth packs, water bottles, towels, and wet clothing everywhere. There was still so much to do, and those kids needed a lot of guidance. We started by flipping over the canoes and putting away the paddles and life jackets, but that was just the beginning.

"I have to speak at the campfire later tonight," I thought to myself. "What am I going to say?"

I would have to come up with something.

chapter 13

like herding goats

"I'm so glad they're finally gone."

For the rest of the morning, we went through the clean-up process. We visited Chuck up at the trail shack, where we put away our gear and scrubbed our dirty pots until they were shiny and clean. Then, it was off to lunch in Starlight Lodge, where we gorged ourselves on real food that tasted absolutely delicious after a week out on the lakes. Then, we were off to visit the camp store, where they had all kinds of Northern Lights paraphernalia as well as candy and soda pop.

Aria and I took the group back to their cabin, where everyone changed into swimsuits. Then, it was off to the sauna—a final ritual that every group got to enjoy before leaving Northern Lights. We led everyone down to the cable bridge and across the channel to Eagle Island. We kept hiking through the woods until the trail curved around to where the sauna had been built by the edge of the lake.

The sauna was a wooden shack next to a long dock that ran out into the water. There was a stove tucked underneath the building and a stack of firewood there to stoke the fire. Smoke was pouring out of a black pipe that ran up the side of the tiny building. The sauna, as I had been told, was the third one built at Northern Lights in the past four years. Apparently, the average lifespan was just a little over a year before it was expected to burn down. So, we were told to enjoy it while it lasted, and of course, try not to burn it down.

As our group packed inside, I threw some fresh water on the hot rocks and shut the door behind me. There was barely enough room for our group to squeeze into the small space where two rows of cedar benches had been built into the sides of the cabin. As we sat in the darkened room, enjoying the intense heat and dripping with sweat, the kids began to talk about the trip.

They remembered paddling in the storm on Lake Saganaga the first day and seeing the shores of Canada in the distance. They remembered seeing eagles soaring in the sky and hearing the loons call out to each other in the evenings. They remembered the pretty waterfalls on Jasper Lake, the tough portages, and shooting the rapids out of Alpine Lake. They remembered Morty and Oliver getting plastered by the crazy seagulls. They remembered star tipping and watching Aria topple sideways into the water. They remembered sailing with the wind across Diamond Lake and finding the campsite with the sandy beach on the north shore. They remembered swimming in the crystal-clear water and picking blueberries high up on a bare rock behind the campsite. They remembered singing in the canoes and having splash fights on the way back to Northern Lights.

The trip had started pretty rough, but after five days out on the lakes, the kids had come through it all with some great memories. As they talked among themselves, I thought of a few highlights for myself: the soaring columns of magnificent white clouds, the clear blue sky reflected on the water, the powerful forces of nature at work in the wind and the waves, the simple joy of stretching out on a sandy beach in the sunshine, and working together to portage canoes and packs from one lake to the next.

The heat in the sauna seemed to have a soothing effect on all of us. When Morty threw another cup of water on the rocks, the air became so hot and steamy inside, it was nearly impossible to breathe.

I called it. "Come on, guys! We're jumping in! Follow me!"

Everyone barreled out the door, hung a left, and raced down the long dock that ended about twenty feet out in the lake. We all jumped into the cool water—arms flailing, voices screaming, bodies splashing and diving and swimming around, and making way too much of a noisy ruckus than was really necessary. Then, we climbed out and went back to the sauna for another fifteen minutes of sweating, and then we did it all over again. It was a great way to end the trip.

After supper, Aria and I escorted our group down to the boat landing to say goodbye. They seemed to have changed from the first day we met them, but the giggling had never completely gone away. They gave us a big group hug before climbing into the Voyageur canoe and paddling off. Aria and I smiled and waved as they joked around, teased each other, and giggled their way back across Diamond Lake to the mainland far away. I would never see a single one of them again for the rest of my life.

"Wow, I'm so glad they're finally gone," I mumbled as I turned to go. "That was quite a trip."

"Crikey, mate!" Aria exclaimed as she raised her hand and gave me a high five. "That was bloody hell!"

"Where'd you learn to talk Aussie like that?" I asked.

"Oh, I got a friend back in Chicago at school," she said. "She's gonna come and visit me in a couple of weeks."

"What's her name?" I asked.

"Esther," replied Aria. "She's my best friend."

"Oh, okay," I said. "That'll be nice."

Later that night, Aria and I talked at the campfire program about our trip with the kids from Milwaukee. I did most of it. Aria pretty much just smiled and nodded. As I talked in front of everyone, it felt weird not to have the students there to back me up, but it was probably for the best. Most likely, they would have stood there giggling like billy goats the entire time. I didn't get too many laughs, but I found it fairly easy to recount all the memories they'd come up with about the trip. I had a feeling they would remember it with great affection and delight. The Boundary Waters always seemed to have a way of creating little miracles like that.

After the trip, I did a lot of thinking about Aria too. What I said to her on Diamond Lake was the absolute truth. I would remember that trip mostly because of her. On the first day of camp, she had won my respect and admiration. Then, on the first trip of the summer, she had won my complete trust, friendship, and undying loyalty as well. Our companionship during the trip eventually gave way to a deep and enduring friendship.

For the rest of the summer, Aria and I were continually bantering back and forth in a way that others couldn't understand or appreciate. I quickly realized that Aria was not only physically and mentally tough, she was also brutally honest, fiercely loyal, and a lot of fun to have as a best friend. I adored her dry, snarky sense of humor most of all. She didn't seem to get along too well with most of the other camp staff, but I didn't mind. As far as I was concerned, Aria was terrific, and when it came to our friendship, I was all in.

About halfway through the summer, I began to wonder how she really felt about me. I think other people at camp were starting to wonder too. She seemed to have grown overly attached. I began to worry about the possibility that she might like me more than just a little bit. For me, the age difference was the big issue, and with Aria being only eighteen, I felt like I had to keep my distance, at least for one more year.

The way I did that, for better or worse, was by always joking around with her. The way I figured it, if we were always goofing around, it would be safe, and nothing would turn serious. Only later did I learn that it only made Aria's affection for me stronger.

Without a doubt, we became good friends that summer. Some of the other camp staff picked up on it, and some of them let me know, in not so many words, that they didn't like it. In spite of that, I didn't worry too much about what the others thought. It was what it was, and Aria was truly remarkable.

What could I do about it anyway?

chapter 14
a vision of beauty

"What? Is she waving at me?"

As the summer moved along, I was out on the lakes with a new group every week. I wasn't in base camp very often, usually just two or three days at a stretch. On my days off, I either caught up on my sleep or I went out on short trips on my own time.

After the trip with the group from Milwaukee, my parents came up for an overnight on Diamond Lake. I was also planning a three-day trip with my uncle and two cousins for later in the summer. It was nice to have my family take an interest in my summer job. They'd never been too interested before, so I was enjoying the unexpected attention from back home.

When I was in base camp, I found myself alone much of the time. It was hard to make friends with anyone when I was never there. The staff at camp had bonded quickly, but any friendships I'd begun during staff training seemed to go up in smoke once the actual groups started coming. To my surprise, the best friend I made at Northern Lights was Aria Hunter. Without her, this story would be over by now. But thanks to her, this is where the story really begins.

Aria and I had a way of going at each other lovingly, relentlessly, and sometimes toxically, ever since that first week of camp when we served together as guides. Aria had just graduated from high school that spring. She had been a camper at Northern Lights in junior high. Ever since then, it had been her dream to work there someday. She couldn't wait to be a canoe guide, so she signed on as a swamper in order to be at camp for the entire summer.

Whenever I was in base camp, we hung out together. She made me feel good about myself. She made me smile. Aria was the only one that summer who could really get under my skin and make me laugh out loud. I'm sure everyone could hear us walking along the trails at camp, with Aria talking a mile a minute, and me just laughing along.

Aria and I were totally different from each other in so many ways. We were from completely different backgrounds. I was a plain white college student from rural Iowa. Aria was a rough-and-tumble teenager from the north side of Chicago. She was three years younger than me, which seemed like a lifetime to me, and she was black too. Her racial makeup and the color of her skin didn't matter one bit to me. I don't think it was a big deal for anyone else either, but the age difference was. Unfortunately, I think it made our friendship a bit questionable for some people at camp.

The more we hung out together, the more paranoid I became about it. I tried not to think about what others thought or what Aria's parents or my parents might think. I just wanted to enjoy our friendship while it lasted—if it lasted. I didn't care what she looked like, where she came from, or how young she was. I just liked her a lot. I was just surprised at how quickly we clicked and became such good friends.

About four weeks into the summer, Aria and I and a bunch of other camp staff left dinner early and hiked down to the dock by the beach. A large group of visitors was arriving that afternoon, and we'd been called on to serve as the welcoming committee.

Cassie had received word that they were crossing the channel to Northern Lights in the Voyageur canoes, so we hurried down the trail through the woods to greet them. Aria was excited because her friend, Esther, was coming that day with an outdoor adventure group from Chicago. They were planning to be at camp for three weeks to help finish off the construction of a new log cabin on the south side of the main island.

Aria had been talking about Esther a lot as the day of her arrival approached, so I knew a few things about her. Esther was a foreign exchange student from New Zealand. She had been in the United States for the past year, taking classes at the University of Chicago.

That's where Aria met her, in a course on environmental justice, and that's where they became friends. Aria encouraged her to join the outdoor adventure group and then spend some time at Northern Lights before she had to go back to New Zealand.

As we arrived at the beach near the dock, the two big Voyageur canoes were slowly coasting in next to the boat landing. There were about fifty people on board the canoes. They started climbing out with their luggage to be led off to their cabins and get settled in. We watched them from the walkway above the beach, waiting to help the new arrivals with their luggage if necessary.

Suddenly, my eyes caught sight of a beautiful girl, tall and slender, standing in the middle of the chaotic scene below. She had dark red hair, lots of it, thick and long, that fell down below her shoulders in wavy swirls that curled up at the ends. She glowed in the late afternoon sun and appeared to be on fire as the light sifted through the long red locks that hung down almost to her waist.

The girl was wearing a black skintight T-shirt, with a jean jacket over the top, army green capris tied up at the knees, and a pair of rugged black hiking boots. She had on a pair of sunglasses that seemed to match her hair and her dark red lipstick. But the most striking feature of the girl was the wave of light brown freckles that swept across her nose in a beautiful arch from cheek to cheek.

She removed her sunglasses and scanned those of us standing up on the beach. I could see her eyes—deep sapphire blue—surrounded by thick dark eye shadow. They seemed to glow with an intense luminescence, like blue flames of fire. As she stood there with her knapsack flung over her shoulder, she looked intimidating, tough as nails, and even a bit dangerous. I couldn't take my eyes off the girl who appeared so fierce and wild and so out of place, standing in the middle of the crowded mass of people below.

Suddenly, the beautiful redhead raised her arm straight up in the air and waved excitedly. "What?" I thought. "Is she waving at me? Yes, she is!" She was looking directly at me. As she smiled, her face lit up, and I caught a glimpse of her dazzling eyes that seemed to reflect the deep blue sky and green pine trees all around.

I looked around and started to raise my hand to wave back, when suddenly, she called out, "Aria! Aria, it's me! I made it!"

Aria, who had been standing behind me, shrieked so loudly it made me flinch and double over in surprise. Aria shoved me aside and lunged quickly past. She ran down to the dock and gave the beautiful redhead a big bear hug. Then, she stepped back and smiled at her. "So, this is Aria's friend," I thought to myself, "Esther, the exchange student she'd met at the University of Chicago."

I made my way through the mass of people and stood nearby as the two girls caught up on their lives. As I watched them laughing and talking, one word kept popping into my head, "Wow!" Esther seemed even taller up close and more fierce than ever. A cluster of silver necklaces hung down over her shirt. They matched the other jewelry she was wearing: a collection of bracelets, three rings, and a pair of large dangly earrings.

Aria suddenly noticed me standing there. With a jerk of her arm, she pulled Esther over and introduced us. "Leo, this is Esther, my best friend in the entire world! I love her so much!"

Esther extended her hand and said with a smile, "Hey, mate!"

I shook her hand, grinned like a schoolboy, and replied awkwardly, "Welcome to Northern Lights."

Aria immediately turned back to Esther and gave her a big shove. "I'm so glad you came!" she shouted. "We're gonna have so much fun! Come on! I'll take you to our cabin."

Apparently, my services were no longer needed, so I turned to go. But then, Aria barked at me, "Leo!" and pointed to Esther's luggage on the dock. Like an obedient dog, I picked up her things and followed behind as they bounded away up the trail.

As Aria talked a mile a minute, I analyzed the introduction, thinking about what Esther said, "Hey mate," and what I said, "Welcome to Northern Lights." I kicked myself and despaired, "Good grief, Charlie Brown! You could have done better than that!"

I thought about the touch of her warm, soft fingers as we shook hands. I didn't fully realize it then, but my fascination with Esther had begun the first moment I'd laid eyes on her. I wanted to know more about her. I wanted to hear what she was saying to Aria up ahead. As I followed along, I took some solace in the fact that I was carrying her backpack, sleeping bag, and pillow in my arms. So basically, I was the bellhop. Whoopee!

At the cabin, I followed the girls inside and dropped the luggage on an empty bunk. Aria continued her mindless chattering. Then, as if by accident, she noticed me standing nearby again.

"Thanks, Leo!" she exclaimed. Then, she shoved me out the door and yelled, "See you at the campfire tonight!"

I stumbled out the door and nearly toppled over into the bushes at the bottom of the steps, twisting my left ankle in the process.

"You're welcome," I muttered as I limped away, a bit hurt at being so rudely excluded like that.

I couldn't think of anything else to do, so I walked back to my cabin. I had been out on the lakes almost every day so far that summer, and I was looking forward to spending a few days in base camp. It would be a nice change of pace. Even so, my heart still yearned to return to the lakes. I knew it wouldn't be long until I got another group and would be out again.

When I got to the cabin, Chuck was there lying on his bunk. He had just returned from a trip with a group of youth. It was the only one he would make all summer. He'd only been out because they were shorthanded that week and needed him to go. He had gladly done it. He didn't especially like being stuck in base camp doing the trail shack job. It was a lot of busywork, packing out the food, making sure everyone got their tents, cook kits, and other gear. I knew where his heart really was—out on the lakes.

I liked Chuck, even though he was a bit rough around the edges. As the summer rolled along, he seemed to be turning into a wild man, ever more hairy, disheveled, and bearded. He hadn't shaved in a long time, and his beard was starting to gobble up his face.

"Hey, Leo," he greeted me, peeking out from under the wide-brimmed hat that was covering his eyes.

"Hey, Chuck," I replied. "Are you going to the campfire?"

"Yup," he replied. "My group's gonna talk about our trip tonight."

"Oh, cool," I said as I crawled up into my bunk.

He rolled out of his and grabbed a towel. "I'm gonna go take a shower," he said. "See you at the campfire."

"Sure, I'll see you there," I replied.

On my first day at camp, Chuck had welcomed me warmly, but it didn't take long to realize he was a man of few words. The time we'd gone out canoe surfing seemed to be a strange anomaly. Since then, our friendship had been limited to just a few sentences at a time, usually only regarding the necessary things in life. I was pretty introverted myself, but he had me beat by a mile.

As Chuck hiked off down the trail into the woods, I relaxed in my top bunk. It was the only place at camp that was my own personal space. I grabbed my old beater guitar like a long-lost friend. Then, I leaned back against the bunk rail and picked out a mellow tune. I treasured those quiet moments, just me and my guitar, surrounded by the pine trees, the sparkling water, and the fading light of the sun setting in the west.

Outside, shadows crept across the still waters of the lake below. The sun had fallen below the trees on the ridge overlooking the cabins, but far away to the east, I could still see its light blazing across the lake in the wide bay that separated the islands from the mainland. The red suspension bridge that spanned the two islands burned brightly in the evening light too, but only for a little while. Soon, it also fell into the shadows as the day came to a close.

The voices of people walking on a trail to the south drifted through the trees. Everyone was making their way to the campfire ring in the center of camp. I wanted to stay and play guitar, but I knew I'd best be on my way to the campfire as well. I tossed the guitar on my bunk and slipped out the door.

"I should at least go make an appearance."

chapter 15

evening campfire

"It was pretty dang exciting, right guys?"

The evening campfire was a nightly ritual at Northern Lights. At twilight, everyone gathered at the big fire ring in the center of camp to sing songs, hear stories, and connect with each other. It was a tradition for the canoe guides who were fresh off the water to be given a chance to talk about their trips. The guides prided themselves in their storytelling skills, which inevitably included some tall tales and juicy details about their adventures in the wilderness.

As I strolled along through the growing darkness toward the sound of the campfire, I wondered what Chuck would say about his trip. From some distance away, I could already hear everyone singing the Moose Song: a goofy little tune about a moose named Fred, who liked to drink his juice in bed. Outwardly, I barely tolerated the silliness that usually made up the typical campfire program. It wasn't really my thing, but deep down, I loved the stories, songs, and laughter that were always a part of it.

A man's voice drifted through the woods as I approached the giant circle of people seated at logs around the blazing campfire. From a long way off, I could tell it was Finn. His hair gleamed in the campfire light as he stood up front to greet everyone. He welcomed the new arrivals from Chicago and the other families and groups that were heading out on the lakes the next day.

We were always happy to see visitors, but as a guide, I was somewhat detached from the activities going on at base camp. I had struggled to develop any long-lasting friendships at Northern Lights, and the summer was already half over. Aria was the one exception, but not surprisingly, we had bonded on our canoe trip. There was a sort of kinship among all the canoe guides, but we rarely crossed paths unless we happened to be in base camp at the same time. We were offsite most of the time, leading groups along the lake routes, often for many days at a stretch. So, each time I returned to camp, I never knew who I'd see there. The base camp staff were always around, but they had bonded with each other, so I always felt a little out of place at Northern Lights.

At the campfire, I settled down on a log in the back. Cassie stood up and introduced Percy and his group of junior high boys, who'd just returned from a trip. Percy was the ultimate wilderness canoe guide: strong, good-looking, funny, and intelligent. Naturally, I disliked him for all those reasons, but he was actually an excellent guide, and he was also greatly admired by many of the young women in camp. His victory in the canoe race earlier in the summer set him apart from the rest of the guys. It wasn't without controversy, but he'd still won by a long shot. To be honest, he dominated the other male guides in every way, and as far as the women were concerned, he had us all beat by a mile, and he knew it.

Percy stood up slowly and gave a long sly smirk at his captive audience. Then, he started in on his adventures with the junior high boys. Almost immediately, he had everyone laughing along to a tale of a fishing mishap that involved a sharp fishhook and someone's smelly underwear. Then, he told another story about almost losing a couple of boys to a crazy moose who didn't take a liking to being offered a ham sandwich. Percy continued on with a hair-raising story of the boys struggling to carry their canoes over a rocky portage into Jasper Lake. Thankfully, they had their hero: good old Percy, who naturally showed up to save the day and keep them from falling down the cliff into the rushing river far below.

For the grand finale, Percy relayed an account of how his group had encountered a stubborn bear on Ottertrack Lake just two nights before returning to camp. The bear had climbed up into the tree where the boys hung their food pack and refused to come back down. All night, they struggled with that ornery bear. They threw rocks and sticks at it. They banged pots and pans together and made a noisy ruckus under that tree, but it absolutely would not budge from its roost high overhead. After many hours of trying, they finally gave up and crawled back into their tents and fell fast asleep. In the morning, when they woke up, the sun was already high in the sky, and that bear was long gone, along with a number of meals they had been counting on. Percy figured it was probably deep in the forest somewhere in the heart of Canada by that point.

"That bear must have been awful hungry!" Percy exclaimed. "That's a reminder always to hang your food pack far away from your tent; otherwise, you won't get much sleep with a bear chomping away on your food all night in a tree directly above you! Right, guys?"

The boys grinned and nodded. Everyone laughed and cheered. Percy was in his element, the center of attention, with everyone's eyes and ears fixed on him. He was having a grand time stretching his tale of adventure, mishap, and pure stupidity out for all it was worth. The boys stood at attention behind him, grinning from ear to ear. They looked up at Percy in admiration, not realizing that they were the butt of most of his jokes. They laughed when everyone else laughed. They smiled when Percy smiled back at them. But clearly, they were famished and exhausted from the trip. Some of the boys looked like they'd been to hell and back, and just needed a good night of sleep, maybe two or three. When he finished, everyone cheered and clapped for Percy and the boys. I cheered and clapped too, but only because he was finally done.

As the campfire moved along, two counselors taught a silly song about a gray squirrel that liked to shake its bushy tail. I sang along halfheartedly, somewhat irritated inside, knowing that I would never be able to tell stories as well as Percy could.

Finally, it was Chuck's turn to talk. He hopped up in front, followed by his group: a bunch of youth from a church in Minneapolis. They lined up behind him as he started in on his tale of doom and disaster. They looked especially worn and weary, bleary-eyed, and gaunt, as if they were slowly coming out of a state of shock.

Chuck, however, looked alive and well. He rolled out his story in chunks and rambled on in a choppy, unorganized sort of way. After finally ending my pout-storm about Percy, I turned my full attention to Chuck, noticing how energetic and animated he became when he was up in front of a crowd. It didn't suit his usual low-key, laid-back kind of style, but it was fascinating to watch.

"So, we went north on our first day, heading for the Canadian border," Chuck began. "The next day, we had a bit of a wind on Saganaga, so we cut south through Zephyer Lake, which didn't help much. I really pushed my group, and it was still terribly windy, so later that day on Knife Lake, we decided to go off-trail and cut through to Nave and then Nabek Lake. It was totally dark when we got into Holt Lake, so we made camp on an island. It started pouring while we were setting up our tents, so everyone piled into one tent and had a cold supper huddled inside. The next morning, we bushwhacked through the woods over to Ogish. That's when Lizzie fell and sliced open the bottom of her foot. We had to do a bit of triage on it to keep her from bleeding to death. Thank God for duct tape! We paddled most of the day in the rain. That's when Jimmy started showing signs of hypothermia. He'd been duffing all day, so we got him out, wrapped him up in a sleeping bag, and force-fed him an entire bag of GORP trail mix. For all you novices out there, that stands for good old raisins and peanuts. Then, we made Jimmy paddle the rest of the day in the rain until we found a muddy campsite on Diamond Lake. On our last night, we left all our dirty dishes out by the campfire to try to get a bear, but in the morning, all we found were a couple of messy chipmunks that seemed to have a bad case of diarrhea. So, we packed up and sailed across Diamond and finally made it back to camp. It was pretty dang exciting, right guys?"

Chuck's group nodded, and everyone cheered and clapped. The kids smiled and limped back to their log and sat down. I cheered and clapped along. "What a nightmare!" I thought to myself.

I'd heard Chuck tell several stories from his last couple of years as a canoe guide, and I was starting to realize why Cassie had finally decided to pull him off the lakes and give him the trail shack job.

In just about every story I heard, tragedy somehow struck. His stories always seemed to include the three main essentials: blood, poop, and hypothermia. I was always a bit surprised because when he led the staff trip at the beginning of the summer, we had a great time. I wondered about it, but I still respected him for his wealth of wisdom and his deep love for the outdoors.

When Chuck finished his tale of doom and disaster, I noticed Aria and Esther sitting across the campfire ring. They were off to my right, two logs down, and behind a little family of four sitting in the front row. Esther was sitting right next to Percy, of all people, and it made me just a little bit jealous.

As we learned another song about a little green frog, I watched the two of them. Percy, of course, was hitting it off with Esther. I could see him laughing, telling jokes, and talking her ear off. Esther smiled and politely responded to him, but she didn't seem to be taking the bait. In fact, she didn't seem to be enjoying the attention at all. From where I sat, she looked downright miserable. I wondered what the big doofus was saying to her to make her so uncomfortable.

As I watched, Esther began to ignore him altogether. Percy, however, seemed undaunted at getting the cold shoulder, and he carried on, oblivious to what I was witnessing. It was intriguing to watch, and for some reason, I was pleased with Esther's reaction. I wanted to know what was going on over there but could only guess from where I sat across the fire ring.

The campfire ended much as it had begun. Cassie stood up and gave a couple of final announcements and then sent everyone off to their cabins. Many people didn't want to leave, and they lingered quietly around the warm glowing embers of the fire. I wanted to check in with Aria and Esther, but they had already taken off back to their cabin. I thought about chasing after them but changed my mind. Aria probably didn't want me following her around with Esther there, so I headed back to my cabin.

The muffled sounds of people talking and laughing in the darkness could be heard all around. There were long lines of flashlights shining and bouncing along the trails, weaving in all directions through the woods. Some people were hanging out on the deck over at Starlight Lodge. Others were making their way down to the cable bridge and across to Eagle Island. I walked quietly back up the hill to my cabin in Pleiades Village and crashed for the night.

After an hour or so of sleep, I woke up when Chuck stumbled in and collapsed on his bunk below. I guessed that it was about midnight. Everything was quiet and still outside. For the next hour or so, I tossed and turned on my bunk and tried to get back to sleep. It wasn't easy. The mattress was hard and my mind was restless. Almost immediately, Chuck began to snore up a storm, which only made matters worse. As I lay awake, I couldn't help but think about everything I'd experienced in such a short time that summer.

It was nice to be in camp for a while, but I really wanted to be back out on the water. I loved the life of a canoe guide: paddling across the open lakes, portaging canoes, looking for campsites, spotting wildlife, exploring the wilderness, and enjoying nature. I loved being away from everything I'd once considered normal, away from the rush of human activity, away from the cares and worries of the rest of the world. I longed to be out there again, but I was content to have a couple of days to rest before going back out.

Base camp could get pretty interesting too.

chapter 16

breakfast with aria

"Heavy on the sausages, eh, Hunter?"

I awoke to the sounds of the North Woods, which every morning seemed pleasantly fresh and new to me. The air was brisk and sweet as it drifted through the screen windows of the cabin. A soft breeze whispered through the millions of pine needles in the trees all around. It sounded distinctly different from the thick, steady winds that rustled through the densely packed cornfields of Iowa.

Down by the lake, I could hear the call of a white-throated sparrow, so common to the Boundary Waters. To me, its cheerful morning song sounded like "My sweet land, Canada, Canada, Canada!" It called over and over again, until from somewhere far away along the edge of the island, a loon whistled a long mournful reply.

"I could stay here forever," I thought, lying motionless on my bunk with my eyes closed. "This is where I want to live someday."

Suddenly, the shrill call of a Canadian jay pierced the still air commandingly from the low branch of a silver birch tree nearby. "Wake up! Wake up!" it seemed to say. "It's time to get up now and get on with the day."

I opened my eyes, just slightly, to let in a little light. Through the screen door of the cabin, I could see down to the lake. A group of canoes passed by, heading out west toward the islands of Diamond Lake, on their way to faraway destinations, distant portages, streams, and waterfalls, all waiting to be discovered. Their paddles thumped gently against the sides of the aluminum canoes as they moved off. The young explorers were talking excitedly, explaining how to hold a paddle and how to properly steer a canoe. They reminded me of the bossy Canadian jay, wild and free, without a care or worry in the world. I listened to the campers talk over each other in a jumble of words as they drifted away, happy to be setting out on their adventure in the wilds of the North Woods.

I rubbed my eyes and sat up in my bunk to look outside and check the weather. The crisp cool air was a sign that it had rained overnight, but only just a bit. The sky was filled with fluffy pink clouds that were drifting lazily eastward. I guessed that it was probably going to clear up and turn into a nice day. I flopped back down again onto my sleeping bag and listened once more to the sound of the breeze whistling through the pine trees overhead. All summer long, those quiet moments washed over me. They never got old. They were always being made new, over and over again.

My sore body, however, snapped me back to reality. My shoulders still ached from all of the portages from my last trip. My skin tingled in various places from being sunburned over and over again, and I was hungry too. I rolled out of my bunk and landed on my feet in the middle of the tiny cabin. As I got dressed, Chuck slid back under his sleeping bag with an irritated snort. Then, he rolled away from the daylight and snuggled up against the cabin wall.

"See you later, Chuck," I said, wishing he were more of a morning person like me. "I'm going to breakfast."

"Yeah, later dude," was all he could manage in return.

I hopped off the cabin steps and strolled down the rocky path that wound along the edge of the ridge above the lake. I walked past the next two cabins identical to mine, each housing two canoe guides for the summer. The cable bridge off to the east creaked out a steady pattern as a long line of campers walked across, heading for Starlight lodge. I navigated my way down the winding path that dropped off from the rocky ridge of Pleiades Village to the beach and the boat landing below.

A couple of canoe guides were carrying packs and supplies down to the beach and stacking them by a group of overturned canoes that were lined up and ready to go by the edge of the lake. They waved lazily to me as I passed by and continued along the trail that worked its way back up through the woods to the main lodge.

On the wooden deck outside Starlight Lodge, I came across Siri and Star just lazing about. They looked happy and hungry, as always. "Hey guys," I greeted them as they watched me go inside.

In the dining hall, breakfast was already being served, so I got in line with the other early risers. At the serving window there was a nice selection of breakfast food: sausages, eggs, toast, strawberry yogurt, granola, and fresh fruit, as well as milk, juice, and hot coffee over at a beverage station in the corner. It was simple food, but exactly what was needed to get you started for the day. I took the eggs, sausages, two pieces of toast, and some jelly. Then, I found a place to sit by myself and quietly eat my breakfast. Seconds later, Aria plopped down across from me and immediately started downing her food, as if it were the last meal she was ever going to get.

"Heavy on the sausages, eh, Hunter?" I commented, staring at her pile of steaming eggs buried in a heap of sausages.

"Shut up, freak," she said bluntly. "I'm starving, and I'm heading out soon too."

"It's supposed to be nice weather this week. Who are you going out with?" I asked.

"Edna," she replied.

"Oh, good luck with that," I said with a smirk. "I hope you make it back alive. How many days?"

"Seven," Aria said as she stuffed two sausages into her mouth followed by a big scoop of eggs. "We'll be back next Monday."

"That is if you don't get strung up by Edna as bear bait out there in the middle of nowhere," I replied, trying to ignore her bad habit of speaking with her mouth full.

Aria shoved another scoop of eggs into her already full mouth and snapped, "Oh, shut up, Leo."

"Edna likes to feed little green swampers like you to big hairy animals in the woods," I replied. "That's what I hear. And if you don't make it back alive, she'll just add your gruesome death to her story at the campfire program."

"Whatever," Aria said as she stuffed two more sausages into her mouth. "I really gotta scoot, though. She'll be a bear if I don't show up soon to help."

"Hey, Hunter, I'm gonna start calling you Bear Bait," I said, thinking that Bear Butt would be a better nickname for my fiery little friend from Chicago.

I looked at Aria and grinned with delight. She was irritable as usual, but she was adorable in the morning. Her dark curly hair seemed to be always on the move, springing up and out every which way as she talked. Her brown eyes flashed like lightning as she looked around the room. Her cute round nose crinkled up as she munched on her eggs and sausages. Her deep cherry lips talked a mile a minute as they curved up and out on the sides. She was solid, tough-looking, and strong, but clearly still a girl at heart.

It was her spunky personality that really stood out to me, though. She bounced and moved and fully expressed everything she was thinking inside. Her actions and speech were always fully animated, even in the simplest things. She was completely different from me—my polar opposite. Maybe that's why I treasured her friendship so much. I loved how we had become such good friends that summer, and I wondered if it would stand the test of time.

"I'm gonna really miss you, Aria," I lamented. "What'll I ever do around here while you're gone?"

"Leo, you love me, and you know it," she teased back, gazing enticingly into my eyes. "We're meant to be together, Farm Boy. This love train's coming whether you like it or not. It's our destiny."

"Bear Bait," I repeated with a grin. "Yeah, that's totally you."

She leaned forward and stuck out her tongue. "You freakin' idiot! Call me Bear Bait one more time, and I'll . . ."

"Bear Bait," I blurted out daringly.

"I'll kick your sorry ass!" she whispered loudly just a few inches away from my face.

"Hey, be quiet," I whispered back. "People might hear you, and then you'll get me fired."

"Good! You deserve it!" she replied with a fiendish grin.

"And then, Hunter," I said, leaning forward slowly, "I bet you'd miss me something fierce."

"Oh, shut up, Farm Boy!" she wailed one more time, but even more loudly than before.

A couple of people turned and looked over at us. I sat upright and stared at Aria with my eyes bulging out. She just laughed, scooped up the last bit of eggs, and stuffed them into her mouth. She slid the last few sausages off her plate onto a napkin and then grabbed two more off mine and popped them into her mouth.

"I gotta scoot!" she said, talking with her mouth full again.

"You just stole my last two sausages," I whined sadly.

"Oh, yeah?" she replied, leaning in close and eyeing me with a devious grin. "I'd steal more than that if you'd let me."

"No, I'm good," I said calmly, grinning back at her like a big brother waiting for his little sister to stop misbehaving.

I was willing to put up with just about anything Aria could dish out. She was such a great friend, and I loved her for it. I just couldn't say it like that, not yet anyway. I had a good idea what people were thinking, though, but I shrugged it off. They could think whatever they liked. I wasn't about to abandon Aria.

"Okay, so I really, really gotta dip this place!" Aria said as she grabbed the napkin full of sausages and stood up to go. "So, Leo, I'll see you Monday, okay? I gotta make a pit stop at the washroom quick and get my butt down to the beach ASAP."

"Okay, Bear Bait," I said, risking a severe beatdown. "I'll still be out when you get back, that is, if you make it back."

Aria frowned and huffed at me, unamused as she pranced off with her dirty plate and a handful of snacks to go.

As she walked away, I called out, "Hey, Hunter, have you seen Esther this morning?"

The question sort of slipped out unconsciously. I'd been thinking about Esther ever since I saw her standing on the dock smiling and waving at me. Actually, I hadn't been able to stop thinking about her. I might have been obsessing about her just a little bit, maybe all night long, but I couldn't tell Aria that.

"Hey, jockstrap!" Aria snapped back at me. "Don't you go and mess with Esther while I'm gone!" She gave me a stern look, so cold and severe, it made me sit up straight like a schoolboy.

"Yes, ma'am," I responded sarcastically as I swallowed my last bite of toast and jam.

"Leo, I'm serious," Aria said harshly. "Esther is *my* friend, and don't you forget that! So, you just keep your distance."

As Aria stared fiercely into my eyes, I realized that she was being totally serious, and I had learned to respect that.

"Okay, Hunter," I replied. "I'll see you Monday then, or Friday, I mean, that's when I'm getting off the lakes."

"Yeah, I'll see you later, Farm Boy," she shot back. Then, with a wicked smirk, she drove her clenched fist hard into my left shoulder and took off for the beach.

I finished my breakfast and walked back out onto the deck. Siri and Star were still there, looking happy and hungry as always. There was a napkin on the ground next to Star, which he was taking a strong liking to. I hopped off the steps and headed down the trail toward the beach. I rubbed my shoulder, which didn't feel so good thanks to my spunky little best friend, Aria.

"This is the life!" I thought to myself.

chapter 17

soup and a sandwich

"I think it was something I ate."

On the way back to my cabin, the pain in my shoulder slowly moved down to my stomach. Suddenly, I didn't feel so well. As I hiked up the trail to Pleiades Village, I quickly turned left to vomit over a rotten log. A few steps farther up the trail, I did the same thing in the middle of a healthy patch of blueberries. When I made it to my cabin, I hesitated to go inside, in case another episode suddenly hit me by surprise. When it seemed to have abated, I went in, only to rush out and let it fly again down the hill toward the lake.

After a couple of minutes, I went back inside. I took a big swig of water out of my water bottle and spewed it out the screen door as another guide came walking by.

"Sorry!" I called out apologetically. "Not feeling so good! Don't eat the blueberries!"

I decided to stay put for the rest of the morning in hopes of feeling better by lunchtime. I curled up in my bunk and slept for a while. It felt good to rest, even though my stomach was churning inside.

When I woke up, Chuck was standing on the steps outside the cabin, holding the door open a crack.

"Hey," I groaned, rubbing my stomach. "What's up, Chuck?"

"Hey, Leo," he replied, pushing the screen door open a little farther. "Dude, you feeling any better?"

"Yeah, kind of," I said. "I think it was something I ate."

"Yup, you're probably right," he replied. "Finn said that some other people got it too."

"Well, that's nice. At least it wasn't the flu," I mumbled.

"Yup, you get better, dude," Chuck said. "Hey, are you still on for your trip in a couple of days? Cassie wants to know."

"Sure, I'll be fine," I replied. "I'm just a little wiped out. Don't tell her that, though. I'll be fine." I understood why Cassie needed to know. I just didn't want to lose out on my next trip.

"Okay," Chuck replied as he shut the door. "Cassie said you stay put through supper and be sure to get some sleep."

He lumbered off down the trail like a lazy grizzly wandering off into the forest. He probably didn't realize it, but I truly admired him. I wouldn't have made a friend like Chuck anywhere but there. He had such a simple way of going about life. He loved the Boundary Waters. It meant everything to him.

One of the deepest talks Chuck and I had was about acid rain. He couldn't believe how human pollution could be allowed to do such a thing. It made him sick to think that the lakes in the Boundary Waters were being affected by the carelessness of society. It showed me that he was deeply concerned about the environment and how people needed to take care of it, not recklessly destroy it.

I admired Chuck for the things that were important to him: living simply, not excessively; caring for the world around him; and once he was gone, leaving no trace that he was ever there. It seemed like a decent way to approach life, and I respected him for it.

But I also wanted to leave my mark on the world somehow, not in a sloppy, messy sort of way, but in a great way. I wanted to inspire people and have an impact on their lives. It's kind of funny to think about how Chuck had done precisely that for me in his simple way, without even trying. Sometimes, I wondered what was really going on in his head—a lot more, I thought, than what he let most people see on the outside.

For the rest of the afternoon, I stayed in the cabin. I was feeling better, but I didn't want to go out and make people nervous about getting what I had, so I stayed put through supper.

I rested on my bunk and listened to what was going on around camp. I could hear people down at the beach playing volleyball. I could hear work going on out west, probably at Cedar Lodge: another bunkhouse that was being renovated for camp guests.

From my cabin up in Pleiades Village, I had a perfect view of the narrows down below. I could see everything that was going out or coming in from the lakes. I watched as Carly paddled out with a group of college students. They were already talking about cliff jumping and skinny dipping, so she'd have her hands full for the week. Then, a big group of families passed by for an afternoon paddle around Diamond Lake. I saw Jim and a few swampers heading it up. I could tell they were happy to be getting off-site for a while.

As evening approached, I started to get bored. I took another short nap, played guitar some more, and wrote in my journal for a while. I was just daydreaming and staring at the ceiling when I heard a knock on the cabin door. No one ever knocked on the door.

When I saw who it was, I was completely floored. I didn't hit the floor, actually. I just sat up on my bunk and watched her try helplessly to get inside. After a few seconds, I jumped down and opened the door because she clearly needed help.

Of all people, it was Esther, standing there precariously on the rickety steps to the cabin. She was holding a bowl of soup in one hand and a sandwich along with a glass of milk in the other.

"Wow, what is she doing here?" I thought to myself as I opened the door to let her in.

"Hey, mate," she said with a smile, carefully balancing the items in her hands. "I didn't see you at tea tonight. They said you were feeling a bit crook. Got the collywobbles, eh?"

"Collywobbles?" I asked.

"Yeah, you know, sick and all," she explained. "A couple of gals in my cabin got it too. They were spewin' up something fierce after brekkie this morning."

"Yeah, I was too . . . spewin'," I replied, guessing that it meant what I thought it meant.

"Oh, grotty business, that!" she exclaimed.

"Yeah, grotty," I repeated, guessing again. "Thanks for bringing me some food."

"No worries, mate," she replied cheerfully. "I thought you might be hungry, so I snatched some take-aways from the kitchen. Sorry, no lollies, though. I could barely manage it all by myself, you know."

"Lollies?" I asked.

"Yeah, lollies . . . you know, treats," she explained. "They had ice cream tonight, but it would have been a lake by the time I got here, so I passed on that."

"Well, thanks," I said, taking the glass of milk from her. "I don't eat a lot of lollies anyway. This'll be just fine."

"Sure, bro," she replied as she looked around the cabin.

Just like the day before, she was dressed to kill. She was wearing another tight T-shirt along with her blue jean jacket, army green capris, and black boots. It was a cramped space inside the cabin, so I hopped back up onto my bunk and watched her set the soup and sandwich down on the little table by my things.

"How did you carry that all the way up here?" I asked.

"Very carefully," she said, giving me a tiny grin. "Would you like to try the soup before it gets cold?"

"Sure," I replied.

"I miss Aria already," she confessed as she slowly lifted the bowl of soup up to me.

I took a bite, then carelessly said, "Well, you've still got me for a couple of days." I suddenly realized I hardly knew her, so I quickly spit out, "Sorry, I say stupid stuff sometimes."

She chuckled softly and replied, "You talk with your mouth full too, don't you, bro?"

I swallowed another spoonful of hot soup, then nodded and replied, "Guilty as charged."

"No worries, I do too sometimes," she said, smiling up at me.

As I ate the soup, it was silent for a minute or so, awkwardly silent. I didn't know what to say, so I just kept busy with the soup. I watched her from my bunk as she leaned back against the wall. She looked as fierce and dangerous as ever. Her red lips matched the sunglasses that were tucked up on top of her head. Her fiery red hair flowed down around her shoulders and even across her face, which didn't seem to bother her at all. The dark makeup around her eyes made them look deep and mysterious. They sparkled like jewels in the fading sunlight as she quietly looked around the cabin.

"So, Leo, this is a pretty sweet crib you got here," she said.

"Yeah," I replied casually. "It's tiny, though. You can barely turn around in the place."

She looked across at the little desk and the rustic shelves built into the wall. "That's your stuff on that side, isn't it?"

"Yeah," I replied with my mouth full, yet again. "Chuck's got that wall, and this one over here is mine."

She got up and took a couple of steps across the floor to have a closer look. I watched as she examined my things—a stack of shirts, some socks, a pile of underwear—everything totally out in the open. Her pretty necklaces gently clinked as she leaned down and looked more closely at my things on the desk—a compass, a flashlight, a small notebook, and my journal, along with my guitar propped up against an old chair. I felt more than a little exposed by the silent examination, but strangely, it was a good kind of feeling.

As she ran her fingers gently across the guitar strings, they made a soft discordant melody. "You play the guitar?" she asked.

"Yeah, a little," I admitted.

"You bring it on your canoe trips?"

"Yeah," I said. "I like to make up songs when I've got the time, usually around the campfire."

"So, you're a songwriter, eh?"

"Well, I'm not sure I'd call it that," I replied. "It's just something I do for the fun of it."

"It's all good, bro, I understand," she said, leaning back against the desk and looking up at me. "I'd like to hear you play sometime."

Suddenly, I realized she was trying to be kind, or maybe not just trying; she actually was kind. Up until then, I hadn't really thought about what sort of a person she was inside. Like every other male at camp, I'd been bowled over by her stunning appearance. Suddenly, she wasn't so fierce and dangerous after all. Suddenly, she was real, approachable, kind, and perhaps even thoughtful. It seemed as if she was actually trying to get to know me. It felt uncomfortable and awkward, yes, but it felt good too. Apparently, she had come to talk to me, not just deliver a happy meal. Her open curiosity made it easier for me to loosen up.

"Do you play an instrument?" I asked.

"Yeah, a few," she replied. "The violin, the mandolin, and a bit of piano too, but the mandolin is my favorite."

Her list sort of blew me away. "The violin, mandolin, and piano?" I thought. "Seriously?" I'd have never guessed. She didn't look like a musician at all, well, maybe a punk rocker, but not a real musician.

"I used to play the piano, but I quit in the third grade," I replied. "Then, I took up the saxophone, but I quit that in the sixth grade when we moved to California for a few years."

"Gotta stop giving up so fast," Esther said with a grin. "Sounds like you get the willies pretty easily, eh?"

"Yeah, I suppose so," I admitted. "I like the guitar, though. I picked it up in high school when we moved back to Iowa, mostly because it was easy, but now I really like playing it."

"Awesome, that's how I am with the mandolin," she replied.

"We should play together sometime," I suggested, but I don't think I really meant it. I was just trying to warm up to the intriguing girl from New Zealand who'd brought a bowl of soup to my cabin.

"Sorry, Leo," she said. "I didn't bring my mandolin to America. I reckon you'd have to go all the way to New Zealand to do that."

"Okay! When should I come?" I joked awkwardly.

"I don't know, mate," she replied, chuckling softly. "It's pretty far away from here, you know."

Esther picked up my guitar and began strumming it quietly. I took another spoonful of soup as she hummed softly and gently plucked a few strings on the guitar.

"You play the guitar too?" I asked.

"No, not really, just a few chords, that's all," she replied as she stopped to switch her fingers on the guitar.

"Well, it sounds nice," I said.

"Thanks, mate," she said as she played another pretty chord.

The quiet simplicity of that moment slowly seeped into me. Esther didn't try to fill the space with empty conversation. She just strummed on my guitar, as if it were perfectly natural for her to be there, without any need for either of us to entertain each other.

A sense of companionship gradually rose up within me. It was a feeling of closeness and comfort, like being back home again with my mom and dad. I wondered about the fascinating girl who was playing my guitar so sweetly. In her own way, she was gently taking care of me with no strings attached. The sweet notes quietly filled the silence between us and drew us closer together.

I watched her down below as I ate my soup. She didn't look up. The afternoon sun drifted through the screen windows and bathed her in golden light. The light mingled with her hair and set it on fire again, like glowing red embers in the growing darkness. Esther stopped playing the guitar and set it back down carefully. She looked up at me again with those beautiful blue eyes.

"So, Leo," she said softly. "Why are you here?"

"Um, excuse me?" I asked as I swallowed the last bit of soup.

She grinned and asked again, "Why are you here, bro?

"Well, I'm not feeling so good," I replied, stating the obvious. "I think it was something I ate, so, food poisoning, yeah."

Esther chuckled politely. "No, goofball, why are you here at Northern Lights this summer?"

"Oh, yeah, sorry," I blurted out, unsure whether I wanted to go there or not. I looked up at the plywood ceiling for guidance, but it didn't give any, so I said whatever came to mind, which usually meant a bit of rambling was in store for the listener.

"Well, I was looking for a change," I explained. "I kind of got stuck in a rut back in Iowa the last couple of years, so when some friends started talking about working at a canoe camp this summer, I got to thinking about it too. When I talked to Cassie about this place, it sounded pretty cool, so I applied for a job and got it. So, now that I'm here, yeah, I love it."

"So, you love it, eh?" she said, leaning back against the desk. "What do you love about it?"

"It's everything I thought it would be and more," I said. "I love the lakes and the trees and being out there on the water. But now, halfway through the summer, for some reason, I think it's more than just about my love for the outdoors. I think I ended up here for a reason. Being a canoe guide is fun and all, but I also have a chance to make a difference in people's lives too, especially the kids that come here. I'm still learning so much, though, so that's kind of a tough question for me to answer right now. I feel like I might need the rest of the summer to figure it out."

Esther grinned up at me. "Well, that was quite an answer, Leo. I didn't expect to get a nice tidy lecture out of you." Her words were direct and revealing. "Do you yabber on to all the girls that way? With long speeches like that?"

I felt a sudden rush of embarrassment. "Oh, no, not really. Well, I don't know . . . maybe." I stared down at the floor and shut up.

"Well, I like how you talk so openly," she said as she flashed her eyes up at me again. "I expected you to be a quiet guy, a kind of woodsy buck who didn't say much. It's just nice to hear what you're thinking on the inside."

Esther smiled and looked around the room again. She seemed so peaceful, so confident in who she was, and so mysterious too. She had been watching me the entire time I spoke, apparently interested. But as I finished off the glass of milk, she glanced away, then outside as if sadly wondering about something, as if disappointed or tired or even bored. Silence slowly crept into the space between us again like an invisible barrier.

"Hey, Esther, I'm sorry," I suddenly blurted out. "I told you why I'm here. What about you? Why are you here?"

"Hmm," she hummed softly as she slowly stirred and came back to life. "That's a pretty big question, bro."

"Well, I've got all night!" I said the words, then realized how awkward the idea sounded.

"All right," she replied as she gazed up and tapped her fingers on the side of the desk. "I'm here because Aria begged and pleaded for me to come and visit her this summer."

"She probably threatened to beat you up if you didn't," I added, trying to make her laugh again.

Esther chuckled and grabbed the edge of the desk with both hands. "Not exactly, but I had to come and see her, so I signed on with the adventure group from Chicago, and here I am."

I loved the way she talked. Her accent was fascinating, not to mention the way she looked. She seemed so incredibly nice. She wasn't at all what I first thought she'd be like: tough as nails, cold, and intimidating. As she talked about herself, she seemed to open up like a flower and bubble over with life and enthusiasm.

"What made you decide to come to the United States?" I asked, curious to know more about her.

"Oh, Leo!" Esther replied as she squirmed against the desk and crossed her legs. "Another big question, eh?" She fussed a bit but still seemed willing to share more.

"All right," she continued. "I was in my second year of studies at the university in Auckland and starting to get interested in certain subjects—astronomy, jazz, and music. I looked into doing an internship or studying abroad somewhere—in England or America. That's when I ended up getting a pretty sweet scholarship from the University of Chicago, so I jumped on it."

"And your parents were okay with it?" I asked.

"It took a little convincing for them to come around," she said. "We agreed that this would be my big OE. My parents don't like it, but they let me do it anyway when I promised that I'd go back home after a year in America."

"Your big OE? What's that?" I asked.

"Yeah, my overseas experience," she replied. "A lot of young people from Down Under do it. It's like a rite of passage for a lot of university students. We go overseas for a few months or a year to see what life is like off the islands. Some never return home, but I'm going back in a few weeks."

"Your parents must miss you a lot," I said.

"My mum and dad?" Esther replied. "Yeah, mate, I suppose so. I'll see 'em soon enough, though."

"How has the past year been?" I asked.

"Actually, it's been a bit dodgy at times," she said. "But overall, it's been pretty sweet. I miss my family a lot, and I miss New Zealand too. Chicago is so much bigger than Auckland, but the classes have been awesome, and there are so many things to see and do. It took a while to get used to it, but now I feel as if it's where I was supposed to be, almost as if I were led there somehow, and here too."

"Well, I'm glad you're here," I said. "I love the way you talk."

"Oh, yeah," Esther said with a little smirk. "That's what happens when you live your entire life on an island cut off from the rest of civilization."

"It sounds cool," I said.

"Right, mate," Esther said. "I apologize in advance if you don't get some of the things I'm saying."

"That's fine," I replied. "You can teach me a few new words this summer if you want to."

"Yeah, bro," she said. "I reckon that'll happen."

She paused and suddenly looked lost in thought, as if there was something else she wanted to say but was holding back. I wanted to hear what she was thinking inside. I was desperate to know more about her—immediately, so I opened the door a little wider.

"So, Esther, why are you here?" I asked again.

She stared at the floor and didn't move a muscle. I waited and watched as the seconds ticked by. Then, slowly, she looked up at me. Behind her dark makeup, her deep blue eyes, and her beautiful freckles, I thought I saw her blushing.

"You know," she replied with a weak grin. "After brekkie this morning, I heard Chuck saying that you got the collywobbles and all. When I didn't see you at lunch, I figured that you'd be hungry by teatime, so I snatched a few take-aways from the kitchen and brought 'em by on my way back to my cabin."

"But no lollies," I said, practicing the new word I'd just learned.

"Nope, no lollies," she replied. "Sorry, bro, maybe next time."

"Well, thanks for thinking of me," I said casually. "I'm feeling a lot better already."

Suddenly, Esther seemed anxious to leave. "Okay, then," she said. "I'd best be on my way. I told Cassie I'd meet her for the evening campfire. Would you like to come along?"

"Oh, no," I blurted out. "I better stay and rest." Then, I thought, "What am I saying? I want to go!" But it was already out there, and I couldn't take it back.

"Okay, no worries," she said as she stood up next to my bunk. "Shall I take your bowl back to the kitchen then?"

"Yeah, thanks," I said, handing it down to her. "Thanks again for thinking of me."

"Sure, Leo," she replied with a soft smile. "Perhaps I'll see you around tomorrow, eh?"

"Yeah, see you tomorrow," I said as she turned to leave.

Esther pushed the screen door open and threw me another pretty smile. "Spotcha later then, mate!"

"Goodnight, Esther," I replied. "Thanks again!"

She shut the door gently and walked away down the trail. I sat on my bunk, thinking through what had just happened. There was more. I could feel it. There had to be more than she was telling me. Why had she come to my cabin with the soup? Why had she asked so many questions? Why had she stayed to talk? Why did she blush when I asked her why she was there? I grinned and flopped back down onto my bunk. I knew why.

She had come to see me.

chapter 18

another sleepless night

"Who could be up at this hour?"

That night, as I lay awake on my bunk, the sounds of the campfire echoed through the trees. The last bit of daylight faded into gray dusk outside and grew darker. I couldn't keep myself from thinking about Esther—her red hair glowing in the sunset, her deep blue eyes examining my things on the shelves, her rosy cheeks blushing as she thought about why she'd come to my cabin. The thoughts kept swirling in my head like a Ferris wheel stuck on go.

Even after Chuck returned and collapsed in his bunk down below, I couldn't stop thinking about Esther, and Aria, then Esther again. Aria's playful threat kept reverberating through my head. "Leo, don't you mess with Esther!" How serious had she actually been? Why would she even say something like that?

I was leaving in a couple of days on another trip, and then probably again soon after that. Esther would be gone in three weeks, and then she was heading back to New Zealand too. The thought of anything developing just didn't make any sense, so why couldn't I sleep? Why shouldn't I pursue her? What was holding me back? Why was I already coming up with excuses? Why was I hesitating?

I couldn't help but think back on the past few years of my life. I'd only been in three serious relationships, but for various reasons, each one had ended painfully. Those experiences were still weighing on me and whispering doubts in the back of my mind.

My bad luck in the past made me overly cautious, and my introverted personality didn't help much, either. At Northern Lights,

I tried to find time to be with other people, but those opportunities were few and far between. I'd given up all hope of making any real friends at camp until Aria and I suddenly hit it off. I liked her a lot, but in the back of my mind, I was still protecting myself and being cautious with how I let people inside. I didn't want to get myself hurt. I didn't want to hurt anyone else either.

Near the end of my freshman year in college, I went through a bad breakup with a girl named Grace. She was wonderful, sweet, and full of life. I thought that she was the one. We would graduate, get married, and spend the rest of our lives together. But as the snow began to melt in the spring, our relationship spiraled out of control. We both said things that we regretted. We both did things that couldn't be taken back. I remember the horrible way we broke up outside her freshman dorm. It was as if we had ripped each other to pieces as we finally broke apart for good. After she left, everything felt so empty, dark, and cold. I was determined never to let that happen again, but I was worried that it would.

I vowed to keep my emotions under control at all costs. I was determined not to let my feelings drive me into any relationship unless I was absolutely sure I would be safe in the end. Over the next two years, I passed on one relationship after another, not letting myself feel anything for anyone, holding everyone at arm's length, carefully maintaining control. I dated a couple of girls, but I'm sure they were confused and frustrated by my actions, which probably came across as being selfish, indecisive, and idiotic. I just couldn't let anyone get too close, for fear I would end up getting hurt again.

I'd come to Northern Lights to escape everything, but those past broken relationships and personal failures were still a part of me. I was still wrestling with feelings of guilt, anger, and self-doubt. Out on the water, I'd done a lot of thinking about my life, but despite all that alone time, I don't think I was any better off. I was still hopelessly confused, still indecisive, still overly cautious, and still holding my emotions on some sort of leash. I really didn't understand why things had happened the way they did, and I didn't know how to explain my feelings to anyone else, let alone myself.

I tossed and turned all night long. Chuck was out like a log. He could sleep through a thunderstorm if he wanted to. I finally grabbed my guitar from down below, picked out a quiet tune, and hummed along softly, letting my thoughts and feelings flow. Playing the guitar always seemed to help. After a while, I clicked on my flashlight and wrote down a few rough lines to a song. It was too mellow, I thought, too depressing. I played it again anyway. It was a sad song, but for some reason, it made me feel better.

Time slipped by unnoticed as I wrapped myself up in the sad lyrics and comforting melody. I had no idea how late it was, and I didn't care. I couldn't sleep anyway. I peered out the screen window by my top bunk into the stillness outside. The moon was high overhead, gleaming brightly in the night sky, casting shadows on the path that ran past the cabin. I thought I heard the sound of footsteps on the bridge down by the lake. I leaned over and looked out again. "Who could be up at this hour of the night?" I wondered.

I looked over to Eagle Bluff, the cliff straight across the narrows, from where one could gain a bird's eye view of everything going on around the camp. I thought I saw a faint reflection of someone standing on the edge of the cliff up there. The dark form was barely visible, but it cast its own small shadow in the moonlight. I blinked my eyes and shuffled around on my bunk to have another look, but the mysterious figure vanished, or it wasn't actually there after all. It was just my mind, seeing things again, things it wanted to see, or maybe, just things it was afraid of seeing.

My thoughts kept returning to Esther. What would she think if she knew I'd been obsessing about her so much? I wondered where she was and what she was doing. Maybe she was lying awake in her own cabin, listening to the soft strums of a guitar far away as it drifted aimlessly across the still waters of the lake.

Maybe she was having a hard time getting to sleep too.

chapter 15

southern style

"So prim and proper and politely off-beat."

When Chuck woke me up the next morning, I was physically shot. I hadn't slept but an hour or so, and it was a restless, dreamless sleep at that. I was groggy and miserable, but I forced myself to get up and get going anyway. I wasn't getting my next group for a couple of days, but I had promised Chuck that I would help him at the trail shack. He had a pile of work to do, and I wanted to be a good cabinmate, so it was up and at 'em!

As I got dressed and headed off to Starlight Lodge for breakfast, I was still thinking about the beautiful redhead who'd walked into my cabin with a bowl of hot soup the previous night. It seemed as if my innocent fascination with Esther had somehow transformed itself into a full-blown obsession overnight.

In the two days she'd been in camp, I'd already learned a lot about her. She talked about being an exchange student at the University of Chicago, being from Auckland, New Zealand, and how her birthday was coming up in a week or so. She'd been living with a family in Chicago for the school year and would be heading back home in a month. She had a gorgeous accent from Down Under that became even more pronounced when she got excited or nervous.

Esther, however, didn't seem to fit in with the Chicago group. In fact, she didn't hang out with them at all, except when they were heading off to the worksite. She tended to be a loner, like me, who went her own way most of the time, usually just listening to what others were talking about.

I couldn't get past her striking appearance. She had that beautiful auburn hair that fell almost to her hips. The wave of freckles that ran across her nose was simply mesmerizing. Her bright eyes seemed to glow like burning coals of flame. I was almost afraid to look into them for fear of being exposed. They seemed to reflect the exact likeness of the blue sky above, or the deep green of the pine trees, or the sparkling ripples of the water on the lakes—or perhaps I was just seeing what I so desperately wanted to see.

Esther had a darker, edgier side to her too. For those first few days, she was always dressed in the same clothes: a skintight T-shirt with a jean jacket over the top, army green capris tied at her knees, leaving the calves of her legs bare, highlighting the rugged black hiking boots that she always wore. Her lipstick seemed to perfectly match the red sunglasses she usually had on as well. Her appearance was tough and intimidating, and it seemed to fit her personality. To nearly everyone, she came across as one tough cookie, more than a bit dangerous, and at times, downright cold and harsh.

But from her visit to my cabin, I knew she could be quiet, kind, and thoughtful too. Her rugged outward appearance seemed to be a sort of mask that hid a more vulnerable personality, which I had a feeling was lurking somewhere deep down inside her.

It was immediately apparent to everyone within earshot that Esther talked differently. She sounded like a Brit to me, which was pretty exotic to a plain-spoken guy from Iowa. Actually, she spoke the way I thought more Americans should speak—polite and proper, but it was her accent that I found so interesting. I patiently waited for her to say "crikey," like Steve Irwin, but she never did. Every now and then, however, something offbeat would slip out, like when she called the ice cooler a chilly bin and the outhouse a long-drop.

For those first few days, I found myself watching Esther more and more, trying desperately to catch what she was saying, no matter how insignificant it might be. I listened, usually from across the room, trying not to be noticed. I was fully aware of my growing obsession with her. I'd be the first to admit it. For me, it was a pathetic, helpless feeling, but it felt wonderful too.

I was fascinated with her southern style, so prim and proper and politely off-beat, but she could be surprisingly sharp at times. The other canoe guides learned to treat her with caution because of the way she'd sometimes react to typical American humor.

Percy experienced it firsthand at breakfast that morning. Since he was tall, dark, and handsome, and more than a bit of a flirt, I had a natural dislike for him. It was pretty obvious he didn't care too much for me either, so when he plopped down across from Esther at breakfast, my ears perked up. He'd already honed in on her the first night she was at camp, and that morning, he was still in hot pursuit. It was mealtime, which always put him in a jovial mood, and he was surrounded by his friends, which only increased his confidence. Unfortunately, he made a lot of strategic mistakes, and that morning his mistake would be to mess with Esther.

"So, Esther!" Percy exclaimed as he sat down. "How is the pretty redhead doing on this beautiful spring morning?"

"I'm fine, but I'm pretty sure it's summertime," she replied coldly. Then, she looked back down at her plate and took another bite of her toast and jam. I got the signal all the way down at the end of the table. It read, loud and clear, "Please leave me alone or go away."

But Percy rarely could stop himself from running a red light, much less anything else in life. He had the feel of a spoiled cat that got fed on time, scratched whenever it wanted, and babied like a precious little cuddle-muffin to the point of insanity. Privilege and entitlement seemed to reek from his every pore, and he was ready and willing to take full advantage of it.

Percy kept staring at Esther, grinning like a happy circus clown. Every time she looked up, he was there, eyeing her like a confused squirrel wondering how to reach the unattainable acorn hanging from a branch so high above. She took it for a while, but finally, she'd had enough of his staring.

"So, mate," she said, looking him coldly in the eyes. "What are you gawking at anyway?"

"Your freckles, darling, they're so adorable," he replied, stumbling carelessly down the slippery slope of his own mind. "Crikey! They look like bread crumbs sprinkled all over your pretty little nose. I wonder if you'd sprinkle some of them on me . . . later tonight?"

"Oops," I thought to myself. "The drop-off came sooner than expected." I watched as good old Percy grinned with satisfaction and waited for the cute redhead to giggle appropriately.

Esther looked up and then calmly said, "So, mate, I've heard from some of the girls yakking around here that you're quite the loose unit. One of them even said you have a nice little patch of freckles on your keister, but that doesn't mean I'm going to compliment you on them. And I certainly don't want you to sprinkle any of your grotty keister freckles on me anytime soon, eh."

Everyone sitting within earshot went completely silent as Percy turned a bright shade of raspberry red and wondered who could have possibly told her about the patch of freckles on his bare bottom. Esther picked up her glass of milk and took a sip as if nothing had happened. She sat there calm and serene until someone nearby cried out, "Oh! Percy! Shot down again!"

All at once, the entire table erupted into a wild cacophony of laughter. As Percy sat paralyzed in shock and dismay, Esther flashed a dry smirk in his direction and continued to munch on her piece of toast and jam. The raucous laughter and relentless joking kept up for the rest of the meal, all at the expense of poor Percy, who finally got up and just walked away. I finished my breakfast with deep satisfaction. Anytime someone could put Percy in his place, it was a victory for losers like me. At least that's what I thought as I watched it all play out from my corner of the table.

The day had certainly gotten off to a good start!

chapter 20

rescuing the redhead

"She was alone, and it showed."

The victory Esther won at breakfast didn't last long. From that moment on, she had the attention of every male in camp, both the camp staff and the guys from the Chicago group. She was attractive, dressed to the hilt, and her Kiwi accent only made her all-the-more desirable. The guys seemed to hover around her like bees trying to pollinate the biggest, most beautiful flower in the field. Meanwhile, the girls in camp looked on with disdain.

Esther tried to brush it off, but it wasn't working. In fact, it only seemed to make matters worse. The guys treated her cold shoulder and sharp comments like a game of chess. They seemed to think she was just playing with them, as if she were available, but only to the best one. To some, she was an irresistible challenge, and they turned her into a competition among themselves, with each guy stepping up to the plate, taking three mighty swings, only to strike out in the end.

The other girls didn't appreciate all the attention she had so easily stolen away from them. They blamed the guys, of course, but they were intimidated by Esther as well. She soon found herself excluded by the girls, which made her even more of a target for the guys, who hounded her relentlessly. It was a bad situation to be in. She had come to see Aria, but on Esther's first full day in camp, Aria left on a week-long canoe trip. She was alone, and it showed.

"That's probably why she came to visit me," I thought. "She was frustrated and alone, under siege by the guys, and she had no one else to turn to." I felt sorry for her, but I couldn't seem to find a decent way to break through the onslaught that always seemed to be buzzing around her. So, I kept my distance, but that probably wasn't the best choice I could have made.

That evening after supper, when everyone was down at the beach hanging out, the guys from Chicago were taking on the girls in a game of volleyball. I was watching from the edge of the woods, still feeling weak from my bout of food poisoning. I watched as Esther stood on the beach near the volleyball court. When one of the girls asked if she wanted to join them, she shook her head "no" at first. That's when all the guys on the court erupted like a volcano.

"Come on, redhead!" they shouted. "Join the girls' team! We need some real competition out here!"

Two of the girls went over to Esther while the guys continued to beg for her to join the game. She hesitated for a minute, but then for some reason, she changed her mind. When Esther took off her jacket and threw it to the side of the court, all the guys let out a thunderous roar of satisfaction.

"Oh yeah!" one guy shouted. "They've got the tough redhead on their side now! Let's go, guys!"

"Yeah!" another one yelled excitedly. "No more mercy! Come on, guys! Let's show 'em who's the boss!"

When the game resumed, it was a mad scramble on the guys' side. They dove for every ball. They shouted and elbowed and bumped into each other. They shoved each other down to get a crack at the ball. They began launching themselves recklessly up into the net to spike the ball down on the girls.

It was actually a pretty good game to watch. The girls were no spring chickens. They gave it right back to the guys for a while. Esther was tall and athletic, and when she got into the front row, she laid down a series of shots that sent the guys diving for cover and falling all over themselves.

"Oh yeah!" one of them shouted. "You just got burned by the redhead!"

"Come on, guys! We can't let ourselves get beat by the girls!" another one exclaimed.

At first, the girls seemed to enjoy the sudden burst of competition, but the guys started to play dirty. They were flying around, reaching over the net, even lunging across onto the girls' side of the court to knock them down. It stopped being just a friendly game and turned into a nasty free-for-all. The girls began to complain about it, but the guys wouldn't play nice. They wanted to win. They wanted to impress the redhead. They pounded away at the net, spiking the ball like maniacs every chance they got, slamming bombs down on the girls' heads from high above.

When Esther let off another shot that sent the guys flying all over the place, one of them cried, "You girls wouldn't be able to compete with us if it wasn't for the redhead! She's the only one over there who's taking this game seriously."

"Oh, really!" one of the girls shouted back from across the net. "Well, you can just kiss my ass!"

That's when things began to unravel into a nasty tangled mess that wouldn't come clean anytime soon. The guys should have known better, but they'd already worked themselves up into a wild frenzy, and besides, they were brainless idiots to begin with anyway. They were clearly more stupid as a group than any one of them could have possibly been alone. But no one seemed to have the ability to think or reason for himself.

Together, they all began to chant the label they'd given their coveted prize, "Redhead! Redhead! Redhead! Redhead!"

As Esther backed away in dismay, a couple of the girls stepped forward and yelled back, "Shut up, you jerks!"

But the guys only chanted all the more loudly, smiling and laughing like clueless imbeciles as they jumped up and down and continued to thrust their fists into the air.

I was about to run down and join the girls in calling them a thing or two, but that's when Carly stepped forward in a rage and faced the guys at the net.

"All right!" she shouted. "If you bozos are gonna act like idiots, then we're out of here!" Then, she stomped off the court, followed by all the other girls, all of them that is, except for Esther.

"We're done playing!" one of the girls shouted.

"Yeah, jerks!" another girl yelled. "Go ahead! Play with yourselves! You're probably really good at that!"

I watched in shock as the line of girls stomped off the beach and marched right past me standing next to the trail. I could hear them cursing under their breath as they hiked back up to the lodge. Down on the beach, however, standing alone on the girls' side of the volleyball court was Esther.

The guys whined and called out, "Come on! We were just having fun! We'll play nice! Come back!"

"Not on your life!" came the reply from the last girl in line.

When they realized that their playthings were not going to return, the guys shifted their attention back to Esther, standing alone on the other side of the net. They stared at her in a merciless stupor, as if trying to get the blood to flow back up into their pitiful brains once again, but they simply couldn't.

One of them cried out, "All right! It's ten against one!"

That broke the ice, and the guys all cock-a-doodle-doo'd again like mindless roosters. They were back to the same old idiotic selves they'd always been, ready to have some more fun with the gorgeous female on the other side of the court.

"Let's see if the redhead can handle all ten of us at once," one idiot shouted as he served the ball across the net.

Esther stood there in disbelief as the ball thumped in the sand and slowly rolled off to the side and out-of-bounds.

"I'm done," she said quietly.

"Come on!" the guys wailed. "We'll split up!"

A couple of them ducked under the net and joined her on the other side of the court.

"All right, let's go!" they cried. "We've got the redhead on our side now, so you guys are toast!"

As they began to play again, Esther just turned and walked off the court. She didn't have any witty reply to the disaster that had just unfolded. She was beyond despair. She was beyond anger. She was embarrassed to the point of tears. In a daze, she walked slowly up the beach toward me as the guys begged for her to return. But she didn't look back. She just kept walking.

As she passed by me, I said, "I'm sorry, Esther, they're just being stupid jerks."

She spun around and glared at me. I could see that she was burning up inside, but she was trying to hold it in. "Whatever!" she yelled furiously. Then, she turned and walked away.

I was shot through the heart. Suddenly, I realized that I'd done nothing, virtually nothing at all over the past two days to be a friend to Esther. She had reached out to me in the cabin, and all I could muster was to stare at her and listen from across the room as the guys circled her like vultures. Just like them, I only seemed capable of treating her like an object of desire, nothing more.

As the imbeciles on the beach continued to plead for the redhead to return, Esther suddenly turned back and stared at me. She stood there alone, strong, and fierce, as if the buzzards on the beach weren't even there any longer.

"I'm sorry, mate. It wasn't your fault," she said.

"That's okay," I replied, but I knew I was the one who should have been apologizing.

"I'm sorry," she said again. Then, she turned and walked away up the trail and back to her cabin.

I should have run after her, but I was paralyzed with guilt and embarrassment. I'd been taught ever since I was a child, that you can't be a passive observer forever. At a certain point, you have to speak up. You have to take a stand for what's right. Sadly, that moment had come and gone a long time ago.

For some reason, I wasn't thinking about myself anymore. Maybe it was Esther's angry words that finally shook me awake. Perhaps it was her undeserved apology and words of forgiveness. Whatever it was, I realized that I didn't care what happened to myself anymore. Anyone who would treat a friend of mine, or anyone for that matter, in such a horrible manner was no friend of mine. I wasn't willing to just sit and watch any longer. I had to speak up. I had to act. I had to stand up and fight for Esther.

The blood rushed to my head as I marched down toward the group of guys still standing around at the volleyball court. They saw me coming and immediately figured it out.

One of them chuckled under his breath and muttered sarcastically, "Look out, here comes the big man himself."

The snide comment only made me hotter, and I glared angrily back at them as I approached. The two leaders of the pack stepped forward to face me. They seemed like two enormous sweaty rats preparing to fight over a piece of cheese.

"Well, look who finally showed up," the bigger of the two said with a sneer. "It's the redhead's little chaperone. Come to save the damsel in distress, have we?"

"Shut up, you idiots!" I yelled at the top of my lungs. "You're just a bunch of jackasses! You know that, don't you? You're all down here rolling around in your own crap, hee-hawing after something you can't have! She's gone already, so why don't you all just go back to your game of shit-ball and shut the hell up!"

After the furious outburst, my courage failed me. I wasn't used to talking like that. Everything else I'd wanted to say seemed to shrivel up as the guys leered back at me. They eyed each other as if amused, and then they just started laughing.

Being laughed at was a killer for me. There was nothing else I could manage to say or do. I turned and walked away across the beach, physically shaking as the guys broke into a chorus of jeers. I heard what they called me as I walked away. I heard what they thought of me. It was a nasty, terrible, and humiliating experience. I wanted to yell a few things back, but it wouldn't have done any good.

Over the laughter, one of them called out, "Hey, big man, chill out! We didn't mean anything by it!"

He wasn't serious; I was sure of it. He didn't really mean it. I kept walking and yelled back, quoting Esther, "Whatever!"

Then, I stopped dead in my tracks as the blood pounded away inside my aching head. I turned around and shouted back, "You know, you're apologizing to the wrong person! You should be apologizing to Esther! Not the redhead, you morons! Her name is Esther! She's got a name! If you really want to make things right, go and apologize to her—that is if any of you jackasses is man enough to do it, but I really don't think any of you are!"

The angry words seemed to come from somewhere deep down inside me, but it wasn't actually me. I heard the words spewed out furiously, as if I were standing right next to another angry young man. I hadn't actually said those words, had I? My head began to spin, and I felt as if I were about to faint.

All of the guys were glaring at me from far away across the beach. I could hear a couple of them mumbling angrily under their breath. They clearly didn't appreciate the loud reprimand, the tidy words of advice, or having their manhood questioned so rudely. I half expected them to come over and beat me to a pulp, but I didn't care. I would have enjoyed it. The sudden rush of adrenalin, anger, and fear pulsing through my veins made me feel invincible.

When they started laughing again, I turned around and walked away, fuming up the trail to my cabin, thinking furious thoughts all along the way. "They're all idiots! They were raised idiots! They'll all raise idiot children!" I thought of all the hateful things I could imagine, but I held the feelings inside. I knew it wasn't a healthy thing to do, but that's just the way I was raised, I guess.

A little later, after I simmered down a bit, I reasoned that some of the guys had just been going along with the crowd. There were a couple of bad apples in the bunch, though. There were a couple of guys who weren't even students at the university, who probably got the rest of them all riled up, to the point that they simply turned into a pack of wolves. They picked out the prey they wanted, and together, they worked tirelessly to isolate it and bring it down. That's what a couple of them were thinking, at least, and I wasn't about to let that happen, not while I was still around.

I felt so weak that night, so completely drained. I didn't go to the campfire. I should have. I should have gone to look for Esther and sit beside her, but I figured that she wouldn't be there either. So instead, I huddled in my cabin and banged away on my old guitar, but it didn't help at all. I took no pleasure in it. The guitar sounded angry and hopelessly out of tune, so I threw it down and climbed up into my bunk. I was so tired. I finally slept, but it was a restless sleep full of tearful regrets, fits of rage, and angry dreams.

I woke at first light, still exhausted, as if I'd been wrestling with a horde of demons all night. Immediately, I thought of Esther. I would be heading out soon on a canoe trip, and Aria wouldn't be back for another six days. The last thing I wanted to do was leave Esther alone at camp to fend for herself.

All that day, I watched Esther, not because I was fascinated by her, but because I was concerned about her. I watched out for her as any good friend should. I was ready to jump in at a moment's notice if she got picked on or threatened in any way. I was prepared to stare down any of the predators who had mistreated her so badly. At breakfast that morning, a couple of the guys gave me dirty looks, but other than that, the situation seemed to have settled back down.

I noticed that three of the guys apologized to Esther later that day, and several of the girls came by to comfort her. After lunch, I talked to Jim about everything that had happened. He reassured me that he would keep an eye out for her while I was gone. Cassie gave me a look from across the dining room that seemed to indicate that she was aware of the situation too.

It appeared, however, that some of the guys in the group had not given up the ghost. When they were around, they circled on the edges like hungry wolves, eyeing Esther as if still hunting prey. It unsettled me to no end, and I couldn't imagine what it did to Esther, who had to work with them each day. She was tough, though. I knew she'd be okay, but it still ate me up inside.

After supper, Finn found me in the lodge. I could tell he knew something was up. He asked a few fishing questions, not about fish, but about Esther. I had a feeling he was onto it and was simply giving me an opportunity to fill in the details. I hesitated, but then I finally did. I told him everything as he listened patiently. It was such a relief to get it off my chest.

When I finished, Finn simply said, "Thanks, Leo. Don't you worry about Esther. I'll take care of it."

I had expected him to say more, but that was it. He was a man of few words, a lot like Chuck in that regard. I would have liked more assurances, but I knew Finn would do everything he could. I'm not sure what he did or who he talked to, but later, Esther told me the problem stopped immediately. It wasn't perfect, but at least it was tolerable, and that's all I cared about at that point.

That evening, I met Esther at her cabin, and we walked to the campfire together. I was still so ashamed; I couldn't look her in the eyes. We didn't say much on the way there or at the campfire either. It just felt good to be near her, sitting beside her as we listened to the stories and songs and silliness. Afterward, I walked her back to her cabin and said goodnight.

She stepped up onto the cabin porch and turned back toward me. "Thanks, mate, for sticking up for me," she said.

"Sure," I replied. "I'm just sorry for not saying anything sooner."

She laughed quietly. "You really told those dipsticks off on the beach, didn't you?"

"You heard all that?" I asked, somewhat surprised. "I thought you were long gone by then."

"Well, you were shouting pretty loudly," Esther said as she slugged me gently on the shoulder. "I heard you spewin' all the way back up here at my cabin, bro."

"You did?" I exclaimed in embarrassment. "Then, the whole island must've heard it."

"Yeah, I reckon so," Esther replied as she opened the cabin door. "I know you talked to Finn too. Thanks. He told me you did, and he said he'd keep an eye out for me while you're gone."

"He did?" I said with a sigh of relief.

"It means a lot," she said quietly, "I mean, to have someone who cares about me."

In silence, I grinned sheepishly up at her like a stray dog begging to be let in out of the cold.

"You know what this means to me, right?" Esther asked, as she looked into my eyes and waited for me to reply.

"Um, sure, I think so," I replied.

"It means you're my special bro now," she said quietly, smiling down at me, standing there in the dark.

"Um, thanks," I said.

As I stood there, she quickly leaned forward and gave me a soft kiss on the cheek.

"Thanks," I said, surprised by the kiss.

She reached out and gently squeezed my cold hand with her warm fingers. "You earned it, Leo."

"Thanks," I said again.

Esther giggled softly at my lack of anything more to say. As she pulled away, our hands dropped slowly apart. "I'll see you tomorrow before you leave on your trip, eh?"

"Yeah," I replied. "I'll see you tomorrow."

She stepped into the soft light of the doorway and let it slowly shut. As I walked away down the path to Starlight Lodge, I could feel her eyes on me. I wondered what she was thinking, what she was dreaming of, and what she was feeling inside. Most of all, I wondered what it meant to be Esther's special bro.

Whatever it was, it sounded good to me.

chapter 21

the trip of a lifetime

"I smelled trouble. Literally, I could smell it."

My next canoe group was set to arrive the following afternoon. I had been looking ahead to the trip with a good deal of apprehension, but in the end, I'd have to admit it was the trip of a lifetime. I'll always look back on it with nothing but joy and affection, but in all honesty, it started out kind of rough.

A few days before the group arrived, Cassie told me about them. She called them "troubled youth" from the Twin Cities. I was getting no swamper to help on the trip. There was no more room, so it was just me: a country bumpkin from Iowa and a bunch of mischievous boys from the inner city. Cassie seemed overly worried about it—or about me—as the day of their arrival approached. Every time she talked about the group of "troubled youth," she would raise her left eyebrow and give me a wild wide-eyed stare. She kept pestering me about the logistics of the trip all the way up to the moment they arrived and hopped off the boat.

I met them on Friday afternoon, and instantly, I smelled trouble. Literally, I could smell it. The smell came from a hodgepodge, ragtag army of fifth and sixth-grade boys from Minneapolis. Almost everyone knows how boys at that age start to give off a peculiar odor called B.O. It's a sort of "get it out of here or so help me" kind of smell. Well, those boys had it in spades. It was endearing at first, but after a while, it kind of grew on you like fungus.

The boys and I made it through the first couple of hours just fine. After we moved into a smelly mosquito-infested cabin near Starlight

Lodge, I gave them a walking tour around camp. In that span of time, I only had to break up one fight and patch up a scraped knee with a couple of Band-Aids. For the most part, the boys seemed quiet and cute, but with a certain degree of city sass as well.

I found it refreshingly different from what I'd been used to growing up in rural Iowa. Cassie, however, kept on worrying. At the evening campfire that night, she pulled me aside and warned me about some of the boys. With a wide-eyed stare and her bleached eyebrows going nuts, she gave me a long list of special instructions.

"Lead with a heavy hand at first," Cassie exclaimed forcefully. "These are tough boys, so don't joke around, don't let them get away with anything, and for Pete's sake, don't smile!"

She said I could lighten up eventually, but certainly not on the first day or two, and then, only if they understood who was in charge.

"You're the leader of the pack!" she exclaimed, poking me in the chest. "That's you, Leo! You need to be firm and assertive with those boys. You need to take charge!"

I felt a little embarrassed at getting a talking-to in the rear of the campfire ring as people filed past. I worried about what they might think. Was he in trouble? Did he do something wrong? As I listened to Cassie give me the talk, my eyes glazed over. I nodded incessantly, almost mindlessly. I said nothing in hopes that her lecture would end sooner, not later. I could tell that she was afraid those boys were going to eat me alive. I wasn't assertive enough. I wasn't strong enough. I was too soft. I was a green canoe guide who didn't know very much. She was dead right on all counts, except for the eating one.

After Cassie's little pep talk ended, I went over and sat down with the boys. Esther snuck in late and sat next to me. She leaned forward and peeked down the log at the lineup of surly sailors I'd be watching over for the next week.

"They're so cute," she whispered. "They look like little angels."

I nodded and grinned back at her. I suddenly wished I wasn't going out with the boys at all, but I kept looking forward, trying to maintain a strong and assertive facade. I was worried about the boys too. They weren't little angels by a long shot. I wondered if they'd seen Cassie's frantic display. I wondered what they had already concluded about me. Their little minds were already churning through the many ways they could take advantage of me; I just knew it. We sat through the campfire, and then it was off to bed. As I got to know the boys, I began to understand why Cassie had been so worried.

When the campfire ended, I stood up and announced that we were going back to our cabin to get ready for bed. That was my first mistake. It would be followed by several more throughout the week. They trudged along behind me on the trail to the cabin like lost boys without mothers. They were tough little cookies; it was easy to see. It oozed out of them like mold on moist bread. They didn't want to go to bed, and I knew it. But I was determined to have it my way.

The boys filed like soldiers up the steps and into our smelly one-room cabin full of mosquitoes. Just getting in the door was a challenge. The last few in line didn't appreciate the fact that they were, in fact, last in line. So, the stragglers tried to sneak forward and make it inside before the other unlucky end-of-the-liners got there. No typical fifth or sixth-grade boy ever wanted to be last. It was a chaotic scene for a few brief seconds, but we managed to survive getting through the door and into the cabin. The screen door took a severe beating in the process, but it would be okay.

Inside, the boys were buzzing around like a beehive that had just been whacked with a stick. The cabin was nicely supplied with hard thin mattresses and a horde of hungry mosquitoes just waiting for us to go to sleep. That's about it, except for the bare bulb dangling precariously from the ceiling.

The boys recognized the entirety of the situation at once. I was just the odd man out, the babysitter, the tardy referee in the game they'd already begun to play. They immediately went about the process of making the stark space their home. They started rolling out their sleeping bags and digging into their over-stuffed duffle bags for all sorts of little knickknacks. None of it had anything to do with sleeping. One kid pulled out a pack of playing cards. Another kid had a little electronic game that buzzed annoyingly. Another pulled out a football and started throwing it around the room.

Like a lion king, I tried to settle the antsy herd of wild hyenas down. They and I knew, however, that it was going to be a life-and-death struggle before that happened. The scene was set. None of the boys knew each other before coming on the trip, and each of them had their own little issues that started popping up all over the place. Each boy was trying to establish his place in the pecking order that was rapidly being formed. No one wanted to be at the bottom of the pile. They just needed a little more time to figure it out. It was time that I was unwilling to give them, but they took it anyway.

What made things even more complicated was the knock everyone heard on the flimsy screen door. When I answered it, all of the boys immediately changed. One kid ran back to his bunk for a T-shirt. Another one elbowed me hard in the ribs.

"Hello?" I said as I pushed the door open a crack.

"Cheers, mate!" I heard the unmistakable voice of Esther outside.

"Hi, Esther," I replied, with a worried glance back at the boys staring at me from around the room. "What do you want?"

"Oh, nothing much," she said sweetly. "I just wanted to meet your troupe of little sailors."

"Is that your girlfriend?" the kid who elbowed me asked.

"She's just a friend," I responded, perhaps a little too quickly.

"No way!" a little kid named Quincy bellowed bravely. "She's your girlfriend."

"No, she's not," I replied desperately, suddenly realizing things were spiraling rapidly out of my control.

"Yes, she is!" Quincy countered. I knew from experience there was absolutely no way to win a word fight with a fifth-grader, ever.

Esther pulled the door open and peeked inside. "How can she not smell that rotten potato smell?" I wondered. It was actually beginning to make my eyes water.

"Why, hello there, mate," Esther said sweetly to little Quincy, standing boldly by my side. She grinned down at him as he stared wide-eyed back up at her. The other lost boys began to gather around too, as if they were being visited by an angel, or a beautiful fairy, or perhaps their long-lost mother.

"Hi," Quincy replied politely.

"So, little fellow, what's your name, eh?" Esther asked.

Her unusual Kiwi accent immediately captivated the entire room of surly city kids. They'd never met anyone who spoke like that before. In fact, they'd never met a real-life punk rocker either, so it was quite the special occasion.

"Quincy," he replied. It was all he could muster as he gazed up at the amazing creature who had just wiggled her way into his stark, smelly, sheltered little world.

Esther held her hand out. "Well, mate, give me five, eh?"

Quincy slapped her hand with eager delight and bravely asked, "What's your name?"

"Esther," she said. "I'm a friend of your guide, Leo, here."

"You like Leo?" Quincy asked in disbelief, getting right to the point. I looked over at Esther, along with all the other smelly sailors in the room. I couldn't believe it either.

"Maybe, maybe not," she replied casually. At first, I was deeply hurt, but her big grin gave away the real answer.

"Are you his girlfriend?" Quincy asked, this time sounding even more skeptical than the last time.

"You're pretty nosy," she said with a cheerful laugh. "You're really cute too!" Esther reached out and tweaked Quincy's nose with her pretty fingers.

"What?" he replied, shocked that the amazing creature had actually touched him.

"I bet you have lots of girlfriends back home, don't you!" she said, setting the little ruffian back on his heels.

"No, not really," he said, feeling the instant pressure from the other boys behind him. "Well, actually, yeah! I got three or four girls who like me."

"I thought so," Esther said with a giggle. "You're quite the cheeky fellow, aren't you?"

"Yeah," Quincy agreed to whatever that meant. "My main woman is Ranita. She's already thirteen and in the seventh grade."

"How old are you?" Esther asked.

"I'm eleven, almost twelve, though," he replied proudly.

"Well, you little stud muffin!" Esther exclaimed. "Going out with older women now, are we?"

"I can handle it," Quincy boasted, hoping for another touch from the angelic creature.

"Well, I reckon you can!" Esther heartily agreed. "Maybe you should put me down on your list too."

"Sure, babe," Quincy replied boldly, beginning to discover his tiny oats lurking somewhere deep down inside.

"Okay!" I interrupted frantically. "Esther has to be going now!"

"No, I'm…" Esther tried to respond.

"So, Esther," I said, turning my back to the room full of hypnotized sailors. "What was it you wanted anyway?"

"I just wanted to say goodnight to you and your little men," she said innocently.

"Okay, thanks," I replied, trying to be calm, assertive, and polite all at the same time. I nudged Esther back toward the door with my arm and held it open for her. It felt a lot like a third date to me.

"Okay, Leo," she said sadly. "I can go now if you want me to."

"Goodnight," I said, grinning nervously as she backed down the rickety steps.

"Those boys are so cute," she whispered as she turned to go. "I want to take Quincy home with me."

"Yeah, thanks for stopping by," I replied, continuing my imaginary conversation with myself. "I'll see you next week. Aria will be back tomorrow or the day after that, I think."

"Goodnight, Leo," Esther said as she waved and smiled at Quincy, who was peeking at her from the window.

"Goodnight, Esther," I replied as I slowly shut the door.

I stood there for a brief moment, realizing that I had to turn around and face the room full of eyeballs that were all fixed on the back of my head. It was going to be rough. I knew what was coming. I just didn't want to deal with it, but there was no way out of it.

When I turned around, the room erupted into a wild frenzy, and a deafening "Whoop!" went up all around me. I was sure Esther could hear it as she walked away down the trail. In fact, I wondered if the entire camp could hear it as well. I couldn't help but grin from ear to ear as the boys went completely nuts. If there had been anything breakable in that cabin, they would have broken it. I was sure they were going to tear the place apart. Toys and footballs were flying around. Pillows and sleeping bags were getting tossed in the air. Boys were jumping off the top bunks onto each other. Others were rolling around and wrestling on the floor.

"She's your girlfriend, right?" Quincy shouted excitedly over the pandemonium.

"No," I replied.

"Yes, she is! She's hot!" another kid exclaimed.

"Hey, stop that!" I replied, desperately trying to maintain control of the ravenous pack of hyenas who seemed to be taking me down for the final kill.

"Where is she from?" another kid asked.

"New Zealand," I replied.

"She likes you!" Quincy said confidently.

"No, she's just a friend," I replied, sticking to my talking points.

"No, she likes you!" Quincy said again. "I can tell."

"She's just a friend," I repeated. I wondered how Quincy could tell that she liked me, but I had to stick to my story, or all hell would break loose, as if it hadn't already.

"That girl likes Leo!" Quincy shouted to a couple of boys standing nearby. "She's his girlfriend!"

"She's just my friend, you little…pipsqueak," I mumbled, staring helplessly around at the chaotic melee.

After Esther's surprise visit, it took forever to settle the boys back down. I had to shout to be heard over the roomful of excited voices that wouldn't stop talking and yelling and sometimes screaming. They were just a wee bit excited, and Esther's visit only amped up their tiny hormone-infused eleven and twelve-year-old bodies all the more. It was a losing battle I had to win, but how? Just as Cassie said, I needed to be firm and assertive. I couldn't smile or give in one inch. I had to be the leader of the pack.

Slowly, I began to take back control of the room. I worked on the boys one by one, starting with the weaker ones first. They were tired, so I had that one thing going for me. Through a series of commands and outright threats, the games and toys gradually got put away or taken away. The boys reluctantly retreated to their respective bunks, but from their perches, they renewed the battle over the bulb. With the boys in their bunks, that was the one last hold I had over them: the light switch. As the minutes ticked by, I warned and threatened and pleaded with the boys to quiet down.

As I struggled to gain control of the situation, I was confronted by the true leader of the pack. It was a big kid they called Squire, who was sitting up in his top bunk, defiantly clicking his flashlight on and off. He seemed to have greater command of the room than I did. When he spoke, the rest of the boys listened. When he shined his flashlight into other kids' eyes, they simply shrunk away. He was the one I had to take down if we were going to get any sleep that night. I eyed him like a hawk as I circled the room and wondered how I was ever going to accomplish that.

Squire sat up in his bunk, blatantly challenging my authority. All the boys knew it. When I said it was time for bed, he said he wasn't tired. When I insisted on it, he said he stayed up past midnight every single night. When I told him that wasn't going to happen, he told me that I could go to sleep if I wanted to, and he would "babysit" the other boys. That really riled everyone up. Squire insisted it would be fine. He'd get some sleep when he felt like it.

For about fifteen minutes, the two of us had a long drawn-out power struggle in front of the other boys, who watched keenly to see who would ultimately win. By some miracle, I finally got all of them, including Squire, to crawl into their sleeping bags, or at least to lie on top of them. Then, after about five more minutes, I called for lights out. That's when the fun really began.

When I flipped the switch, Squire immediately turned on his flashlight and began to talk to the kid in the next bunk. Then, someone else clicked on their flashlight. Then, someone belched. Obviously, that was followed by a chorus of laughter from everyone in the room.

I tried to quiet them down and told them to turn off their flashlights again. When they did, I said, "Okay, now let's get some sleep."

But in the dark, Squire mimicked me and clicked his flashlight on and off again. That was followed by another bout of uncontrolled giggling. Flashlights clicked on and off, followed by giggles, then more flashlights, then more giggles. It went on and on. I kept telling them to be quiet. Some tried to lie still, but eventually, they'd get the wiggles, and the giggles would break loose all over again.

I was determined to wear the boys out. After all, I had no other choice. As the giggles subsided, one kid said he couldn't sleep. Then, two other boys said they couldn't sleep either. Then, someone farted. That was followed by another eruption of laughter and a spray of flashlights around the cabin. Then, someone complained about a nasty odor coming from the corner of the room. He got blamed for it himself by another kid. That led to a heated argument and some chest-thumping. When the first kid told the other one to shut up, I had to jump out of bed and make sure things didn't escalate into fisticuffs or another late-night free-for-all.

Things settled down for about ten seconds until someone farted again. The giggling erupted again, and a fresh wave of flashlights sprayed the ceiling. When that was followed up with a fresh chorus of farts, I lost my cool and shouted for everyone to be quiet. I'm sure they must have heard me all the way down outside Starlight Lodge. They probably were having a pretty good laugh about it too. I'm betting Cassie was probably down on her knees at that very moment, praying to Saint Christopher for my safety as well.

All of this went on and on, in the dark, for what seemed like an eternity. I barely knew them and was still just learning their names, let alone their peculiar personalities, and there I was, being asked to not let them get away with anything. It had taken only one hour, and I was already at my wit's end. Finally, I told the boys that the next person to talk was going to lose his flashlight. It happened immediately. Squire laughed and then clicked his flashlight on and off.

I got up, marched straight over to his bunk, and stuck out my hand. "Give it," I said, looking him sternly in the eyes.

"No," he whispered back defiantly. Everyone watched the final showdown in suspense to see what would happen next.

"If you don't give me your flashlight," I said, "I'm going to tell my boss, Cassie, about you. And she said at the campfire tonight that if any of you boys so much as step out of line, she'll make you stay here and do chores all week while the rest of us go on the trip of a lifetime. So, Squire, it's time for you to choose. Which is it going to be?"

"What?" he asked.

"A week of chores with Cassie, the witch queen, or the trip of a lifetime in the Boundary Waters."

Squire squirmed in his bed. "She's a witch queen?"

"Yes, she is," I said firmly as I looked him straight in the eyes and waited for him to make the biggest decision of his life. "And Squire, she will eat your eyeballs for supper tomorrow night if you so much as wipe your nose without asking for permission."

After a long silence, he finally said, "Okay, I'll be quiet. Just let me keep my flashlight . . . please."

I stared at him in the dark and let his apology sink in. His final please was exactly what I was looking for. It was a sign of weakness. We both knew it, and he had uttered it in a way that gave me complete authority over his miserable little life.

"You just promised to be quiet and keep your flashlight off," I sternly reminded him. "Do you swear to do that?"

Another long silence, then, "Yeah, I swear."

"All right," I said seriously. "But if you don't keep your promise, then I'll have to keep mine." I turned to the rest of the boys. "And that goes for everybody else too."

The room was silent and dark from then on out, but I could tell that the boys were still restless. They kept squirming around in their bunks, swatting mosquitoes, all the while desperately trying to remain true to their word. I was worried one of them was going to slip up and start giggling or turn on a flashlight, so I gave them something they weren't expecting.

"Since you boys are being quiet and keeping your flashlights off," I said quietly, "I'm going to tell you a story."

Immediately, the room became silent. Several of the boys flipped over in their bunks and eagerly waited for me to begin.

I told them a story about my dog, Suchi, who was my best friend as a child. Suchi was a great dog, but she loved food more than she loved me or anyone else. I told the boys how she snatched a bunch of sizzling hamburgers right off the grill while everyone was saying the table prayer before a picnic. Then, I told a story about how I got stuck under a snowbank, playing with Suchi in my backyard. She tried to dig me out, and then she went and barked at the back door to get my dad to come and save my life.

Then, I told a couple of stories about my adventures with my best childhood friend, Josey, who always seemed to get us both into the craziest scrapes. According to my stories, we were like the modern-day version of Tom Sawyer and Huckleberry Finn.

Then, I told the boys a creepy story about a creature called the Watermelon Baby, who haunted the woods of a camp I'd worked at in Iowa. The story was actually just something I made up on the fly, but it really seemed to freak out one of the boys—Squire. The rest of the boys, one by one, had slowly drifted off to sleep sometime earlier in the storytelling marathon, but I could see Squire on his top bunk still leaning on his elbow in the dark.

When I finished the story, he didn't move. Then, knowing he was risking a week with Cassie, the witch queen, he nervously whispered to me across the room, "Leo, I can't sleep."

I knew he knew he was risking the trip of a lifetime, but I got up anyway and went over to his bunk. "Are you okay, Squire?"

There was a long silence. "No," he whimpered.

"What's wrong?" I asked.

"That story," he replied, "the one about the Watermelon Baby, it's kind of freaking me out."

"Oh, I'm sorry, Squire," I said gently. "Would you like me to tell another happier story just for you?"

There was another long silence. No one else stirred in their bunks. Everyone was asleep except for Squire and me.

"Yup," he whispered quietly.

"Okay, buddy," I said. "This one's just for you."

I proceeded to tell Squire every other story I could think of from my childhood memories—stories from my father's repertoire, stories from my rough years in junior high, and even some I simply made up to try to get him to go to sleep. After another hour or so, I asked one more time, "Squire, are you asleep yet?"

Finally, there was no reply, just the gentle breathing of a big tough sixth-grade boy sleeping in the top bunk of a smelly cabin full of a bunch of other smelly tough kids. I crept back to my bed and slid down into my sleeping bag.

"Man, this is going to be a great trip," I thought to myself.

We took off the next morning on our trip of a lifetime, and it turned into precisely that. We were out for seven days, and we had a blast. For an entire week, those boys and I explored the North Woods by canoe. We went everywhere and experienced just about everything possible in the Boundary Waters.

First, we paddled north to the Canadian border and had lunch on an island outside the United States. It was the first time any of them had been in a foreign country. Then, for two days, we traveled southwest, winding our way through a series of remote lakes where we saw no one. Our favorite was Topaz Lake, where we paddled around and explored islands and bays scattered in every direction. We spent the afternoon fishing, but the wiggly boys caught nothing at all.

Then, we canoed west on Knife Lake for miles and miles to visit the place where the Root Beer Lady used to live. I told the boys that before the lady left, she hid a stash of chocolate Hershey bars and soda pop somewhere on the island, and we were going to find it. For the entire way, the boys refused to believe me. When we got there, they hopped out and immediately started to look around.

By some miracle, I happened upon a stash of chocolate bars and two bottles of Mountain Dew hidden somewhere near the canoes. The boys couldn't believe their eyes. They tried to get me to reveal the secret spot, but as a Northern Lights canoe guide, I was sworn to secrecy. We sat around, eating our Hershey bars and sharing the Mountain Dew for a while. At that point, I knew I had those boys eating out of the palm of my hand.

The next day we ventured south to Kekakabic Lake and an area farther out than most groups could afford to go in just five days. We had a time getting there, though. I decided to portage into Sema Lake, then look for an unmarked trail to Kekakabic. Chuck would have been proud of me. We ended up bushwhacking through a swamp for over a hundred rods. When I finally found the lake, I was so worn out I simply walked straight into the water with the canoe on my back and went for a nice long swim. Then, I went back to retrieve the boys who were stuck along the swampy trail in the woods.

After a week on the lakes, the boys and I bonded for life. They were still a handful at times, but most of our issues went out the window when we got a bear one night right after we'd all gone to sleep. The bear didn't get our food, but our pots and pans took a beating from a kid named . . . oh, now, what was his name?

Shorty will do, I suppose. Anyway, one of the pots was so badly bent out of shape, we had to stick chewing gum in the bottom of it to keep it from leaking. I paid the price for that when we got back to camp, but it was worth it.

As we unloaded the canoes back at base camp, my thoughts immediately went back to Esther again. "What had she been doing while I was gone?" I wondered. "Will I see her at dinner or maybe at the campfire afterward? Yes, she'll be there! When are these boys leaving? The sooner, the better—I need to see Esther!"

Okay, so I had a major obsession going on. It was a weakness of mine, for sure. Usually, I kept it under control, and it probably didn't look nearly as bad as it sounds.

Anyway, was I thinking about Esther again?

"Yup."

chapter 22
getting beat up on the beach

"Cross my heart and hope to die!"

As I stood on the beach and watched the boys carry their paddles and life jackets back to the shed, I was greeted by Siri and Star: my two buddies from the first day at camp. They ran up to me, panting happily and wagging their tails, as if they'd been waiting for me all morning. When two boys began to swordfight with their paddles, I thought I should probably go and do something about it, but before I could, Aria surprised me from behind.

"Hey, Farm Boy!" she exclaimed. As I spun around, she jabbed both of her fists hard into my chest. "How was your trip with your little men?"

Esther stood next to Aria, smiling. She covered her mouth with her hands and quietly laughed, enjoying the sight of me getting sucker-punched by my so-called friend.

"Aria, hi!" I replied, rubbing my chest. "The trip? Actually, it was great. We paddled north along the border all the way to the Root Beer Lady's old place. We got a bear the next night, and then we got lost in a swamp trying to find Kekakabic Lake. Yesterday, we went cliff jumping on Diamond Lake, and then we sailed home today. So yeah, it was a blast!"

"Too bad I wasn't along with you guys," she said. "I could've spiced things up a bit." She faked a punch at me, making me flinch again as Esther grinned.

"Yeah, I could've used your help," I agreed, still rubbing the sore spot in the middle of my chest. "Some of those boys were really scared of the woods. You could've held their hands on the way back to the throne. They would've loved that."

"So, Leo, seriously," Aria said, ignoring my lame attempt at a joke. "Esther and I sort of have a proposition for you to consider. It's kind of a favor, a little one. You'll say yes; I know it."

"So, Hunter, you're using my actual name now and propositioning me?" I said, gazing into her big brown eyes. "After all these weeks, Aria, this is exactly what I've been waiting for. Why did it take so long for you to realize how much you loved me?"

Aria stared back at me and rolled her eyes. "Leo, seriously," she said. "We're just wondering if you'd think about a little idea we had." She glanced at Esther, who was grinning back at her excitedly.

"Yeah?" I replied, mildly interested. "So, what is it?"

Aria took a big breath and said, "We thought, maybe, you might consider taking your best friends in the entire world, which of course, would be Esther and me, out on the lakes for an overnight paddle when you get back from your next trip?"

"Oh man, Aria, I don't know," I moaned. The idea seemed entirely ludicrous to me. Cassie would never allow the three of us to do a trip together. It was totally out of the question.

"Oh, Leo! Puh-leeze!" Aria began to beg furiously. "I'll love you forever and ever, cross my heart and hope to die! Think about it, Leo, a trip with just the three of us!"

I gave her crazy request a second thought. The idea of getting to spend more time with Esther, and Aria too, of course, was enticing. But there were too many hurdles to get over, Cassie being the biggest one of them all. She would never go for the idea. I knew I had to break the bad news to them, but I didn't want to.

"I don't think it's gonna work out," I replied. "I don't even know when I'm going out next."

"We do!" Aria shouted, straight into my face. "We talked to Finn, and he's okay with it! He said you're heading out Sunday with a group, and you'll be back on Thursday. And your next trip doesn't leave until the following Sunday, so you've got three days in there where you're free to take us!"

"Wow, Hunter!" I exclaimed. "I should hire you as my booking agent. You know my schedule better than I do. So, what did Cassie have to say about it?"

I waited for the proverbial shoe to drop, but Aria just grinned as if she'd won the state lottery.

"I know you won't believe this," Aria said, "but Cassie told us to have a nice trip!"

Aria and Esther stood there beaming with delight. They couldn't keep from smiling and looked like they were ready to burst wide open. I couldn't believe it!

"What?" I muttered in disbelief.

"Cassie said we can go!" Aria squealed. Then, she turned to Esther and together, they both let out an earth-shattering scream.

The two of them made quite an embarrassing scene right there on the beach in front of my boys, who suddenly seemed keenly interested in what the three of us were talking about.

"Are you serious? Cassie is okay with it?" I asked.

"Yeah, buddy!" she said triumphantly. "Finn told her it was okay! So, we can go! Can you believe it?"

I stood there, wondering why Finn would dare to go over Cassie's head like that. "Finn okayed it? How on earth—"

"Come on, Leo!" Aria exclaimed as she poked me in the stomach and grinned excitedly. "I'll be nice to you for the rest of the summer. It's the only chance for Esther and me to camp out on the lakes before she leaves, and it's her birthday on Friday too! You've got three days, so we could even go for two nights and make it a three-day trip."

"Well," I said slowly, sizing up Aria as she pleaded with me.

She seemed so desperate and needy. Wasn't that a nice change! And then there was Esther, standing right beside her, waiting for my answer—her beautiful eyes gazing excitedly into mine, looking so amazing and incredible.

"Please, Leo!" they both begged. "Puh-leeze!"

I tried to keep from grinning to play it out a little longer and make them beg just a little bit more. Finally, I couldn't help but smile.

"Okay, I'll do it," I replied.

Immediately, Aria and Esther launched themselves into me and began jumping up and down with excitement, screaming at the top of their lungs. That was the exact response I was looking for, but suddenly, I found myself getting squished in the middle of a very out of control Aria-Leo-and-Esther sandwich. Siri and Star began to run around and bark as the girls jumped wildly up and down.

I tried to fend them off as I shouted, "Just let me bring my—"

Suddenly, Aria's shoulder came up and bonked me squarely in the nose. All at once, the lights went out. The next thing I remember was seeing Aria hunched over me with Esther peeking at me from behind her shoulder. I had a sudden feeling of déjà vu.

"Sorry, Leo," Aria said with a laugh. Then, she added apologetically, "I always find a way to hurt you, don't I?"

"Oh, it's okay," I said, grinning up at her. "I enjoy all the physical affection you give me. That's why I love you so much."

I looked past Aria to Esther standing behind her. Her blue eyes were fixed on me. I got lost in her gorgeous red lips, her long wavy hair, and those pretty freckles that swooped across her nose from cheek to cheek. My head was spinning from that knock to the nose, or was it just Esther? I shook my head to clear away the stars.

"Are you all right, Leo?" Aria asked.

"Yeah, I'm fine. Just help me up," I replied.

I had played it pretty cool, but I was definitely excited about the trip. I tried to get up, but my head was still spinning. I sat down again and kept on going until I was all the way down on my back again, lying in the sand.

"We'll plan everything," Aria said, standing over me. "I'll get the permit and gear, and we'll pack the food too."

Esther broke in quietly, "What was it you wanted to bring, mate?"

"What?" I asked as I felt my nose, which was starting to ache.

"You said you wanted to bring something on the trip?"

"Oh yeah," I said, coming back to myself. "My guitar; I'll play it in the canoe while you guys paddle."

"Oh, I get it," Aria said, suddenly reverting back into her old self as she stepped down hard on my chest. "You think you're gonna duff the whole way, huh? That's fine, Farm Boy, we can handle all of the manual labor if you want us to."

"Great, that's great," I said. "I'm just looking forward to a nice safe trip with you two lovely ladies."

I grinned up at them as I lay there helplessly trapped under Aria's boot firmly planted on top of my chest. I was in heaven, and I had a feeling that things were only going to get better.

"That's what I thought," Aria said, lifting her boot off my chest. "You better get up now, Farm Boy. Your boys are looking a little worried about you over there."

Aria and Esther walked away, talking excitedly about the upcoming trip. Siri and Star followed along behind them as they disappeared on the trail up to Starlight Lodge.

I lifted my head a little bit and looked around. Sure enough, there was my group of curious boys—staring at me, wondering what just happened and how I got beat up and stomped on by my supposed girlfriend and her personal bouncer. Was that how every canoe guide was greeted after a trip in the Boundary Waters?

I waved at the boys to reassure them I was okay. Then, I slowly got back on my feet and walked over to them.

"She likes you," Quincy said. "I told you so."

"No," I replied, trying to play it as cool as humanly possible. "We're just friends. That's all there is to it."

"Yeah, right!" Quincy said.

He clearly didn't believe me. He was a smart kid, but there was so much he didn't know.

The same went for me as well.

chapter 23

love triangle

"We need to know which way you want to go."

The boys and I had a full day of work ahead of us. We dropped off our sleeping bags and personal items at the cabin. Then, we hauled our camping gear up to the trail shack. Chuck was there to greet us with a cheerful smile. He swung into action and had those boys cleaning the pots and pans, hanging up the wet packs and tents, and putting away all of our gear in a wild frenzy. Afterward, the boys gave him a big group hug and said their goodbyes.

Then, we were off to the sauna. We stopped at our cabin to change into our swimsuits and grab our towels. As we crossed over on the creaky bridge, the boys stopped in the middle to jump up and down just for fun. When we got to the sauna, there was a mad scramble to get inside. As usual, nobody wanted to be the last one.

It was already hot and steamy inside, but I threw another full cup of water on the sizzling rocks just for good measure. I'd been living with those smelly boys all week, and I was excited to finally get rid of the stench that was beginning to seep into my skin. The boys sat in the steamy darkness and soaked up the warmth as they reminisced about their trip of a lifetime in the Boundary Waters.

Suddenly, I heard the voices of Aria and Esther coming down the trail. "Oh no, not again," I thought. "This is the last thing I need right now." But sure enough, the girls opened the door and peeked inside. When they saw nine pairs of beady eyes staring back at them, they laughed and closed the door. As they walked down to the end of the dock, I wondered, "What could they want now?"

"Yo, Leo," Quincy said, elbowing me in the ribs, "I told you, that girl likes you."

"Yeah, I heard you," I replied, trying to avoid another word fight with the bullheaded kid.

As we sat there roasting in the sauna, I fended off another barrage of questions from the curious boys. I tried to play it down, but I had a hunch as to why the girls were there.

"Come on, guys! Let's go jump in the lake!" I finally said.

"You just wanna see your girlfriend!" Quincy said.

"Maybe I do, maybe I don't," I replied. "We've gotta get out of here anyway before we all shrivel up and die! Let's go!"

The whole gang piled out of the sauna and ran down to the end of the dock, where they all jumped in the lake . . . all except for Quincy, that is, who strolled coolly by my side down the long walkway to have a chat with the ladies-in-waiting. Quincy and I both agreed; they looked mighty fine in their swimsuits. When Esther saw us coming, she smiled and gave me a little wave of her hand.

"See, I told you so," Quincy insisted again.

"You know, Quincy," I replied smoothly, "I think you're right. The redhead likes me. But the other one, Aria, she keeps showing up whenever you're around too."

"Yeah, so?" Quincy said toughly.

"Well, big guy," I hinted, "I think she might have a thing for someone else, if you know what I mean."

"A thing?" he wondered aloud.

"Yeah, I think Aria really digs you," I replied.

The girls got up and began walking back up the dock toward us. As they passed by, Aria gave Quincy a wink and a smile.

"Hey, little man," she said, "I'll see you around."

That was all it took for Quincy. He tossed his towel up in the air and took off at a dead sprint down to the end of the dock. With a loud "Whoo-hoo!" he jumped off and did a cannonball into the lake.

"Man, he's a cute kid," Aria said, looking me straight in the eyes. "Why do I keep falling for the cute ones?" She gave me a long cold stare that sent a shiver down my spine.

"You just made Quincy's day," I said with a nervous chuckle. "That'll be the highlight of his whole summer."

"Yeah, I know," she said with a thin smile. "I have that effect on guys, don't I, Leo?"

"Um, yeah," I replied, wondering what she was getting at.

"That little kid sure is cute!" Esther said. "Too bad, he smells like a stinky codfish."

"Give him a few years. He's gonna be a real hunk," replied Aria.

"Like me?" I asked.

"Yeah, right!" Aria exclaimed cynically as she turned to go. "Keep on dreaming, Farm Boy!"

"What?" I said innocently. "What did I say?"

"Come on, Esther, let's go hop in the sauna," Aria said as she pulled her friend along up the dock.

"Leo!" she called back to me. "Come up when you get the chance. We need to talk some more."

"Sure, just give me one sec," I replied, wondering what was eating at Aria. She seemed more than a bit upset.

Esther glanced back as Aria pulled her along. She smiled and waved at me again. That was all it took for me. I tossed my towel up in the air and took off at a sprint down to the end of the dock, where I did precisely as Quincy had done.

With a loud "Whoo-hoo!" I leaped off the end of the dock and came crashing down on the boys with my own version of a cannonball belly flop. I could hear them screaming with delight as I came back to the surface. I was screaming too.

After playing in the lake for a while, I got out and asked the lifeguard to watch the boys. Then, I ran up the dock and climbed into the sauna. It took a few seconds for my eyes to adjust to the darkness. Aria was sitting on the far side of the room directly opposite from me. Esther sat back against the wall in between the two of us.

A tension hung in the steamy air. Aria didn't say anything for a long time. She didn't seem to be her usual self. I wondered what could have happened in the last hour to change her mood. All sorts of possibilities began to swirl around in my head.

The reality of the situation I'd placed myself in suddenly dawned on me. I'd be spending three days in the Boundary Waters with Esther and Aria. It would just be the three of us for three days straight. Aria clearly liked me, but I couldn't stop thinking about Esther, and she was caught somehow in between the two of us. I began to wonder if I really wanted to go on the trip after all.

Aria finally spoke up. "So, Leo, we've got a few more details to talk about in regards to the trip."

"Oh, so that's why you followed me all the way over here to the sauna," I quipped, trying to lighten the mood. "I thought you were just stalking me or something."

"Yeah, right," she said dryly. "We've been stalking you?"

Aria gave me a long blank stare across the dimly-lit room. She was hinting at something that I think we both knew was happening. After another awkward silence, I got up and threw a cup of water on the rocks. I sat back down and watched the steam rise up, avoiding any eye contact with her.

"So, Leo, we need to know which way you want to go," she said.

"Which way? I have no clue," I replied.

"Well, that's pretty obvious, dingbat," she said. "So, you need to decide ASAP."

"Why me?" I asked, getting a bit irritated. The discussion seemed to be turning into an argument on two completely different levels, and Aria wasn't making things any easier.

"Because you're the canoe guide," she replied. "And we need to get an entry permit before we leave. I just need to know which lake you want to put in on, Diamond or Sag?"

"I don't know, Hunter. What's the weather looking like for next week?" I replied, all business.

"It's supposed to be nice all this week," Aria said. "There's a chance of storms next weekend, though."

"That could be an issue," I said, thinking out loud. "Wind or rain could slow us down and really mess things up. We'll just have to go for it and hope for the best."

"So which entry should I get?" she asked again.

"Well, where would you like to go?" I asked.

"I'm fine with whatever," Aria said, still cold as ice.

I was getting nowhere with Aria, so I turned to Esther and asked, "What would you like to see on our trip?"

Talking to Esther in front of Aria suddenly felt strangely awkward. Aria was watching both of us like a hawk. It was as if she were second-guessing the whole idea of the trip just like me.

Esther didn't seem to be aware of the tension in the air. She simply said, "Well, I'd like to see some waterfalls and the northern lights, and I'd like to visit Canada too."

She talked so sweetly in her Kiwi accent. I was excited about the surprise trip, and I was looking forward to getting to know Esther too. I held my excitement in as best as I could. After all, Aria was right there, staring back at me . . . or was she glaring at me? I couldn't tell. It was difficult to see in the steamy darkness, and I was beginning to sweat up a storm.

Esther spoke up again. "Leo, there's just one more little thing I was wondering about."

"What is it?" I asked.

"There's a lake," she answered. "I saw it on a map. It's called Esther Lake, just like my name. I was wondering if we could go there so I could swim in it on my birthday."

"I know where Esther is," I said. "But it's pretty far out there, and we only have three days. I can't guarantee that we'll be able to get there and back in time. What day is your birthday?"

"It's on Friday, the 14th of July," she said cheerfully. "I'll be turning twenty-one on that day."

"Well, we can sure try," I said with a smile. I suddenly realized that I'd do just about anything to make Esther happy.

She grinned happily and grabbed my hand that was resting on the bench next to her. As she squeezed my hand, I could feel the heat coming from Aria across the way.

"Awesome, Leo!" Esther exclaimed excitedly. She leaned over and gave me a playful nudge with her shoulder. "That would be totally sweet, bro!"

And that just made it worse. Man, it was getting hot in there! I was ready to bail out and go jump in the lake by myself, but the girls weren't ready to let me go, not just yet anyway.

"So, Saganaga it is," Aria said, still staring coldly across at me. "Hopefully, we don't get too much wind like the last time we were up there. Remember that one, Leo?"

"Yeah, it could be bad," I replied.

I knew Aria was referencing the trip we'd done together earlier in the summer. It brought back a ton of great memories. They all flashed before me in a split second, all the good times we had shared on that trip just a few weeks earlier. I glanced up, then quickly back down again, somehow trying to avoid the icy gaze I knew she was giving me from across the darkened room.

"Okay, we'll head north on the big lake first," I said. "We'll hit Monument Portage on the Canadian border and then play it by ear. Hopefully, the weather holds long enough for us to make the turn back east to Diamond Lake."

"Aw, sweet as, mate!" Esther exclaimed, squeezing my hand again. She grinned happily at Aria. "That's totally sweet, eh?"

"Yeah, totally," Aria said, giving Esther a friendly grin.

I breathed a sigh of relief to have that little conversation over and done with. I was relieved when Aria smiled across at me too.

"Thanks, Leo, this means a lot to us," she said.

"Sure thing, Bear Bait," I replied. "I'd do just about anything for you; you know that."

I felt a rush of relief as Aria and I seemed to clear the air. At that moment, we'd both come to a sudden realization. I wasn't able to clearly define it, but I knew that Aria and I would talk it out sometime in the future because that's what good friends do.

"Come on, lovebirds," Aria said. "Let's go jump in a lake!"

Aria sprang up and kicked the door open. She screamed at the top of her lungs as she raced down the dock and leaped into the lake. Esther and I bailed out of the sauna right behind her. We couldn't help but shout and scream too as we lunged out into the cool clear water while the boys watched us from the dock.

"It doesn't get much better than this," I thought. "It couldn't possibly get any better, could it?"

Quincy gave me a wink and a nod from his perch on the edge of the dock. I could tell he was jealous. There I was, hanging out with two amazing women, swimming and splashing around in a beautiful lake, living it up all summer long, while he was getting ready to go back home. I would miss his spunky little persona and how he always seemed to find a way to keep me on my toes. Thankfully, I still had Aria around to challenge my preconceptions.

I hopped out and let the girls keep swimming in the lake. I had to get the boys out of there anyway. They were too distracted by Aria and Esther to do much of anything except stare. I led the little sailors up the long dock and down the trail back to base camp. They didn't stink anymore, but they still jostled for position in the line as we hiked along. No fifth or sixth-grade boy likes to be last in line, ever.

At the campfire program that evening, the boys and I stood proudly up in front of everyone. We told our stories of fighting off the bear, of discovering the hidden stash of candy bars in the woods, and cliff jumping on Diamond Lake. We stretched it a bit, of course. The audience at the campfire probably wasn't sure if they could believe us or not, but you could tell it was all true, just by looking into the bright but sleepy eyes of those eight wonderful boys.

There was so much that happened on that trip. We could have talked for hours about all the fun things we did, like learning to make home-made pizza over the fire, swimming around and playing water tag in Knife Lake, smoking out our clothes to fend off mosquitoes, playing a game called "Wolf" in the woods, singing silly songs in the rain, thumb wrestling in the canoes, and getting chased down the portage trails by some crazy canoe guide with a big canoe on his back. We did a lot of quiet things too, like calling to the loons, enjoying the beauty of nature, listening to stories around the campfire, having deep conversations about friends and family, and talking about becoming young men of character and integrity.

There were many more things we could have shared about that trip, but it's too long of a story to tell. Someday, maybe I'll explain the whole thing, including what happened on the portage into Pickle Lake, the games we played in the thunderstorm on Jasper, and the bathing beauty we passed by in the waters of Ogishkemuncie. But that isn't what this story is about, so it'll have to wait until another time.

After the campfire, the boys and I went straight to our cabin. There was no wrestling match to get them to sleep. We were all so tired; we slept like logs. I'm sure our dreams were full of amazing sunsets, refreshing waterfalls, hungry bears, lonely loon calls, warm sandy beaches, and beautiful women. At least that's what I was dreaming about as I drifted off to sleep that night.

In the morning, I was refreshed and ready to go again. The boys were heading out first thing, so I got them up early and marched them down to the dock to see them off. I would miss Quincy and the rest of the boys I had become so attached to in our short time together. It had been a great trip, and I knew those boys would remember it for the rest of their lives.

It truly had been the trip of a lifetime!

chapter 24

hanging out together

"It's too late to back out now!"

After I said goodbye to the boys, I ran up the big wooden steps that led to the bridge and watched them cross over to the mainland. Aria and Esther had asked me to wait for them at the bridge so we could go to Morning Light together and then talk about our trip at breakfast. I hung out by the steps as people passed by on their way across the bridge to the open-air cathedral.

I didn't have a watch on, but I knew the girls were late. I was just about ready to take off when they finally showed up. It was nice to see that Aria was in a better mood. Esther looked incredible as usual. Underneath her jacket, she was wearing a short top that left a thin band of midriff showing just above her waist. Her hair was freshly washed and piled up in a bun on top of her head.

"Hey, Farm Boy!" Aria called out. "Are you ready to go?"

"Sure," I replied. "I've only been waiting here for like an eternity. We better get a move on!"

"I was ready a long time ago," Aria said, rolling her eyes in Esther's direction. "But Cinderella, here, took an hour-long shower this morning, and then she had to put her face on!"

I grinned at Esther and said, "You look very nice."

"Cheers, mate," she replied. "So do you!"

Aria moaned as she ran up the steps and took off across the bridge. The two camp dogs, Siri and Star, were hot on her heels again that morning. Those two dogs had taken a definite liking to their new best friend and smoked sausage provider.

"After you, my dear," I said, motioning for Esther to go ahead of me. I followed behind the girls and the two happy-go-lucky dogs as we bounced across the bridge to Eagle Island.

At Northern Lights, every day began with an all-camp gathering, called Morning Light, which was held at the open-air cathedral on the bluff overlooking the lake. Morning Light was a camp tradition, just like the nightly campfire programs, which had been going on since the camp's inception. Usually, it was led by one of the camp staff or a canoe guide who was off the lakes for a few days. Whoever led it could do anything they liked, but usually, it was short and sweet—a simple reading, a quiet song, and a brief message by the leader. There was always time for quiet reflection after the message too. Whenever I was in base camp, it was one of my favorite things to do.

The bridge bounced and swayed and squeaked as we walked across on the creaky boards along with other sleepy campers and staff. Early in the morning, sometimes you could spot mallard ducks or a family of mergansers swimming near the shoreline. It was clear and crisp that morning, and the lake was peaceful and calm like glass. The trees far across the channel to the east were still dark green as the sun crept slowly up into the sky behind them.

As we came to the other side of the bridge and continued into the woods, the forest floor came to life with all sorts of colors, sounds, and smells. Almost always, a chickadee or white-throated sparrow offered a cheerful greeting as hikers passed through its nesting space nearby. Flowers and ferns covered the ground that glowed bright green in the sunlight. Bunchberries held on to their bright red clusters, which most people wouldn't touch since they weren't very tasty. They were pretty to look at, though, and they always cheered me up.

Young blue spruce and balsam fir trees filled out the understory, while the larger pines towered overhead. The delicate leaves and pine needles mixed together to create a tapestry of forest greens of all shades and colors. The air was sweet with the smell of pine sap, wild roses, wood lilies, and a variety of daisies scattered along the path. I loved the sounds of the birds and the sight of fresh growing things so early in the morning. I had been gradually learning to identify most of the flowers, trees, and birds found in the North Woods, but almost every day, I was surprised to discover another flower or plant or bird that I'd never seen before.

The path meandered around toward the east until it climbed steeply up into a grove of majestic white pines. They towered overhead and shaded the entire landscape all around. As we climbed up the last stretch to the open-air cathedral, we joined a host of others seated on benches under the pavilion, quietly soaking up the new day. Starlight Lodge was barely visible through the trees across the narrows. The eastern edge of Diamond Lake could be seen stretching south for two or three miles. As the sun rose in the sky, it sent beams of misty light through the trees into the pavilion.

Cassie stood up and greeted everyone. Then, she read a poem by Robert Frost, entitled "The Road Not Taken." Just like most other mornings, the songs and readings were new to me. They made me think about my life and what I wanted to be and do.

I appreciated how Northern Lights was a place where you knew you were surrounded by a bunch of shameless tree huggers and nature lovers. The people were deeply spiritual too. They valued the rustic lifestyle, the simple ways of doing things, and taking care of the earth. It all resonated with my own spirit. I felt like the world needed more time and space like that, to be away from everything, to be silent and still, to appreciate the natural wonders all around us and set apart from everyday life.

As I sat there listening to Cassie, I closed my eyes and let her words drift through my mind. The words of the poem mingled with the sounds of the surrounding forest. The time of peaceful reflection reminded me of what I was doing there at Northern Lights. It was more than a job. It was a calling to care for others, to treat the earth with respect, and to connect with all of life. I looked forward to that time each day. Some days, I wished we could just sit there in silence and let the sights and sounds of nature be the speakers, but most often, the leaders had plenty to say.

Cassie shared some thoughts about what the poem meant to her. She did a good job. I could tell how much she loved working up there.

I wondered if I would ever find a job like that, maybe someday in the future. I didn't know. There was a lot of pressure on me to be somebody, to get a good-paying job, start a career, and do well in life. Working at a camp didn't seem to fit with what I was being told by others, but it sure was tempting to at least think about the possibilities every once in a while.

I miss those quiet walks through the forest to the open-air cathedral. I wish I could walk to work like that every day. It would change everything about me—how I think and talk, how I deal with stress and conflict, how I treat others, and how I view myself and the world around me. Everyone could benefit from a morning nature walk through the woods, not to mention an evening campfire or a quiet sunset to help focus on the deeper things in life. I remember telling myself that I should make those daily rituals a regular habit in my life, but they came and went, and for the most part, were lost to me. Still, the memories of those quiet, peaceful mornings have had a way of giving me comfort even today.

When the program at the cathedral ended, everyone walked back across the bridge and made their way to Starlight Lodge for breakfast. Aria, Esther, and I got our food, and then we sat down at the end of a long table near the windows overlooking the lake.

"So, Leo," Aria said as she munched on a blueberry muffin. "After I knocked you out on the beach yesterday, Esther finally told me what happened when I was gone last week,"

Esther suddenly looked up in surprise. Her eyes opened wide as she stared nervously at her friend sitting next to her. I watched with curious interest from across the table.

"She told you what happened at the volleyball court?" I asked.

"No, not that," Aria replied casually. "She told me that you two went on a couple of hot dates together."

"What?" Esther blurted out, looking embarrassed and somewhat angry. "I never said that, you little liar!"

Aria just ignored her and kept right on going. "Yeah, she said she's already had a nice, little visit to your cabin, or crib, as she called it, Farm Boy."

"Aria!" Esther exclaimed. "Quit your yakking, girl!"

"That's a place I'd sure like to see someday," Aria continued. "I hear it's pretty cozy, Leo, your little crib, but you've never invited me up for a visit. What was the special occasion?"

"I had food poisoning," I replied, a bit irritated and yet mildly amused as well. Esther was turning bright red as Aria totally ignored her and kept right on my tail with more juicy details.

"She said you guys sat together at the campfire too," Aria said as she grinned deviously at me from across the table.

"Ahh, Aria!" Esther exclaimed furiously. "You're being mean as cat's piss! You little—"

"Yes, I am," Aria replied, staring calmly across at me. "I'm just wondering what happened later that night. Did you two lovebirds hold hands around the campfire in the dark, or what?"

"Aria! Belt up, girl!" Esther pleaded frantically.

"Did you try to kiss her, Farm Boy?"

"Bloody hell!" Esther erupted. "Aria, shut your big mouth, or I swear I'll—"

"Yeah, Hunter, we made out like love-starved bandits in the woods," I replied calmly, trying not to show any hint of a smile. "Esther's quite the good kisser, you know. It got pretty intense. She was tearing my shirt clean off my back. I finally had to do the right thing and just run for it."

Esther glanced over at me in disbelief, unable to stop either of us from discussing her imaginary love life like two sick psychotherapists in an upscale coffee shop.

"Good thing I wasn't around," Aria said calmly. "I would have beaten the snot out of you, Leo."

"Well, that's why I went for it when I did, Hunter. With you out of the way, I knew I had Esther all to myself. And man, she's an amazing woman, let me tell you."

"Leo!" Esther cried frantically. "You filthy bush oyster! Both of you blockheads, stop it this instant!"

"It's okay, darling," I replied, as my head started to spin out of control, almost as if I'd been socked in the nose again by Aria on the beach. "We can tell Aria all about it now. It's about time she found out about us anyway." I reached out for Esther's hand, but she snatched it away and then swung it back straight at my face.

"Leo! You dirty dipstick!" Esther cried as she slapped me across the face with her open hand. I was so surprised it sent me flying backward, tumbling onto the floor like a flimsy rag doll. In the process, my plate of food went flying everywhere too.

Esther's slap shouldn't have surprised me. After all, I deserved it. Everyone nearby looked over and wondered what the three of us were up to. As I sat up on the floor, I started to laugh, and then Aria started to laugh too. I'm sure we looked absolutely ridiculous, but I didn't care what anyone thought. That kind of thing could only happen with Aria, and it was fun to get crazy with her sometimes, even if it meant that I looked like a complete idiot.

Esther glared at both of us and huffed, "Well, you two blokes are quite the jokers, aren't you! How can you guys even do something so mean like that?"

"I'm sorry, Esther!" Aria said, still laughing. "I can't help it. I'm just a horrible person sometimes."

"You got that right, sister!" Esther exclaimed.

"But Esther," Aria said, "I never thought you'd go and take out Farm Boy, here, with one mighty swipe of your hand!"

"I didn't mean to do that, but he certainly deserved it!" she said, glancing down at me still on the floor.

"Yeah, but it was totally sweet," Aria replied. "I couldn't have done a better job myself."

"Well, I'm learning from the master," Esther said, and then she began to laugh along with Aria.

"Oh, I've got so much more to teach you. Believe me!" said Aria. "We're gonna have such a great time next week."

"Straight up! I can't wait!" Esther exclaimed, still bewildered at what had just happened.

"But, we gotta stop smacking Leo around like this," Aria added. "We won't be able to go on our trip if we put our canoe guide in the hospital between now and then."

Speaking of Leo, I was just beginning to pick myself up off the floor, along with the remains of my breakfast, which had been scattered all over the place. I couldn't believe it had only taken a minute, and the girls were somehow already making up with each other after that insane fiasco.

"Hey, Farm Boy!" Aria called down to me. "Are you okay? Or do you need your mommy to kiss your owie for you?"

"I'm fine," I said, sliding back up onto the bench with my empty plate and a handful of food scraps. "I just didn't expect Wild Thing, here, to full-on deck me."

"Oh, does it hurt? Maybe Esther could kiss it and make it all better," Aria teased.

"Hey now! Stop already!" Esther exclaimed, as she elbowed Aria hard in the side and glared at her.

"Whoa, girl!" Aria yelped, trying to defend herself. "I'm done! I'm done! I promise!"

"Well, you better be!" Esther said angrily. "I'm not telling you anything ever again!"

"I'm getting some more food," I mumbled, grabbing my plate. "You two lovely ladies have a nice day now, okay?"

"Hey! Don't leave yet!" Aria called to me. "We've gotta talk about our trip some more!"

"I'll be right back," I promised.

As I walked across the hall to the serving counter, the girls went back to chatting about something or another. I couldn't believe what had just happened. I could barely remember it after that humongous open-handed slap from Esther. I remembered hearing how the two of us had gone on a date or something like that, and then I kissed her? No, Aria got that all wrong. It was Esther who kissed me. I'd never have forgotten that. It sure seemed like Esther took it pretty personally, whatever it was. I wondered what all the drama was about. There had to be more going on there than met the eye. I'd have to admit, I could be pretty dense sometimes, so anything was possible. Did I actually say that Esther and I made out like bandits in the woods? Good grief! What was I thinking back there?

I chuckled to myself as Andie dumped another pile of steaming eggs onto my plate.

"Pretty hungry today, aren't we, Leo?" she inquired.

"Yeah," I replied. "Could you throw a couple more sausages on there too? I think my first two flew out the window."

"Sure thing," she said. "Have a nice day, Leo." Andie flashed a friendly smile at me as I walked away.

"You too, Andie, thanks," I replied.

I walked back to the table where the girls were sitting eerily calm and quiet. I sat down and looked across at them, huddled there like two innocent cherubs in the children's church choir. They grinned back at me in silence, and then suddenly, they both broke into hysterical, uncontrolled laughter again.

"Holy cow, this is gonna be quite the trip," I muttered miserably under my breath.

"That's right, Leo!" Aria exclaimed, rather loudly. "It's too late to back out now, Farm Boy! We're all yours!"

I looked around to see if anyone heard Aria . . . and yeah, some of them did. I ducked my head down and tried to finish my second breakfast in a hurry. The girls kept giggling and whispering to each other across the table. Suddenly, I felt like I was back out on the lakes with a bunch of clueless billy goats, just counting the days until the nightmare would be over.

I looked up at the girls, grinned politely, and said, "I'm so glad I've got you two nutcases as my best friends here at camp."

They just looked back at me and laughed. I suddenly realized I was going to have to survive three days out on the lakes with the two nuts across the table from me. "Oh no," I thought to myself.

After breakfast, Esther had to go with her service group to the south side of the island. Aria and I didn't have anything to do that day, so we decided to go along and help out. As we hit the trail, cute little Star and the bigger older Siri jumped right in alongside us. Aria dropped a handful of sausages for them beside the path. They stopped to devour the treats, and then they raced like greyhounds to catch up to us again as we hiked through the woods.

It was a long trek south on a trail that led through an old forest, thick with dozens of large downed trees. They were the ones that had been knocked over in a windstorm that occurred on July 4th some years earlier. Packing winds in excess of ninety miles an hour, the storm came out of the west and wreaked havoc from the eastern edge of North Dakota all the way across Northern Minnesota. There wasn't a lot of structural damage, but they said the straight-line winds blasted a path of devastation ten miles wide straight through the Boundary Waters. Over twenty-five million trees were uprooted or knocked down in the process. The damage was catastrophic.

The Big Blowdown, as it was called, had the U.S. Forest Service scrambling to create firebreaks through the downed timber to stop any future forest fires from burning out of control. The amount of fresh fuel that remained on the ground several years later, was a constant source of concern. Any small fire could suddenly burst into a wildfire and spread quickly to other areas of the forest.

The Forest Service had done quite a bit of logging on the mainland south of the islands to address the concerns. Some work had been done at Northern Lights as well, but I wondered about the thick, dense forests on the south side of the island. No one wanted to cut down the remaining pine trees standing so tall and majestic there. The hope was that any future fire would somehow spare the islands, and the camp would make it through unscathed. I wondered about it, though. There were thousands of acres of wind-damaged forests out there, waiting like dry kindling for the first match to be struck.

When we reached the construction site, we came out of the woods into a clearing that overlooked yet another stellar view of Diamond Lake. The new cabin was being constructed on a rocky ridge about fifty yards from the lakefront. The crew was doing work on the inside of the building, hanging and mudding drywall. I didn't know how to do any of it, but a couple of crew chiefs got us working inside, and soon we felt like pros.

Esther was thrilled to have us along for the day. Her time since the volleyball incident had been rough. For several days afterward, she spent most of her time feeling isolated and alone. When Aria got back and heard what had happened, she went straight to Finn to talk about it. He graciously made a command decision and went over Cassie's head, giving Aria permission to stay on base camp to be with Esther for the rest of her time there.

I just couldn't believe that the girls had somehow convinced Cassie to let us go on our own three-day adventure into the Boundary Waters. I never thought she would have allowed it, but apparently, a miracle had happened, and the trip was definitely on. Aria and Esther couldn't talk about anything else, and things with both of them had been getting more and more interesting.

I had another trip coming up soon, but I wasn't thinking about it. All I could think about was the trip with the girls. I had a feeling it would be fun, but I wondered how we'd get along. Aria seemed conflicted about something. Esther seemed clueless about everything. And I was both conflicted and clueless. I had no idea where I was in regard to either of them.

I just wondered what would happen next.

chapter 25

ask me anything

"You don't have to answer if you don't want to!"

That evening after supper, Esther, Aria, and I hung out on the bridge for a while. We watched the sun drop behind the islands in the west as the clouds in the sky gradually changed from orange to pink and then to a dusty blue. As it grew dark outside, we decided to go up to the Crow's Nest, which was a lounge located above the camp office. It's where the camp staff went to relax in their time off.

When we walked in, the place was packed with people. Some were playing cards at tables. Others were spread out on a couple of old couches. There was even a group sitting on the floor in the corner with guitars and a mandolin, singing folk tunes. It was so noisy and crowded, we just turned around and walked out again.

"Well, everyone saw that," Aria said as we walked back down the stairs and wondered what to do next.

"It's okay," I replied. "They can think whatever they like."

"Hey, I've got an idea," Esther said. "Let's go across to Eagle Bluff. No one will be over there."

Aria and I glanced at each other. We didn't have any better ideas. "Sounds good!" we replied in unison.

We followed Esther through the woods and across the bridge to Eagle Island. We took a left at the trail on the other side and followed her up a steep and windy path. It was dark by then, so the trail to the top was hard to follow. In spite of that, Esther ran ahead, leaping over rocks and racing around trees as if she could see in the dark. Meanwhile, Aria and I stumbled along behind her on the path.

"I should have brought a flashlight!" I shouted, as I tripped on a rock and nearly biffed it.

"Nah! We'll be fine," Aria replied as she caught a root in the trail and tumbled forward onto the ground.

"Hunter, slow down," I said, helping her back up. "You're gonna get us both killed."

"Whatever," she replied. "Let's catch up to Esther."

The last hundred feet of trail was a steep climb up a series of large stone steps built into the hillside. At the top, the forest opened up into a picnic area with a few tables and benches scattered around. A grove of tall pine trees towered overhead, growing right up next to the cliff. In the daytime, Eagle Bluff was a destination for casual hikers and a nice shady resting spot. At night, it was a cool observation point with a perfect view of base camp across the way.

By the time we got there, Esther was already standing dangerously close to the edge of the cliff that dropped steeply down to the lakeshore below. She was gazing across the narrow channel at the lights of the cabins and lodges scattered around the camp. I could see the bridge we had just crossed over to the southeast next to the beach and the boat landing nearby. The seven cabins in Pleiades Village, directly across the channel, were all dark. Two people with flashlights were walking up the trail toward them. I could hear them talking to each other as if they were only ten feet away.

"It's so high up here!" Esther said. "You can see everything."

"Hey, Esther, don't get too close to the edge," I said as I walked up and tried to grab her hand, but she snatched it away.

"It's okay, Leo, I'm not going to jump!" she said, taking a step back. "Besides, I can fly anyway if I want to."

"How did you get up here so quickly?" I asked, still out of breath.

"It was a breeze, mate," she replied. "I can see quite nicely in the dark, especially when the stars are shining so brightly."

I looked at Esther, and I totally believed her. The makeup around her eyes seemed to make them glow like blue flames in the darkness. The lights from the cabins were sparkling in them like hundreds of fireflies falling out of the night sky.

"I've been up here a couple of times before," she added.

"When?" I asked.

"Usually at night in the dark," she said, creeping closer to the edge. "I sneak up here when everyone's asleep." Esther slowly inched forward and whispered loudly, "Then, when I'm all alone . . . and no one is looking . . . I jump off and fly away!"

All of a sudden, she lunged up to the very edge of the cliff, threw her arms out, and screamed at the top of her lungs. Aria screamed too and jumped forward to grab Esther. I tried to grab one of her arms, and Aria went for the other one, but she was waving them so wildly we both missed and almost tumbled off the cliff.

"Easy, mates!" she exclaimed. "Didn't you want to see me fly?" Esther grinned at us as we both hung on to her in fright.

"I know you can fly and all," said Aria. "But you'll fall straight to your death if you get any closer."

I pulled Esther away from the edge and suggested, "Why don't we sit down back here on a bench."

"All right," Esther agreed as she grabbed on to my hand. "Leo, you're always looking out for me, and so are you, Aria. I love how you guys are determined to keep me safe."

We carefully backed away from the edge and sat down on a wooden bench that looked out over the bluff. Somehow, I ended up sitting between the two of them in the process, with Aria on my left and Esther on my right.

"I'm glad you guys are here with me," Esther said, still looking out across the narrows.

"Sorry it hasn't been the dream vacation I promised," Aria said.

"It's been all right," Esther replied.

We could see the dock and the beach below. The moon was beginning to rise above the bridge to the east, where a couple of people were watching it. We could see the lights of Starlight Lodge and several other cabins scattered throughout the camp on the other side of the lake. The faint chatter of voices could be heard from the Crow's Nest, drifting through the woods and across the narrows.

"Well, this is fun," Aria said dryly.

"I've got an idea," Esther suggested. "Let's play a game."

"What kind of game?" I asked.

"Ask Me Anything," Esther said excitedly. "It's where you take turns asking each other questions. You can ask anything you want, but you don't have to answer if you don't want to. It'll be fun! I'll start, and then you guys can go afterwards. So, just think of some questions for me, and when you're ready, ask me anything."

Aria wasn't too excited about it, but I was. If there was one thing I wanted, it was to find out more about Esther, so I started asking her question after question. Aria gradually warmed up and joined in.

Esther was pleased that we agreed to play her game. As we bombarded her with a stream of questions, she happily answered each one. We asked about all sorts of things: What's your favorite color? What's your favorite drink? Favorite song? Class at the university? Restaurant? Hobby? Movie? Pet? Songwriter? Sport? Food?

Esther answered everything with cheerful delight: forest green, Foxton Fizz, Waiting On The World To Change, astronomy, the Soul Shine Café, horseback riding, Finding Neverland, cats, Peter Mayer, and volleyball, of course.

She had trouble choosing just one kind of favorite food. She seemed to have an endless list that included things I'd never heard about, such as Kiwi burgers, potstickers, Jaffas, and Hokey Pokey ice cream. Some of it took a bit of explaining on her part, which she enjoyed immensely. I learned so much about Esther in such a short amount of time. I only wished I could remember it all.

At first, I thought the game should've been called "Favorites," but as it went along, it turned a shade more serious. We learned that Esther's role model was her great uncle Fritz who helped her grandparents immigrate to New Zealand. The person she most admired was Nelson Mandela. She had her first boyfriend in the sixth grade. His name was Stanley Buttons, and he was a redhead like her. She also had her first kiss in the sixth grade, with none other than that lucky son of a gun, Stanley.

When things got more personal, Aria glanced at me in the dark, then asked, "Esther, do you have a boyfriend back home?"

I listened carefully as Esther hesitated. "No, not really," she finally said. "I mean, I don't think of the bucks as—"

Aria chimed in loudly. "What does that mean? Not really? Either you *do* or you *don't*, girl! So, which is it?"

"No, really," Esther insisted. "I don't have a steady boyfriend. I've got blokes who are friends, but they're not what you'd call boyfriends. They're my bros, you know. We hang out like this. I have a few besties too—you know, Aria, like you and me. I'd love for you guys to meet my friends in Auckland someday."

I tried to sit still as she talked about her boyfriends. It wasn't easy, but I kept it under control. I had another question ready to go when she finished gushing about all her friends back home.

"Esther," I finally said. "If you could write a book about anything, what would it be about?"

She thought for a few seconds. Then, her eyes lit up as she replied, "I'd write a book about the stars and constellations of the southern hemisphere—about their stories, how they were named, and especially their history before the European explorers arrived and renamed them. The sky down under is so lovely."

"What's your favorite constellation?" I asked.

She smiled brightly and said, "The Southern Cross is my favorite by a long shot. It's so beautiful. You can't see it this far north, though. The sky looks completely different down there."

"I've got one more question," Aria said. "What's the most amazing thing you've ever done in your life?"

Esther thought about it briefly, then smiled. "You know, this right here is sweet as, mates! Being here with you guys—talking about our lives, taking the time to get to know each other. This is what true friendship is all about."

"Cool," Aria said. "That's totally cool, Esther."

"Spot on," Esther said, grinning back at her. "Now it's your turn. I've got heaps of questions for you too."

"Oh no," Aria moaned, shrinking back on the bench as we pelted her with questions. Aria put up quite a fuss at first, but eventually, she warmed up and answered everything we threw at her.

She gave quick, concise answers to her favorite color, drink, song, class, etc. Aria tossed her answers back at us like bags of peanuts at a Cubs baseball game: chocolate brown, Coca-Cola, Fallin' by Alicia Keys, environmental ethics, Gino's East Pizza, shopping, Million Dollar Baby, dogs, Aretha Franklin, volleyball, and Chicago-style pizza, of course.

Martin Luther King Jr. was the person she most admired. She had her first boyfriend in the eighth grade. She kissed a boy in the first grade, but that relationship didn't last very long. She had no boyfriend back in Chicago and no decent prospects to speak of.

"How about someone you look up to?" Esther asked. "Do you have a role model that sticks out in your life?"

"My mom," Aria said immediately. "Besides her, though, it would have to be Hazel May Patterson. She's the strongest woman I've ever known. She's a rock at Holy Family there in Cabrini Green. In those tough times when I was little, she took all of us kids under her wing and helped us make something out of our lives. She'd watch us when my mom had to work on the weekends. She'd even pick us up and take us to church sometimes. It was Hazel who found some money and arranged for me and a bunch of other girls to come up here to Northern Lights one summer when we were just out of the eighth grade. She probably doesn't know how much she changed my life. Without her, I don't know if my mom could've survived. I don't think I would have either."

"Are you still in touch with her?" I asked.

"I haven't seen her for a while," Aria said. "I really should go and look her up when I get home. I should take her out to eat sometime and tell her how much she's meant to me. Chicago is such a tough place to grow up. I can't imagine what might have happened to us without our church family."

"I still don't know much about Chicago," Esther said. "It's so big. If you were in charge, what would you do to change things?"

"Oh, thanks, Esther! Give me a hard one!" Aria complained, reaching around me to give Esther a friendly shove.

"Uh-huh!" Esther grinned back innocently in the darkness.

"What would I do?" Aria thought out loud. "I have no idea. Maybe I'd stop all the gang-banging going on in the city, or help the homeless people, or maybe build more shelters, or start programs to help them get jobs. I don't know. That's an impossible question!"

"I'm sorry, girlfriend," Esther replied, suddenly on the defensive. "I didn't mean to upset you."

But Aria was all wound up, and she continued her rant. "I mean, millionaires are sitting up a hundred stories high in skyscrapers while homeless people beg in the streets below. Educated yuppies are living just north of the University of Chicago while there's extreme poverty on the South Side. Rich megachurches and shopping malls are being built out in the suburbs while dilapidated, run-down buildings are falling apart in places like Cabrini Green, where I grew up. It's all such a mess! I wouldn't want to be in charge. Who would ever want to do that? I don't even want to think about it."

"I'm sorry. I was just curious," Esther said sadly.

"Oh, it's all right. I'm fine," Aria said as she began to settle back down. "I've lived with it my whole life. It's nothing new. I just rather not think about it right now."

We sat quietly in the darkness, looking out at the lights across the lake. It seemed as if we needed a break from the game we'd been playing. I sat still, waiting for the girls to start in on me next, and of course, they eventually did. It seemed as if they'd made a mental list of about a hundred questions each. I had trouble keeping up with them as they asked me one after another. What was my favorite color? My favorite drink? My favorite song, class, restaurant, etc.

I had always been a bit nervous about talking about myself, but it felt good to know that Aria and Esther were interested in me. I replied as quickly as I could with my answers: sapphire blue, Mountain Dew, Annie's Song by John Denver, entomology, Pizza Ranch, guitar, the Lord Of The Rings trilogy, dogs, James Taylor, basketball, and Canadian bacon pizza, of course.

I couldn't keep the number of role models down to one. I had to include my grandfather, my uncle, and a church youth worker from high school. For some reason, I passed on the question about the person I most admired. I had someone in mind, but it just didn't seem like the right time and place to talk about it.

The girls wouldn't let me off the hook, though, when it got to my past relationships. I blushed in the darkness when Aria and Esther got me to confess that I had my first girlfriend when I was in kindergarten. Then, they gave me another hard time when I admitted that I hadn't kissed a girl until I was in the tenth-grade. I was waiting for Esther to ask me the all-important question, but Aria beat her to it.

"So, Leo," she said. "You have to be totally honest with us now, and no lying." She turned and stared at me. "No lying, okay, Leo?"

"Okay, okay," I replied.

"So, Leo," Aria said slowly. "Do you have a girlfriend?"

I sat there in silence. I could feel both of them staring at me, just waiting for the golden egg to drop.

"No," I finally admitted. "I don't have a girlfriend."

I was going to say more, but for some reason, the answer caught me off-guard. "Why didn't I have a girlfriend?" I wondered. "Why didn't I have more than one? Why had all of my past relationships end so abruptly and tragically wrong?"

"Come on, Farm Boy!" Aria suddenly erupted. "You have to give us more than that! Who was your last girlfriend? What was she like? When did you break up with her? Why did you break up with her? Did she dump you? Did you dump her? Are you still friends? Come on, Leo, answer the questions!"

"Um," I mumbled in the dark, trying to think of how to answer the first question. "That's a lot of questions, Aria. I didn't know I was gonna get ambushed up here tonight. Okay, if you really need to know, my last girlfriend was—"

"That's all right, mate," Esther interrupted. "You don't have to answer if you don't want to."

"Come on, Esther!" Aria cried. "Let's get some answers out of the sucker while we've got him trapped!"

I glanced over at Aria, mildly amused and somewhat irritated. She had just called me a sucker. How completely typical of her. I cleared my throat and prepared to give a nice long speech on all of my past relationships, beginning with the cute little brunette in kindergarten. And there was a long list after that, a really long list. We would've been there all night.

"No, Aria, it's fine," Esther said. "I can tell Leo's uncomfortable talking about it."

Aria put up quite a fuss, but Esther eventually calmed her down. We'd be spending three days together soon, she said, so Aria would surely get more information out of me then. Her reasoning seemed to appease Aria only a little, but she finally stopped hounding me. She heaved a long exasperated sigh and then sat there visibly pouting on the bench next to me in the dark.

"Hey, Leo," Esther said, "I have one more question for you. I hear you playing . . . I mean, I know you like to play your guitar in your cabin sometimes. If you could write a song about anything at all, what would you write about?"

"If I could write a song?" I wondered aloud. "I don't know, maybe one about the stars in the night sky or one about the northern lights. Maybe I'd write one about how it feels to watch the sunset or about an early morning paddle on a misty lake."

"Choice, bro!" Esther exclaimed. "That would be sweet as, mate! You should write about all those things!"

"I'll do it if you write your book about the stars," I replied.

Esther turned toward me and thrust her hand out in the dark. "It's a deal, mate!" she exclaimed.

I grinned and shook her hand, or to be exact, she shook mine excitedly, almost violently. As her warm fingers wrapped around my hand, I could feel the energy flowing through her veins. Her eyes beamed at me with enthusiasm, a deep sapphire blue. She seemed to bubble over with life and light as we shook hands. There was something special in her touch. I could feel it . . . literally.

As we sat there together, I couldn't stop thinking about Esther. I was starting to sense something happening between us: a friendship, yes, but something more, something deeper and more meaningful. I wasn't exactly sure what it would end up being, but I was bound and determined to find out.

We stayed up there on Eagle Bluff for another hour or so, watching the lights in the cabins go out one by one. Soon, all we could see were the lights in Starlight Lodge in the trees above the bridge. It was getting late, so we found our way back down the trail with a little help from the sliver of moonlight overhead. We walked across the bridge, and the girls went off to their cabins.

"Good night!" I called to them as I walked across the beach toward the trail to Pleiades Village.

"Good night, Leo!" they called back in unison.

"See you tomorrow, Farm Boy!" Aria cried.

"Yeah, right, Bear Bait!" I replied.

When I got to the edge of the woods, Esther called one last time from far away. "Good night, Leo!" she shouted. "You have very sexy hands, mate!"

I could hear them laughing as they walked off to their cabin.

"Oh, man!" I thought to myself. "How am I ever going to get to sleep tonight?"

I climbed up into my bunk and listened to Chuck, snoring up a storm down below. It must have been an hour or so before he finally rolled over on his belly and suffocated himself for a while. Then, he rolled back over, and the snoring picked right back up where it left off. It was okay. I couldn't sleep anyway.

All I could think about was Esther. I ran through all the things she'd said earlier, over and over again. I wondered why she hadn't joined Aria in getting me to talk about my ex-girlfriends. I wondered what kind of a song I should write for her. I lay wide awake on my sleeping bag, thinking about Esther. I know, I already said that once or twice before, but it's true.

It was just one of many more nights like that.

chapter 26
the wild bunch

"What about the hair?"

Whenever we were in camp at the same time, Aria, Esther, and I hung out together. I wasn't around that much, but still, it had been noticed by Cassie and the other base camp staff—the three of us sitting together at lunch, hanging out at the beach, or walking the trails around the islands. Apparently, someone had come up with a special name for the three of us. I wouldn't have ever known about it, except for Chuck, who mentioned it to me in our cabin one day.

"You know, Leo," he said calmly. "I heard they're calling you guys the Wild Bunch."

"What?" I asked. "The Wild Bunch? Why?"

"I don't know, just because," he replied. Chuck had a way of analyzing everything perfectly. "It makes sense, you know. You guys are always together, and there's sort of a family resemblance going on between you three. As for wild, well, I don't know what that refers to, but you guys do sort of act a lot alike."

"I don't act like Aria or Esther," I replied. "I don't look like them either. In fact, none of us look anything alike."

Chuck grinned, and in his subtle way, he summed it up with a single pointed observation. "What about the hair?"

"The hair?" I thought to myself. "What is he talking about? And who is he to talk?"

I was staring at the hairiest man I'd ever seen in my entire life, and there he was, talking about *my* hair? I wasn't offended by Chuck's comments; they just didn't make any sense to me.

Over the next couple of days, I thought about Chuck's reasoning for the goofy title Aria, Esther, and I had somehow acquired without even knowing it. He didn't say another word about it, and I didn't either, but I began to wonder if he was onto something. When it came to our hair, all three of us did have a particular flair for the dramatic, each in our own unique way.

Esther was the most outstanding of us all. She had that glorious head of long wavy red hair that flowed down over her shoulders almost to her hips. You could see it a mile away. Aria, too, had a generous helping of curly brown hair that shot up and bounced around like an active volcano on top of her head, with pretty strands exploding every which way, eventually falling down around her shoulders. And finally, I guess I'd have to admit that I had my own version of an explosion going on up there as well.

It's kind of difficult to explain, but ever since I was a kid, my hair had always been a little out of control. It was golden brown like sandpaper, slightly curly, and thick as molasses. It was fairly long too, coming down to my shoulders, and even longer when it was wet. Of course, I blamed my mother for it.

For as long as I can remember, my hair was longer than most other boys at school. It's how my mom liked it, and I simply accepted it as if I had no say in the decision. My mom was the one who cut my hair, and she liked it long, so it didn't get cut very often. I actually enjoyed the fact that she liked it that way. So, between the two of us, I kind of had a hippie hairstyle going on, and when I was away from home, it only got longer.

On most days, I usually let my hair do whatever it wanted except for a quick run-through with my fingers. It had the look of a lion's mane, especially first thing in the morning. In college, when it grew out longer, I would occasionally tie it into a ponytail until I could get home and convince my mother to trim it up.

She would inevitably resist. "Oh, my Cielito!" she'd say, using the pet nickname she'd given me as a baby. "It looks so nice on you, Leo." She'd fuss over me, tugging here and there on my scruffy locks as she commented on how handsome I looked in long hair.

As a result, my crazy head of hair just grew longer and longer. That's how I showed up at Northern Lights at the beginning of the summer, with my hair down to my shoulders, unkempt and messy, looking like a hippie who needed a haircut and a shave. To be honest, after seeing Chuck and a few of the other camp counselors, I thought I fit right in, but apparently, I'd underestimated the lion's mane that had been sprouting up on top of my head.

After obsessing about my hair, Esther's hair, and Aria's hair for a while, I finally concluded that our crazy hairstyles were clearly deserving of the Wild Bunch title. But there was probably something else that I didn't notice all that much, but other people might have, especially when they saw the three of us together around base camp. It wasn't how the dogs, Siri and Star, seemed to follow us around everywhere. It wasn't our late-night escapades. It wasn't our strange and sometimes rough sense of humor. It was something the three of us didn't notice all that much, but everyone else did. We all had a conspicuous case of . . . the freckles.

Esther's face was thick with them. She had a spray of pretty tan freckles that swooped across her nose from cheek to cheek, and they didn't stop there; they ran down her neck to her arms and hands as well. Aria had a freckly face too, just not as overwhelming as Esther's. They amounted to a few little dark spots sprinkled across her cheeks like crusty breadcrumbs. I also had a few sunspots splattered across my nose, just a few, but enough to place me neatly into the Wild Bunch category, especially considering the thick head of hair I was sporting to go along with them.

Other than that, I was pretty average looking, at least that's how I felt about it. I was just another reasonably tall, mostly skinny, almost grown-up, big kid who was lucky enough to get hired as a canoe guide at Northern Lights Adventure Center for the summer. There were plenty of other camp staff who looked a lot like me: tall blue-eyed blond Scandinavians from the Upper Midwest.

Well, my eyes were actually green, and my hair wasn't blond, and I wasn't a full-blooded Scandinavian by a long shot . . . all of which left me feeling fairly unremarkable. So, the title they'd given us was a bit of a surprise. If Chuck hadn't mentioned it, I never would have noticed anything unusual about the three of us. But the more I thought about it, the more it made sense.

As I turned the Wild Bunch title over in my mind, I realized we had one other similar characteristic as well. All three of us, in our own unique and peculiar ways, seemed to be . . . outsiders.

I was painfully shy. I kept to myself most of the time out of pure necessity. I tried to socialize and hang out with others, but for some reason, it was extremely difficult for me. I just wasn't as outgoing as most people. I looked for ways to escape group gatherings, only to wander off by myself and not do much of anything important or necessary, other than to be by myself. I didn't really know why. That's just the way I was designed, I guess, needing that alone-time more than most other people.

My two best friends were my guitar and my journal, even though I didn't have much of anything important to say or sing about. But that's what I often did, especially that summer, until Aria and then Esther showed up. They seemed to have an uncanny knack for recklessly breaking into my private space and invading my lonely little bubble with carefree abandon. It was as if they recognized something like themselves in me. So, the three of us—the Wild Bunch—were outsiders together.

I could understand why people felt that way about us, but I knew there was a lot more to us than what others probably thought. I really don't know how to explain it. We just came alive around each other. I guess you could say we were like three lonely lions, driven out of the larger pack, only to find comfort and companionship in each other. We were the Wild Bunch. It was a label we laughed about, came to accept, and ultimately carried with us each day with a certain sense of pride. After learning about it, I decided not to cut my hair for the remainder of the summer.

My mom would have been so proud of me.

chapter 27
killing time

"Sunday, Monday, Tuesday, Wednesday."

The time spent with Esther and Aria began to affect everything I did, including my next canoe trip. The one with the boys had been a fun distraction, but since then, I was having trouble focusing. I was out on the water with another group, but my thoughts kept drifting back to base camp and the girls.

The group was from a health institute in St. Paul—five mentally challenged youth and two supervisors. It was a relaxing trip. We set up camp in the southwest corner of Diamond Lake on a tiny island near the mile-long portage into Paulsen Lake. From our island base, we went out on several short excursions nearby while they fished and fished and fished some more.

For the most part, the two supervisors simply sat around and watched the campers. But when anyone caught something, they would swing into action and help clean and cook it up. We had more fish for supper on that trip than all of my other trips combined. It was a pretty lazy trip for me, but everyone seemed to be having a good time doing a lot of mostly nothing.

All week long, I couldn't help but think about what Esther and Aria were up to back at camp. They had to be packing up the food for our trip, along with the cook kit, tarp, tent, and other supplies. I wondered if they got an entry permit for Saganaga Lake or if it would be Diamond Lake instead. I wondered about the weather too. We would need the perfect conditions to do the long route around to Hanson and Esther Lakes in just three days.

I counted down the days in between the fish fries: Sunday, Monday, Tuesday, Wednesday, and finally Thursday. The time passed by slowly on that little island in the southwest corner of Diamond Lake, but finally, after five lazy days, we packed it up and headed back to camp. I was excited to see the girls again.

As we paddled around the tail of Turtle Island, I half expected to see them standing on the beach waiting for me to return, but they weren't there. The beach was completely empty as we coasted slowly in and ran our canoes up on the sand.

We unloaded our gear, put the paddles and life jackets away, and hiked up to the trail shack for pot scrub as usual. It had taken us longer than expected to get back that day, and by the time we finished all our chores and got packed up to leave, it was already late in the afternoon. The chaperones were anxious to get going, so we rushed to get them to the boat landing by five o'clock for the last ride back to the mainland.

It was unusual for me to think about the actual time of day and the need to make an appointment. Out on the lakes, time was never a consideration. The unspoken rule for a canoe trip was to leave all watches and any sense of a schedule behind at camp. We got up each morning at first light, stopped for lunch when we were hungry, then went to bed only after all the chores were done and we felt tired. I loved being free from the clock all summer long. It was refreshing to live each day so completely unfettered like that.

Still, I wondered about Aria and Esther. It was late, and we needed to get going. I wondered if our plans had been scrapped for some reason while I'd been away. I stopped by their cabin, but they were nowhere to be seen. I was filthy, so I hiked up to the bathhouse for a quick shower. I thought about shaving, but decided to go with the scruffy look. Then, I headed for Starlight Lodge to catch the tail end of supper and hopefully find the girls.

The clock was ticking, and I was just killing time.

chapter 28

into the north woods

"We're going tramping in the wop-wops!"

As I was hiking up the trail to Starlight, I finally ran into Esther and Aria. I felt the urge to give each of them a hug, but at the last second, I just smiled and decided to play it cool.

"Hey, Leo!" Aria exclaimed. "Where've you been? We've been looking all over the place for you."

"I was seeing my group off," I said. "We were a little behind schedule. So, what's up? Are we still on or not?"

"Yeah, buddy!" she said excitedly. "We're all set. Esther and I got everything packed and ready to go."

"When do you want to take off?" I asked.

"Two hours ago!" Aria shouted, giving me a big shove in the chest. Esther laughed as Aria jumped around and shouted, "Come on, Leo! We've been waiting all week for you to get back. Let's dip this place and scoot on out of here!"

"You mean, right now?" I asked.

"Yeah!" Aria said, giving me another shove. "Are you ready for this?" She turned to Esther and yelled, "Are you guys ready for this?"

"All right!" I replied. "Give me ten minutes. I need to grab some stuff at my cabin. Then, I'll meet you down at the beach."

"Okay, that's what I'm talking about!" Aria shouted. "We'll see you there in five!"

She and Esther took off running down the path, leaving me standing there. Aria suddenly stopped, turned around, and yelled back, "Come on, Leo! Get a move on!"

As the girls disappeared into the woods, I could hear them chattering excitedly on their way to the beach. I made my way down the same trail behind them. Then, I cut left on a little path that led the back way to my cabin. I grabbed my sleeping bag and filled a small plastic bag with some extra clothes, a swimsuit, rain poncho, flashlight, my journal, and a map. That was more than enough for a three-day marathon out on the lakes.

When I got to the beach, the girls were standing there waiting for me. Aria was chomping at the bit. Actually, it was a big piece of beef jerky, and she looked like she wanted to deck me.

"It's about time, Farm Boy!" she cried frantically. "We've been waiting here for like an hour!"

"Oh, chill out, cuz," Esther said as she grinned at her friend and then at me. "We're pretty stoked about the trip, Leo. We've just been waiting all day long for you to get back."

"All week long!" Aria corrected her.

"Yeah, bro!" Esther exclaimed. "We're just a wee bit excited, eh?"

"Well, I'm ready to go," I replied. "Just stay away from me, Hunter. I don't want another bloody nose."

"No problem, Farm Boy!" she said. "Come on, let's go."

"Where's all our stuff?" I asked, looking around the beach for the packs and the canoe.

"It's over at eagle landing by the cathedral," Aria said. "Come on! Let's get a move on!"

"Why is it over there?" I asked.

But Aria had already taken off. She sprinted ahead as Esther and I followed behind and tried to keep up. By the time we got to the bridge, she was already halfway across. We ran across the bridge, which creaked and bounced up and down as we chased after Aria. When we got to the other side, she was bounding down the trail to eagle landing, which was a smaller, more remote, rocky beach with a big square dock where a pontoon boat was tied up. The canoe was there as well, resting halfway in the water, already loaded and ready to go.

"Throw your stuff in, Leo, and let's shove off," Aria said almost frantically. "It's getting late already."

We pushed the canoe out into the water and jumped in. Aria took the bow and let me have the stern. Esther nestled down in the middle compartment with the packs and my guitar, which I had almost forgotten at my cabin. We paddled around the eastern edge of the island, staying close to the shore for a while. We could hear the voices and laughter of everyone up in Starlight Lodge as we quietly slipped away. The voices slowly faded off behind us as we rounded a rocky point on the east side of the island. I turned the canoe out into the lake and aimed it straight across toward a low spot in the tree line on the eastern shore.

Aria was a strong paddler. The canoe lunged forward each time she took a stroke in the water. I struggled to keep pace with her, but gradually got in sync, taking a break every once in a while to just lie back and use my paddle as a rudder. Esther leaned back on the packs in the middle of the canoe. She looked around excitedly at the ripples in the water and the scenery that was constantly changing as we skimmed across the lake.

The sun was already hanging low in the west as I aimed the canoe across the lake toward a small gap in the shoreline. We cruised through a bit of rapids in the passageway, then on into a narrow channel that led due east to a boat landing and a public campground at the end of the Gunflint Trail. We could see the road and the boat access down by the lake in the distance, but that was as close as we would get to civilization for the next three days.

I swung the canoe to the left, following the sound of some gentle rapids that connected Diamond Lake and Gull Lake to the north. We paddled into a calm area above the rapids and cruised ahead slowly into a small opening along the shoreline. It was an overgrown portage marked by a few wooden planks near the edge of the water. Most people crossed over to Gull Lake via the boat landing, but I wanted to avoid the people and the parking lot over there. Either way, we'd have to carry our packs and canoe across to the next lake, and the portage was a little shorter of a hike.

Just before the canoe scraped on the rocks, Aria jumped out into the shallow water and grabbed the side of the boat to guide it in.

"All right, you guys, let's do this!" she said excitedly. "We've got a long way to go before we rest tonight."

Esther climbed forward, clutching the side rails of the canoe. Then, she stepped gingerly into the water. I moved the canoe a bit closer to shore and then stepped out into the water too.

"This is so unreal!" Esther said excitedly. "We're going tramping in the wop-wops, you guys!"

"This ain't nothing like the prairie I used to play in as a kid," Aria said as she lifted a pack out of the canoe. "Man, this is heavy, Esther! What did you pack in there? You're entire wardrobe?"

"Nah, just a few things for the bush," Esther replied. "My togs and a towel, a jumper, an extra jersey, some bug spray, my jammies, my jandals, an extra pair of knickers of course, plus some biscuits, a bag of scroggin, and a torch."

"What the?" Aria said, shaking her head in disbelief.

"You'll see!" Esther said with a confident smile. "I reckon it'll all come in handy when we get out there."

"All right, girlfriend, whatever!" Aria replied as she lifted the pack up high for Esther to carry.

"Crikey!" Esther exclaimed as she slipped into the shoulder pads. "This thing *is* heavy!"

I jammed the two paddles under the front thwart of the canoe. Then, I grabbed the other pack and carried it to shore. I lifted the pack up behind Aria as she pushed her arms through the shoulder straps and bounced it up high onto her back.

"Come on, Esther! Follow me!" Aria called as she hunched forward and lunged up the trail into the woods. Esther slowly turned and followed along behind, lugging her own heavy pack.

"See you on the other side, Farm Boy!" Aria called back to me.

"What about the waka?" Esther asked.

"Don't worry about that. Leo's got it," Aria replied.

I turned back to the canoe, still floating in the water. "Okay, here we go," I whispered to myself. "I can do this."

This was the tough part about traveling by canoe in the Boundary Waters: getting your canoe from one lake to the next. Most of the portages were laden with rocks and roots, swampy puddles of mud and muck, and sometimes whole logs or downed trees across the trail. All along the way, leafy green branches reached out into the narrow sliver of daylight that fell onto the path.

Portaging a canoe was always a challenge, but as the summer progressed, I was growing to appreciate it for what it was: lifting the canoe out of the water, swinging it overhead, and letting the shoulder pads drop down slowly around my neck; feeling the weight of the canoe, and balancing it as I stepped left, then right, trying not to fall over; then lunging forward step by step up the trail, carefully navigating the twists and turns along the way.

With that being said, portaging a canoe was also probably my least favorite activity as a guide. The view from underneath was somewhat limiting and often downright dangerous, with the forest floor passing by below. Almost always, a pesky mosquito was buzzing around my face as I moved ahead, unable to do much of anything except keep going forward. There was really no way to stop. Doing that would just prolong the pain that was steadily building in my shoulders. So, I'd simply keep trudging along with my arms outstretched underneath the canoe, gripping the side rails with my fingers, and pulling down on them to keep it level. By the end, my shoulders would be burning like a forest fire. The experience was something that was seared into both my mind and my body. The aching, sore muscles served as a reminder long after a trip was over.

Yet, it was something I learned to value and appreciate about being up there on the lakes. I enjoyed everything about it: the challenge of trekking off into the wilderness, traveling from lake to lake through narrow portages that led to remote places farther and farther away from civilization—away from people and traffic, away from assignments and classes and appointments to keep, away from the hustle and bustle of the world and everything that came with it.

Thankfully, our first portage was a short one that just skirted around the rapids and came out below them. When I got to the other side, I waded straight out into the water until it was about knee-deep. Then, I pushed the canoe up quickly and threw it off my shoulders to the right, letting it flip over and fall back into the water with a loud satisfying smack.

"There you go!" I said, happy to have the first portage behind us. "Let's load 'er back up and keep going."

The girls dropped the packs back in as I pulled out the paddles and steadied the canoe. It took a lot of teamwork to do a portage right. It was hard work, but it built character. You can tell a lot about a person when you're faced with a tough portage. Our first one was only about fifteen rods long. There would be longer and tougher portages ahead, and I was wondering how Esther would handle them.

Once we were back in the canoe, we moved north again. We paddled around a point, then kept going through a channel with enormous black rocks sticking up out of the water and others visible below the surface. We had to be careful not to scrape the bottom of the canoe. Aria leaned forward and directed me to steer right or left to avoid running aground. The channel opened up into a small lake with an island in the middle. We paddled across the open water, skirting the island on our left, and continued north into another narrow channel that was just outside the Boundary Waters.

There were private cabins tucked away in the trees on both sides. Several had docks and boat ramps leading down to the water. We passed a couple of other canoe outfitters along the way as well, but we saw no one out and about at that late hour.

The channel became even narrower as we passed a rocky outcropping with a weathered sign posted there, welcoming visitors to the Boundary Waters Canoe Area. We made our way through another narrow passageway where more rocks were hiding just below the surface. Eventually, it opened up into a wide channel that continued north as far as the eye could see.

We quietly paddled ahead in silence, taking in the beauty all around. The channel widened out considerably, and we eventually found ourselves paddling into the southeastern section of Lake Saganaga, the "lake of many islands" as the Chippewa so appropriately described it long ago. It extended for several miles northwest up into Canada, deep into the Quetico Provincial Park that bordered the Boundary Waters to the north. We could see islands up ahead in a bigger part of the lake and more islands off to the west as well. It was unusually calm and quiet on the water, with barely a hint of a breeze. It was a welcome treat on such a large lake.

When we passed a small island on our left, the enormous lake opened up for miles and miles to the west. The tiny ripples on the surface of the water reflected the glistening rays of pure white sunlight that shot directly into our eyes. Esther flipped down her sunglasses and smiled back at me. It was such an amazing sight. I had to squint and look away to keep from being blinded.

As the sun began to set in the west, it dipped behind a line of tall white pines on an island far away, casting long shadows that stretched eastward for miles across the lake toward our canoe. The islands in the west slowly fell into darkness, but the treetops still glowed in the last remaining sunlight. Behind us, the trees on the eastern shoreline had turned a deep forest green, and the water reflected their waning glory in the last few seconds before the sunset.

We stopped paddling and watched in silence as the sun slowly dropped down onto the horizon. Esther grabbed her camera and snapped a couple of photos. For the last few seconds, we could actually see the sun moving ever so slowly . . . down, down, down behind the trees in the faraway distance, and then it was gone.

"That was sweet," Aria said quietly.

"Faaaaaa!" Esther exclaimed softly. "That was a stunning one."

"Totally," Aria replied.

"Thanks, nature! You are ace!" Esther exclaimed.

"Just wait, it's not over yet," I quietly said.

The sky grew more colorful as the sun sank beneath the horizon. The vibrant shades kept transforming from soft blues high above to deep orange and yellow in the west. Golden cloud formations glowed brightly in the sky far away. Above us, rosy pink whiffs of watery mist drifted eastward in the upper atmosphere, still reflecting the direct light from the distant sun. The circumference of the evening sky in every direction—north, south, east, and west—gradually faded to a dusty blue with shades of purple off to the northeast.

We watched for a little while longer. Then, I dipped my paddle into the water and moved us forward again, aiming the canoe at an opening between two large islands far away in the distance. When Esther asked to switch with me, I was happy to oblige. We carefully swapped places as Aria steadied the canoe. Esther started paddling right away, happy to have something to do, but as the canoe curved sharply off to the left, I heard Esther curse under her breath.

"This paddle isn't working right," she complained as she tried to keep the canoe going straight ahead.

"Switch sides!" Aria called from the front as we floated dangerously close to some submerged rocks.

"This is hard!" Esther cried as she flipped her paddle across to the opposite side and splashed water all over my back.

"Come on girlfriend!" Aria called again. "Go right!"

Esther paddled frantically, flipping her paddle back and forth from one side to the other, getting me soaked in the process. I didn't mind, but my guitar was getting wet too. When I spun around and peeked at Esther, she threw me a frustrated look and tugged on the paddle again. I had to bite my lip to keep from laughing out loud.

I tried to explain how to do a J-stroke with the paddle to keep us going straight. At first, she struggled with the technique. The canoe curved aimlessly off to the right and then back left as it made large sweeping arcs in the water. Esther didn't give up, though. Eventually, she calmed down and had us moving forward again.

As we continued northwest, we passed by several more islands of different shapes and sizes, scattered across the southern section of the lake. When we paddled through the opening between the two large islands, suddenly, we saw how enormous Lake Saganaga actually was. Far away to the north, across miles of open water, we could just barely see the Canadian shoreline in the growing darkness. The wind had completely died down. The lake fell silent and still as it reflected the last remaining light in the evening sky.

It was exactly what we'd been hoping for all along.

chapter 23

starry, starry night

"This is pretty amazing."

As we moved northwest into the vast open body of water, the deep purple sky seemed to melt like heavy wax and fall into darkness. The far-reaching expanse of the lake loomed up all around us and appeared to swallow our canoe like an ever-expanding black hole. I had an intense urge to speak up and ask the girls to paddle harder. I felt as if we needed to get across to the other side as quickly as possible, but I kept quiet as the lake slowly overwhelmed us and drew us farther and farther away from shore.

All of my past experiences warned me of the dangers of lingering out in the middle of such a large body of water. My instincts were telling me to stay close to shore, not to get drawn too far out into the middle of the giant lake, and to be wary of the wind and waves that could blow up at any time, creating a dangerous and impassable barrier for anyone caught out on the water. But that evening was completely different from all the other times I had been there. The lake was completely calm and silent.

"It's like the lake is asleep," Aria said quietly.

"Yeah, it's usually so windy," I replied. "This is such a nice surprise. I've never been out here in the middle of the night."

"Life is full of surprises, especially when you start looking for them," Esther said. "It happens when you break away from your routine and do something completely new."

"That's how I feel about this summer," I said. "I could've stayed in Iowa, but I felt like I needed to experience something different."

"Well, mate, this is totally different," Esther replied.

"The whole summer has been that way," I said. "I can't help feeling like I was meant to be here, as if it were fate that I'd end up here on this lake with both of you."

"Leo, I sure wish you would talk more," Esther said. "You're not what I thought you'd be like at all."

"What did you think I'd be like?" I asked.

"I had you pegged as just another bogan," she replied.

"A bogan? What's that?" I asked.

"You know, a redneck, a hick," she explained. "A guy who's just interested in trucks and partying and drinking."

"Wow, that's not me at all," I said. "I'm a hick, probably, and I've got an old Chevy back at home, but drinking and partying are things I almost never do."

"Yeah, bro," she said. "I'm probably more of a bogan than you. I've done my share of partying with my friends back home."

"There's nothing wrong with that," I replied.

"Yeah, I know," Esther said. "Actually, my friends are pretty sweet. You'd like them, I think, but you're not like them at all."

"What am I like?" I asked, curious about her take of me.

"You're quieter, gentler, and less crazy than I thought you'd be," she said. "You're more of a deep thinker. You feel things down in your heart, almost on a spiritual level. I reckon you hold a lot of your thoughts and feelings inside too."

"Yeah, I do that," I admitted. "I keep a lot of things to myself. I've been doing a lot of journaling lately. Sometimes, that's the only way I can let my feelings out. I'm not very good at sharing my thoughts and feelings with other people."

"That's okay. That's why I'm here," Esther replied.

"Why you're here?" I asked.

"Yeah, mate," she said. "I'm pretty good at getting people to talk. I just keep asking questions until I get what I want."

"Get what you want?" I asked.

"Yeah, I just keep at it until I get people to open up and share what they're thinking about," she explained.

"You've done a pretty good job at that already," I said. "You have a way of getting Aria and me to talk when we don't want to."

"Yep, but there's one egg that's been pretty tough to crack," she replied. "I'm not a quitter, though. I'll just keep chipping away at it until the walls come tumbling down."

"You mean, like . . . me?" I asked.

"Yeah," she said with a chuckle. "You don't have to say anything you don't want to, bro. I'm just warning you about what I'm like."

"Okay, Esther," I replied. "Whatever you say, but I'm just warning you that you've probably met your match in me."

"Met my match, eh?" she replied.

"Yeah, I'm pretty tight-lipped these days," I said. "It's only gotten worse over the past few years; just ask any of my friends. So, I'm sorry if you don't end up getting exactly what you want."

"I don't know, mate," she replied optimistically. "As I said, I'm pretty good at getting what I want."

I glanced back at Esther in the back of the canoe. I wondered if she already knew something. I wondered if she were reading my thoughts, the ones I was trying to keep hidden from her.

"Yeah, bro," she said, throwing a confident grin in my direction. "You're the one who might need to be careful. You just might have met your match in me. I reckon there might be a few more surprises in store for you too, if you just loosen up and let your guard down a bit. You never know what might happen. Things can get pretty amazing if you put yourself in the right situation."

"Pretty amazing, huh?" I replied, grinning back at her.

"This is pretty amazing," Aria said from up in front as she tilted her head back and gazed up at the starry sky above.

As we'd been talking, the sky had been getting darker and darker, and a few stars were beginning to shine in the growing darkness. I set my guitar down, leaned back, and looked up. Esther stopped paddling, and so did Aria. We paused far out in the middle of the lake and just sat there looking up into the night sky. We watched silently, almost reverently, as the heavens gradually came to life high above. The planets and the brightest stars were the first to appear, but they were soon followed by hundreds and thousands more, all across the vast expanse. Our canoe drifted aimlessly on the water as we gazed up in awe, floating in the middle of the calm glassy lake with the nearest shoreline miles away.

The Milky Way, with its millions of stars, crossed the sky from north to south, as if splitting the heavens into two halves. I could see the Big Dipper to the north, almost directly ahead, hanging low in the sky. Looking off to the right, I could make out the North Star, as if set apart and alone in an empty area of the sky. That was all I knew of the constellations, nothing more, except for maybe the Little Dipper, which I could find, but it would only be a guess. I didn't know how to identify any of the other constellations in the sky. I'd never taken the time to learn them in school or on my own, and I didn't want Esther or Aria to find out how little I knew. I waited for one of them to start pointing out some of the constellations, but neither of them did. It was as if we'd been struck speechless by the incredible sight spread out above us. It filled the entire expanse of the sky from the eastern shoreline all the way across to the western horizon.

As the sky grew darker, the stars became even more crisp and bright. Their twinkling lights reflected on the lake that stretched out before us like a giant mirror. It felt as if we were flying through the heavens themselves, with the stars high above and the stars deep below in the waters of Lake Saganaga as far as the eye could see.

All I could hear was the water dripping from our paddles and the gentle rocking of the canoe on the lake. A loon in the distance let out a lonely haunting cry that echoed across the lake and bounced off the islands far away to the south. As we watched in silence, I could hear Aria quietly utter her amazement. I could hear Esther behind me softly breathing as she looked all around up above. For the longest time, we just sat silent and still with our mouths open wide, as if drinking up the peaceful moment. In the west, it was almost completely dark, but the stars were so bright, we could still see for miles and miles across the lake in every direction.

When I turned to sneak a glance at Esther in the back of the canoe, she was looking straight up into the sky with her head tilted back and her mouth pooled open wide. It was as if she were receiving a great blessing that was being poured out upon her from above. The starlight flickered in her eyes, sparkling like diamonds as she took it all in with complete joy and pleasure.

"I love this," she said quietly, lifting her arms straight up into the evening sky. "It's so beautiful, so incredibly beautiful."

Aria turned around in the canoe and gave us both a euphoric smile. "I know, isn't it just so amazing?"

It was humbling to be surrounded by so many incredible things: the vast universe in the brilliant sky above, the twinkling stars reflected on the glassy lake below, the quiet spirit of Aria sitting up in front, and the amazing beauty of Esther overflowing in the back. In the silent stillness, it felt as if my heart, my mind, and even my soul were filled to overflowing by the amazing sight.

It was a time of wonder under the starry, starry sky.

chapter 30
holy family

"It's family time."

In the darkness, I could just barely make out a peninsula in the distance, called American Point, and a large island nearby. We needed to go around the point and then southwest along the edge of the lake to where a number of campsites were located. I told the girls to aim for that spot, and they started paddling again. We had a long way to go before we would even begin looking for a campsite, so I grabbed my guitar and started playing a quiet tune. I hummed along softly as the girls moved the canoe across the lake.

I could feel Esther's eyes on me as I played. She was paddling steadily, but she was completely silent. I had a feeling she was listening to me as she steered the canoe through the water.

"Leo," she said softly from behind. "Who are you, mate?"

"Um," I balked at the open-ended question. "What do you mean?"

"I don't know. Just tell me a bit about yourself," she said.

"Okay," I replied uneasily. "I'll be a senior at Concordia College in the fall. I'm majoring in biology and history, and I'm studying to be a teacher. But I really love nature, so I'm thinking about getting a job where I can use my bio degree outdoors."

My answer seemed dry and lifeless. I wondered if Esther felt the same way about it too.

"But *who* are you?" Esther persisted. "I mean, what made you who you are, eh?"

"You mean, like my family and where I grew up?" I asked.

"Yeah, totally," she replied. "Whatever, bro."

"Well, I was born in North Dakota, but we moved to Iowa a couple of years later. My dad is a Lutheran pastor, so we moved around every once in a while. He had two small churches in North Dakota. Then, we were at a big one in Des Moines. Then, he got a job as a camp director near Story City, Iowa. I loved it there. It was so much fun running around all summer with my friends, going fishing, playing outside with my dog, and riding my bike to town. But after a few years, we moved to California. Then, when I was in high school, we moved back to Iowa. That's when I graduated and went off to college.

"Wow, that's a fair amount of gallivanting around," Esther said. "You never got to hang about in one spot very long, did you? Where do you feel like your true home is?"

"I don't know," I replied. "Nowhere, I guess. I never had time to put down roots anywhere. All that moving . . . I didn't like it. I think it kind of shaped who I am now. It made me more of a loner, but more independent too, and maybe more self-reliant."

"I see that in you," Esther said. "What about college? Have you made some good friends there?"

"Oh yeah," I replied. "I like Concordia, but I wonder how long those friendships will last. We all graduate next year, so I think I'm sort of holding back a bit. To be completely honest, I've kind of struggled with relationships my entire life."

"Have you been hurt in the past?" Esther asked.

I hesitated, wondering how much to share with her. For some reason, I felt safe, even with Aria quietly listening up in front.

"Yeah, I suppose so," I confessed. "That's probably why it's so difficult for me to let people get too close. I tend to put up walls to protect myself. I know it's not healthy, but I do it anyway. Even now, there's a lot I'm not telling you. It's as if I'm automatically filtering it out in some way, to keep the more personal stuff inside and only share what seems safe to me."

"Yeah, mate, I do that too," Esther said reassuringly. "I reckon everyone does that to a certain degree."

"Yeah, I suppose so," I replied. "I'm pretty good at it, though. I kind of enjoy keeping to myself, or maybe I've just become used to it.

After I graduated from high school, I spent that first summer back up in North Dakota, working on my uncle's farm. I worked dawn to dusk, feeding cattle, pitching hay, cleaning out stalls in the barn, driving the combines, and hauling grain to town. I worked mostly by myself. In the evening, when the old-timers settled down in front of the TV set, I'd go out on the porch and watch the sunset and play my uncle's guitar. That's when I started keeping a journal too. I'd walk the hills in the evenings, feed the horses in the pasture, and play with the dogs. That summer on the farm sort of reminds me of this one—being outdoors most of the time, dealing with the weather, working with my hands, and spending a lot of time alone. It was hard work, but I loved it, and I love this too."

"Yeah, I reckon you do," Esther said. "I see it in how you talk about things and how you treat other people. You seem to be at peace here. That's so important."

"Yeah, this is a pretty awesome place," I replied.

"What will you do when the summer ends?" she asked.

"I'll go back to school for my final year, but I don't want the summer to end." I stopped talking, realizing I'd said more than I'd planned. "What about you, Esther?" I asked. "Who are you?"

"Oh, Leo," she chuckled softly. "That's a mighty big question. I wouldn't know where to begin."

"You started it," I insisted. "Now it's your turn to spill the beans."

"Spill the beans?" she asked.

"You know," I replied. "Talk about yourself and reveal all the secrets you've been keeping from us."

"Oh, righto!" Esther said as she took another stroke with her paddle. I could tell she was thinking about what to say, so I waited quietly and let her have as much time as she needed.

"All right, Leo," she began with a deep sigh. "For starters, I suppose I'd have to go back at least two generations to explain a few things first."

"That's okay," I replied. "We've got all the time in the world."

"All right," she said. "My grandparents lived in Czechoslovakia before World War 2, and when it started, they saw what was beginning to happen in Germany and the occupied countries. They were Jewish, so they had no choice but to flee, and thankfully, they got out in time. They moved to France first, but when Germany attacked, they left there too and ended up halfway around the world in New Zealand. That's where my father was born and where he met my mum. They got married, and then they had me and my little sister Anna."

"So, you've lived in New Zealand all your life?" I asked.

"Yep," she replied. "I've lived in the same house for as long as I can remember. My parents still live there in Auckland: the biggest city on the north island. I like it, but we're so far away from the rest of the world. That's why I came to the United States to study. I've always wanted to travel and meet people and have exciting new adventures. But I never expected to end up out here in the middle of nowhere, exploring the border of Canada. I never would have guessed I'd be with you two either. You're my pals—Leo, my special bro, and Aria, my bestie from America."

Aria suddenly came to life up in front. "You got that right, cuzzy!" she exclaimed. "We're gonna be besties for life. I'm coming to visit you in New Zealand someday too."

It was nice to hear some of Esther's story. I'd been dying to know more about her, and as she talked, it made me feel full and satisfied, just like a hot bowl of oatmeal in the morning. I set my guitar down, stretched out in the middle of the canoe, and gazed up at the stars as Esther talked about her life back home.

After a while, she called up to Aria. "What about you, cuz? We've hung out a lot this year, but I still don't know much about your family. What are some things that have shaped who you are?"

"Sorry, sister," Aria replied immediately. "I'd rather sit this one out if you don't mind."

"Come on, Aria, please!" Esther begged from the back of the canoe. "Don't be a party-pooper!"

"Why don't you ask me in a few years? I'll have more to say by then," Aria replied stubbornly.

"Aria!" Esther cried. "Leo and I both bared our souls. Now it's your turn to spill the beans!"

"Aw, applesauce," Aria muttered under her breath. "I knew this was coming the whole time, I guess."

"What did you say, Hunter? Applesauce?" I asked.

"Oh, nothing," she replied. "It's just something my mom taught me a long time ago." Aria paddled for a while, thinking and swearing quietly under her breath. The minutes ticked by in silence.

"Come on, cuz," said Esther. "We're waiting."

"I don't have anything to say," Aria complained.

"You can tell us. You're safe with us," Esther insisted.

"Oh, good grief," Aria replied with a heavy sigh. "All right, cuzzy, I'll do it for you, but just this once."

Aria took a big breath, and then she began to talk. "I grew up in Chicago since I was a baby," she said. "We lived on the northwest side over by Cabrini Green in a pretty rough part of town. I remember going to church a lot. It was a place called Holy Family. It was a tiny church in the middle of the projects surrounded by a bunch of high-rises, which were mostly all run-down with busted windows and bullet holes in the walls. There was trash all around the place and lots of gangbanging going on. The city was moving people out, tearing down the high-rises, and building new upscale apartments. My dad left when I was little, so I don't remember him much. Things got pretty tough after he left. My mom was happier, but life got harder."

"We ended up moving to the North Side," she continued. "It's another high-rise apartment closer to the lake. My mom works hard as a secretary downtown. She always gets home late and all worn out, but she takes good care of my little brother and me. She's such a strong woman, and I love her to death. I don't know what I'd do without her. After we moved and I was in high school, I had to make new friends in a different school, but it wasn't easy for me. I think the move toughened me up, though.

"I can't imagine that, Aria!" Esther exclaimed. "You mean you weren't always such a tough little cracker?

"The next few years were pretty difficult," Aria replied. "I think the move might have saved my life because I got away from my old friends back in that rough part of town and ended up spending more time at home with my mom. We kept attending Holy Family in Cabrini Green, though. That church family was so important to my mom and us kids. It was like a lifeline. The people there are so strong and loving and supportive. It's not so much the religion I like; it's the way the people care for each other."

"Do you still go to church there?" Esther asked.

"Yeah," Aria replied. "My mom takes us whenever she can, but sometimes she has to work on weekends. That old neighborhood in Cabrini Green is changing so fast now. It's going upscale, so I just hope the church survives. I miss the people there a lot."

"Hey, Hunter," I chimed in. "You should take me there when I visit you in Chicago this next school year."

"Anytime, Farm Boy!" she called back. "Indiana State isn't that far away. I could catch the train some weekend and show you around!"

"Sounds like a deal to me!" I replied.

"You can stay with my family on the North Side," she exclaimed. "You'd love my mom and my brother too. We'd have to ride the "L" downtown, try some Chicago-style pizza, and visit the Bean too!"

"Hey, mates!" cried Esther. "I'll be gone in a couple of days, and you two will still be here, having so much fun without me."

"Hey, sister!" Aria replied. "No one's forcing you to go back to that little island on the other side of the world. Just call home and tell 'em you're staying in Chicago with me."

"I have to go back," Esther said. "I have to finish my degree, and my plane leaves in just a little over a week."

"I'm gonna miss you, cuzzy, and you too, Leo," Aria said sadly from up in front. "At the end of the summer, we'll all be in different places. It's gonna be so weird."

We paddled for a while in silence, thinking about the big changes coming in each of our lives. We floated quietly by a campsite that was occupied. Two canoes rocked back and forth down by the shoreline, and a campfire could be seen up by the trees.

"I can't believe Cassie let us do this trip," Aria said quietly. "Esther, this is a pretty awesome end to your year in America, isn't it?"

"Totally," she said. "But it wasn't Cassie; it was Finn."

"What?" Aria asked.

"I got permission from Finn," Esther said. "Cassie never would've said yes, but Finn's my buddy. He's such a big sweetheart."

"I thought you talked to Cassie," Aria said.

"Nope, it was Finn," Esther replied. "We owe him big-time."

As we moved along, I enjoyed listening to the girls chatter back and forth. I didn't have much to say, but they did, and they were always more entertaining than I could've ever been. As they talked, a feeling of contentment came over me. I felt like I was making friendships that would last a lifetime. I wondered, though, how I'd feel about it when we went our separate ways.

"Hey, you guys," Aria said, "I know it's only half over, but this has been the best summer of my life, and you guys are the best friends I've ever had. I miss my mom and brother, but it's so nice to have you guys with me. You're like my summer family."

"Straight up!" Esther replied with delight. "This is a family trip, cuz! It's family time."

Aria suddenly stopped paddling. Then, she spun around and looked at both of us sitting in the back of the canoe.

"I don't know what I would've done this summer without you guys," she said. "Esther, you're so awesome. Without you, I would have failed environmental ethics last year. You're like the sister I never had. And Leo, I love you like a brother."

"Thanks, Hunter," I replied with a grin. "You beat up on me just like my big sister used to when I was a kid."

"No, seriously, guys, you're like family to me now," Aria said.

"Aw, Aria!" Esther replied. "You know we love you too!"

We skimmed across the calm lake in the dark. As I thought about what Aria said, I realized that I felt the same way too. I couldn't explain exactly how, but I felt like Esther and Aria were closer to me than my own sister and I had ever been.

"You're my family," Aria said, "my holy family."

chapter 31

camping in the dark

"This isn't looking too good."

The girls kept us moving northwest across Lake Saganaga toward American Point. I got the map out along with my flashlight and started looking for campsites. As we approached the point, we could hear the ripples washing over the rocky shoals that stretched out into the lake. It was unsettling to know that there were rocks just below the surface in that area, and we moved cautiously ahead to avoid getting snagged on them in the darkness.

As we rounded the point, the breeze picked up slightly. Canada was not far off, just a mile or so across the channel to the north. The plan was to find a campsite on the American side that night, hopefully before we had to portage out of Saganaga. I counted five campsites on the map along the last stretch of the lake. Esther steered the canoe closer to the shore so we could see them in the darkness. We cruised by one, then two, then a third campsite—all occupied.

We moved on, still hopeful that one of the remaining sites would be open. We passed by a tiny island on the Canadian side and floated into the first bay of Saganaga. A few weeks earlier, I had stopped at the island with my group of boys. We had our lunch there and enjoyed making a clandestine visit to Canada as well.

I thought about the possibility of stopping there again and pitching a tent just for the night, but I was still hoping for one of the remaining sites on the American side. We still had a chance, but they were popular sites coveted for their northern exposure, great views of the stars, and if you got lucky, possibly the northern lights.

"Leo, this isn't looking too good," Aria worried as we floated past another occupied site. "We're running out of campsites."

"There's one more up ahead," I replied. "If it's taken, that's it. We'll just have to portage into Swamp Lake."

"There are a couple of campsites in Ottertrack Lake, but that's two portages farther up," Aria said.

"Yeah," I replied, "I don't want to portage in the dark."

Aria was worried, and I was beginning to lose hope as well. All three of us sat up in the boat, nervously eyeing the shoreline in the darkness. I was comparing the map to the landmarks, which were barely visible, trying to locate the last site that was supposed to be somewhere nearby.

Aria pointed to a cluster of large rocks that jutted out from the shoreline. "That's gotta be it right there," she said.

I could just barely see a sandy spot off to the side where canoes could be pulled up onto the shore. The trees looked a bit sparse and worn too, which was a typical sign for a campsite.

I pointed to the spot and said, "Esther, pull in there." She aimed the canoe straight for the sandy opening, and we floated in.

Aria hopped out before the canoe touched ground and whispered, "I'll go check it out." She walked up through the trees and returned a few seconds later, all smiles. "It's open, guys. We've got ourselves a campsite for the night."

We unloaded the canoe and pulled it up onto the shore. Then, we hauled our packs up by the fire grate and looked around. It was a big rocky campsite with a lot of open space. Aria dug out a bag of granola bars and dried fruit, even though we weren't that hungry. It was nice to have a place to rest, but we were too tired to do anything about it. We sat on the logs by the fire grate and nibbled on the food as a gentle breeze picked up off the lake.

Suddenly, Aria looked up in surprise and exclaimed, "Hey, you guys, there aren't any mosquitoes here!"

"Too right!" Esther replied. "No mozzies!"

"They must have gone to bed," I suggested. "Either that or the breeze is driving them into the woods."

Mosquitoes were a constant presence in the Boundary Waters. They were everywhere—on the portage trails, around the campfire in the evenings, and down by the lake. They especially liked to hover around the throne back in the woods, but none of us was interested in going to look for that right away.

"Do we have to set up a tent?" Aria whined. "Why don't we just crash right here?"

I glanced over at Esther for her opinion. She was smiling and nodding at Aria as if to say, "Yeah, here would be great!"

"All right, fine with me," I said, looking around for a soft spot to sleep. "Let's throw our tarp down in that grassy spot right over there and get some shut-eye."

"What about our food pack?" Aria asked.

I'd forgotten about that. I wondered at the risk of not hanging it in a tree. Bears were wandering all over that area, and it would ruin the trip if we lost our food on the very first night. It's just that I was so tired, and I had no desire to hang a pack in the dark.

"Yeah, we better do it," I finally said reluctantly. "Aria, can you find the rope in the equipment pack?"

"Sure, buddy, coming right up!" she said, swinging into action.

It was something we both had learned to do without much thinking at any given campsite, usually right after supper. Aria opened one of the packs and began digging through it for the rope. Meanwhile, I fished around for a small rock by the fireplace. When she found the rope, she tossed it to me. As I went to work securing it to the rock, Aria grabbed her flashlight and walked back into the woods. Esther followed her, and together they roamed around the campsite, eyeing trees for suitable branches.

"That one looks decent," Aria said, shining her flashlight on a large branch about twenty feet up. It was sticking straight out from a big pine tree. "Leo, bring the rope over, and let's get this done." She aimed her flashlight up at the branch and waited for me.

"It's pretty high," I complained. "I don't know if I can do it."

"Come on, Leo," Aria said. "It'll work, and besides, I gotta go find that throne pretty soon."

I practiced my throw a couple of times; then I heaved the rock up at the branch. The rock and the rope shot up into the darkness above, but it missed and came crashing back down.

"You can't even do this in broad daylight," Aria said as she shook her head. "I don't know how you'll ever get it in the dark."

"You can try it if you like, Hunter," I replied, getting ready to throw the rock again.

"Man, I really gotta go now," Aria said, sounding more urgent. "Hurry up, Leo! Toss that thing and get it this time."

I heaved the rock up again, but it came crashing down like before, dangerously close to the girls.

"For crying out loud, Leo!" Aria exclaimed, shining her flashlight in my eyes. "You're gonna kill us with that rock!"

"I'm doing the best I can!" I shot back. "Besides, I can't see a thing, now that you blinded me with your flashlight."

"Hey, mates," Esther said softly in the dark. "How about you let me give it a go, eh?"

Aria and I glanced at her as if she were a toddler who'd just witnessed her parents fighting over what to have for supper. I picked up the rock and handed it to her. Then, I turned on my flashlight and shined it at the branch up above.

As Esther practiced her throw a couple of times, I started to get worried. "That's not how you do it," I thought, but she was bound and determined to give it a try.

With a mighty swing, Esther heaved the rock underhand like a softball, sending it careening like a meteorite high up into the trees. I lost sight of it with my flashlight as it shot off to one side, pulling the rope along with it up into the darkness.

I heard Aria scream, "Dang, Esther!" as we scrambled away and waited for the rock to come crashing back down, but it never did.

"Esther, you maniac!" Aria shouted. "What did you do?"

"I don't know," she said, still holding the end of the rope that went straight up into the darkness above.

When she tugged down on the rope, Aria cried out, "No, Esther! Don't do that!"

We heard a tree branch crack, and I panicked for a split-second, expecting the rock to come tumbling back down, but it didn't.

"Hey, there it is!" Aria cried.

I shined my flashlight at Esther, and sure enough, there it was: the rock still attached to the rope, dangling in the air a few feet above her head. We followed the rope up with our flashlights and found where it had caught on a big branch off to the left, then swung back over another smaller branch right above us.

"Good job, Esther! You did it!" Aria exclaimed.

"Straight up, cuz!" she said with a smile. "I guess I know how to chuck a rope, eh?"

I wanted to say a few things, but I held my tongue. I gave the rope a tug and eyed the small branch it was caught on. It didn't look good, but Aria was already running to get the food pack. She raced back with it and threw it on the ground. Then, she pushed the rope through the ears, tied a big knot, and hoisted it up.

"Here you go, Leo," she said. "You guys heave it up while I pull."

"Okay," I replied skeptically. "I just hope the branch holds."

Aria grabbed the end of the rope and walked back toward the logs by the fire grate. Esther and I lifted the pack above our heads and tried to push it up, but it tumbled down between us. We tried again, and as Aria pulled, she lifted it about six feet off the ground.

Esther looked up at the pack and said, "That's good, right?"

I gave it a slap and replied, "If I can reach it, so can a bear."

"Come on, Leo!" Aria yelled, still straining on the rope. "Find some branches and get it up there already!"

Esther and I scrambled to find any sticks lying around. It took a while. Finally, I found a couple decent ones back in the woods.

"Hurry up! It's getting heavy!" Aria shouted.

As we poked the branches into the bottom of the pack, I shouted, "Okay, Hunter, pull now!"

Aria heaved on the rope as we pushed up on the pack. Suddenly, it shot a good ten feet straight up and stayed there.

"Way to go, Esther!" I exclaimed, giving her a high five.

"Excuse me!" Aria called to us. "A little help here!"

We looked over and saw Aria's legs sticking straight up in the air. She was lying on her back behind one of the logs by the fire grate, still clinging to the rope for dear life. She looked ridiculous lying there, hanging on to the rope and staring up at the stars in the night sky. I walked over and shined my flashlight into her eyes.

"That looks great, Aria," I said with a smirk. "You just hold it there while Esther and I go lie down and get some sleep."

Esther came up behind me and giggled.

"Leo!" Aria yelled. "Grab the rope right now, or I swear I'm gonna stuff you down the throne head first!"

"All right, Hunter," I said with a chuckle. I reluctantly grabbed the rope and tied it off to a tree nearby.

"We did it, mates!" Esther rejoiced. "That was pretty easy, eh?"

Aria slowly rolled back over in the dirt and got to her feet again. "Yeah, but I gotta find that throne ASAP," she moaned. "Anyone want to go with me?"

I looked at her, but thankfully, Esther volunteered to go. As the girls dug out the toilet paper and went off in search of the throne, I laid the tarp out on the grassy spot near the fire grate. Then, I rolled out my sleeping bag and flopped down on top of it.

"We made it," I sighed with relief. I folded my arms back behind my head and gazed up at the stars. I could hear Aria and Esther back in the woods, taking their sweet time.

Then, in the darkness, I heard Esther slap something and shout, "Get away, you nasty mozzies!"

"Esther, stop smacking me!" I heard Aria yell back. "Just hand me the TP, quick!"

"There's no way in hell I'm going back there tonight," I quietly mumbled to myself.

"Ah, life in the North Woods!"

chapter 32

stargazing

"Sorry, I have no idea what you're pointing at up there."

By the time the girls got back from the throne, I was ready to sleep, but apparently, they weren't. They fumbled around the campsite for quite a while—getting their sleeping bags out, brushing their teeth, changing into their pajamas, and doing all sorts of other things. As they shined their flashlights around and whispered in the dark, I couldn't figure out what they were doing, but I was content simply to lie back and look up at the stars. Finally, they brought their sleeping bags over and settled down next to me.

It wasn't something I usually did: sleep outside in the wilderness. It just didn't feel right. I felt like we should have set up the tent, but I was too tired to do it. I'd never gone camping alone with two young women either, but for some reason, that wasn't bothering me one bit. The stars were sparkling in the sky up above, and a nice warm breeze was blowing gently off the lake, keeping the mosquitoes away. It was a perfect night to be outside.

We lay on top of our sleeping bags like three spokes of a wheel, with our heads close together in the middle of the tarp. Even though I was physically tired, I was still on a high from the events of the day. There we were, the Wild Bunch, in the middle of the Boundary Waters, witnessing a beautiful sunset, finding a campsite in the dark, and finally, gazing up at the night sky chock full of stars.

The experiences out there in the middle of nowhere simply overwhelmed our senses. It seemed as if the beauty and grandeur of creation were baptizing us, and we were being reborn to new life.

It was exciting to know that we had two full days ahead of us where anything might happen. We were totally free. We could do anything we wanted to.

We rested together in the open air, taking in the warm summer breeze and gazing sleepily up at the stars blinking and twinkling high above. The sky was clear and dark, which made all of the stars—even the tiniest ones—shine all the more brightly. There were so many of them. "Where did they all come from?" I wondered. "How were they formed? How far away were they?"

"This is pretty sweet, eh?" Esther said. "I'm camping out in the star hotel with my besties!"

"Yeah, it's a perfect night for stargazing," Aria replied.

"Hey, mates," Esther said excitedly. "Tell me, when you look up into the sky, what do you see?"

"I see thousands of beautiful stars," Aria said. "They look like dancing fireflies to me."

"You know what I see?" Esther replied. "I see an amazing night sky full of stars and planets, millions of them, and countless galaxies in every corner of the universe, which is constantly changing and ever-expanding. I see dozens of constellations, each with stories to tell about heroes and heroines, gods and goddesses, creatures and myths. There are stories from every culture on earth and legends passed down to us through history, some familiar and some very different from our own. We are part of that story, that history, just a small part, and it's such a gift to get to see it from our own tiny perspective right here in this place. It's so totally sweet."

"Whoa, Esther, you see all that?" Aria said.

"Straight up!" she said, glancing at us lying next to her. "I can see it, and I can feel it too. I see the stars reflected in your eyes too, both of you. The stars in your eyes look so delightful."

Aria and I listened as Esther gushed about her love for the stars and the classes she'd been taking at the university. She talked on and on as it flowed out of her like a mighty flood.

Esther stretched her arm out and pointed straight up. "Do you see that star, the really bright one right there?" she asked.

We scrunched in closer to Esther and followed her arm up into the sky. "That's Vega. It's *my* star," she said softly.

I could see it off the tip of Esther's finger, an extremely bright one shining almost directly above us.

"It's your star?" I said, a bit confused.

"Yeah, well, I claim it anyway," she said with a grin. "It's got part of my last name in it, so it's mine. It's twenty-six light-years away from earth, so the light we're looking at left Vega twenty-six years ago, and it's only now reaching us here on earth."

"What is a light-year again?" I asked.

"It's the distance light travels in one year's time," she replied.

"So that light was sent out before I was even born," I said.

"How old are you?" Esther asked.

"I turned twenty-one in July last summer," I replied, starting to enjoy the little astronomy lesson.

"I turn twenty-one tomorrow!" Esther happily reminded us.

"So how far does light travel in a year?" I asked.

"How far do you think it can travel?" she replied.

"Maybe a billion miles?" I guessed.

"You're not even close, bro!" Esther said. "In my class, I learned that light travels over six trillion miles in just one year!"

"So how far is that anyway?" I asked.

"It's like this," she replied. "If the circumference of the earth is twenty-five thousand miles around, then traveling six trillion miles would be like going around the earth about seven times . . ."

"What?" Aria exclaimed. "That can't be right!"

". . . in one second, that is," Esther said with a smile.

"Well, that helps a lot! Thanks, Esther, you're a freakin' genius!" exclaimed Aria.

"That's right, cuz!" Esther said with a laugh. "So that's like two hundred and fifty million times around the earth in one year."

"Okay, now I get it! Thanks!" Aria snapped back. "I'm just a dumb high school kid, remember?"

"No kidding," Esther heartily agreed. "It's really, really far! Does that help you understand it any better?"

"No, not really, but thanks for trying," replied Aria.

I tried to wrap my mind around how far six trillion miles might be. It was totally impossible, and to think light had been traveling from Vega for twenty-six years. My tiny brain simply couldn't fathom what that even meant.

"Hey, you guys," Aria whispered excitedly. "The Big Dipper over there looks like it's pouring water down on Canada."

She pointed over the lake to the northwest. Sure enough, the big pot was tipped slightly to the right, as if it were pouring its contents onto the lake below.

"It's actually called Ursa Major," Esther said. "That's Greek for Great Bear, but most people call it the Big Dipper. So, do you chaps know how to find Polaris?"

"You mean the North Star?" Aria asked. "No, I've never even looked for it. How do you find it?"

"Here's how," Esther said. She pointed to the two stars at the bottom of the Big Dipper and traced a line with her finger across the sky to a little star shining due north of us. It sparkled in an area of the sky that was nearly void of any other bright stars.

"That's it right there," she said.

"I see it!" Aria replied. "It's right above those trees over there!"

"Yeah, right!" Esther exclaimed. "It's actually the end of the tail of Ursa Minor, or the Little Dipper, as most people call it."

"How do you find that?" Aria asked, slowly warming up to the stargazing lesson.

"Go up a bit, and you'll see two faint stars," Esther said, pointing at the next two stars of the handle. Then, she kept going to four more stars that formed the bucket of the Little Dipper.

"See the little rectangle?" she asked. "That's it right there."

Aria looked for a couple of seconds, then exclaimed, "Hey, I see it! Yeah! It looks like it's pouring water back into the Big Dipper down below." Sure enough, the little bucket was tipped up on its handle, as if pouring its contents down into the Big Dipper.

Next, Esther showed us Draco the Dragon: a long line of stars that wrapped around the Little Dipper and then curved up to a small cluster of four stars that formed the head of the dragon. At first, I had trouble seeing it, but when Esther said that it looked like a giant number 2 in the sky, suddenly, I could see it there just as she said.

Aria was fascinated with the stargazing activity, and she asked Esther to show us more constellations. As I watched Esther lying next to me with her long slender arm pointing up into the night sky, I was fascinated too. "Why did she love the stars so much?" I wondered. I gazed at her outstretched arm. The freckles on it seemed to blend in with the blurry stars above. As I listened to her talk, I followed her pretty arm as it moved around the sky.

Next, Esther drew an imaginary line from the two stars in the Big Dipper across to the North Star. Then, she continued the line out farther, about half that distance to another bright star.

"That's the tip of the throne of King Cepheus," she said. "It looks like a big house in the sky." She pointed over to the right and outlined four other fairly bright stars, and connected them to the first one. The five stars were easy to see, and they looked like a house that was tipped over on its side to the left.

From there, Esther led us farther east to Cassiopeia: a giant W in the sky that was easy to see; then over to Andromeda, which appeared like a crooked tower lying on its side; and then Perseus, which looked like a giant K hanging low in the eastern sky. Once we had located all those constellations, Esther told us a Greek myth about Andromeda and the mythical characters in that part of the sky.

"So, this is one of my favorites," Esther said as she shuffled around on her sleeping bag and prepared to tell us the story.

"Once upon a time," she said, "there was a beautiful princess named Andromeda. All of the young princes wished to court her for marriage, but her mother, Cassiopeia, wouldn't allow it. One day, as Cassiopeia bragged about her daughter's great beauty, Neptune, the god of the sea, became enraged. To punish Cassiopeia, he sent the sea nymphs to capture Andromeda and chain her to a cliff by the ocean to be sacrificed to Cetus, the sea monster. But before she perished, a brave young prince named Perseus appeared, riding the winged horse Pegasus across the sky after killing the evil witch, Medusa. When he saw Andromeda, he rescued her by using the head of Medusa to turn Cetus into stone, sinking it into the sea. Perseus and Andromeda fell in love, and they lived happily ever after. When they died, they were placed in the sky next to each other. Cassiopeia was put nearby too, next to her husband, King Cepheus. She was placed upside down on her throne, though, as punishment for her vanity."

As I listened, I couldn't believe how much Esther knew about the stars. I loved listening to her talk about all the constellations. I tried to keep up with her as she pointed out one after another. I finally got lost when she pointed to the constellation of Lyra.

"Do you see it?" she asked. "It's straight above us, right there."

"No, I can't see it," I replied.

"Just follow my arm straight up, mate," she said. "It's right there, six pretty stars right above us."

I looked, but I still couldn't make it out. "Sorry, I have no idea what you're pointing at up there."

"Here, bro," she said. "Give me your hand. I'll help you."

I reached up next to Esther's outstretched arm that was still pointing up into the sky. She wrapped her hand around mine and pushed my index finger up next to hers. She led my hand straight up to Vega, the brightest star, and together we found the five other stars in the beautiful little constellation of Lyra.

Then, Esther led my hand over to Hercules, shaped like an hourglass; then to Bootes, the herdsman, shaped like a teardrop; and farther over to Corona Borealis, shaped like a crown in the sky; then down to Virgo, lying low over the lake in the west.

Aria, who had begun to feel a bit left out, finally reached up and joined us. Together, the three of us moved around the sky, learning all the constellations of the northern hemisphere. We listened to Esther as she told us one Greek myth after another and pointed out the individual stars related to each one. I had never done so much stargazing in my entire life.

Aria was the first to fall asleep. Her hand slowly slipped down and dropped into her lap. Esther and I could hear her breathing heavily as she slept, still lying on top of her sleeping bag.

"I love the stars in the northern hemisphere," Esther said. "In New Zealand, we can't see the Big Dipper or the Little Dipper."

"What can you see?" I asked.

"Corona Australis and Centaurus," she said, "but the Southern Cross is the most beautiful constellation I've ever seen."

"What else?" I asked, peeking at her out of the corner of my eye. I felt like I was witnessing the most beautiful thing I'd ever seen too.

"You can't miss Sirius. It's the brightest star in the sky. It's in the constellation Canis Major, the Big Dog. You have the Big and Little Dippers in the north. In the south, we have the Big and Little Dogs. If you visit New Zealand someday, I'll show them to you."

"Are you serious?" I joked. "I'd like that, but I hardly know you."

Esther either didn't get the joke, or she was drifting off to the land down under. "One of my other favorites is the constellation Carina," she said. "It means the keel of the boat. There's a sail, and a compass, and a poop deck attached to it too."

"A poop what?" I asked.

"A poop deck, you bloody buffoon!" she replied.

"The poop deck is attached to a bloody balloon?" I joked.

"You big bugger, Leo, really!" Esther exclaimed.

"Well, at least that's a little better," I replied. "I'd rather be a big bugger than a big booger." The words came out wrong, but it didn't matter. I grinned and glanced over at her.

"Leo! You big nincompoop!" she said, elbowing me gently in the side. "You have no idea what you're saying, do you."

I looked over at her as seriously as was humanly possible and asked, "So, Esther, you're calling me a nincompoop now?"

"Yup," she said with a grin.

"Where did you learn to say such a naughty word like that?" I asked.

"From Daisy, the six-year-old daughter of my host family in Chicago," she replied.

"I thought so," I said seriously. "You know, Daisy has an extremely foul mouth for a six-year-old girl from Chicago."

"Too right," Esther replied with a chuckle. "Daisy taught me some other naughty American words this past year too."

"Well, I can't wait to hear them," I said softly.

"Well, I can't wait to use them," Esther said defiantly.

"Okay, I dare you," I replied, elbowing her gently in the side. "Let's hear another one right now."

"Okay, I accept," Esther said with a grin. "If Daisy were here right now, she'd probably say . . . you were being a really big pooper."

"So, I'm a big pooper now; is that what Daisy would say?" I asked, pretending to be offended.

"That's right. You're being a really big pooper," she replied.

"So," I said slowly, gathering all my wits about me. "Let me see if I can make this crystal clear."

"Yes, please do," she replied. "I need you to make it crystal clear."

"So, Esther," I said, clearing my throat. "What I think you're saying is that you'd like a big nincompooper to come down to New Zealand and take a peek at some giant poop deck up there in the dog-infested sky. Would that be a correct assumption or not?"

"Leo, you're such a goofball!" she exclaimed, nudging me in the side again. "What am I ever going to do with you?"

I was wondering the same thing. What *was* she going to do with me? I was thinking of some things we could do, but it wasn't the time nor the place. I tried to get serious again, but it wasn't easy.

"I'm sorry, Esther," I said, trying not to laugh. "I just can't help myself sometimes."

"No worries, Leo," she replied. "I like your stupid jokes."

"Why, thank you," I said. "I like your nerdy astronomy lessons."

I wanted to tell her a few other things I liked about her. She was so fun to be around. I just couldn't believe we were lying there together, and she was letting me get away with being the big nincompooper that I knew I was. She seemed to be playing right along with me. I wanted to keep at it, but I took the high road instead.

"What's the bright star right there next to Virgo?" I asked.

"That's not a star," she said. "It's a planet. That's Jupiter."

"I thought it was just another star," I replied.

"Did you know that it rains diamonds on Jupiter?" Esther asked.

"It does what?" I exclaimed.

"Scientists think that lightning storms turn gas into chunks of graphite in Jupiter's atmosphere," she explained. "Then, they become hailstones of diamonds as they fall to the planet surface."

"It seems like it always boils down to burning balls of gas, in one way or another, up there in the sky, doesn't it?" I said with a chuckle.

"So, you've seen *The Lion King*, eh, bro?" she asked.

"Aaah! Mah-bagya!" I cried loudly. "Gimme some ah yah peaches ya mahmwa!"

"What in the world, Leo!" said Esther. "What are you doing now?"

"Just quoting Pumbaa or whoever sang that little ditty," I replied.

"Well, you're a very nice singer," she said with a laugh. "I'd like to hear you sing one of your real songs sometime, though."

"Oh, I don't think so, but thanks anyway," I said. "Just don't get me started on all that bloody bugger stuff again, or I swear—"

She elbowed me hard in the side again. Esther and I kept pointing up into the starry sky with our fingers intertwined together, moving from one constellation to the next. It felt so good. I didn't want it to end. Finally, we dropped our hands back down to our sides, but Esther kept my hand tucked inside hers.

"I've never seen the stars shine as brightly as tonight," she said.

"Why not?" I asked, feeling the warmth of her soft hand holding on to my cold fingers.

"My hometown of Auckland is a city of almost two million people," she said. "It's bright there all the time, and in Chicago, it's even brighter. The sky just looks purple there, with only a few of the most brilliant stars shining through the city lights."

"Like your star, Vega?" I asked.

"Yeah, mate," she replied. "Vega is my favorite. Did you know the earth is moving toward Vega at about twenty clicks a second?"

"Really?" I replied. I had no idea what that meant.

"Yeah," she said. "It'll become the North Star about fourteen-thousand years from now." She grinned and then laughed at all the facts she had stored up inside her head.

"Esther, you're incredible," I finally confessed. "Up until now, the only things I could find were the Big Dipper and the North Star."

"That's okay, Leo," she said, giving my fingers a soft squeeze. "I'm happy to be the one getting to show them to you for the first time."

"How did you come to love the stars so much?" I asked.

"I fell in love with them when I took my first astronomy class at the university in Auckland," she said. "I'd like to get a degree in astrophysics when I return to New Zealand."

"Well, now I do too!" I exclaimed.

We both had a good laugh. As we lay there holding hands with our heads snuggled so close together, Esther kept on talking about the constellations in the Northern Hemisphere. Then, she raised her arm and pointed straight up one last time.

"Leo, give me your hand again," she said. "I'd like to show you one more constellation."

As I raised my hand and slid it back up inside hers, she pointed up and whispered softly, "Do you see that?"

In a daze, I followed her beautiful arm up to her delicate fingers surrounding mine. I could go no further. All I could see were her fingers wrapped around mine and her long gorgeous arm covered in a myriad of freckles.

"See what?" I whispered back.

"The stars right there," she said, pointing to the Milky Way. "See the line of four bright ones, crossed by another line in the middle?"

I focused my gaze back up into the sky. "Um, yeah," I replied slowly. "I see it, I think."

"That's Cygnus the Swan," she said. "It's the Northern Cross."

"It's directly above us," I replied.

"Yeah, straight up, eh," Esther said. "The base of the cross is the long neck of the swan, and the shorter end is the bottom."

"The bottom?" I whispered.

Esther giggled and nudged me in the side again. "Leo, it's a mystery, they say, when you see the Northern Cross flying through the heart of the Milky Way."

"It's what?" I mumbled, trying to sort out what Esther had just said. I couldn't figure out what she was talking about. Wouldn't the Northern Cross always be in the Milky Way?

Slowly, she lowered our hands back down to the ground. Then, she turned toward me and whispered, "You'll know it when you see it, bro. And when you do, you'll be in for a lovely surprise."

She grinned and gazed back up into the sky. I lay there next to her, just trying to keep up as she pointed out more stars and constellations, explaining little details and obscure facts about various astronomical theories. I listened, enjoying the sound of her voice as I tried to fight off sleep at the same time.

"Leo, you know how fascinated I am with the stars," Esther said. "How about you? What do you like learning about?"

The question took me by surprise. "Um, I don't know," I said.

"Come on, Leo," she said. "There's got to be heaps of things. What are some things you find fascinating in life?"

"In life?" I asked incredulously, thinking that narrowed it down by, like, zero percent. "Well, I like reading about ancient history, especially Greek and Roman history," I said. "I like playing guitar for a campus fellowship group that's pretty interesting, and I love everything I'm learning up here at Northern Lights too."

"We're talking *like*, Leo, not love, not just yet, at least," she said, flashing a smile at me again. "So, what else do you like?"

"Um, let's see," I replied, trying to think. "I like hanging out with my friends at school and volunteering at a food shelf downtown too. I like working on my car, and . . . well . . . I like you."

I suddenly froze in silence. I hadn't meant to go there so carelessly. I wondered if she'd ask me why I said that, and I tried to think of a response as the silence between us grew. My words hung there for a while as we both gazed up at the stars high above.

Esther didn't seem to mind the silence. She didn't ask me what I meant either. After an awkward minute or two, I decided to blaze ahead and bounce the question back at her.

"Esther, what are some things you like?" I asked.

She grinned and gave a big sigh, as if she'd been waiting for me to ask. "Oh, there are so many things," she said. "I like hanging out with my mum and dad, and playing with my little sister, Anna. I like chilling with my high school mates, Cas and Polly. I think you'd like them too.

I like hanging out in Auckland and exploring New Zealand. It's so sweet there—the mountains, the coastline, the ocean, and the beaches. But it's so far away from the rest of the world."

As I listened to her talk, I wondered about Cas and Polly, and how good of friends they were. I wasn't so sure that I'd like them as much as she thought I would.

"And I like Chicago," she continued. "The classes at the university are awesome, especially the astronomy class. And of course, I like Aria too. She's the best friend a girl could ever ask for."

Esther paused as if she were thinking about how to say something else. Then, she spoke softly and deliberately. "Yeah, mate, I like you too," she said. "I reckon I like you a lot."

Esther didn't move, but she squeezed my fingers tightly in hers as she kept looking up at the stars above. My body rushed with adrenalin as I lay there next to her. I wanted to lean over and give her a kiss, but I wasn't sure if liking a girl in New Zealand meant the next step was to full-on kiss her or not. My mind raced with all kinds of ideas about how to respond, but it all got lost in a jumbled mess up in my head. Neither of us said anything for a long time. That didn't matter to me. It just felt wonderful to be there, lying next to her, holding hands, and looking up at the stars in the sky.

After a while, Esther finally squeezed my hand one last time. "Goodnight, Leo," she whispered.

I was falling again, drifting off to sleep in a heavenly bed of bright stars twinkling in the beautiful night sky high above.

"Goodnight, Esther," I whispered back.

As we drifted off to sleep, the moon slowly rose in the eastern sky just above the whispering pine trees. Esther kept her warm, soft hand wrapped around my cold fingers.

We fell asleep together for the first time.

chapter 33
wild surprises

"What the hell am I doing?"

A few hours later, I was up and at 'em. The morning light always seemed to wake me up, even if I hadn't gotten much sleep the night before. It's just the way I was made, I guess.

The girls were still sleeping soundly. In the night, Esther had snuggled up to Aria, and they were both almost completely covered inside their sleeping bags, all except for Esther's feet that were sticking out at the bottom of her bag. I sat up and looked at her toes. There were tan lines from her sandals crisscrossing the tops of her feet, and her toenails were painted a deep red that matched her lipstick and sunglasses. Her feet were dusty and dirty, but still so pretty.

I thought about starting the fire and making breakfast, but I figured the girls might want to sleep for a couple more hours, so I decided to go out in the canoe and explore the lake. Without making a sound, I lifted the canoe into the water and stepped in ever so carefully. Then, I kicked off the shore and coasted quietly out onto the glassy lake. I brought two cooking pots along to collect water for breakfast and dishes afterward.

It was a peaceful morning. The sky was baby blue with no clouds to speak of. The gentle breeze from the previous night had stopped entirely, and the lake looked like a giant mirror, reflecting the trees, rocks, and cliffs all around. Far away near the southern shoreline, a solitary loon floated on the water. It was no surprise to see loons everywhere in the Boundary Waters. They built nests along the edges of all the lakes and often could be seen with two or three fuzzy chicks trailing behind in the water, or sometimes even getting a free ride on their mother's back.

I paddled along the eastern shoreline, where I collected a few dead branches for the fire. Then, I quietly paddled out into the lake, trying not to make a sound. On the map, it looked like a giant hand, and there was an island that made a sort of gap between the thumb portion of the lake and the fingers. That's where I was headed.

On the way, I stopped in the middle to collect water. To do that, the pot first had to be swished around and around to clear away any floaties on the surface; then it was dipped under. I filled both pots—some for drinking, some for cooking, and some for washing dishes. I usually drank water straight out of large lakes, but this was an area of Saganaga that was smaller and shallower, so we'd boil our water or treat it with tablets before drinking any that morning.

As the island drew near, I floated along, looking at the shoreline on the right side. There among the bright yellow water lilies near the shore, two painted turtles watched me nervously. They didn't move an inch, but I could see their little eyes fixed on me. They sat motionless on a dead log, basking in the warm rays of the early morning sunshine. I knew that any sudden move on my part would send them diving for safety, so I paddled by slowly. I stared back at them as I floated past into the channel between the mainland and the island.

Suddenly, I heard a snorting sound and a splash in the water up ahead. I'd been staring down those turtles for so long; I hadn't been watching where I was going. When I turned to see what it was, I froze in horror. Standing directly in front of me was a huge female moose wading in a shallow part of the lake. She stared at me curiously as she munched on a mouthful of dripping water lilies.

"Holy cow!" I thought to myself. "What the hell am I doing?"

As the canoe floated straight toward her, I suddenly realized how much danger I was actually in. If I kept going straight ahead, in a few seconds, I would end up directly underneath the giant moose. During staff training, we were taught that bears could be handled easily, even scared away if necessary, but a moose was totally unpredictable and extremely dangerous. I'd even heard a couple of stories that summer about people getting trampled by angry moose. They weren't inherently mean, but they didn't like to be startled, and things could get ugly in a hurry.

Unfortunately, the canoe was heading straight for the long legs of the moose just a few feet away. As I floated toward her, the big female towered over me. Her long lanky legs stuck up out of the water higher than my head. I realized I couldn't merely cruise by and pet her as I passed. Something had to be done immediately, so I dug my paddle into the water and pushed it sharply forward to turn the canoe to the right, aiming for the deeper open water. Then, I took a big stroke and tried to gain momentum to get away.

It didn't help. Suddenly, the moose was right on top of me. I must have made her nervous, because she jerked her head back, let out a snort, and stepped forward in the water toward my canoe. That was enough for me! In a panic, I bailed out and plunged headfirst into the water, tipping the canoe, the firewood, and the waterpots into the lake as well. I stayed under for as long as I could hold my breath, maybe an entire minute or so. Under the water, I could still see the legs of the moose standing there not far away.

Finally, I couldn't hold my breath any longer. I came back up, surrounded by the branches I'd collected, the upturned canoe, and the cooking pots floating upside down in the water. Thankfully, I had drifted out into the lake a safe distance away from the moose. She looked unfazed. She was standing in the same exact spot, still munching on the water lilies, with her big black eyes staring down at me curiously. She must have watched the strange spectacle unfold, wondering the whole time at the unusual behavior of the terrified human in the silver canoe.

I grabbed my paddle and the pots before they sank to the bottom of the lake. Then, I flipped the canoe over and crawled back inside. It was an arduous task to paddle the canoe full of water to the edge of the lake, where I could finally get out and flip it back over. I noticed that the turtles hadn't moved a muscle during the entire episode. As I struggled with the canoe, they watched me cautiously from the safety of their perch on the log.

"You're welcome," I mumbled gruffly at the two unimpressed critics. "I hope you guys enjoyed the show."

When I finally got back into the canoe, I continued south through the channel. Then, I rounded the island and paddled back across the lake toward the campsite. I was sopping wet, unnerved, and more than a bit humiliated at my misfortune . . . or perhaps it was pure stupidity on my part. I refilled the water pots in the middle of the lake, then coasted quietly into the sandy spot by the campsite. I made sure not to make a sound as I pulled up to shore.

I tiptoed past the girls who were still out cold underneath their sleeping bags. I snuck back into the woods and quickly changed my clothes. Then, I went for a hike to find the throne and gathered some more dry wood for the fire. When I came back, Esther and Aria were still fast asleep, so I set to work on breakfast.

I had a feeling the girls would be hungry when they woke up. I knew I was. It had been a long paddle the night before, and then we'd stayed up for a couple more hours after that too. I thought about how Esther held my hand as we looked at the stars together. She said she liked me. I wondered what that meant. I wondered if it meant as much to her as it did to me.

I worked on the fire and mixed up a batch of pancake batter. Then, I boiled a pot of drinking water and another one for dishes later. I loved the quiet mornings on the lakes. I enjoyed cooking over the fire too. It was those times of solitude before anyone else was awake that seemed to energize me the most and renew my spirit. I needed that time to think, listen, and talk to myself. I wondered what new surprises the day would bring.

I felt ready for whatever it might be.

chapter 34
hot tang in the morning

"This is some mighty sweet jungle juice."

When Aria and Esther finally woke up, they yawned and stretched like two lazy cats waiting to be scratched and fed. By then, I had breakfast all laid out on the upturned canoe nearby.

"Good morning, sleepyheads," I said cheerfully. "Welcome to the land of the living."

"You're a geek," Aria mumbled as she gave me a scowl and flopped back down face-first into her sleeping bag.

"Good morning," Esther said with a long, slow yawn. She stretched her arms up high over her head, then rubbed her eyes and stuck her legs straight out on the ground in front of her.

"I'm sore from sleeping on this rock," she said. "I could really use a back scratch right now."

She looked so warm and delicious sitting there on top of her sleeping bag—her red hair all tangled up, her sleepy eyes blinking in the morning light, her hands rubbing her body, the same hands that held mine the night before.

"Leo, bro, what's for brekkie this morning?" Esther asked.

"Breakfast?" I said, resuming the guessing game. "I've got pancakes and syrup ready to go, and Chuck packed us three tangerines too."

"Johnny cakes? Choice, bro!" she exclaimed, poking Aria in the bottom. "Get up, cuz! It's time to get your A into G!"

Aria slowly sat back up. She was still half asleep, and she looked atrocious. Her hair was squished flat on one side, and on the other side, it was standing straight up in the air.

"Hey there, girlfriend," Esther said with a chuckle. "You're looking totally skux today."

"Thanks, how'd you sleep?" Aria replied, rubbing her eyes.

"Sweet as, cuz!" Esther said. "Like a box of budgies!"

"Awesome," Aria said sleepily.

"Straight up, eh!" Esther exclaimed. "Hey, girlfriend, let me have a squiz of that map, eh. Gizza geez!"

"Here you go, cuzzy," Aria said, blindly tossing the map in the air.

"Ta!" Esther said with a grin.

"Tata back at you, girlfriend," Aria replied, dropping back down in a heap on her sleeping bag.

"You're completely stuffed, eh, cuz?" Esther said.

"I guess so," Aria mumbled slowly with her face still buried in the sleeping bag.

"Beached as, eh?" Esther persisted.

"Sure am," Aria replied. "I'm totally wiped."

As I stirred the syrup, I listened to the girls chatter away. I had no idea what they were talking about. They sat there for a while. Then, they went down to the lake to look around. Then, they made a trip to the throne. Then, they came back and brushed their hair and puttered around on their sleeping bags again. I couldn't figure out why it took so long to get ready for the day.

Eventually, they made their way over to the fire. I was still babying the home-made syrup as it began to boil. It was made out of a cup of brown sugar and a squirt of vanilla, all packed up for us in a little plastic baggie by Chuck, our beloved trail shack coordinator. The pancakes were still fairly warm since I'd taken care to cover them with a lid and keep them close to the fire.

The girls were impressed with my cooking skills. I was just happy to do it, knowing Chuck would have been proud of my efforts. Chuck also packed us a bag of Russian tea for breakfast. It was a mixture of sugar, cinnamon, instant tea, and a generous amount of powdered Tang mix. It had a way of making you feel warm all over. We sat around the fire, warming up and downing the best pancakes in the world at that moment in time.

"This is some mighty sweet jungle juice," Esther said, sipping away on her cup of hot Russian tea. "I'll take another cup, thanks."

"Sure, here you go," I said, filling her cup with another helping of the sugary mix. "It'll really give you a kick in the morning."

"Man, I'm so tired," Aria complained. "I don't know how you do it, Farm Boy. How can you get up at the crack of dawn after last night? It must have been midnight before we fell asleep."

Esther glanced over at me and grinned from behind her steaming cup of hot tea. "Yeah, Leo," she said. "I'd really like to know how you do it, mate."

"Man, she looks hot!" I thought to myself as she sat there scrunched up next to the fire in just a sweater and jammy pants. She giggled softly and held the cup up in front of her mouth. Her sunglasses, which were riding on top of her head, suddenly dropped down onto her nose with a plop.

"Oh, crikey!" she exclaimed. Then, she straightened the sunglasses and blew into the steamy cup of tea, which immediately fogged up her glasses. She giggled again and kept sipping away on the tea.

"It must come from milking all those cows at six o'clock in the morning," I said sarcastically. "It's kind of hard for a farm boy, like me, to break old habits."

"Yeah, right! You never milked a cow in your life!" Aria scoffed.

"Maybe I have, maybe I haven't," I said. "But I've never been able to get much sleep if it's light out. I must be a morning person."

"That's right," Esther said. "You're a little sun sparrow, Leo, up and chirping away at the crack of dawn. I heard you shuffling around this morning getting things fixed for us."

"I was trying not to wake you guys up," I replied. "I figured you'd need your beauty sleep."

"Yeah, right," Esther chuckled. "See what it did to Aria here. She's looking mighty skux deluxe this morning!"

"Oh, leave me alone," Aria grumped. "I'm a night owl. I've tried to break my late-night habits, but it's so hard to do."

"Not if you have someone to talk to," Esther said, giggling again from behind her hot cup of tea and foggy sunglasses.

"I've tried coffee, but it tastes like crap," Aria said.

"How would you know that?" I said, going straight for the toilet.

"Shut up, Leo!" Aria complained. "Is this what you're like when you don't get any sleep?"

"Yeah," I confessed. "I'm always a potty-mouth on no sleep."

"Keep your trap shut then, or go to bed earlier," Aria snapped.

"I'm such a big nincompooper," I mumbled with a grin.

Esther giggled from behind her hot steamy sunglasses. "Man, she looks hot," I thought. "It looks like she's on fire over there."

"I've tried going to bed earlier," Aria continued. "But I never can get to sleep, and I end up tossing and turning all night long."

"You were out cold last night, cuz," Esther said. "Thank goodness I had Leo there to keep me company."

"Whatever!" Aria replied with a scowl. "I just have a hard time breaking old habits. You know, back in junior high, I had a big problem with swearing."

"And you don't now?" Esther said with another giggle.

"Well, it's still a work in progress," Aria admitted. "It used to be a lot worse until my mom heard me one day. We talked it over, and I agreed to cut it out and start talking like an adult."

"What does that mean?" Esther asked.

"Like a normal person," Aria replied. "You know—happier, less angry, less depraved. At least that's how my mom described it. You guys know I'm carrying a lot of baggage. It's probably from my upbringing—my nonexistent father, my so-called friends, and transferring to a new school in junior high."

"I know, that's rough," I said, turning serious. "I went to three different high schools myself. It's not too much fun."

"I dealt with it by talking tough," Aria said. "It didn't help, though. I think it just made me even angrier. After a while, I started to expect my life to be horrible, so it started coming out of me all the time—angry thoughts, bad words, and hateful speech."

"Not even, ow," Esther said sympathetically. "You were really packing a sad, eh, cuz?"

"Yeah, I was pretty depressed," Aria replied. "I didn't want that to become my new normal. I never went around swearing as a kid, so why did I start doing it in junior high?"

"Most of my chums back home swear all the time," Esther said. "It's part of the lingo, you know. So, you really think it's bad?"

"Well, it's not good, that's for sure," Aria replied. "It's not the best choice I could be making, as my mom would say."

"I think your mom is pretty smart," Esther said.

"When you think about it, yeah, it's bad, dirty, even filthy," Aria admitted. "I know I slip up sometimes, but I'm trying to honor my mom. Actually, she helped me pick out some better words to use instead of the really bad ones."

"Like what, Hunter?" I asked, fascinated to be getting a lecture on swearing from none other than Aria herself.

"Oh, like applesauce and fudge-pops," Aria replied, trying not to laugh as she said the words. "My mom and I picked out a few of my favorite foods and turned them into euphemisms."

"Awesome! That's totally sweet!" Esther exclaimed.

"Yeah, well, it's kind of weird, if you ask me," Aria said. "My mom seemed to like it, though."

"I want a food euphemism," I begged like a spoiled baby.

"Okay, Farm Boy," said Aria. "What's your favorite food?"

"Um, I like Russian tea, and these tangerines are pretty sweet too," I replied enthusiastically.

"That'll work," Aria said. "When you're upset, just say, 'tangerines!' And when you get really mad, you can say, 'Russian tea!'"

"Ha!" I laughed. "Hot tangerines! I love it!"

"How about you, Esther?" Aria asked, suddenly eager to share her mom's idea with the two of us.

"Oh, I don't know, cuz. Sometimes I swear a lot. It'd be a tough habit for me to break," replied Esther.

"Come on, what's your favorite food?" Aria insisted.

"All right, let me see," Esther pondered. "I like fizzy drinks and potstickers dipped in barbecue sauce."

"We can work with that," Aria said. "When you get angry, just shout, 'Potstickers!' or 'Fizzy pop!' or something like that."

"I don't know, cuz," Esther said. "I reckon I'll just stick with Leo on this one and go with hot tangerines."

I grinned and blurted out, "Hot tangerines! Esther, you're looking potsticking sweet this morning!"

Aria let out a long, miserable groan. "Maybe this wasn't such a good idea with nerd-man sitting right over there."

"Fizzle sticks," I replied. "Aria, why do you have to be so fudge-popping negative all the time?"

"Okay, moving on!" Aria said.

"Yeah, mate, I'm totally with you, sister!" Esther said coldly.

"Potstickers," I mumbled. "You guys are no fun in the morning."

"Hey, Esther, how about you?" Aria asked. "What's been the hardest habit for you to break?"

"Oh, girlfriend," Esther replied, suddenly feeling put on the spot. "I don't know. You'll have to let me think about that one for a sec." She took a sip of her tea and sat there for a minute. Then, she said, "I think a hard thing for me has been trying to stay positive and not let people get me down."

"What?" Aria exclaimed in disbelief. "Are you kidding me? You're the happiest person I know!"

"Well, I'm actually referring to my oldies," Esther said. "You know, my parents, and mostly, my dad—he was pretty hard on me, growing up and all. We haven't always seen eye to eye. In fact, lately, it only seems to have gotten worse."

"Why's that?" I asked, trying not to appear overly curious.

"Well, my dad thinks I've made some rather dodgy decisions in my life," Esther replied as she gazed into the smoldering fire.

"Like what?" Aria asked.

"I haven't exactly been the perfect daughter," Esther admitted. "My dad wanted me to be a lawyer or a doctor or something like that. Then, he wanted me to marry some college professor in Auckland. Yikes! I just about died and went to hell for turning that one down! So, we've had words about my career, my choice of friends, and even who I date. It goes on and on with him. My mum is quiet about it all, but I still get the feeling she's on board with my dad anyway."

"It sounds to me like they're just trying to control you," Aria said. "It's like they don't trust you or something."

"Maybe they're afraid of losing you," I offered. "Maybe they're having a tough time letting you go."

"I know they want the best for me," Esther said. "They just have a way of meddling into every little detail of my life. They're always knocking the way I dress and who I hang out with. They're still trying to tell me what to do, what to believe, how to behave, and even what career to choose."

"It's your life, not theirs," Aria said coldly.

"It's mostly my dad," Esther continued. "If I don't agree with him all the time, he up and throws a wobbly. I don't know what'll happen when I get back home. He was spewin' up a storm when I decided to come to the U.S. in the first place. When I go back, I'm worried he'll still be angry, and it'll all come around again."

"You have to live your own life," I said. "Your parents just have to learn to accept that and love you for who you are."

"I love how you see it like that, Leo," Esther said. "That's right proper of you, but that's not how my oldies see it."

Aria leaned over and nudged Esther. "Why didn't you tell me about it before?" she asked.

"I don't know," Esther said. "I guess I don't like to yak about my problems. It's a lot more fun just to be happy and enjoy life."

"Esther, that's who you are," I said.

"Sure, bro, that's who I want to be, but sometimes life can sort of mess things up, eh?" she said. "So, Leo, how about you? What are some things you struggle with?"

"Oh, I don't know," I replied. "I don't swear too much, and I get along with my folks most of the time. A few years back, though, I made a New Year's resolution . . . well, actually, it was just something I decided to do, or I mean, I decided not to do."

"What the?" Aria exclaimed. "What the freezing fudge-pop are you talking about, Farm Boy?"

"Yeah, I know," I said with a chuckle. "I tend to ramble. I just have a hard time talking about myself sometimes."

"No kidding!" Aria exclaimed. "You're talkin' in Greek parables half the cotton-picking time! You know, it's a miracle you've got any friends at all."

"I've got you, don't I?" I replied, smiling back at Aria.

"And me too, bro!" Esther added.

"Whatever," Aria huffed. "You guys are both weird."

I ignored Aria and continued. "I was just going to say that when I was in junior high, or maybe the tenth grade, or it might have been when I was a junior in high school, I don't know—"

"Spit the fudge-pop applesauce out for Pete sakes alive, boy!" Aria shouted. "We don't got all day, you know!"

"Okay, yeah," I said, taking a big breath of fresh air. "When I was younger, you see, I was kind of . . . a bully."

"What, you?" Aria began to laugh. "You've got to be kidding me!"

"Well, I was a bully in a friendly sort of way," I replied.

"Now, I've heard it all!" Aria exclaimed. She seemed strangely delighted to hear my sorry confession, but she still didn't know if she could actually believe it or not.

"No, really, Hunter," I said. "When I was in high school, I kind of teased my friends a lot. It was always just for fun, but sometimes it got out of hand. I remember one day, I was up to my usual self, and things got a little crazy with a couple of my friends. I ended up sucker-punching a kid named Jack. I didn't mean to hit him hard. It was just supposed to be a fake punch, but for some reason, I didn't stop myself in time, and I wound up knocking the wind out of him. He ended up on the floor, gasping for air. It probably wouldn't have affected me so much, but when he finally recovered, he was furious. That was it. He never talked to me again."

"Wow, Leo, I can't believe you bush-whacked some guy and totally knocked him out," Aria said with an admiring grin.

"Straight up, bro!" Esther said with a nod. "Congratulations!"

"You guys, that's not the point," I said. "After that happened, I decided that I wouldn't ever hit anyone ever again, and that kind of translated into everything else too—how I treat people, how I relate to them, even how I talk about them."

"Hey, Leo, I punch you all the time," Aria said. "You must think I'm such an awful person."

"No, Aria," I replied. "I love all that physical affection you give me. Seriously, my mom hugged me all the time, so when you slug me, it actually makes me feel good."

"Oh, really?" Aria said. "Well, in that case, Farm Boy, I'm gonna have to take you down, right now. Come on, let's go!"

As Aria stood up and took a step towards me, I spoke up in a hurry. "That's okay, Hunter! How about you just surprise me every now and then, like you've been doing. That seems to be working just fine."

"All right," Aria replied, backing off. "I'll just give you something to remember me by every once in a while. And now that I know it makes you feel so good, I think I'll go ahead and make sure you really feel the love."

"Aria!" Esther exclaimed with dismay. "Don't beat poor Leo up, you . . . you little sausage biscuit!"

"What was that you just said, cuzzy?" Aria asked as she slowly turned and gave Esther a quizzical look.

"You know, like what you said, you sausage biscuit pop!"

"Are you trying to say applesauce fudge-pop?" Aria asked.

"Yeah, that's it!" said Esther.

"That's not really how it works," Aria replied.

"Oh, I think it is, you saucy fudge-pop biscuit sausage!" Esther replied with a silly smile.

"Holy cow!" I said with a laugh.

"And then there's that little bit of profanity from the Iowa farm boy himself!" Aria exclaimed.

"Yeah, bro!" Esther chimed in as she began to laugh. "You gotta cut that 'holy cow' shit out, Farm Boy!"

"What? Now you're calling me, Farm Boy, too?" I complained with a wide-eyed look at Esther sitting there so cutely.

"Straight up!" she exclaimed defiantly. "You big biscuit sausage fudge-pop!"

"If my mom heard you swearing like that, I think she'd kick your sorry little applesauce back to grade school!" Aria said.

"Hot tangerines!" I exclaimed. "Both of you girls are driving me freaking fudge-pop crazy!"

"Both of you are bloody buffoons!" Esther exclaimed. "You guys know that, don't you?"

We all had a good laugh. For some reason, the silly play on words tickled my funny bone, and I couldn't stop giggling. I tried to stop, but every once in a while, I'd break out laughing again for no reason at all. Aria and Esther kept swapping fudge-pop sausages and hot applesauce biscuits back and forth until the holy cows came home, and I just watched with tears in my eyes, unable to stop chuckling at their crazy talk. An hour later, I was still giggling like a little schoolboy when we started packing up to go.

Aria stuffed her gear down into her pack and then made the big announcement, "I'm going to the throne, you fudge-pop applesauce biscuits, so hold on to your sausages until I get back."

"All right, Bear Bait," I called back. "Have fun mooning the mosquitoes back there in the woods." I knew she was too far away to even think about coming back to give me a beatdown.

There wasn't much to do after breakfast except pack up and load the canoes, but the rope we'd used to hang the food pack was not cooperating. I had lowered the pack down earlier to get our breakfast out, but the rope got tangled around a branch high up in the scraggly pine tree. The more I pulled, the tighter it got.

Esther came over and asked me what the trouble was. When I explained the predicament, she smiled and said, "It's okay, mate. I'll go up and fetch it down for you."

"You'll what?" I asked. "How are you gonna do that?"

"I'll climb on up and get it down, bro," she said, patting my shoulder like I was back in kindergarten. I could tell she had something to prove, so I stepped back to watch.

Esther went over to the tree and examined it carefully. Then, all of a sudden, she attacked it like a bear hugging a telephone pole and shimmied straight up the trunk to a big branch sticking out about ten feet off the ground. She swung a leg over the branch and pulled herself up into a seated position. Then, she stood up on the branch and continued to climb until she was perched right over the spot where the rope was caught. I watched from below as she loosened the knot and dropped the rope down to me.

Then, she worked her way back down, climbing like a koala bear from limb to limb. She swung down from the last big branch and then dropped to the ground, where she stumbled and fell straight into me. I tried to catch her, but she barreled right through me, knocking us both to the ground in a heap.

"Nice," Aria said dryly. "You two are so pathetic."

"Thanks for catching me, Leo!" Esther exclaimed with a smile. "That was right proper of you."

"I didn't catch you. You knocked me over," I replied.

"Yeah, nah," she said. "I was aiming for you the whole time, mate. So, you served your purpose."

"I served my purpose?" I asked, pretending to be offended.

"Yeah, I was trying to land right on top of you," she said, still smiling happily. "You're a good boy."

"You got that right," Aria said as she closed up one of the Duluth packs and started to giggle.

"I'm a good boy?" I replied, acting offended again.

Esther stood up and chuckled. "I don't know, but I'm bettin' you're one hell of a fizzy fudge-pop, bro."

"He's quite the steamy little sausage biscuit, ain't he?" Aria said with a cynical laugh.

"Sweet tangerines, you guys!" I exclaimed. "Enough with the freaking fudge-pop lingo already!"

But we just couldn't seem to stop it. As we got ready to go, we started right in on the funny food euphemism speak again. It was almost impossible to stop the silly talk once it got started. I'm not sure if Aria's mom would have approved of it or not.

As I cleaned up around the fireplace, the girls chattered away and packed up their things. They had quite a time getting everything back into their pack. It seemed as if their things had somehow expanded and multiplied overnight. To make more room, Esther pulled out her jacket, slipped it back on, then rolled up the sleeves. Aria pulled out a rain jacket and tied it around her waist. Lightening the load didn't seem to help all that much, though. Aria finally pounced on top of the ornery pack like a professional wrestler and squished it down as Esther scrambled to fasten the straps.

Afterwards, the girls sat there exhausted and rested for a while. Then, the chatter started up again right where it'd left off. Aria talked away as she gathered her hair into a kind of ponytail high on her head and tied it with a bandana. Esther began to talk about how excited she was that it was her birthday. Neither of the girls seemed to be in any rush to get going. As they continued to go about their business, I was more than content to just watch and listen.

I couldn't stop thinking about how Esther climbed the tree earlier. I'd always been attracted to strong women who loved the outdoors, but Esther just kept surprising me over and over again. I'd climbed trees before when I was a kid, but I'd never done it like she did—tackling it head-on like a bear and shimmying straight up the trunk. As I watched her climb that tree, I learned a couple of valuable lessons: First, how to climb a tree with your bare hands. Second, how amazing Esther was beginning to look to me.

I had a feeling it was more than that, though. I was beginning to feel funny in the head. After getting knocked down by Esther, it seemed like I couldn't shake a feeling of slight dizziness. As we hauled our packs and the canoe down to the lake, Esther kept smiling at me sweetly. I thought about all the times she'd expressed her interest in me—bringing me supper on that first night, kissing my cheek outside her cabin, holding my hand while we were stargazing, and then telling me she liked me. Suddenly, I realized what was going on. I was falling, literally, head over heels for her.

"Oh no," I thought. "Here we go again!"

chapter 35
monument portage

"Oh, you're stuck, you say?"

By the time we got on the water, the sun was already high in the sky. It looked as if it would be a good day for traveling west. There was only a slight breeze in the air along with a few fluffy white clouds overhead. We were grateful for the nice weather because we had a big day ahead of us and a long way to go.

There were several difficult portages along our route, starting with the first one just a mile west of our campsite. It would be the easiest one of the day. Within a half-hour we were there, sitting in our canoe and looking over at the next lake. It was just a few yards away across a narrow isthmus of rock that divided the two lakes.

"Let's just carry the canoe across," Aria suggested.

Esther and I agreed. Together, the three of us picked up the canoe, along with our packs still inside, and carried it across to the next lake, where we set it gently back into the water.

"That's one portage down, only ten more to go," I announced.

"They won't be as easy as this one," Aria said.

She was right. The next one, called Monument Portage, was eighty rods long and built right on the Canadian border. It was a rocky trail that climbed slightly to a ridge and then dropped back down to the next lake. There were two monuments along the trail that marked the American and Canadian sides of the border. The portage was only a few hundred yards ahead and already in sight.

As we paddled across the little lake, we were startled by a low-flying loon directly overhead. It gave out a strange hooting sound, then flapped its wings wildly as it swerved off to the right. We looked up and over to the north side of the lake just in time to see it crash into a long branch of a pine tree. I only caught the tail end of the peculiar tragedy as the loon dropped straight down out of the tree. With an awkward splash and a wretched squawk, it plopped like a rock into the shallow water near shore.

We watched and waited to see if it was okay or not. The bird flopped around in the water for a few seconds; then it righted itself and let out a mournful cry, "Ah-woo-oo-oo!" It was the saddest, most miserable bird call I'd ever heard.

We looked around and wondered what had just happened. Apparently, the show was over, just as abruptly as it began. The loon floated calmly in the water near the shoreline, preening itself or perhaps checking for any broken bones. Then, it just sat there and softly hooted as if life were back to normal. We looked at each other and then slowly broke into confused laughter.

"What was that?" Esther asked. "A baby eaglet?"

"No, a crazy loon!" Aria said. "I've never seen one do that before."

"Do loons always come in like that?" Esther asked. "That bird had the whole lake to land in, and it hit that tree bang on!"

"It must not have seen us when it was coming in," I suggested. "Maybe it tried to pull up, but it was too late, so it crashed into the tree branch and fell straight out of the sky."

"Hard out, bro!" Esther exclaimed. "That was a bit suss!"

"Sorry, loon! We didn't mean to scare you!" Aria cried sadly across the calm water.

"You should see one when it takes off," I said. "It's just like a plane barreling down an airport runway."

"What?" Esther asked.

"Yeah, it takes a loon about a hundred yards to get into the air," I explained. "It flaps its wings like crazy as it sprints on top of the water. It takes forever, but eventually, it gets airborne."

"That sounds like quite a show. Will we get to see one take off like that?" she asked.

"I don't know," I replied. "Maybe, if we get lucky."

We paddled on toward Monument Portage, which was directly in front of us. There was a wooden platform jutting out into the lake that looked like a large homemade dock. It was half-submerged beneath the surface of the water as if slowly sinking into the lake. The platform was surrounded by tall swampy grass that was growing along both sides of a long narrow walkway that ran straight to shore about two hundred feet away.

The trick was to stay on the walkway and never step off into the grass. I had learned that valuable lesson a couple of trips earlier when an eager kid stepped off by mistake and immediately sank up to his waist in the swampy muck. We pulled him back out, but he never did recover his shoes, which I'm sure, joined an abundance of other footwear down at the bottom of the swamp.

I warned the girls about the dangers of the grassy swamp as we pulled up next to the submerged dock. We unloaded our packs and climbed out onto the safety of the wooden platform. I was getting ready to lift the canoe when Esther spoke up.

"Hey, mates, I'd like to try portaging the canoe all by myself on this one," she said.

I gave her a skeptical look and replied, "How about I carry it for a while, and then maybe you can give me a break on the trail somewhere."

"Yeah, nah!" she said. "I'll lug it the whole way, if you don't mind me slogging along at my own pace, eh?"

Aria and I looked at each other and agreed to let Esther give it a shot. I flipped the canoe over onto the dock and lifted the front end up over my head.

"Okay, Esther," I said. "Go ahead and step into the harness, and I'll lower it onto your shoulders."

Esther hurried to slip underneath the canoe. She felt for the harness pads attached to the center rail; then she stepped forward to position them over her shoulders. I carefully lowered the front down and then let go. To my surprise, Esther grinned and immediately took off at a good pace up the dock toward shore.

"Are you okay?" I asked. "It'll get pretty heavy, you know."

"No worries, mate! She'll be right!" Esther exclaimed.

"Are you sure you don't want someone to go with you?" I called after her as she scampered away.

"Nah, it'll be a piece of piss!" Esther shouted back. She hopped off the dock and was soon completely out of sight, heading up the trail and into the woods.

"A piece of piss?" I replied, giving Aria a confused look.

"Yeah, she's just saying it'll be easy, like a piece of cake," Aria explained. "Except, in this case, it's like taking a piss."

"Okay, if you say so," I replied. I still didn't understand the whole piece of piss thing, but whatever.

"All right, let's get going," Aria said as she grabbed one of the Duluth packs. "Here, Leo, help me get this on my back."

"Yeah, we better catch up to Esther," I replied. "It's a pretty long portage." I held the pack up behind Aria as she wiggled her arms into the shoulder straps.

"Chill out, Leo, she's got it," Aria said reassuringly as she turned and took off up the dock. "You gotta learn to relax and give these things time to work themselves out."

"What things?" I said, hoisting the other pack onto my back and grabbing my guitar. "It's an eighty-rod portage!"

"Come on, Farm Boy! Get a move on!" Aria shouted as I raced to catch up to her.

We walked along the trail for quite a while with no signs of Esther anywhere. I started to wonder where she could have gone as we passed the first monument along the path. It was a large silver post about three feet high, square in shape, and sticking up out of a concrete pad. We didn't stop to look at it. We just kept on trudging ahead up the trail, looking for any signs of Esther.

When we reached the second monument near the peak of the portage, I began to worry about her. Going downhill was easier than going up, but it was trickier too. We'd seen no sign of Esther anywhere. We continued on, declaring that Esther was somehow related to Wonder Woman and was probably waiting for us down at the water's edge on the other side of the portage.

Then, we saw her canoe lying in the middle of the trail. It was just sitting there upside down, and Esther was nowhere to be seen. We looked around for her, but she was gone.

"Esther!" Aria called into the woods. "Where are you?"

We listened for a few seconds, waiting for a response. Then, from underneath the overturned canoe came a low muffled reply. "No worries, mates, I'll be along in a jiff."

We waited for Esther to move, or crawl out, or say something else to explain herself, but the canoe didn't move, and she said nothing more. Aria and I looked at each other and then turned our attention back to the canoe. We weren't about to leave her there.

"Would you like a hand?" I asked, finding the situation to be somewhat humorous.

"Nah, I'll be all right," came the pleasant reply, followed by more silence. We both continued to stare at the canoe.

"Well, what are you doing under there?" I asked.

"Just sitting here," Esther replied.

She said sitting, but it sounded strangely peculiar to me, sort of muffled and slurred, like another word similar to "sitting" but not quite as politically correct.

"You know, Esther, most people go a ways off the trail to take a sit," I said, beginning to crack up. "It's more discreet that way."

Aria glared at me, then snapped, "Leo, you jerk!"

We stared at each other for a couple of seconds. Then, we both started to laugh. We looked back at the canoe again with Esther still "sitting" there underneath it.

"Okay, mate," Esther finally said. "I reckon you could grab the front and lift it back up for me, thanks."

"Are you sure you want me to do that?" I replied, still holding to the nasty theme. "Have you finished sitting under there, or should we wait until you're done?"

"All right, wise guy!" she exclaimed. "You got me, Leo! Just don't expect me to save your bum the next time you get stuck."

"Oh, you're stuck, you say?" I teased, halfheartedly trying to regain my composure and better judgement.

I slowly lifted the front of the canoe, revealing poor Esther, squatting down underneath it like a squished pile of steamy pancakes. Her yellow life jacket was jammed forward over her head like a pad of butter gently sliding down on top of her long red hair that oozed out like thick maple syrup in every direction. With great effort and a good deal of complaining, Esther stood up, straightened her life jacket, and tried to rub the mud off her bare legs and knees.

I held the canoe up high over my head, trying to appear humbly concerned. It wasn't easy, because inside I was feeling quite satisfied with myself, like the witty superhero that I knew I was.

"All right, there you go, Esther," I said with a smirk. "I'd be happy to take a sit now."

Aria couldn't help but laugh from behind the canoe. Without saying a word, Esther glared at me and then moved back under the canoe. I tried to sober up, but I was still giggling like a schoolboy.

"I'm sorry, Esther," I apologized. "I'm just teasing you . . . well, you know . . . because I like you."

Oops, there it was again, out in the open. My true feelings for Esther somehow slipped out by mistake, or possibly, pure stupidity. I knew it would happen, just not at that critical and somewhat tender juncture of the trip.

Esther threw me a sarcastic grin from under the canoe. "Oh, really? You like me, Farm Boy?" she snapped back.

She stepped forward into the harness, then wobbled unsteadily to the right as the canoe came down on her shoulders. I grabbed on to the side of the canoe to help stabilize it as Esther stepped back to the left and struggled to regain her balance.

"Oh, bust it!" she shouted as she pushed down on the front of the canoe to level it out again. She stood there with her feet spread out wide, visibly shaking under the weight of the canoe.

"Are you sure you're going to be okay?" I asked one more time. "I'd be happy to take it from here."

"Straight up, Farm Boy! She'll be right!" Esther said fiercely as she stared straight ahead with a determined look. "I'm good as gold! Let me go, bro!"

I hesitated but finally took my hands off the canoe.

"Okay, Esther," I warned. "Just don't ask me to save your butt the next time you get . . . stuck."

I suddenly realized I had stepped over the line one too many times, maybe more, so I finally shut up for good, but it was already too late. I moved aside as she walked up next to me.

"Okay, wise guy!" she snapped. "Thanks a heap!"

Out of the blue, Esther's fist shot out from under the canoe and punched me squarely in the stomach. It took me by surprise and knocked the wind completely out of me. I buckled over and smacked my forehead on the side of the boat, which sent my John Deere hat flying straight up where it came to rest on top of the canoe. Gasping for air, I dropped down on my butt beside the muddy trail. The heavy Duluth pack, still strapped to my back, slowly pulled me over on my side and pinned me to the ground. In a huff, Esther stomped off, leaving me to wallow in my own misery.

In between gasps for air, I called out to her. "Wait! My hat! It's on top of the canoe!"

"Watch it, Tootles!" Esther yelled back. "I just might have to save your pathetic bushman's arse next time!"

I sprawled helplessly in the mud as Aria walked forward and looked down at me with a bewildered stare.

"Good grief, Leo, what is going on?" she asked.

"I know, I deserve it," I said, still gasping for air.

"I told you, Farm Boy," she replied with a grin of satisfaction. "Don't mess with Esther." Then, she took off down the trail, leaving me there to think about that little nugget of wisdom for a while.

"What's a bushman's arse?" I called to Aria.

"Oh, Farm Boy!" she called back. "You've got one! Totally! And it's mighty fudge-poppin' cute too!"

I lay back down in the mud for a while, wondering how to get back on my feet again. I tried to stand up, but I couldn't get the pack dislodged from the sticky mud patch to which it was glued. After several attempts to roll this way and that, I finally gave up and rolled back onto my side, letting the pack have its way with me. As I struggled to yank my left arm out of the shoulder strap, I suddenly realized that a stranger was standing there watching me. I looked up at the curious hiker, who was smiling pleasantly down at me.

"Need a hand, eh?" he asked politely.

"No, I'm fine," I said and resumed my wrestling match with the stubborn pack, which by then had become a living entity still clinging to my body. It seemed to have a personal grudge against me and an intelligence that apparently surpassed my own.

"All right then, have a nice trip, eh," the happy hiker said as he walked away, whistling a merry tune.

I lay there for a while—paralyzed, frustrated, and alone. I'm sure I mumbled a few horrid curses at the nasty pack as I lay helplessly in the mud beside the trail that wound up and down somewhere along the inhospitable wilderness of the Canadian border. Another cheerful hiker, carrying a canoe, walked by and laughed under his breath as he lumbered forward down the trail.

"Canadians," I thought. "Why are they always so happy?"

chapter 36

mermaids and pirates

"Second star to the right and then straight on till morning!"

After finally escaping from the Duluth pack, I made my way down to the lake where the girls were waiting. They were already floating in the canoe about twenty yards offshore.

"Are you coming, Farm Boy, or should we just leave you there?" Esther called indignantly.

"I'm sorry, Esther!" I cried. "I know, I'm an idiot!"

"What took you so long anyway?" she said, pretending to be offended. "Were you pashing on that Canadian girl back along the trail, or what? She was pretty cute, you know."

"What? I didn't see any girl on the trail!" I exclaimed.

"Making out in the wop-wops!" Esther mused openly. "I'm bettin' hard cash on it. Aria, what do you think, girlfriend?"

"Nah, he wouldn't even know what to do!" Aria shouted in my direction. She flashed her eyes at me and grinned as if to say, "Leo, you're in so much trouble."

I stood helpless and pitiful on the shoreline, reeking with embarrassment, knowing there was nothing I could do or say to get out of the muddy mess I'd dug for myself back along the trail.

"I'd really like to come with you lovely ladies!" I cried.

"Oh, we're lovely ladies now!" Esther teased sarcastically. "First, the bro says he likes us. Then, he calls us lovely ladies. What do you think about them apples, Aria?"

"Things are getting way too touchy-feely for me," Aria said dryly.

"Please, come and pick me up," I begged from the edge of the water. "I really don't want to starve out here in the wilderness!"

"I don't know," Esther replied as she pondered the request, not yet satisfied with my attempt to make good. "What else might the grotty poofter think of us?"

Assuming she meant me, I gave a big sigh and sucked it up. "Okay," I said. "I think you are sweet and nice and intelligent, and of course, extremely beautiful, and I would really, really like to get in the canoe with you and get going now."

Esther grinned deviously and asked, "Who exactly are you talking about there, Leo? Me or Aria?"

"Oh, good grief!" I thought. "I'm still not off the hook."

"Um, both of you," I replied, "but of course, each of you in your own special ways."

"And extraordinary ways?" Esther added.

"Yes, and extraordinary ways," I agreed wholeheartedly.

"And spectacular ways?" Esther egged me on.

"Yes, and spectacular ways," I cried, about to lose my mind. I walked into the lake, still lugging the muddy pack, which was getting heavier by the second.

"I'm so sorry for making fun of you, Esther," I begged. "I'll never say such horrible things about you ever again. I honestly didn't mean to hurt your feelings, but now I see that I did. I'm an idiot. I'm not sweet or nice or intelligent or beautiful or spectacular like you. I'm just a stupid man, and I'm so, so sorry."

Esther finally had what she'd been waiting for, a pathetic apology from a pathetically embarrassed idiot who finally realized how stupid and insensitive he was. She moved the canoe forward, grinning from ear to ear as I waded in the water, looking like a wet rat that just lost a wrestling match with the Swamp Thing.

"Smile, Leo!" she called to me as the canoe drifted in.

"Huh?" I wondered, looking up. "Oh, no! Please, no!"

"Oh, yeah!" she chuckled. "Say cheese, you dirty dipstick! I want to remember this amazing cracker of a day!"

Esther snapped a photo of me standing in the lake. I tried to smile, but I probably only managed a pathetic grimace instead.

"That's a keeper for sure!" she exclaimed with a smile.

"That was really sick, Leo," Aria said as they pulled up next to me.

"I know, but I really need a ride," I said. I threw the pack in, along with my guitar, and lunged over the side into the middle of the canoe. "Thanks for stopping to pick up your long-lost friend."

"Yeah, no problem," Aria said with a satisfied smirk. "You're an idiot, but I still love you."

"Back at you, Bear Bait," I replied, heaving a sigh of relief at not getting left behind. "I'm really feeling the love right now."

"Thanks, Farm Boy," she said. "You know, we couldn't leave a hunk like you standing around alone like that in the woods. The moose up here in Canada might start to get ideas."

"You shouldn't talk," I replied. "You're pretty fudge poppin' cute yourself, Hunter."

"Crikey, mates!" Esther exclaimed. "Now, who loves who in this happy little love triangle we've got going on here?"

"I don't love anybody," Aria replied with a cynical laugh.

"Oh, I don't know, cuz," Esther insisted. "I've noticed you cracking onto a certain joker quite a few times now, girl."

"Come on! Give me some props, girl," Aria replied. "You're the one who's been on cloud nine for the past week or so."

Speaking of clouds, as I listened to the girls talk, I had my eye on the sky. In the west, long streaks of thin wispy clouds were slowly stretching eastward in the upper atmosphere. They looked like silky white strands of hair curled up at the ends. It was gorgeous out, but I knew what the delicate wisps of cirrus clouds meant.

A change in the weather was on the way, possibly rain later that day or the next. I didn't worry too much about it, though. There was no use in fretting about the weather, at least not yet anyway. It was too nice outside to care. The sun was shining down on us in the blue sky above. We would deal with it when the time came.

As I drifted back to the conversation at hand, I had no idea what the girls had been talking about. I tried to figure it out, but like so many other times, I was just desperately trying to catch up. I knew I'd always be the outsider in conversations that were so esoteric. Still, it was a pretty sweet spot to be in. I strummed away on my guitar as the girls carried me lazily across the lake under the hot sun to a land of make-believe far, far away.

"Yeah, right!" Esther exclaimed. "You were too! You're just getting a wee bit snarky about it, girl."

"Oh, yeah, there I go again," Aria said sarcastically. "You know I'll always love you more than I could love any man!"

"Oh, Aria! I love you too, sweetie!" Esther cried. "You're my best friend in the whole entire world."

"You're mine too!" Aria replied.

I had to admit, the way the girls carried on back and forth was pretty entertaining. It reminded me of my trip with the lost boys from Minneapolis a few weeks earlier. At times, it looked like they'd almost come to blows, and then ten seconds later, they were back loving on each other again.

Whatever it was the girls had been talking about, I had no desire to jump into that hot mess. I was more than content to simply lay back, strum on my guitar, and let the girls hash things out for themselves. I knew my place. I was just the boy captain of a ship with two surly sailors who couldn't keep their foul mouths shut. I happily settled back for a sweet ride across the next lake as they talked up a storm and did all the work for me.

"Bust a gut, girlfriend!" Esther cried from the stern. "Let's get back on this little Tiki-tour of ours! You know, I'd like to get to my lake before the sun sets tonight!"

"Two thumbs up, sister!" Aria cried. "Which way is it, Leo?"

"Second star to the right and then straight on till morning!" I cried in my captain's voice from my cozy perch on the poop deck.

We moved out of the swampy bay into Ottertrack Lake: a long slender body of water that stretched for five or six miles southwest along the Canadian border. I would've liked to take it all the way down and do a hop, skip, and a jump over a short portage into Knife Lake, but Esther had taken command of the ship.

She had her heart set on swimming in Esther Lake on her birthday, which she had been constantly reminding us was that Friday—

and Friday had finally arrived. I'm not sure if I actually believed it, but that's what she said, and at that point, I wasn't in any position to argue. After all, she was in the back steering the canoe, and I was just the cheap entertainment curled up between the Duluth packs playing guitar to pass the time. I should have been more careful on that Friday. I should have known better, but I was just along for the ride as Esther flew off into Neverland like a delirious child who believes in talking dogs and flying fairies.

"I'm so excited!" Esther squealed as we floated into the portage off Ottertrack. "My lake is right over the next hill!"

On the other side of the portage was the lake she had begun to claim as her own. It was named Esther Lake after all, and she had finally arrived to let the whole world know it belonged to her.

The portage to get there, however, was not an imaginary piece of cake. It was only eighty rods, but for most of the way, it climbed steeply upwards through mud and rocks, then over mucky puddles near the top. Then, it was a steep descent back down. Thankfully, Aria shouldered the canoe and took off bravely up the hill.

"I bet you're ready for this one," I said as I loaded a pack onto Esther's shoulders.

"Too right!" she exclaimed with glee. "I can't wait to see my lake!" She marched off up the trail like a happy whirlwind, chatting cheerfully to herself. I grabbed the other pack and followed behind.

We caught up to Aria at the top of the hill, and she needed a break. I walked around to the front of the canoe and grabbed on to the bow as she lowered the back end down. She stepped out from underneath the canoe, then took the pack off me and hoisted it on her own back. Then, she held the canoe up for me to carry the rest of the way. The two of us had swapped out like that quite a few times on the trip earlier in the summer. The kids in that group didn't especially like carrying canoes, so we did most of it, and it had become routine.

Esther trekked on ahead excitedly as Aria and I followed behind down a steep, deeply-rooted trail that fell sharply off and ended at the glistening waters of the lake below. When we got there, Esther was flittering about like a fairy high on pixy dust.

"It's my lake. It's so pretty. I love it!" she kept saying over and over. She was giddy with excitement and beaming from ear to ear.

Actually, the spot where the portage ended was near a swampy bog with mosquitoes buzzing around everywhere. There were dozens of dead cedar logs floating off to the east where the wind had pushed them over time. The mosquitoes were relentless, so in a rush, we tossed our packs into the canoe and took off again.

I took the stern and let Esther duff in the middle to enjoy her lake. We paddled hastily out of the buggy portage to escape the mosquitoes that were desperately trying to keep up. The lake gradually opened up into a long beautiful stretch of water that extended southwest for about two miles. I studied the map to make sure we didn't go shooting off into a deceptively large bay on our right. I was also looking ahead to locate an island we had to go around that had a couple of nice campsites at both ends of it.

"It's my lake!" Esther said over and over again. "I love it. It's so pretty!" We listened to Esther express her undying love for her lake as we paddled along and laughed at her silly expressions.

After a while, Esther calmed back down. She stretched out in the middle of the canoe, enjoying the ride of a lifetime across her very own lake. As I paddled, I couldn't help but notice her lying there in front of me—her body sprawled out on top of the packs, her arms dangling loosely over each side, her fingers trailing in the water—head back, eyes closed, grinning contentedly, and soaking up the warm rays of glorious sunshine. She was so completely and utterly carefree, so exuberant about life, finding joy and pleasure in each moment of her own human existence as it came to her each day—like a great blessing bestowed upon her from above simply to open and enjoy.

As we moved across the lake, I wondered how many relationships she had been in and how serious they were. I wondered why she was flirting with me so freely and if she really wanted me to pursue her, to kiss her, or more. Or was she just playing with me? Did she even know what she was doing? Did she even care? There was so much about her I didn't know, but I was still helplessly fascinated, still wildly obsessing, and I was ready to pursue her if she let me.

As we paddled into the big open part of the lake, Esther began to stir again with excitement. To my utter delight, she started taking her clothes off. I just kept paddling and tried not to stare. Esther resumed her adoring descant for the lake as she stripped down to her swimsuit: a pure white bikini that looked amazing on her body.

Aria called back, "Esther, are you okay back there, girl?"

I couldn't help but respond immediately and rather exuberantly. "She's fine, Aria, just fine!"

Without giving us any warning, Esther stood up in the canoe, threw her arms out wide, and shouted, "It's my birthday!"

Then, with a scream, she leaped out of the canoe, straight into the lake. We just about tipped over during the spontaneous celebration, but thankfully, the canoe managed to stay afloat.

"Okay, then!" Aria shouted into the air as Esther sank under the water. "That's my girl!"

Esther surfaced and screamed at the top of her lungs, "Oh, Aria! It's freezing! But it feels wonderful!"

"Happy birthday, cuzzy!" Aria shouted back. "You're the one who wanted to swim in Esther Lake, remember!"

"Come on, Aria!" Esther replied desperately. "Get on in here!"

I looked up at Aria and asked, "You're getting in too?"

"Yeah, we sort of had a bet going," she said, grinning back at me. "A couple of nights ago, she told me that if we made it to Esther Lake on her birthday, she was going to, um . . ." Aria hesitated. "She said she was going to jump in the lake and go for a swim."

"So?" I asked, still bewildered.

"So," Aria hesitated again, "I promised to jump in with her."

"So, what are you waiting for?" I asked.

"Well, if I jump in, she might do something else," Aria tried to explain. "So, I'm not really sure if I want to encourage her or enable her . . . or whatever."

"What in the world are you talking about?" I asked. Her words made no sense to me, but I was getting used to it.

"Oh, nothing, probably," she muttered as she stripped down to her bathing suit: a dark green bikini that sparkled in the sunlight.

"Awesome!" Esther cried with delight. "Jump on in!"

I steadied the canoe as Aria stood up and then lunged over the side. She stayed under for a long time, but I wasn't worried. I could see her in the water below, moving like a dark shadow, coming up directly under Esther. "She's a good swimmer," I thought. "She looks like a big green frog or maybe a hungry crocodile."

Suddenly, Esther screamed and sank under the water. At the same time, Aria shot up to the surface, laughing hysterically. Esther popped up right after her and proceeded to attack her fiercely. The two girls splashed wildly in the lake like two carefree mermaids, laughing and screaming and having a wonderful time.

"You tried to drown me!" Esther shouted with glee. "Is this what I get on my twenty-first birthday?"

"What are best friends for?" Aria exclaimed, taking off away from the canoe. "Come on, girlfriend, let's get away from Leo."

"Why?" Esther cried as she followed Aria.

"You know!" Aria shouted as she swam away. "He's too much of a grown-up to appreciate what we're gonna…" I couldn't make out anything else as the two girls swam furiously away.

They kept swimming until they were nearly a hundred yards away. It looked as if they'd be out there for quite a while, so I crept forward and took Esther's cozy spot in the middle of the canoe. There was hardly any wind on the calm lake. The sun was warm and bright. It was a perfect time to enjoy a little catnap.

I took in a big breath of fresh air and stretched out in the canoe just as Esther had earlier, letting my fingers dip into the calm water, soaking up the warm sunlight. The canoe rocked gently back and forth, slowly spinning like a dry leaf on the lake as a slight breeze inched it to the south. I closed my eyes and let my starry-eyed mind go anywhere it wanted to. I began to think about Esther again—sweet, romantic thoughts—beautiful, enchanting thoughts.

"She's like a swan flying in the sky," I thought. "I'd like to see her soar across the heavens. I'd like to hold her close and kiss her pretty lips." I snatched a glance at the girls swimming far away. Then, I closed my eyes again and drifted peacefully off to sleep.

When I awoke, I was a mile high, flying through fluffy white puffs of clouds, looking down on the glistening waters below. I was so far up that I could see Hanson Lake to the south and other smaller ones off to the east and west. Far below in Esther Lake, a tiny silver boat floated aimlessly in the clear blue-green waters. I could see immense rock formations lurking under the water's surface in various places, and dark deeper areas farther out in the middle of the lake, where two creatures appeared to be heading farther and farther away from the little boat. They were swimming around in circles, lunging in and out of the water, and splashing each other with their tails—two beautiful mermaids playing in a sea of make-believe.

I began to slowly descend back down out of the sky when suddenly, I noticed a group of red boats—four of them—coming up from the south, out of a narrow passageway next to a long slim island. They appeared to be pirate ships on the high seas, loaded down with filthy sailors and plunder of every kind. As they approached, I could make out a black flag attached to the bow of the lead ship. There were rough-looking bearded men in the ships, and they were moving quickly across the water, making a beeline straight for the two playful mermaids. A panic swept over me as I suddenly realized the mermaids were in grave danger.

Then, all of a sudden, I felt a jolt, as if I were plummeting straight out of the sky. I jerked awake in the canoe—still alone, still rocking gently on the calm water. I gazed up at the fluffy clouds floating by peacefully in the blue sky above. I felt the warm sunlight on my skin. "Life is fine," I thought to myself. "Yeah, it's mighty fine." I closed my eyes and began to drift off to sleep again.

"Hello there!" a deep and melodic voice suddenly called out to me from across the water somewhere nearby.

"Hey!" I blurted out as I sat up—my heart pounding—somewhat embarrassed to be caught off-guard. Coming up on my left were four canoes—nine people, all men, a fishing party probably. They were drawing up closer than I'd have liked, closer than they should have.

"Hello!" the man in the lead canoe called out again. "You got some swimmers with you?"

He looked grim and melancholy as he eyed me carefully and chewed on the short remains of a fat cigar. A smaller man in the front of the canoe chuckled slightly as he cleaned his spectacles in his chubby little hands. They looked like two tiny skylights reflecting the sunlight directly into my eyes.

"Is he doing that on purpose?" I wondered.

I looked around in every direction, but Aria and Esther were nowhere to be seen. "Um, yeah," I tried to explain. "I did, but I don't know where they're at right now."

"Thought so," the lead man replied as the others in his party eyed me and my canoe. "We saw 'em up here when we were back a ways. They must have gotten away from you, huh?" The men looked on starkly as I mulled over how exactly to respond.

"Um, yeah, I guess so," I agreed halfheartedly. I didn't especially like being questioned by strangers on the lakes. Their cold dark eyes stared back at me suspiciously.

"They're fishing for more," I thought. "They should've kept their distance too. They should have known better."

For a second, I started to panic again, as if someone had shaken me awake out of a terrible nightmare. Where had the girls gone?

"Come along, Tom," one of the men finally said as he baited the hook on his fishing pole with a worm that looked like a wiggly noodle. "Let's be on our way, captain."

"Well, you take care then," the lead man said in an overly dramatic fashion. "I sincerely hope you find your missing swimmers." He swung his paddle back into the water and heaved a heavy sigh. Like obedient dogs, the other men followed suit.

"Safe travels," the little man in the front chirped as he tipped his hat towards me. The gloomy party of fishermen paddled off in a long line—one behind the other as if they were playing follow-the-leader. They began to hum a jolly tune as they moved swiftly away across the big open part of the lake.

Still dazed and confused, I scanned the surface of the water all around for any sign of the girls. A wave of desperation swept over me as my heart began to race wildly like a broken clock deep inside my chest. Then, I felt a tug on the canoe—a real tug that time. Then, suddenly, a hand shot straight up out of the water near the bow of the boat, then another, followed by the heads of Esther and Aria—both of them gasping for air.

"Are they gone yet?" Aria whispered hoarsely.

I stared at the two girls, clinging for dear life to the front of the canoe, sucking in fresh air in such a frenzy, it was as if they'd been holding their breath for a half an hour.

"Where have you been?" I asked, more than a bit confused.

"We got the willies when we saw them coming!" Esther blurted out, still gasping like a racehorse. "We swam for the canoe and when they got close, we ducked underwater!"

"We stayed down there this whole time," Aria exclaimed. "Why didn't you get rid of them sooner?"

"I don't know. I didn't know where you were," I replied.

"Really? You didn't know?" Aria said harshly. "Couldn't you see us down there?"

"I don't think so," I said, considering carefully what to say next. Then, I finally admitted, "Actually, I was daydreaming. I was having a sweet dream about two pretty mermaids."

"You were daydreaming!" Aria shouted. "A sweet dream about two mermaids? You big jerk!" She swung her arm and splashed a tidal wave of water up at me in the canoe.

"Yeah, daydreaming," I replied, irritated at receiving the surprise bath and getting yelled at besides.

"So, you didn't see us, eh?" Esther repeated the million-dollar question in a slightly less hostile manner.

"No, I didn't see you," I said obediently, giving the correct answer to the all-important question of the day.

"Really? Not once?" Aria asked again.

"No, not until right now," I said, pleading my case. "I swear, I didn't see you until you popped up right next to the canoe."

The girls glanced at each other and slowly grinned. Apparently, I had finally convinced them of the truth.

"Good!" they said in unison.

"You're sure you didn't see us?" Aria asked again.

"No!" I shouted back. "Why do you keep asking me that?"

"Oh, never mind!" Aria said as they grinned at each other again, looking suspiciously naughty.

"Leo," said Esther, gazing tenderly into my eyes. "Would you do just one more thing for us now, bro?"

"Okay, what?" I asked.

"First, you have to promise that you'll do it," she said.

"Promise to do what?" I asked, completely confused at that point.

"Just promise, Leo, okay?" she insisted.

"Okay," I mumbled. "I promise." I rolled my eyes as the girls just stared cautiously back at me. I knew we weren't going anywhere until they were completely satisfied with my response.

"I promise!" I yelled, repeating the correct answer even louder to reassure them that I was totally on board with whatever it was that I was about to do because I was promising to do it.

"Okay," Esther said. "Turn around and look the other way."

"Why?" I asked dumbly.

"Leo, you promised!" she shouted frantically. "Just turn around and look the other way until we say so."

At that moment, if it had been Aria or any other person in the entire world, I would have lied through my teeth, but for Esther, I was willing to do just about anything. Still, I heaved a loud frustrated sort of sigh; then I flopped over on the packs and waited impatiently for the mystery to run its course.

I heard the girls duck under the water and then nothing. It was completely silent, just like I was back floating on the lake by myself, not only ten minutes before. What were they doing down there? I had no idea, so I just stared at the bottom of the canoe.

Suddenly, up they came, back to the surface of the lake. The girls looked up at me and then broke into laughter. For some reason, they were in a much better mood than before.

"What's going on?" I asked.

They glanced at each other and grinned again. I waited for an explanation, but they just ignored me and kept right on laughing.

“Leo, hold on to the boat,” Aria said as she swam to the back of the canoe. “I’m getting back in.”

“Me too,” Esther said, clinging tightly to the bow of the boat.

As both of the girls struggled to get their bodies up and over the sides, I hung on for dear life. The canoe rocked precariously back and forth and almost tipped over a couple of times. It was a terrifying process to watch . . . or listen to. Like a good boy, I closed my eyes and politely looked away. It wasn’t hard to imagine what was going on. It was just better not to see it. There are some things that just aren’t fit to watch, and that was probably one of them.

After all, I’ve never been a fan of horror movies. They give me nightmares, and I didn’t want to have any nightmares that night, so I just looked away and let the gruesome process run its course. Still, I couldn’t help but hear the painful soundtrack as the girls worked their way back into the canoe. I was just glad when it was over.

Once they were safely back on board, the girls grabbed their clothes and got dressed in a flash. In fact, they dressed in such haste, it looked as if their very lives depended on it. Once their lifejackets were on, they swung into high gear. They raced us down the lake like a speedboat, past the island campsites and on toward the narrow channel that linked Esther to Hanson Lake.

Along the way, I twanged out irritating little tunes on my guitar and tried not to think about what had just happened. Maybe I was just an innocent country hick from the corn fields of Iowa, but sometimes those two big city-slickers could really be weird.

“So, what was all that about anyway?” I finally asked.

“Shut up, Leo,” came Aria’s terse reply.

“What did you guys do back there?” I asked.

“Nothing,” she responded.

“What?” I asked again.

“Shut up, and play your guitar,” she said. “It sounds nice.”

Thus ended the brief question and answer segment of the trip. Esther kept quiet as she paddled furiously along with Aria. Neither of them seemed eager to shed light on the subject, so I stopped asking and just accepted it for whatever it was.

Actually, I knew what it was. I was just jealous that I'd been so rudely excluded. There was no hope for me, and I knew it. Esther had claimed the lake for herself, and it made me just a bit jealous. It's true. I wanted a part of it for myself. It was her birthday, I guess, so she had a right to do whatever she pleased. Still, I felt excluded. I know, I said that already, but it just kept digging at me. So, I played dumb for the rest of the way across the lake.

To be completely honest, I was just trying to get the girls to open up and let me in on the secret. But they wouldn't budge, so I stopped asking and just let it go. It was a lesson I was still trying to figure out for myself. After all, it wasn't what they'd done that was bothering me. It was something I was trying to sort out in my own head. Whatever it was, it was damned confusing!

To make matters worse, as we passed through the channel into Hanson Lake, Esther turned around in her seat and took one last look back at her very own lake and bid it a fond farewell.

"Goodbye, my beloved lake!" she cried. "I will remember you with deepest affection for the rest of my life. You are my greatest and truest love, as far as lakes go, and I'll treasure the intimate moments we've spent together, now and forever. Goodbye, my lovely, romantic lake! Goodbye! Goodbye! Goodbye!"

As Esther gave her touching farewell speech, I drifted off into my own version of never-never land and imagined she were speaking the words directly to me. When she finished her speech, Esther put both of her pretty hands to her big red gorgeous lips and threw an excessively dramatic and sloppy kiss off to Esther Lake. Then, we paddled through the narrow channel into Hanson Lake. "What will happen in this one?" I wondered.

"Anything is possible if you just believe!"

chapter 37
spirits in the wilderness

"You mean like God and stuff?"

We had a nice tailwind on Hanson Lake that pushed us gently to the south. Halfway across, we stopped for lunch at a campsite along the western shoreline near the portage up to Cherry Lake. While I waited for the girls to come back from the throne, I explored the site. It was one of my favorites. I had seen it on my second guide training trip at the beginning of the summer, and then I ended up camping there two weeks later with another group.

As I walked around the campsite, it felt eerily quiet. I couldn't hear the slightest noise—no birds chirping, no wind in the trees overhead, not even the girls back in the woods. I stepped on a fallen twig that snapped so sharply under my foot, it made me jump. As I walked around looking for the tent sites, I could hear the sound of my heart beating in my chest, but nothing else.

I came upon an open area back in the woods where the ground was covered with pine needles and old leaves that looked like skeletons. It seemed as if they had been lying there for a long time. On top of the leaves were some small birch branches, just little twigs actually. It appeared as if the twigs had been placed there on purpose in a circular pattern that reminded me of a compass. It seemed peculiar, so I knelt down and brushed away the leaves to take a closer look. What appeared was a circle of white stones hidden underneath the dead leaves. The stones looked like milky quartz, and each one was about the size of a quarter. They were arranged in a circle, perfectly spaced apart, and buried neatly in the soil at ground level.

It was a startling discovery that filled my mind with questions. Who could have placed them there? How old were they? What was their purpose? I couldn't answer any of those questions. For some reason, a feeling of deep sadness and death washed over me. Suddenly, it was as if I were not alone in that quiet, secluded spot in the woods. I felt as if I were being carefully watched and examined by ancient spirits from long ago. A chill ran through my body and up to my cheeks as I knelt in silence beside the circle of stones.

Ever since then, I've had an eerie feeling about that campsite, a feeling that there was something mysterious going on there, something much older and more knowledgeable than me, something deeply spiritual lingering in the silence there from the long-ago past.

As best as I could remember, I placed the leaves and twigs back where I'd found them. Then, I went back to the rocky slope by the lake and waited for the girls to return. When they did, they sat down, one on each side of me. Together, we looked east over the water. It was a high spot with a majestic view of the lake. A large island with high cliffs was off to the northeast. Beneath the cliffs, huge black boulders jutted up out of the lake, each with dark red streaks running down the sides of them. The streaks on the rocks looked as if they had been painted on by a giant hand, and their reflection drifted out onto the lake like a long stream of blood. The lake felt ominous, alive, and mysterious as it stretched out before us.

Aria dropped back on the rock and closed her eyes. Esther sat with her arms around her knees, looking out over the deep dark lake. She was thinking about something; I could tell. I leaned back on my elbows and stretched my legs out on the big flat rock, waiting for her to spring whatever it was on us.

"Leo," she finally said quietly. "What do you believe? I mean, what do you believe in?"

The deep open-ended question caught me off guard. "You mean like God and stuff?" I asked.

"Yeah, sure . . . whatever," she replied.

"Well," I hesitated, unsure of what to say and how to say it. "I grew up in a pretty traditional home, and we went to church."

"So, do you believe it?" Esther asked.

"Um, yeah," I mumbled. "Sort of, I guess."

"Really?" she said.

As I thought it over, I didn't want to say anything else. My faith was something I kept to myself for the most part. It was deeply personal to me, which was why I felt so at home at Northern Lights. The people there were definitely spiritual people, some overtly Christian, others not so much, but I felt safe there, probably because there was a profound sense of respect for everyone's beliefs.

Esther smiled reassuringly and nudged me in the side. "You don't have to talk about it if you don't want to, bro."

"Yeah, I think that's it for me," I said. "Maybe I'll say more later."

"No worries, bro," Esther replied.

"What do you believe in?" I asked, knowing she was waiting for me to throw the question back at her.

Esther took a big breath of fresh air and gazed out over the calm, peaceful lake. "Love," she said quietly. "I believe in love."

Aria suddenly let out a loud groan and buried her face in her hands. "Now there's a rosy picture that we all can appreciate," she complained bitterly. "Wait a sec, can you two lean in and smile so I can get a nice, happy little picture of the both of you."

Esther leaned forward and gave a worried look over at Aria sitting on the other side of me. "What's wrong?" she asked.

Aria sat up, sighed heavily, and then leaned back on her arms. "Esther, you say you believe in *love*. And Leo, here, says he believes in God and stuff, or no, actually he . . . um, yeah, *sort of* does."

Esther and I glanced over at Aria as she stared out at the lake in silent agony. "What the hell, you guys!"

Aria's bitter outburst shamed Esther and me into painful silence. I thought about her cynical comments. I'm not going to lie; they hurt, but I deserved it, after the pathetic way I described my faith. I knew what I believed. I just didn't want to stick my neck out too far, so I went with the limp noodle version, but I was getting thrown up against the wall anyway. Aria sure knew how to test her overcooked spaghetti. I hung there—stuck to the wall—waiting for someone a little more understanding and forgiving to come along and scrape me off before I hardened up there in place forever.

Esther was visibly upset. She sat there, biting her lower lip and silently gazing out at the lake. Then, she glanced back at Aria and ventured bravely ahead. "So, what do *you* believe in?"

Aria sat there in complete silence for a few agonizing seconds. Then, she blurted out, "I don't know! I wouldn't say it the way you guys did, though. It's hard for me to believe in God or love, or for that matter, a loving God, when there's so much suffering going on in the world. It all just seems like a big pipedream to me."

"I don't think you have to blame God for all the suffering in the world," Esther said as calmly as she could.

"Why the hell not?" Aria yelled out at the lake, lying silent and still before us. "He created this mess, didn't he?"

"I'm sorry," Esther apologized. "I didn't mean to rattle your cage. I didn't even mean for this to turn into a discussion about religion. I was just curious, that's all."

Aria leaned forward and glanced over at Esther, who looked like she was about to cry. "It's okay, Esther. It's not your fault. I'm just ranting again, as usual. I'm just sick and tired of people trying to ram a certain brand of religion down my throat."

"Like what?" Esther asked.

"Well, like Leo, here, I was raised in an old-fashioned gospel kind of way," she said. "I've heard plenty of fiery sermons in my day. But all that hot air from the pulpit never seems to amount to much in real life. There's a lot of talk about God's love, serving the poor, and turning the other cheek, but most people keep right on hating, suffering, and dying. Nothing seems to change, at least not in my neighborhood, so it's kind of hard for me to buy into a religion that claims to have all the answers."

Aria went silent again, so I spoke up. "So, Esther, what *do* you believe? It has to be more than just love, don't you think?"

"Yeah, you're right," she said. "Saying it like that wasn't really fair." She paused and thought it over again. "But love really does sum it up for me . . . sort of."

"What do you mean?" I asked.

"Well, first, I'd say that I totally agree with Aria," Esther said as she glanced cautiously over at her friend. I slid back a little to get out of the way and let them see each other.

"It seems as if a lot of people are trying like mad to put God in a box," Esther continued. "They're trying to come up with their own definition of God or faith, and then they use that definition to exclude everyone else, or they use it to control those who are in and condemn those who are out. I just think God can't be shut up in a box like that. I mean, look at where we are, and for that matter, look at the entire world around us. Look at the universe and all the millions of galaxies spinning out of control, so far away we can't even comprehend how far away they actually are. The creator of all this would have to be pretty big, and we're sitting here on a rock in the middle of nowhere trying to describe God to each other."

"But we're talking about what we believe in, right?" Aria said, hopelessly lost in her own thoughts. "So, we have to believe in something, or nothing, or whatever. I don't even know what I'm talking about right now, so how could I ever know what I'm supposed to believe about God?"

"I like what Jesus said," Esther replied tentatively. "He said that God is all about love, just like a loving father, and that God loves the world and everyone, not just some people, but everyone in the whole world. So, if God does that, then we should too."

"Esther, aren't you Jewish?" I asked. "Since when do you buy into something so Christian like that?"

"Hey, he was Jewish when he said it," she replied. "It was only later that people turned it into a stuffy religion. Besides, when someone says something brilliant, I'm totally on board."

"But if God loves everyone, why is there so much suffering in the world?" Aria asked.

Esther gazed out at the lake. "I think God is bigger than anything we can imagine or put into words," she said. "I don't think I'm up to blaming God for all of my problems. I'm not up to giving God credit for all of my blessings, either. It's a two-way street, I think."

Esther glanced over at me and asked, "Leo, you get me, don't you, when I say I believe in love? You've both heard American preachers say that God is love, eh? So, how strange is it for me to say that I believe in love just like you believe in God?"

Esther waited for us to respond, but neither of us said anything. We both just gazed out over the lake lying silent and still before us. What Esther said seemed to ring true to me, but I was deep in my own thoughts, mulling over what I believed and how that played with what they were saying.

"God and love," Esther continued, "I think they're both a lot alike. When I say I believe in love, it's just easier for me to understand. Somehow, it makes more sense that way. It's more down to earth and real to me. Love gives me something to hold on to and something to live for."

"That makes a lot of sense to me," I replied. "Without love, life can be pretty cold sometimes."

"But with love, life is suddenly full of hope and meaning," Esther replied. "So, when I say I believe in love, I'm just saying that it's my driving force. It directs how I approach life, what I do each day, how I treat people, and what I choose to do with my life. That's what I mean when I say I believe in love."

"Yeah, that's cool," I said. "I think God would be okay with that. I know I am. I'm more than okay with it, like you need my approval or anything. I'm just saying . . . cool . . . yeah."

"You goofball," Esther said as she tipped me over into Aria.

"You're the goofball," I replied, pushing her back. "Miss 'I believe in love,' and then you give us a whole sermon on it."

"Ahh!" Esther groaned as she pushed me harder and knocked me back into Aria again. "Leo, you big fudge-pop!"

"If I'm a fudge-pop, then you're an applesauce biscuit!" I exclaimed as I gently shoved her back.

"Ugh, so here we go again," Aria moaned in disgust. "You two mysteriously communicating again on some higher spiritual level, and me, forced to watch it in some weird state of terrified shock."

Esther laughed and said, "Yup, that's just the way it is, cuz!"

Aria grinned or grimaced, or maybe both. "Well, how can I argue with that?" she blurted out as she pushed me back into Esther's lap and then gave her friend a high five over my head. "All that you just said, sister, I'm right there with you. I believe in love too . . . well, sort of . . . I don't know, maybe." Aria rolled her eyes at me and asked, "What other choice do I have?"

"Well, Esther," I said, pushing myself back up. "You really have a knack for getting to the bottom of things, especially all the way out here in the middle of nowhere."

Esther suddenly sat up prim and proper. "It's just what you do when you're way out in the wop-wops."

"The what?" I asked.

"The wop-wops," she replied, flinging her arms out at the lake. "You know, the middle of nowhere!"

"Okay," Aria said with a long sarcastic sigh. "Let's thank Esther for that nice little break from paddling. Why do I suddenly feel like all the troubles in the world magically disappeared, just like that—poof! They're gone, and everything in life is fine and dandy again."

We all laughed, but I knew Esther was right. That *was* what you did when you were out in the middle of nowhere. You talked about everything you couldn't back at home. The Boundary Waters was the perfect place to ask deep and mysterious questions. It was a place to wonder and dream about life, about how the world could be a better place, about how it could be full of beauty and peace just like the pristine lakes and undisturbed forests all around us.

As we walked down to our canoe, Esther said, "All I did was ask a simple question, Aria, and you up and threw a wobbly."

"That's right, sister," Aria replied. "Didn't you know there are two topics people don't ever talk about here in the good old U.S. of A?"

"What's that?" Esther asked.

"Religion and politics, of course!" Aria shouted as she threw her arms up in the air and nearly whacked me in the head.

"Hey, that reminds me," Esther said as she raised her hand and suddenly became prim and proper again. "I was wondering what you guys thought about the last presidential—"

"Nope!" Aria cut her off. "No way, sister! We're not going there. Not here! Not back at camp! Not ever! So, you can just stuff that one back in your pocket, or your panties, or wherever you like, but I'm not gonna let you start talking politics, not out here!"

Esther grinned. "I'll just send it down the long-drop, eh, cuz?"

"Great idea!" Aria exclaimed. "That just about sums up what I would've said anyway!"

We hopped into the canoe and set off into the lake. As we paddled south, I noticed what looked like a dark canoe far away on the eastern shoreline just to the right of the big island. It was barely visible, floating in the shade of some overhanging cedars in the water.

"Someone is probably fishing," I thought, but then a strange feeling came over me. Whoever was in that canoe had been watching us. A little later, I glanced back over my shoulder, but it had disappeared back into the shadows, as if the person didn't want to be seen. I wondered who it could be. Whoever it was, thankfully, was behind us. We continued south and were soon coasting up to the portage at the southern end of Hanson Lake.

We had talked about the portage a couple of times already. It was the longest and toughest one of the trip—a hundred and twenty rods long. The path ran along the edge of the lake, then dropped steeply down along a trickling stream that spilled over mossy green rocks in the woods to the west.

As we pulled up, the mosquitoes swarmed around us, just like at the last portage. I swung the canoe up onto my shoulders and took off in a rush as the little bloodsuckers dove in right beside me. They zipped under the canoe and attacked my arms, neck, and legs at will. I tried to move fast enough to keep from getting bit, but slow enough to avoid stumbling over the rocks. At times, it was best to simply stop and let the flying demons zoom past, then swat the ones that landed and were looking for a suitable place to bite. Then, it was off and running again down the steep trail.

Large cedar trees grew in abundance beside the stream. I found myself weaving around the trunks, trying not to bang into them. They were everywhere, but they were also a blessing in disguise. I discovered that I could easily wedge the front of the canoe between two close trees, drop the stern, and then slip out underneath for a short break. About halfway along the trail, I hung the canoe up between two trees. Then, I walked back to check on the girls.

Esther saw me coming down the trail and exclaimed happily, "Already done, eh?"

"Yeah," I lied. "I just came back to help you two stragglers out."

"You already did a hundred and twenty rods?" Aria questioned me in total disbelief.

"Yeah, it's a cinch, all downhill," I lied again. "It goes pretty fast if you run the whole way. You're almost there."

"No, we're not," Aria replied. "You're such a horrible liar!"

"Okay," I confessed. "I'm just taking a break. The canoe got so heavy that I decided to hang it up."

"Wimp!" Aria said, insulting me directly. She always had a knack for getting straight to the point.

Suddenly, a big burly man came strolling by carrying a Duluth pack on his back, a second one flung over his chest, and a canoe on his shoulders as well. We all stepped aside as he said hello and thanked us for letting him pass. I walked on behind the girls as they gushed over the burly mountain man, whom they immediately dubbed Hercules. And he was so handsome too!

When I got to the canoe hung up between the trees, suddenly, my idea didn't seem so impressive after all. I reluctantly climbed back underneath and lifted it onto my shoulders.

"Only sixty rods to go," I mumbled to myself, feeling very small, very inadequate, and very wimpy.

As I plodded along, the mosquitoes swooped underneath and attacked me again. I could see the stream in the trees off to my right, but I was stuck under the heavy canoe, focused on the jagged rocks, large tree roots, and muddy patches along the path. I had done the portage a couple of times before. It was just as long and painful as I remembered. All along the way, the canoe bounced up and down on my sore shoulders. As the rods piled up, I found myself pushing up on the sides of the canoe to adjust the weight onto a different part of my shoulders, a part that wasn't quite as sore, but doing that quickly lost its effectiveness. Of course, I didn't want to stop again because that would only prolong the ordeal.

I lifted up the front of the canoe and tried to catch a glimpse of the lake, wondering where it was and why it was taking so long to get there. My neck and shoulders were burning and aching. I kept moving forward, afraid to stop again, for fear of collapsing or toppling over under the weight of the heavy canoe.

As I neared the end, the next lake slowly came into view, and I breathed a sigh of relief. Water never looks so good as at the end of a long portage. A cool breeze greeted me as I stepped gingerly into the water. I heaved the canoe up and off to the side, letting it drop happily into the lake. I reached back and rolled my sore shoulders around, trying to loosen up the kinked muscles. It was a satisfying end to another challenging portage.

"What took you so long?" Aria asked in a blatant attempt to further humiliate me. "Did you get lost or something?"

She and Esther were basking in the sun on a wide sandy beach nearby. Aria was just rubbing it in. It was her way of letting me know how much she cared about me. I could appreciate that. I looked out at the beautiful lake that stretched before us. I was more than happy to trade a brief moment of pain and fatigue for a few days of peace and tranquility on the lakes.

"Yeah, I could do that again! No problem!"

chapter 38
crossing knife

"That was quite the willie-waw, wasn't it!"

We stretched out on the sandy beach for a while and soaked up the sunshine. It was a brief reward for making it through the toughest portage of our journey, but there was still a challenge ahead. We were sitting at the east end of Knife Lake, which stretched some twenty miles to the west. There were all kinds of channels, bays, and arms to the massive lake that sliced across the landscape. The big blue waters sparkled in the afternoon sunlight.

"It's all downhill from here!" I said, smiling at the girls.

"Yeah, right!" Aria replied sarcastically. "Now, we've just gotta get across Knife Lake."

Aria knew exactly what we were up against. The long paddle west on Knife wasn't the easiest thing in the world, and I had a feeling it wasn't going to be easy that day either. Throughout the afternoon, the wind had been gradually picking up. On the beach it felt great, but out on the lake it was a different story. The wind was blowing directly against where we wanted to go. That just meant more work for us, and we were already tired.

We had about three miles to go, and most of it was straight into the wind, but the reward that awaited us was unlike anything else we had encountered. In fact, the girls had been talking about it off and on for the past three weeks: Eddy Falls. It was a highlight for almost every group I took out on the lakes. When people heard the waterfalls were large enough to climb up into and stand under, they were immediately sold. We were too.

After kicking back on the beach for a while, we paddled out of the peaceful bay and hit the wind. We moved steadily west for about two hours. The gusty breeze made it extremely slow and exhausting. For every stroke of our paddles, the wind pushed the canoe backward a bit, so any amount of forward progress had to be earned. We weren't floating across a glassy lake anymore. It was real work, and the choppy waves weren't making it easy on us either.

We struggled west, moving through a channel that gradually became larger and wider. By the time we rounded the last point that opened up into the biggest part of Knife Lake, the wind had picked up even more. I had experienced the wind on other trips that summer. It moved up the long lake out of the west and seemed to pick up speed as it blew east into the smaller channels.

The last stretch of paddling we had to do was straight south across a mile of open water. On the far shore, we could see our destination: the portage into Eddy Lake. It stood out on the shoreline because of the large boulders down by the water. I could see a group of people standing there, loading up their canoes. Eddy Falls was there too, hidden in the trees off to the left. The waves, however, had turned into whitecaps out in the middle of the lake. The next hour or so would be the biggest challenge we'd face all day. We floated in the relative shelter of the north shoreline, nervously eyeing the windy lake and considering our options.

"We're going out there?" Esther said nervously. "I reckon that'll be quite a mission, eh?"

"We'll have to paddle farther west and then cut back with the wind. It'll be safer that way," I suggested.

"Yeah, but we could shoot straight across too," Aria said. "It would save us a lot of time."

"The waves are nasty today," I pointed out.

"We can handle it if we stay close to shore," she replied.

"That won't be a problem," I said, glancing off to the east. "The wind will push us over there, and if it has its way, it'll push us all the way over into the rocks along the shoreline."

"We can make it across," Aria insisted.

"It'd be smarter to go farther west," I said one last time.

"Come on, Leo," Aria said confidently. "We're both experienced canoers. We can make it."

When I looked over at Esther, she grinned with excitement and agreed, "Come on, bro, let's give it a buck!"

"All right," I said. "But if we tip, don't say I didn't warn you."

I had to admit, the shorter route straight across was tempting in spite of the choppy water. We would need to keep close to the eastern shoreline just in case we tipped in the water. The more sensible option was to paddle farther west for another mile or so, and then make the turn with the wind at our backs.

With any other group, I would have insisted on taking the safest way, but with Aria there, I was willing to give her idea a try. I trusted her strong canoeing instincts and her judgment on the lakes. Besides, I'd never tipped over in rough water before, which probably made me feel invincible. I'd done dangerous things like that before and survived, so it wasn't that big of a deal to just go for it.

As we made our break for Eddy Falls, it was about a hundred yards out where the wind and the waves really hit us. The canoe began to rise and fall with each big wave, immediately making me second guess our decision. Whitecaps sprayed across the canoe's right side as it heaved up and down and sideways in the giant swells of water. We hugged the eastern shoreline, but getting too close to it was also risky. The waves were pounding away on the rocky beach, ready to tear into the bottom of the canoe if we got too close.

Up in front, Aria was paddling like an Olympic athlete, moving us steadily forward. I was in the stern, wasting a lot of time and energy just trying to keep the canoe from tipping over. I had to keep my body moving back and forth, leaning into the wind as I paddled like a maniac, then leaning the other way as I desperately tried to keep the canoe at a forty-five-degree angle to the waves.

If I turned too far to the left, the waves would swamp us. If I turned too far to the right, the wind would keep us from going anywhere. It was a balancing act to keep the two forces in mind, kind of like living with Aria and Esther over the past two days.

While Aria and I worked the paddles, Esther gripped the sides of the canoe and encouraged us. She pointed out the waves as they rolled in and gave us a running commentary.

"Watch out for that wave! Here it comes!" she called out. "Look out, mates! Here comes another whopper!"

Each wave looked as if it had the ability to swamp the canoe. The whitecaps crashed into the side of the boat and sprayed us as we painstakingly made our way across the lake.

"Keep paddling, mates!" Esther cried from her perch in the middle of the canoe. "Oh, crikey! Here comes another one! Keep paddling, Aria! Watch it, Leo! Here it comes!"

It was easy to see that Esther was living her best life. The danger we faced only made her more alive, excited, and fierce. I listened to her with admiration, but I didn't have time to say a word in the back of the canoe. The wind and the waves were so loud, no one would have heard me anyway. There was no time to panic either. The hour of testing we endured crossing that windy section of Knife Lake was one of those times when we had to simply trust in our abilities and count on each other to know what to do. It was both terrifying and thrilling at the same time.

At first, it seemed like it was taking forever, but we slowly worked our way along. As we drew near the shore on the south side of Knife, we could finally relax a little bit. I turned the canoe in line with the wind and then let it push us east into a shallow bay near the shore. Before we hit bottom, Aria hopped out and pulled the canoe up into the rocks near the portage. We had made it!

"That was a nasty one!" Aria said excitedly. "We made it across, but just barely! How are you doing, Esther?"

"Oh, girlfriend! That was quite the willie-waw, wasn't it!" Esther cried with sheer delight.

"You liked that, huh?" Aria said, smiling at her excited friend.

"That was unreal!" Esther exclaimed. "We almost totally carked it out there a couple of times!"

"Carked it?" Aria asked.

"Yeah, mate," she said. "You know . . . died!"

Esther glanced back at me with her eyes wide with excitement. "I was terrified out there!" she went on. "That was so totally sick! I'm just glad I didn't have to steer the canoe!"

I just sat there and smiled back at her. I was completely shot from the last stretch across the lake. My hands were shaking from the strain. My back ached, and my arms felt like wet noodles. I could tell Aria was totally exhausted too, but she was already digging into her pack and pulling out a towel.

"Come on, guys!" she shouted. "I'm sweating like a pig. Let's go jump in the waterfalls!"

"Yeah! Sweet as!" Esther replied as she jumped out of the canoe and dashed away after Aria. Apparently, she didn't need a towel.

"I'll see you guys in a little bit!" I called after them, but they were already long gone. I let out a heavy sigh of relief. We had made it to the halfway point of our trip, just barely, and a dip in the falls would feel mighty good.

As the girls disappeared into the woods, I rummaged around in the pack for my towel. I found Esther's towel too. It was fun hanging out with two beautiful women in the wilderness, but sometimes a man needs his alone time, so I took my time.

It was nice to know we had the hardest part of the trip behind us. It would be a cinch making it back to camp from there. We still had a long way to go, but it was almost all straight east. Based on all the other trips I'd been on that summer, I knew there'd probably be no more serious wind or waves to deal with, and with luck, the weather would hold off one more day.

I felt like I could finally relax.

chapter 39

eddy falls

"Watch this!"

Instead of taking one of the well-worn paths from the portage over to the falls, I followed the streambed straight up to them. Crystal clear water flowed around large boulders and over smooth stones of deep red, golden yellow, and ashen gray. At every turn, tree branches and slippery dead logs blocked the way up through the stream. It was something I was getting used to—the random array of undisturbed forest, left alone to sprout, shoot up, grow old, and die without ever being cut down, mowed, or manicured. It was a beautiful labyrinth of rocks, branches, dead logs, leaves, and water everywhere, just as it had always been for as long as anyone could remember.

I slowly worked my way up the shallow stream into the cool shade of the towering pines and cedars that grew all around the falls. The sound of rushing water roared in the distance as a fine spray of mist blew into my face. The pools of water gradually became larger and deeper as I made my way farther into the forest. Large downed trees were everywhere, blocking the way. I had to zigzag back and forth to keep going. I hopped over a dead log, slid underneath another one, and shimmied around a large boulder. The sounds of people shouting and laughing drifted through the forest along with the noise of the rushing water that kept getting louder and louder.

Huge black boulders suddenly loomed up directly in front of me. They were precariously stacked on top of each other in a jumbled mess, as if a giant toddler had done it just for fun and then crawled away to find something else to do. Green mossy patches and large cedar logs, some alive and some dead, lay across the boulders that rose at least a hundred feet above the lake. Roaring waterfalls poured through low spots between the rocks, splashing into crystal clear pools scattered at various elevations. Everything was dripping wet. Water flowed down everywhere, trickling through the cracks and crannies, rushing ever downward on its way to the lake below.

The unique beauty of Eddy Falls made me want to stay there for the rest of the day to climb around and explore it from top to bottom, but it was proper etiquette not to linger in a place like that too long. The waterfalls were a popular destination located next to the portage into Eddy Lake. To leave canoes and packs sitting around the portage, taking up needed space for hours on end, was discouraged. No one said anything about it, but most people seemed to abide by the unspoken rule.

There were a few other people there as well. A family of four was exploring the pools at the base of the falls. A couple of others were climbing higher up and out of sight. It didn't take long to find Aria and Esther. Even before reaching the waterfalls, I could hear them through the trees, laughing and screaming over the roar of the water. They were standing in a large pool about twenty feet up, smiling and splashing around as water gushed down on top of them. When I showed up, they waved excitedly down at me.

"Leo, come up here, bro!" Esther cried eagerly. "This is totally sweet! Watch this!"

She plunged her entire body back into a waterfall that poured down through a gap between two huge rocks. I could see her smiling underneath the flowing water that shot up in every direction. A few seconds later, she popped out again, beaming with ecstasy.

"See!" she yelled. "It's so much fun!"

Aria plopped down in the same pool off to the right, where another smaller waterfall poured down in front of her face. She sat there, delighting in the cool refreshing shower.

"Come on, Farm Boy!" Esther shouted. "Get your arse up here!"

I stripped down to my swimsuit in a hurry, thinking about how Esther was starting to sound more and more like Aria. It annoyed me, but it didn't slow me down at all. I jumped into the stream and waded across to a big mossy rock. Then, I climbed up to the pool to join the girls. The water was splashing all around us with such fury, we had to shout to be heard.

"Hi, gorgeous!" I yelled. "Isn't this awesome?!"

"Totally! I love this!" Esther exclaimed as she gave me a big hug. "Leo, you little ripper! This is sweet as, mate!"

"Yeah, thanks!" I shouted back with a humongous smile.

"Here, hold my sunnies!" she said, handing me her red designer shades. "Watch this, Leo!"

She backed into the rushing waterfall again as it fell down on top of her head and sprayed out all over the place. She smiled from inside the falls and thrust her arms out to each side. She looked so ridiculously silly. I couldn't help but laugh. The water was freezing cold, but it felt great.

Esther popped back out and yelled, "You try it, Leo!" She just about knocked me over as she stumbled around in the pool and shoved me back into the waterfall.

"Watch this!" I yelled, mimicking her as I smiled and thrust my arms out to each side. I could see her laughing through the wall of water pouring down over my face.

I noticed that Aria had jumped up and was waving at me along with Esther. I popped out and yelled, "I'm freezing!"

"It's my turn, Leo. Get your butt out of there!" Aria shouted.

I stumbled out of the way to let her move into the prized spot. Aria slid back under the water until it was pounding down on her.

"This is amazing!" she shouted as the foamy water splashed up and sprayed out in every direction.

It was nice to see Aria having such a good time. I wanted her to be happy, even more than I wanted her to like me. I wondered why she was often so rough and sarcastic around me. It seemed to be a disguise she always wore. I knew she had a hard time getting along with other people. I was just glad to be there for her, and I treasured our friendship. I was worried about it too, but not at that moment. Eddy Falls was simply a time to have fun.

Staying close together, we climbed around to the left side of the falls through the ice-cold water. We tiptoed across rocky ledges and carefully slid over slippery logs as we made our way through the jumbled maze and climbed up higher. In many places, we had to hold on to each other to keep from falling. It felt good to grab on to each other, to feel the physical strength of Aria and Esther, to actually touch them, even for so short of a time. It meant a lot to me to be held on to and supported by my friends. It meant they were watching out for me, as I was watching out for them. It was a simple silent lesson, but a powerful one to me.

Esther found a smaller waterfall pouring down over a smooth boulder into a shallow pool. She plopped down on her back and slid behind the arching wall of water. Aria joined her under the falls. The two girls leaned back on their elbows as the water crashed down in front of them. Their long legs stretched out like toothpicks in the shallow pool as they waved frantically at me, standing outside. I could tell they were shouting at me, but the water was so loud, I couldn't understand a word they were saying.

I leaned down closer to the falls and shouted, "I can't hear you! What did you say?"

Suddenly, Aria's hand popped out through the water and pulled me straight down. I plunged helplessly down and landed on top of them with a giant splash. They laughed as I rolled over and leaned back between them under the roaring waterfall.

"What did you say?" I asked again.

"I said, get your butt in here, you idiot!" Aria shouted.

We rested inside the shallow pool, enjoying the privacy of the little watery cave for a while.

"This is so cool, you guys!" Aria said.

"Straight up!" Esther replied. "This is what it's all about!"

"What is it all about?" I asked.

"Being friends, bro!" she said. "Having fun and hanging out with my besties! Enjoying life! Holding on to each other and taking care of my two best friends in the whole entire world!"

"Yeah, it's so awesome to be here!" Aria said.

"I don't ever want this to end!" Esther exclaimed, smiling joyfully at Aria and me.

"Yeah, this is awesome," I heartily agreed. "But I think my toes are starting to turn blue."

"Mine too!" Aria exclaimed. "Let's get going."

"Okay, but remember this, mates!" Esther replied. "Don't ever forget it! It's been the best day of my entire summer!"

Aria crawled back out, but I didn't want to leave. The cold water felt so good on my shoulders and sore back. Besides, it was exhilarating to be under there with Esther lying next to me. I have to admit, I was having a hard time keeping my eyes off her. As we lay there together, I thought I could see a tattoo down on the right side of her belly. It looked like a pattern of blue dots. She had freckles everywhere, so it was hard to tell. I didn't want to be caught staring, so I tried to focus on something else, but it wasn't easy.

"It's freezing in here!" I shouted.

"No, it's wonderful!" Esther exclaimed.

"I pictured you as a black bikini type of girl!" I shouted, for lack of anything else to say.

"You what?" she asked.

"I thought you'd be wearing a black bikini!" I shouted.

The realization of how ridiculous that statement was suddenly swept over me like the waterfall pouring down on both of us. It only emphasized what I had been focusing on the entire time. I suddenly worried that Esther might notice it, but she simply beamed back at me and laughed.

Without a doubt, she looked amazing in that bathing suit, but it was more than that. She was completely changed. Gone were the rugged clothes, the dark eye shadow, the black boots, and the tough look. There she was in the middle of the wilderness in a white bikini without any makeup on and smiling like a little school girl who just got an ice cream cone. Over the previous twenty-four hours, Esther had undergone a complete transformation without my even noticing it until right then and there. I blinked my eyes and had to look again. It was beautiful!

"You look different," I shouted to Esther, trying to justify my comment about her bikini. "I mean, I've never seen you without all your makeup on before."

"Yeah, mate!" Esther shouted. "This is the real me, I guess. I'm just good at hiding it most of the time!"

"You don't need to hide it from me," I replied.

"Thanks, Leo!" she shouted back.

She gave me a big wet hug, then scrambled out from under the waterfalls. I stayed there for a while longer, gazing out at Esther's long slender legs, shimmering on the other side of the glassy wall of water. The rush of the falls faded into the background, and the dizzy feeling returned as I thought about how beautiful she was to me. Everything around me became strangely surreal.

I thought of all the qualities I adored about Esther: her playfulness, her silly mannerisms, her inquisitive nature, her carefree attitude, and her childlike joy for life. It wasn't just her beautiful body that I was attracted to, it was everything about her. She was so full of life and joy and light. It was like playing with a white swan who was so pure and innocent and wild. It was dreamlike, and I was struck speechless in that moment of sheer ecstasy.

For a few seconds, I drifted off into a blurry fantastical daydream until I felt someone tugging on my foot. It was Esther, outside the waterfalls calling to me. I didn't want to go, but it was time to leave that amazing spot at Eddy Falls.

We made our way back across to the larger falls and stopped to plunge in one last time. None of us wanted to leave. As I climbed back down, Aria and Esther stood under the big waterfalls, leaning back into the rushing water. As the girls played in the water, I noticed that a group of boy scouts had shown up below. I watched the boys standing there all in a line—their eyes wide, their mouths hanging open as they stared at the incredible sight they had stumbled upon in the middle of the wilderness: two bathing beauties in bikinis, standing before them in all their glory.

The girls were oblivious to the audience below. They stood like goddesses under the water rushing down over their glistening bodies, all sopping wet, adjusting their bathing suits, fixing their hair, and rubbing their skin—a lot of skin, sparkling and shimmering in the misty rays of sunlight that sifted down through the trees. It was like the Garden of Eden, and the boys were all one and the same: Adam, naked and unashamed. I chuckled as I made my way down toward the boys who didn't seem to know I was even there.

"Hey there, boys!" I called out to them with a smile and a wave. "Are you guys having a nice trip?"

"Yeah, nice, really nice," one boy said as he stared at the girls in the waterfalls up above.

"Aria! Esther! Come on!" I shouted. "It's time to let another group have a turn in the falls."

The boys watched as the girls climbed down. They couldn't take their eyes off of them as they dried off and got dressed.

Aria noticed their fascination and decided to engage them. "Hey boys," she said, but they just kept right on staring.

"Hey, runts!" she finally shouted. "You freaks better get your butts up into the waterfalls ASAP before I have to chase you up there and throw you in myself!"

The boys suddenly snapped out of it, but it seemed as if one or two of them were considering the idea of lingering behind in hopes that Aria would follow through on her threat.

As the boy scouts explored the waterfalls, Esther snapped a couple of photos of the three of us at Eddy Falls. Then, we bid the amazing spot goodbye. We grabbed our gear and made our way back out to the canoe. We felt renewed, refreshed, and clean. Still, I was starting to feel it in my body. It had been a long day, and it was time to start looking for a campsite for the night.

Esther's birthday was coming to a close.

chapter 40

canoeing on jenny

"Anyone want to join me?"

We portaged up past the falls and set out on Eddy Lake. We were happy to let the wind do most of the work as it pushed us southeast nearly all the way across. On the other side, we skirted a rocky point and then drifted into a quiet cove where we found the portage into Jenny Lake. It was an easy portage, just fifteen rods, but we were running out of steam. When I got to the lake, I walked the canoe into the water all the way up to my waist and threw it off to the side. Then, I threw myself in as well and slowly sank under the surface as the girls looked on from the shore.

"Are you okay?" Aria called when I came back up.

"Come and pick me up out here!" I replied as I swam backward farther out into the lake.

"Okay, but you're gonna owe me one!" she shouted back.

The girls hopped in the canoe and coasted out on the water. As they skimmed up beside me, I grabbed the canoe and gave it a sudden jerk straight down. Aria and Esther both screamed and grabbed on to the sides of the canoe.

"What are you trying to do? You'll tip us over!" Aria shouted.

She splashed me with her paddle, almost whacking me in the head. I pulled myself up and flopped into the middle of the canoe.

"All right, ladies, take me home!" I cried in my captain's voice.

Esther giggled up in front, but Aria gave me another splash with her paddle and said, "You jerk!"

"I love you too, Aria," I replied. "Let's do this again sometime."

As they paddled out into the lake, I lay there, dripping all over the packs and my guitar. I was completely spent from the day's adventures. When we reached the middle of the lake, the girls stopped and let the canoe drift on the water. We soaked up the last warm rays of sunshine as it sank lower in the west.

"So, do you guys want to call it for today?" I asked.

"Yeah, I'm bushed," Aria replied. "Let's find a campsite."

"How about you, Esther, what do you think?" I asked.

"Sure, bro," she said. "I'm pretty stuffed myself."

The map showed two campsites on Jenny. I could already see one of them across the lake. It looked like a dark cave in the middle of a long stretch of cedar trees along the shore. There was a rocky point there too, which was always a good sign of a nice campsite.

"Let's go check it out," I said, pointing to the southern shore.

The girls paddled us over to the site, which to our delight, was vacant. Aria ran the canoe hard up onto the shore.

"Oops," she said, as the canoe grated on the sandy bottom.

All three of us just sat there in the canoe and let the realization slowly sink in that our work for the day was finally over.

"I'm too tired to get out," Aria moaned.

"I'm too tired to move my arms and legs," Esther replied.

"I'm too tired to do this," I said, giving the canoe a shove down in the water. The girls didn't even move.

"You're gonna pay for that, Farm Boy," Aria groaned. "I'm just too tired to do anything about it right now."

I rolled out into the water, slowly grabbed a pack, and carried it up into the campsite. It had a cozy campfire ring with hewn logs neatly set around the cooking grate. There was a pile of dry kindling stacked by the fireplace too. To find a site already stocked with wood was rare, but it was always a welcome sight.

The girls brought the other pack up and then had a look around. I pulled the canoe halfway up onto the shore, with plans to go out later to get fresh water. The campsite had a small rocky point on the east side of the beach. It was a cozy site with a nice view of the northwest where the sun was sinking low in the sky.

The girls set up the tent while I unpacked the cook kit and got the fire going. We had my favorite meal that night: homemade pizza. It was made with pizza dough smeared on an aluminum plate, topped with spaghetti sauce, slices of smoked sausage, and thick slabs of cheese. By the time we had the pizzas ready, the coals in the fire were glowing hot. That was the perfect time to bake the little pizzas to perfection, each with another plate flipped over on top of it to make a sort of oven. It took some time, but it was worth it.

"Where did you learn to cook like this?" Esther asked.

"Chuck," I replied. "He taught me everything I know."

"Chuck, eh," she said. "Wow, that chap is a flippin' genius. This pizza really hits the spot."

"Not as good as Chicago-style pizza, but not bad for the wop-wops, eh, sister?" Aria said.

"Not bad at all, cuz," Esther replied with her mouth full of a sloppy bite of the homemade pizza.

It was nice to hear remarks like those from the girls. As a canoe guide, compliments on the food were rare, and so were words of thanks. The food always got eaten, but that was because everyone was famished from the long days of hard work. Comments about the meals were usually more along the lines of simply being thankful for something to fill our starving bodies rather than the food's quality and taste. The one thing I got compliments on all the time, however, was Chuck's coffee cake recipe.

"I'm gonna make you guys something really special tomorrow morning," I announced.

"Aren't you going to tell us what it is?" Esther asked, still working on the last slice of her pizza.

"You'll just have to wait and see, but I bet you'll like it," I said.

"Okay, Leo, keep your secrets," she replied. "I'd like to have a squiz at your work tomorrow morning, though. You didn't bother to wake me up this morning. I felt so lazy."

"You were out like a light," I said. "I thought about tickling your toes, but you looked so adorable lying there under your sleeping bag. I didn't have the heart to wake you."

"If I'd been awake, I would've gotten up and helped you with brekkie," she said with a smile.

"Okay, tomorrow morning then," I replied. "If you don't get up, I'll be sure to tickle your toes."

"Sounds lovely," she said with a tired grin. "Go ahead and tickle them if you want to."

"If you wake me up, Leo, I'll punch you," Aria said sternly.

"No problem, Bear Bait," I said. "I won't touch you; I swear. I wouldn't want to deprive you of your beauty sleep."

"I'll wake her up in the morning," Esther said. "I'm sure she wouldn't hit her best friend, right cuz?"

"Oh, I wouldn't, would I?" Aria replied, flashing her bright eyes at Esther sitting across the way.

"You could never hurt me, cuz!" Esther cried.

"No, I suppose not," Aria said. "But I could tickle you 'til you pee your pants!"

"What? You wouldn't dare!" Esther cried.

"Oh, I can think of a lot of things worse than that!" Aria said.

"Like what?" Esther asked.

"You don't even want to know," Aria replied.

After supper, we worked on the dishes for a while. The only problem with cooking a nice meal was the clean-up afterward. It took a long time to scrub all the burned pizza crust and cheese off the plates, but in the end, it got done, and we were full and happy.

After dishes, I put a pot of water on the fire for tea later. The girls hung the rope for the food pack before it got too dark. We didn't have much food left, so it was pretty easy to pull it up.

As the sun went down in the west, we looked on from the campfire ring. The wind died down considerably as the sun fell lower and lower on the horizon. I was tired, but for some reason, I had the urge to paddle out and watch the sunset on the water.

"I'm going out in the canoe," I said, looking around at the girls. "Anyone want to join me?"

I was disappointed when they both shook their heads. They just sat there staring at the fire, as if in a trance. They were bushed. I was too.

Suddenly, I didn't feel like going out, but I did anyway, leaving them behind by the fire. Most of all, I'd wanted Esther to join me, but she and Aria were so tired, and it was still so very hot.

I pushed off into the lake and let the canoe glide straight out into the calm water. Jenny was a small lake in comparison to Diamond and Sag, but for some reason, it was one of my favorites. On the map, it appeared like an exploding star or firecracker with four long arms shooting off to the north, south, east, and west. We were camped on the south side of the biggest part of the lake, and I felt the urge to do some exploring.

I paddled west into the middle of the lake, enjoying the light of the early evening sky as it faded into a deep rosy pink above the trees not far away. I moved the canoe over to the southern shoreline and skirted the edge, looking at the different aquatic plants and chunks of rock sticking up out of the water. Cedar trees lined the entire length of the shoreline. White water lilies floated among a patch of lily pads in the shallows. Everything was calm and peaceful.

I watched a pair of loons glide ahead of me about fifty yards away. They sank down low in the water and cautiously stared back at me with their dark red eyes. They dipped their heads into the lake, then popped them back up again and eyed me nervously. As I drew closer, they dipped their heads quickly in and out of the water until one of the loons finally had enough. All of a sudden, it lunged forward and dove under the surface. The other one waited for a second or two; then it followed after the first one.

They hardly made any ripples as they dove gracefully under the water. I stopped paddling and looked around in the growing darkness, waiting for them to come back up, but they never did. Eventually, I started paddling again, following the shoreline farther to the west. A minute or so later, I heard the loons calling from behind, hooting softly to each other. They had passed swiftly under my canoe and surfaced safely behind me. I grinned and quietly moved on.

I'd always had a fondness for Jenny Lake. It was on the main route most guides took as they led their groups out west. It was an inconspicuous lake that everyone had to pass through to get to the more exotic locations deeper in the backcountry of the Boundary Waters. With Eddy Falls just one portage away from Jenny, the pretty lake seemed to get overlooked.

Jenny was a beautiful lake. It had a hidden bay accessible through a narrow channel just off the main canoe route. I never saw anyone go there because they were probably only interested in passing through on their way west or heading straight back home. I'd never been in the hidden bay either. It was back the other way, so I turned the canoe around and paddled back east along the southern shore.

As I coasted past our site, I saw the coals in the fireplace still glowing, but I didn't see the girls anywhere. It seemed odd, so I turned into shore and hopped out to look for them. I peeked inside the tent. Then, I listened for their voices back in the woods, possibly off visiting the throne—but still no one. I walked back to the campfire ring and tossed a couple of cedar sticks into the fire to keep it going. As I knelt by the fire, I heard voices out on the lake.

It was almost dark by then. I couldn't see anything in the light of the campfire, so I walked down to the shoreline and peered out across the lake. I could just barely make out the heads of the girls bobbing in the water about fifty yards offshore. "What are they doing back in the water?" I wondered. It was still warm outside, but I wouldn't have gone for a swim at that time of night. Even so, there they were, swimming in the middle of the lake.

They always seemed to find more to explore!

chapter 41
swimming with the loons

"That's right, just a little bit closer."

"Hey, Leo!" I heard Aria's voice calling from the lake. "Leo, come out here and swim with us!"

"What are you guys doing out there?" I called back, as if I didn't already know.

"We're swimming, you idiot!" she shouted. "Come on, Leo! Come out and join us! It'll be fun!"

"Aren't you guys tired by now?" I called back. I was played out, and I had no interest in getting wet again.

"It's so nice in the water, Leo, come and swim!" It was Esther's voice that time. I thought about what it would take to change back into my wet swimsuit, but I resisted the thought.

"No, I'm good!" I shouted back. "You guys should come in now. It's getting dark!"

"Please, Leo!" Aria begged. "The water feels so nice, and it's still so hot outside!"

"I don't know," I replied, still unconvinced.

The girls kept on pleading with me until it started to become downright annoying. "Good grief," I thought. "They really want me to go out there for some reason."

"Leo, please! Come and save us!" Esther begged. "We're so tired! We're drowning out here! We can't make it back to shore."

Esther had a unique way of stirring my heart more than Aria ever could. I thought again about going in, but I held my ground there by the canoe on the shore.

Aria called one last time, "Leo, just come out and pick us up in the canoe. If you do, I'll give you a backrub in the tent tonight. Just paddle out and pick us up! We're so tired, Leo, please!"

It was a tempting offer, and I wouldn't have to get wet after all. My shoulders ached from all the paddling and portaging earlier in the day, and a backrub would feel mighty fine. She'd finally got to me.

"All right, Aria," I shouted. "I'll do it, but don't forget that I'm counting on that backrub later!"

I pushed the canoe into the water and hopped in one more time. It seemed as if I had been pushing and pulling and lifting that heavy canoe around all day long, and as a matter of fact . . . yes, I had indeed been doing that. But even so, there I went one more time out on the lake in the dark just for them.

I could barely see the girls as their heads bobbed up and down in the middle of the lake. There was a faint light shimmering on the surface of the water. I looked to the southeast behind me and saw the moon, peeking above the trees directly over our campsite. I paddled slowly out toward the girls, who were treading water and talking to each other. As the canoe slowly floated up next to them, they smiled up at me from the lake.

"All right, hop in," I said cautiously. "Just be careful not to tip the canoe over."

They stared at each other for a couple of seconds. Then, together, they screamed at the top of their lungs and pulled the edge of the canoe straight down, launching me—head first, arms flailing, legs kicking—into the cold dark water of the lake. When I resurfaced, the girls were swimming away, laughing and screaming with delight. I swam frantically after Esther, but she was already far away, so I spun around in the water and went after Aria instead. She just laughed and waited for me to get close. Then, she ducked under the water and surfaced in another spot safely out of reach.

"I'm swimming out here with a pair of crazy loons!" I thought. "I'll never catch either one of them."

"You can't catch us!" Aria shouted as she swam around and made fun of my pathetic attempts to grab on to her.

Aria lifted something up in the air. Then, she threw it over to Esther, who was treading water by the canoe. Esther looked at it and screamed as she tossed the mysterious object into the boat. Then, she dove under it and swam away on the other side.

"What are you doing?" I cried, getting suspicious. "You guys are up to something!"

"Wouldn't you like to know!" Esther called back fearlessly.

I ducked under the canoe and came up directly in front of her. She screamed, then splashed me and giggled as I slowly moved toward her. When I tried to grab her arm, she thrashed around wildly in the water and swam off. I pursued her, but she got away—shrieking with delight, kicking frantically, and creating an enormous tidal wave of water that splashed up into my face. She was such a good swimmer, and it was impossible to get a hold of her.

"I'll never catch her like this," I thought. I stopped and let myself sink under the surface of the water, where I pulled my T-shirt off. Then, I came back up and threw it into the canoe.

"Oh, Leo!" Aria exclaimed. "What are you doing over there? Are you getting naked in the water too?"

"Yeah!" I shouted. "Watch out! I'm coming after you next!"

I tipped the edge of the canoe down and looked inside. There on the floor were the girls' swimsuits. I suddenly realized they were out there swimming around in the lake buck naked!

"Are you actually skinny dipping?" I cried out in surprise.

"Aah! He found out!" Esther screamed with excitement. "He saw our togs in the canoe!"

"Be careful, cuzzy! Don't let Farm Boy catch you!" Aria yelled as she swam up behind me.

Aria moved closer to me, laughing hysterically; then she dove under the water. I lunged after her, but she was already long gone, hidden in the lake somewhere out of reach, just like the loons I had seen earlier that evening.

I ducked under and swam for a long time underwater in the direction of Esther. When I popped up next to her, she screamed in terror and swam away in another flurry of splashing foam. I grabbed at her legs, her feet, and then just her toes, but trying to catch her was like trying to catch an out-of-control hurricane. I scrambled around hopelessly beneath the water, trying to grab on to her, but she was a good swimmer and easily escaped. Finally, I gave up and just watched her swim off. From a safe distance away, she turned back toward me and beamed with satisfaction.

"Leo, you'll never catch me!" she yelled. "If you took your togs off, I reckon you might be able to, though!"

"I'm not skinny dipping with you guys!" I shouted.

"Aw, come on, Leo!" she cried. "It's completely dark outside."

"Yeah, right! It's as bright as day out here!" I replied, looking around at the moonlight shining on the lake.

"Aw, mate!" she exclaimed. "How about you give it a go!"

I'd about had enough. Actually, I was completely spent from the game of tag, or keep-away, or whatever it was that we were playing out there in the middle of the lake. I swam slowly back to the canoe, trying to catch my breath.

"All right, if you guys won't let me catch you," I gasped, "I'm heading back in, and I'm taking the canoe with me." I gave the canoe a big shove from the stern, sending it shooting off like a rocket toward shore. Then, I swam slowly after it.

Aria, who had slowly moved closer to me in the water, quietly said, "I'll let you catch me, Leo."

I glanced over at her, calmly treading water nearby. She seemed completely serious. Everything became quiet and still as I moved closer to her. Aria simply grinned and waited for me to draw near. I could feel Esther's eyes watching me closely as I approached Aria, who was waiting in the water just a few feet away.

"Closer," Aria said calmly. "Come closer, Leo. That's right, just a little bit closer."

I suddenly noticed how cute she looked, gazing at me with her big brown eyes, waiting for me to swim just a little bit closer. Her face was dripping wet and glistening in the moonlight. Her arms and hands moved slowly and steadily on the surface of the water. Her skin flashed brightly, rich and golden, in the ripples moving out from her body.

I could see her, not in the water, but in my mind. I suddenly realized how strong and vibrant and beautiful she was—right there, just a few feet away, waiting for me to come just a little bit closer, waiting for me to reach out and touch her.

Suddenly, Aria's eyes grew full and bright. With a ferocious splash, she lunged straight at me and pushed me under the water. I scrambled around and shot back up, frantically trying to grab on to her, but she slipped back under and pushed off my chest with her feet. I grabbed at her foot and then her toes as she screamed and flailed wildly about in the water. Seconds later, she slipped out of my grasp and swam away, leaving me gasping for air.

"You'll never catch me!" Aria declared boldly from the safety of the open water far away.

"I had a feeling about that!" I replied in frustration. "So, why do I feel like Charlie Brown right now?"

"Oh yeah!" she shouted defiantly. "You've got feelings, Farm Boy, just not for me!"

I didn't have the energy to argue my case or chase either of them anymore. I was a sitting duck and barely able to stay afloat. The girls swam circles around me as I continued to tread water, just trying to keep from sinking to the bottom of the lake. They came in closer and closer, poking me and splashing me in the face.

"We're so happy you decided to join us!" Esther shouted.

"Are you guys actually skinny dipping?" I asked.

"Why would you think that?" asked Aria.

"I don't know," I replied. Suddenly, I realized they had their bathing suits on after all. "What a couple of sneaks!"

"Are you skinny dipping?" asked Esther.

"No, I've got my shorts on," I said, ever so thankful for that fact. The thought never actually crossed my mind, but if it had, I'm sure it would only have ended in further humiliation.

"Come on, Leo! Take 'em off!" Aria shouted as she swam in closer, taunting me relentlessly as only she could.

"No, I'm done," I said. "I'm gonna die if I stay out here any longer." I swam toward the canoe as it floated away toward shore.

"Come on, Leo!" Esther called. "Stay and swim with us. Don't leave us out here all alone."

"Yeah, we need you!" Aria chimed in. "We need someone to pick on and make fun of!"

I gave the canoe another shove toward shore, then slowly swam after it. I was completely spent. The girls finally gave up on me. They splashed around and laughed out in the water as I reached the rocky shore and pulled the canoe back up onto the bank.

"You two are such little sneaks!" I shouted to them as I held up the wet T-shirts in the bottom of the canoe.

They laughed at me from far away in the water. It's too bad I wasn't a better swimmer. I had no chance of catching them, and they knew it. They swam around a little while longer in the lake as I stoked the campfire and waited for them to return.

After a while, I heard them whispering down by the canoe. Then, out of the darkness, they appeared, tiptoeing through the campfire ring wrapped in their beach towels.

"Hey, Farm Boy, thanks for coming to rescue us," Aria said with a devious smirk.

She threw her wet T-shirt straight at my face as she passed by. It got me all wet and then plopped down into the dirt.

"Oh, that's really gross," I said, picking it up with my fingers. It looked a little familiar to me.

"Aw, a little dirt never hurt anybody," Aria replied.

"Here you go," I said, holding it out to her.

"No, you keep it, Leo," she said. "It's yours anyway!"

The two girls scampered away, laughing on their way back to the tent. I threw another stick into the fire and watched it burn. I plucked the strings on my guitar, thinking, "Aria's backrub is sure gonna feel good later on tonight."

I'd stay up as late as necessary for that!

chapter 42
campfire stories

"This'll be a good one."

As the girls changed in the tent, I set my guitar down and started whittling on a couple of long sticks of cedar. I shaved the bark off the ends and set them next to the fire grate. When the girls returned, they seemed relaxed and refreshed.

"Hey, do you guys want to make s'mores?" I asked.

"Sure, I'm starving," Aria said.

When I handed her a stick and the bag of marshmallows, she said, "Aw, Leo, how nice! You carved me a roasting stick?" Aria tossed the stick to Esther and said, "Here you go, cuzzy." Then, she stuffed a handful of marshmallows into her mouth and blurted out, "Thanks, Farm Boy, you think of everything."

Esther laughed at her crazy friend as she put a marshmallow on the stick and shuffled over beside me. "This is fun," she said as she held it over the fire. "I haven't roasted marshmallows in like forever."

When her marshmallow immediately burst into flames, Esther gasped in horror and yanked it out. "Crikey! It's on fire!" she cried. "What do I do? What do I do?"

She waved the flaming torch frantically around in the air above her head until the marshmallow finally flew off the stick and landed in the dirt right in front of Aria.

"You have to eat it now," Aria said with a smirk.

"Yeah, right," Esther replied. "I don't think so, sister."

"Oh, yes, you do," Aria insisted as she pushed the smoldering black mass toward Esther with her toes.

"I don't want it now!" Esther shrieked as she tried to kick the dirty marshmallow back toward Aria.

"You cooked it! Now you have to eat it!" Aria declared, giving the crispy glob of deliciousness another flick with her big toe.

The two girls proceeded to have a little shoving match with their feet and the disgusting ball of goo right in front of the campfire. Aria finally won the match when the marshmallow got permanently squished to the bottom of Esther's bare foot.

"Oh, thanks, Aria. That's quite lovely," she whimpered.

"What are friends for?" Aria replied with a scowl as she grabbed a couple more marshmallows and stuffed them into her mouth. "Now, all you gotta do is lick it off."

While they had their food fight in the dirt, I'd been slowly roasting another pair of marshmallows over the fire. I placed them in between two graham crackers and carefully slid half of a Hershey bar through the middle of the gooey sweetness.

"Here you go, Esther," I said. "This one's for you."

"Cheers, mate!" she replied, smiling with delight.

"Oh, I see how it is!" Aria wailed, her mouth stuffed to overflowing with marshmallows. "You never made me a s'more on our trip a few weeks ago, but here you go, making one for Esther!"

"I'll make you one, Aria," I said calmly. "How do you like 'em? Golden brown or charred to a crisp?"

"Raw," she said. "Just make me a raw one, and I'll be fine."

"Okay, a raw s'more coming right up," I replied, reaching out to her. "Toss me the bag."

Aria chucked the bag straight at my face. I caught it, but one of the marshmallows went flying out and away into the woods nearby.

"That's for all the starving chipmunks," she declared emphatically. "I bet they like to eat 'em raw too."

I pulled out two marshmallows and made a raw s'more for Aria. "This'll be a good one," I said, squishing the marshmallows into a gooey mass with my fingers and smearing it on top of a graham cracker. I topped it off with a piece of chocolate and then handed it over to Aria.

"Thanks, weirdo. It's perfect," she said. Then, she shoved the entire thing into her mouth and devoured it whole.

"You're disgusting. You know that, right?" I muttered.

"Yeah, but you love me anyway, Farm Boy," she replied with a chocolaty grin.

"How could I not love that?" I said, setting up another pair of marshmallows on a stick. "Who wants another one."

"Me!" came the quick reply from both girls.

We lazed around the campfire, making s'mores and poking fun at each other. The darkness had closed in all around, but the fire was comforting. We stared into the flames as they crackled and danced inside the fire grate. Aria kept adding cedar branches to keep it going. The cedar burned down to red-hot coals, which had a sweet, smoky aroma that filled the air all around us.

"Hey, if you don't want the mosquitoes to get you, just do this," I said, standing up. I took a big breath, closed my eyes, and leaned into the smoke. After a few seconds, I stepped back out and grinned contentedly. "Mosquitoes can't stand smoke."

"Now you stink like a campfire," Aria complained.

"But the mosquitoes are gonna bite you, not me," I replied.

"Yeah, right," she said as a mosquito landed on her leg and hopped around to find the perfect spot to draw blood. "At least I won't stink like a forest fire."

Esther stood up, took a big breath, and thrust herself into the smoke. She stood there for a long time with her eyes tightly shut.

"Girl, get out of there! You're gonna die of smoke inhalation!" exclaimed Aria.

Esther backed out and blinked her eyes. "Like that, eh?"

"Yeah, that's the way to do it," I said. "We'll both send all the starving mosquitoes over to Aria now."

"Sweet, bro," Esther replied with a grin. "I love the smell of smoke. I can't stand them mozzies, though."

We sat around the campfire, talking quietly as the night went along. Esther picked up my guitar and began to strum a few chords, soft and sweet. To see her playing my guitar only strengthened the kinship

I already felt with her. What was mine was hers. She could have anything she wanted—if she wanted it. As she strummed on the guitar, one of the loons out on the lake sounded out a long lonely call that echoed across the still water. I felt just like that loon, but I didn't know how to let it out. I sat in peaceful silence as I listened to the crackling fire and the soothing sounds of the night.

I mixed up a cup of tea and sat down across from the two girls, who had finally calmed down. They both seemed so different than what they were like back at camp. Esther was gently swirling a stick in the dirt as Aria sat beside her, braiding a part of her long hair. They seemed like long-lost sisters who cared deeply for each other. It made me feel even more like the outsider I knew I was. I watched jealously as they went about their girl-bonding time without me.

I couldn't help but notice again how Esther looked completely different from the first day when she'd arrived. Gone were the rough clothes, the black boots, and the red sunglasses. Gone was the dark makeup as well as the lipstick. It all had been replaced with a plain white T-shirt and a pair of blue jean cutoffs. She didn't look tough, intimidating, or fierce anymore. Her sunburned face glowed as she talked cheerfully in the campfire light. She seemed to be shining from within—bubbly and bright—gently listening and laughing along with Aria one minute, then being silly and crazy the next.

We were tired from the long day, but the campfire seemed to give us energy. Maybe it was the Russian tea we were drinking. Esther was on her second cup of the thick sweet brew overloaded with sugar. She was talking a mile a minute—smiling, laughing, and joking around. Her blue eyes flashed in the firelight—bright and beautiful—as if they themselves were on fire, surrounded by her long red hair that seemed extra-curly after the swim in the lake.

"Hey, Leo, this is one sweet bush telly you made for us," she said as she stared into the fire.

I thought about it and realized she was referring to the campfire. We huddled around the warm fire, inching closer and closer as the air outside gradually cooled down. The red-hot coals and dancing flames were mesmerizing. None of us seemed ready for bed.

"Hey, Esther, we should have some fireworks to celebrate your big day," I said as I grabbed a stick and stirred the coals in the fire.

We watched as a spray of fiery sparks shot up and danced around brightly before disappearing into the night sky. Esther looked up and smiled as she rested her chin on her knees. I grabbed my guitar and sang a gentle "Happy Birthday," prompting Aria to join in with a sweet harmony and a melodic run to finish it off.

"Best birthday ever," Esther said with joy as she gently applauded the surprise performance. She hugged her knees tightly and closed her eyes as a single tear rolled out from under her lashes. We sat in silence for a while as our eyes returned to the dancing flames.

"Hey, Leo," Esther said, glancing over at me. "If you could be anything you wanted, anything at all in life, what would it be?"

"You mean like a lion or something?" I asked.

"No, goofball," she laughed. "I'm talking for real, eh?"

"Oh, I don't know," I replied, mulling the idea over in my head.

"Come on, Leo!" Esther said as she poked me with the stick. "You always clam up when I ask you things."

"No, really," I insisted, fending off the pokey stick, which kind of hurt. "I have no idea whatsoever."

"Ahh!" Esther groaned and rolled her eyes. "You guys are just so impossible sometimes!"

"What about you?" I asked. "You go first, and I promise that I'll think of something."

"Okay, I guess," she moaned and closed her eyes. "Let me see. If I could be anything . . . I'd be a pretty white swan." She laughed and said, "Okay, I went. Now it's your turn, Leo."

"What? That's it?" I griped.

"Well, if you can be a lion, then I can be a swan," she said.

"Come on, how about giving us a real answer," I insisted.

"All right," Esther said, gazing into the fire. "If I could be anything, I'd be a girl who's free, totally free. I'd be free from all my worries, free to live and love as I see fit, and free to be whoever and whatever I want to be. To live like that would be so amazing."

"Esther, you're already all of those things," Aria said.

"Oh, I don't think so," Esther countered seriously. "Maybe I put on a grand show, but there's plenty you chaps don't know about me. How about you, Aria? What would you be?"

"Wait a minute," Aria fussed. "You can't just say that and then not give us details. What exactly don't we know about you?"

"Oh, I don't know," Esther said, staring into the fire. "I've got a lot of baggage I'm trying to off-load from my past, I guess. I'm trying to change, but it gets a bit knotty sometimes."

"Like what?" Aria asked.

"I don't feel too comfy yakking about it right now. Maybe I'll clue you in sometime later," Esther replied.

"Sure, girlfriend," said Aria. "You don't have to explain anything to me. I'm just curious, you know."

"So, Aria, what about you," Esther said. "If you could be anything you wanted in life, what would it be?"

I knew Aria didn't like being put on the spot any more than I did, but I was interested in what she'd say. She took some time to think as the campfire crackled and popped. I had a feeling we weren't going to bed anytime soon, so I threw a few more sticks on the fire.

"I don't know," Aria finally said. "I don't even know what I want to do in life yet or what kind of career I'll end up having. But your question made me think of something else."

"What's that?" Esther asked.

"Respect," said Aria. "I want to be treated with respect and valued for who I am. I can't stand it when people tear me down for no good reason at all, just because they feel like it or just because they're idiots. It makes me want to scream straight into their faces to make them wake up and see how stupid they're being."

"Is that why you beaned Percy with the volleyball?" I asked.

"Yeah, maybe," Aria said with a proud grin. "But you gotta stick up for your friends, you know."

"We didn't even know each other back then," I pointed out. "So, why did you do it?"

"I couldn't stand seeing you get treated like that," she said. "I know how it feels, so I decided to teach old Perky a lesson, I guess."

"You knocked him out and scared the crap out of everybody else too," I replied. "You should've heard them talking about it later. Nobody dared to go near you after that."

"Hey, it's the price you pay, sometimes, for standing up for what's right," Aria said. "It all turned out for the best anyway. Look at us."

"Yeah, Hunter, you certainly got my attention," I said with a smile.

"Leo, how about you?" Aria said. "Have you thought of anything yet, or are you still chicken to talk in front of a couple of girls?"

"Ha ha, funny!" I said sarcastically. I stared into the fire and thought for a few seconds. I couldn't think of anything worth mentioning, so I just said what popped into my head.

"I would be here with you guys," I replied. "I would be doing this. It's times like these that make life worth living. I don't really care what I end up being in life—a teacher or something else maybe. Still, it could never replace this right here, sharing moments like this with good friends, just hanging out around the fire, far away from the concerns and expectations of the world."

We sat in silence for a long time, listening to the crackling fire and the sounds of the night. It was almost perfectly still outside, except for a breeze that had gradually been picking up throughout the evening. We could see the stars to the north reflecting off the glassy lake, but the clouds were building in the west and beginning to block out the night sky. The loons that we'd heard earlier had stopped calling too. Something was coming, a change in the weather perhaps. It felt as if a storm was on its way, or at least the chance of a shower.

As we sat around the fire, staring into the flames, there was a peacefulness that seemed to invite a deeper intimacy and openness. We gazed silently at the fire. Somehow, we knew that what each of us longed for was indeed present there. At that moment in time, we were truly loved, respected, and free.

A little later, Esther stirred again. I could tell she had something on her mind. I watched her think it through, wondering what it might be. Then, sure enough, a couple of minutes later, she spoke up.

"Leo, bro," she said quietly. "Let's have a yarn—you know, a story, maybe one from your childhood, eh?"

I was getting used to Esther's random questions and quirky inquiries. It was always a complete surprise to me, but I appreciated the way she did it with such carefree abandon.

"I'll tell a story if one of you goes first," I replied. Esther and I looked at Aria, who nodded reluctantly in agreement.

"All right," Esther said as she bit the side of her lower lip. "I'll need some time to think, though. Aria, you go first, okay?"

"All right," Aria said as she slowly sat up and leaned forward. "I've got one I think you guys will like. So, you both know I grew up in Chicago my whole life. I never got outside the city, except on school field trips to the lake or downtown to visit one of the museums. Then, one summer, my mom talked me into going on a camping trip to Northern Lights. It was with a bunch of junior high girls from my old neighborhood. At first, I didn't want to go. I was intimidated by the other girls, and I was scared to be away from home."

"When I got up here, all the trees and water and open space really made me nervous. It totally freaked me out when we paddled across to the islands in that big canoe, but by then, there was no way to escape. When we met our canoe guide, Susie, straight off, I thought there was absolutely nothing I had in common with her. She was too happy, too polite, and too blond to be real. I didn't sleep all night. It was way too quiet in the woods outside."

"Well, the next morning, we packed up and shot straight out on the lakes. I played it cool, but all that water scared me to death. Susie really challenged us. She was one tough chick. I remember the first portage. She grabbed a canoe and helped me get it on my shoulders. 'You can do this!' she shouted in my face. It jolted me awake, and I thought, 'Damn right, woman, I can!' I carried that canoe across the portage all by myself. On the other side, I could see it in Susie's eyes; she was really proud of me. From then on, I was sold. It took the other girls a little longer to come around, but Susie kept at 'em."

"She was the strongest woman I'd ever met and brave too. But she was hard on us girls and really demanding when it came to chores and pitching in. She came down on us when we screwed off, but she still loved us. I was so impressed with her kindness, her love for the outdoors, and most of all, her patience with us ornery city girls."

"We tried our best to sabotage that trip. We gave her heck, but she just kept on loving us, and by the end of the week, we were all crying and teary-eyed and stuff. I didn't want to go back to the big city, where life was so harsh. I wanted to stay there and be just like her. That's why I'm here now. I want to influence other kids in that same way. So, there you go. That's my little story for you all, I guess."

When Aria finished and looked up, Esther was gazing straight at her, beaming with joy and admiration. "That's so awesome," she said. "And now here you are, living out that dream you had as a kid, eh? You're just so amazing, girlfriend!"

Esther shuffled over and gave Aria a big hug. "I love you so much, sweetie pie!" she gushed. "I'm so glad you're in my life."

Aria blushed and pulled away from Esther. "I love you too, you weirdo! Now, give me some space, all right?"

Esther leaned back and beamed at Aria again. Then, she gave her another hug. "Oh, girl, I could just eat you up!" she cried.

"Okay," Aria said. "Now it's time for someone else to spill their guts. It'd better be good too, or I'm gonna kick some ass."

"All right, I can go next," I said.

When the girls looked at me, I suddenly felt very exposed and vulnerable. It wasn't in my nature to talk about myself in front of other people, but I dove in anyway.

"When I was about six or seven years old, our family moved from North Dakota to Iowa," I said. "But each summer, we'd go back up there to visit my grandma and grandpa. They lived way up in the middle of the state, and it was a long boring trip that took an entire day. We would start out before the sun came up and just drive and drive and drive. By the time I woke up, we were usually driving northwest on I-94 past the Twin Cities somewhere, still heading for North Dakota. It was so flat up there. It was just about as flat as Iowa, but it was so wide open and windy with all those fields of wheat and barley and oats."

"Anyway, my favorite part of the trip was when we would visit my grandparents' cabin on Strawberry Lake. It wasn't a very big lake—

about as big as this one—but I loved it there. It was like a little oasis in the middle of all those dry hills and rolling prairies."

"My grandmother, Elsie, she was my favorite. What a crazy lady! She'd always welcome me with a big hug. She'd pull me straight into her chest and say, 'Oh Leo, you are getting so big and tall! What a handsome boy you are!'"

"She was always smiling, laughing, and joking around. She'd poke fun at everyone, especially me, probably because I was so quiet and serious all the time. But I loved her silly ways. She had a way of lighting up a room with her quirky personality and goofy take on life. She liked to tell corny jokes, cheat at cards, and sing too. She didn't seem to care if she was in tune or not. I just remember her crackly voice and her laughter filling up the cabin on that lake. I think that lake cabin was her favorite place on earth."

"Well, one day, Elsie got it in her head that she wanted to go fishing. She was always talking about fishing. She was always trying to get everyone else to go with her too, but that time, she had it in her head that I needed to go. So, I did. There was no way of getting out of it, because if she got it in her head that I had to go along, I was going whether I wanted to or not. So, we loaded up the fishing gear and rowed out onto the lake in Old Ironsides. That's the name she gave the old rusty rowboat of hers. As I rowed that boat out on the water, Elsie sat across from me, beaming with excitement as she got everything ready for our fishing expedition. She couldn't stop talking about where exactly to go on the lake, how to bait a hook, and the kinds of fish we were gonna catch."

"We finally dropped the anchor in the east bay of the lake and started fishing. As I fumbled around with my pole and the worms, Elsie dropped a line and started right in on fishing. I remember watching her catch one fish right after another—one, then two, then three, four, five, six. It was like the fish were starving or something. It was as if they couldn't wait for her to drop that hook down into the water. I could almost see those fish under the water. They all must have been scrambling around and wrestling each other to be the first to get a bite of that poor worm. It never had a chance."

"I bet my grandma strung up a dozen fish before I got a single bite. I think she saw it in my eyes—my disappointment, my feeling of not being good enough, of not measuring up. That's when she set her fishing pole down and focused entirely on me. She helped me bait the hook; then she talked me through the whole process of casting the line out, reeling in the slack, and then waiting patiently as the bobber moved around and bounced up and down on the water. Elsie and I sat there in Old Ironsides, whispering to each other, her hands holding mine, helping me move that pole around and reel in the line ever so slowly. It was just my grandma and me. It felt so good being out there on the lake with her watching me try to catch my first fish."

"When I got a nibble, I got really nervous, but Elsie laid her hands on mine and calmed me down. We waited—silent and still—as that fish nibbled away on the worm down below. When it finally took the bait, my bobber sank all the way under the water, and I got so excited! My grandma squealed with delight, and then she coached me on how to gently coax that fish in, letting it pull some, then reeling the line in, bit by bit, until we could see it darting around under the surface of the water, still fighting for its life. Then, I lifted it out of the lake as my grandma scooped it up in a big net."

"She grabbed on to that slimy fish as it wiggled and squirmed in her hands. 'Oh, that's a big one, Leo!' she cried. 'What a nice fish you caught! It's a bullhead, and a big one too! We're gonna have a feast tonight!' She carefully twisted the hook out of its little mouth and then strung it on the line with the rest of her fish. I remember her smiling and looking at me with such pride and joy. Her eyes were wide with excitement. 'Are you ready to catch another one?' she asked."

"So, we fished some more. I think I caught two more bullheads that afternoon. My grandma got back to fishing too. She probably pulled in another stringer full of fish, at least two dozen in all. Yeah, Elsie was quite a lady. It's those moments I had with her, just the two of us alone, that stand out in my memory—when she focused all her attention on me, all of her enthusiasm and joy for life, along with her vibrant personality and quirky ways. It's those special moments that really stick with me. I think that's where I got my love for being on the water. She passed it off to me out there in that old fishing boat. Her smile and laughter and funny ways just beamed straight across into me. And now I'm here, still thinking about it, wishing I could be back out there on Strawberry Lake, sitting across from Grandma Elsie in Old Ironsides, letting her hold my hands and teach me how to fish for the very first time."

When I finally wrapped up my story, I looked up and immediately saw Esther sitting there, grinning back at me from ear to ear. I half expected her to leap out of her seat and attack me as she'd done to Aria, but she simply crossed her arms over her chest and let out a big sigh. Her eyes beamed with joy and pride and excitement, just like my grandma so long ago. I could see the same qualities in Esther that I admired in my grandmother—an intense joy for life, a love for the outdoors, and a way of living simply with such carefree abandon and graceful contentment.

"Awesome," Esther said. "That was a mighty sweet yarn, bro."

"Yeah, that was nice, Leo," Aria said as she stared into the fire. "Your grandma sounds like a pretty cool lady."

"Yeah, mate," Esther said, still grinning at me. "I think that I understand your grandma pretty well."

"She's kind of goofy, but I love her a lot," I replied.

"I'd like to meet your grandmother someday," Esther said as she smiled contentedly from across the fire ring.

Her warm smile seemed to signal something deeper and more meaningful to me. I smiled back and wondered what else she was thinking. I wondered what she'd be like when she was a grandmother. I wondered if she might like to go fishing with me sometime too.

"Okay, it's my turn, mates," Esther said as she turned serious and gathered her composure. "I reckon I'm a lot like you, Aria. I grew up in Auckland, a city of almost two million people on the north island of New Zealand. We lived in the heart of the city, so my earliest childhood memories are mostly of our backyard, our big dog, and playing in the streets with the other kids."

"When I was little, I remember going on a trip with my parents out into the back-country to my uncle's ranch. It took half a day to get there, but it didn't seem very far, because we sang songs, told stories, and stopped for lunch along the way."

"I remember bunking in the guest house. It was just a little shanty with one big room and a fireplace on one end. We slept on the floor around the fireplace. It was fun. My uncle had horses, chickens, a dog, and a bunch of cats. I loved the cats. They followed me everywhere and were so cute and cuddly."

"I remember tramping in the bush and spotting rabbits, squirrels, and birds in the trees. My sis and I liked to play in a little stream that ran alongside the paddock into the woods. We played in the water as the horses watched over us nearby."

"One evening, we had a big bushfire outside in the meadow. I remember hearing all the night sounds and listening to my rellies weave yarns around the fire. I'll never forget seeing the stars in the sky for the first time—actually seeing all of them—so bright and sparkly up in that beautiful black sky. It wasn't like the purple haze of Auckland with just a few stars scattered about. There were hundreds of stars covering the entire sky, thousands of them, too many to count, and all of them blinking down on me as if to say, 'Hello, little one! Welcome to the universe!'"

"I had studied about nature in school, but that was the first time I got to experience it for myself—to see it, feel it, and touch it. It's like our time here in the Boundary Waters. So many people read about this place or hear stories about it, but so few get to come up here and experience it for themselves. I reckon even fewer take the time to venture out into the wayback—far away from civilization, from the city lights, and other people."

"I enjoy being out here in the wop-wops, having all this fun, but it's the quiet times that I love the most. It reminds me of those times playing in that stream as a child. I'm free to do whatever I want. I can shape my future into anything I want it to be. And I'm with some of the best mates I could ever ask for, who are here with me, being silly and goofing around, letting me be myself, letting me share my childhood stories around the campfire. The past three weeks have been so sweet. I don't ever want to leave you guys."

When she finished, Aria wrapped her arm around Esther's side and gave her a big squeeze. "You're the best friend ever," Aria said as she leaned her head on Esther's shoulder. "I love you so much."

"I love you too," Esther replied.

Suddenly, Aria stared at Esther's legs and frowned. "Look at your legs!" she yelled as she slapped Esther's thighs in a violent frenzy. "You're getting eaten alive by mosquitoes!"

"Hey, stop it, cuz!" Esther screamed. "Stop it now! Is this what I get for baring my soul to you?"

"Yup," Aria said, giving her leg a final whack.

"Ouch!" Esther yelled. "Stop hitting me, Aria! That's worse than the little mozzies themselves!"

"I'm just getting you back for last night," Aria replied.

"Well, I'm gonna go change out of my togs and put on a jersey," Esther announced, hopping to her feet. "Toss me your torch, Aria, so I can go find my stuff in the bivvy."

"Here you go," Aria said, handing her flashlight to Esther.

"Cheers, mate!" Esther replied as she pranced away to the tent. "You guys can stay out there and get eaten alive if you want to, but not me! I'll be back in a jiffy!"

"Well, those were some pretty sweet bedtime stories, huh, Leo?" Aria said with a smirk. "Now we've bonded over our touchy-feely childhood memories. Life doesn't get any better than that."

"You loved it. You just don't want to admit it," I replied.

"Yeah, I guess so," she said, staring into the fire.

The lake was calm, but I could hear the low boom of thunder far away to the southwest. It wasn't a surprise. Storms passed through the lakes region all the time, and the weather was always changing. It could be bright and sunny one morning, and by the afternoon, rainy and cold. Then, it might clear off overnight and do it all over again. The rumbles of thunder meant that we might get some rain that evening, but it'd probably blow over by morning.

You had to always take it one day at a time.

chapter 43
just friends?

"I was just wondering."

As Aria and I waited for Esther to return, I moved down next to her, closer to the fire. It was warm and bright, and it kept some of the mosquitoes away. We sat there quietly, listening to the wood crackle and pop, throwing a stick in every once in a while. After about ten minutes, I began to wonder what happened to Esther.

"I don't hear anything," I said, gazing sleepily into the fire.

"Me neither," Aria replied, just as sleepily.

"Maybe someone should go check on her," I suggested.

"I suppose you mean me?" Aria said dryly, heaving a long sigh.

I didn't move or say anything. I just stared into the fire as Aria slowly pulled herself up and shuffled off to the tent. I heard the zipper open and then shut. Then, Aria returned and sat back down.

"Well, what's up? Did you find her?" I asked, trying not to appear too interested.

"Yeah, she's out," Aria said, going back to staring at the fire.

"She's out? You mean, like, at the throne or what?" I asked.

"No, Valley Girl," replied Aria. "She's out, like a light."

"Oh, okay, I was just wondering," I said.

"I know, Farm Boy," she replied, speaking directly to the issue at hand. "You're really obsessed with her, aren't you, Leo?"

"No, I'm not," I said, lying through my teeth.

"Hey, Leo, I just want to say thanks for taking us on this trip," she said, ignoring my lie. "It means a lot to Esther and me."

"No problem," I said. "It's been pretty fun, yeah?"

"Yeah," she said quietly. "By the way, I'm sorry for chewing into you so much these past few days."

"That's okay," I replied.

"It's just me being me," she said. "It's who I am, you know. It's just what I do sometimes . . . well, most of the time."

"Hey, I'm fine," I reassured her. "You don't have to apologize."

"It's just my way of dealing with stuff," she said as she tossed a stick into the fire. "Like when my dad left, it was just me, my mom, and my little brother. I changed after that. Life wasn't as much fun anymore. It got colder, harder, and tougher. I think I had to adjust to survive . . . mentally and emotionally."

"I understand, Aria, at least I'm trying to," I said.

"Yeah, cool," she said. "So, when I call you an idiot or a wimp, I'm not trying to be mean, you know. It just comes out opposite all the time. I'm just trying to say that I like you."

"Oh, you love me, and you know it," I replied with a silly smirk.

"I don't know, Leo," Aria said, still serious. "This thing we've got going this summer, I think a part of me is still so afraid. I say things to keep you guessing or to keep you at a safe distance."

"Why do you think that is?" I asked.

"It's not easy to explain," she said with a sigh. "Maybe it's because I know when the summer is over, you'll be leaving, just like my dad left, and I'm just trying to prepare for that."

"Hey, Aria," I broke in. "We can stay in touch through the school year, and then I'll see you back here next summer."

"I don't know," she doubted openly. "You're heading back to college, and I'm going down to Indiana this fall."

"We'll stay in touch," I assured her.

"I don't know," she said again. "You're going one way; I'm going another. They're in opposite directions, Leo."

We sat there staring into the campfire for a long time. The cedar branches crackling in the hot flames were comforting. They filled the space between us with soothing sound and light.

"You know why I like you, Leo, right?" Aria asked.

"Because I'm such a ripped stud-muffin?" I replied.

"No, doofus," she said. "It's because you see all of me, the whole package, not just my outward appearance, like my body and stuff."

"Really? How so?" I replied, wanting to hear more.

Aria let out a deep sigh and said, "I mean, when we're together, I feel like you see me for who I am, both inside and out, and I honestly believe you care about the real me. You've always accepted me as I am, not just who you want me to be."

"Oh, I love you, Aria," I said, replaying the lame old line again.

"Shut up, Leo," Aria shot back in disgust. "Look, so many people I know—they only see me on the outside. Teachers see my mind mostly. Adults see my age. The canoe guides see me as a swamper, and the older guys just see my body."

"Yeah, I struggle with that one too," I admitted.

"You do?" Aria asked as she looked up at me and grinned.

"Yeah," I said, being careful to keep my eyes on the fire.

In the silence that followed, I wondered about our friendship. I wondered how Aria felt about me. I thought I knew, but Esther had come flying into the picture, and it was starting to get awkward. I thought about what Aria meant to me. I wasn't sure. The fire was comforting, but it didn't answer any of my questions.

"Leo," Aria said, breaking the silence. "I don't know how to explain it. I just like being with you. You see me for who I really am. I can feel your love for me—the real me—and it feels good. I don't think I can explain why I say and do the things I do. So, all I'm saying is, I think you're cool, and thanks for sticking by me."

I kept my eyes on the fire. It was a big surprise to hear her express her feelings so openly. Her words made me feel good too.

"Thanks, Aria," I replied softly. "I'm glad we became friends this summer. I've enjoyed our friendship, even with all the beatings and name-calling you dish out all the time. I love everything about you. This summer wouldn't have been the same without you here to keep me grounded and on my toes too."

"Thanks, Leo," she said as she stared into the fire. "But you're not telling me everything.

"I'm not?" I tried to keep my eyes on the fire, but I couldn't.

"I know what's going on, Leo," she said plainly, looking up into my eyes. "Esther is pretty awesome. I knew that when I first met her. Maybe that's why I didn't want to share her with you. I didn't want you to steal her away from me, but that's what's happening, and it's okay. I'm happy for you guys."

"I won't steal her away from you," I said. "I couldn't do that. You and I know there's plenty of Esther to go around."

"Yeah," she agreed. "Esther really takes up a lot of space in the old canoe, doesn't she?"

"Yeah, I think she's got more spunk than both of us put together," I said with a chuckle.

"That's why I love her so much," Aria said. "And that's why you do too. So, don't let me get in the way, Leo. I might say a lot of nasty stuff to you, but you know I still love you, right?"

"Yeah, I know," I said as I leaned over and wrapped my arm around her shoulder. "You're awesome, Bear Bait, really."

"Shut up, Leo," she said, blushing a bit. "You're killing me here. You know that, don't you?" She glanced up at me just inches away. She looked so pretty and sweet, sitting there so close to me.

"Hey, it's getting late," she finally said. "We better hit the sack."

"What about your promise?" I asked.

"My what?" she replied.

"You know, the promise you made when you guys were swimming in the lake." I hoped she hadn't forgotten.

"Oh, yeah!" she exclaimed. "Okay, sure! Let's go! You know, Leo, I've been dying to get my hands on you all summer."

"Yeah," I said with a grin. "You've been smacking and punching and knocking me down ever since we first met. So, here's your chance to really make it hurt. This had better be good!"

Aria grinned and said, "I'll make you beg for mercy before I'm done with you, Farm Boy!"

"Well, I can't wait!" I replied, jumping up and heading for the tent with Aria hot on my heels.

I was really looking forward to that backrub.

chapter 44

backrubs and tattoos

"She was really trying to hurt me."

As I unzipped the tent, Aria kicked me in the seat and exclaimed, "Get in there, Leo! I'm gonna work you over good!"

"Ha! I'm ready for it!" I said as I stumbled in, tripping over Esther who was lying on her sleeping bag in the middle of the floor.

"Are you guys finally coming to bed?" Esther asked as she rubbed her eyes and looked at us in the dark. She was still in her white T-shirt and blue jean shorts.

"Sorry, Esther," Aria whispered. "It's Leo's fault. He's such a klutz. We weren't trying to wake you up, believe me."

"No worries, cuz," she said as she yawned and stretched like a sleepy cat. "I didn't want to fall asleep and leave you guys alone. I was just so stuffed, you know. What's going on?"

"I'm giving Leo that backrub I promised him," Aria said. "Hey, girlfriend, maybe you could give me one after that?"

"Totally," Esther said with a smile. "I'd be happy to, cuz."

I stretched out on my sleeping bag and waited for Aria to pounce on me. She did with a mighty thump and then set to work on my shoulders. It felt so good, getting my sore muscles worked over after a long hard day. My entire body ached, and Aria's powerful hands moved up and down ferociously all over my back, making me groan and flinch and cry out for mercy. It was pretty obvious that she was really trying to hurt me. It felt wonderful.

When she was done, she flopped over onto her sleeping bag and said, "There you go, Leo! That's all there is; there ain't no more!"

"Thanks," I mumbled as I lay there, unable to move. "Now I have something nice to remember you by." I felt like a squished worm reveling in the beating it just took from a shoe that rendered it completely flat and utterly helpless on the pavement. I felt soft and warm and wonderful all over.

"All right, sister," Esther broke in eagerly. "You're next."

She jumped on top of Aria and poked her in the side, making her squirm and squeal. Then, she dug her fists into Aria's upper back and started working her way down. I watched as Esther moved over Aria's body, rolling her knuckles, chopping away at her shoulders, and scratching her back with her long fingernails. She worked Aria over for a good fifteen minutes. Then, she finished it off with a long gentle rubdown. I looked on jealously, wishing it were me that Esther was touching. When she was done, she quietly leaned over and checked to see how Aria was doing.

"There you go, girl," she whispered. "How did that feel?" There was no response. Esther waited a few seconds and then whispered again, "Aria, are you asleep?"

Still, there was no response, just the sound of Aria breathing, thick and steady. Esther flashed her eyes at me as she carefully slid off of Aria's legs and moved over to her own sleeping bag in the middle of the tent. She lay there for a couple of minutes as I waited to see what she would do next. Esther turned her head toward me and grinned when she saw that I was still awake.

"Hey, Leo, we're alone now," she whispered.

"Yeah," I whispered back. I was so tired, but still, I just had to ask, "Esther, do you want a backrub?"

She grinned and nodded silently, then rolled over as I sat up next to her. I hesitated for a moment, realizing that I was about to put my hands onto Esther's body. It was both thrilling and terrifying to be there with her—a girl so alive and carefree, so fascinating, and so incredibly beautiful. Slowly and carefully, I lowered my hands onto her shoulders as if her body were an ancient relic I'd been forbidden to touch up until that very moment. I let my fingers sink into her warm skin as I soaked up the soft tenderness of her body.

Esther's wavy red hair was everywhere. As I rubbed her back, she flipped her hair off to the side, but there was still so much of it. She had tied it up in a loose bun after swimming in the lake, but it was still thick and long and glorious. As she lay on her sleeping bag with her head tilted to one side, I could see the pretty arch of freckles sprinkled across her nose and cheeks in the flickering firelight. I could see freckles on her shoulders as well, running under her white top and down the outside of her arms.

As I rubbed her shoulders, I noticed what appeared to be a tattoo below the back of her neck. It was a cluster of little blue-green dots that ran under the collar of her shirt. I leaned over and tried to make out what they were, but I couldn't tell in the dark.

"Hey, Esther," I whispered. "Do you have a tattoo on your shoulders back here?"

"Yeah, bro," she said. "Would you like to take a peek at it?"

Before I could say anything, she hunched up on her elbows and pulled the shirt off over her head. Then, she flopped back down onto her sleeping bag, using the shirt as a pillow.

"Go ahead, mate, have a squiz," she said. "It's a tattoo I got a few years back in Auckland."

I panicked in two ways at once. First, I thought Esther was going to wake up Aria, and I desperately didn't want that to happen. Secondly, the realization that Esther had just taken her shirt off hit me like a ton of bricks. A sudden rush of electricity shot through my body as I stared at her bare back and listened to hear if Aria was still asleep. Thankfully, Aria didn't stir. She was still breathing quietly on the edge of the tent. But Esther was suddenly naked . . . well, not completely, but it felt like it to me!

"Leo, can you see it?" she asked. "The tattoo?"

I wasn't even looking at the tattoo, not right away at least. What I was looking at was her gorgeous body, lying there completely exposed, with just the thin strap of the bikini—the only thing between my hands and her silky skin. I hesitated, at first, to even touch her. Slowly, I leaned over to look for the tattoo again in the darkness.

"Leo, bro, do you see it?" she asked again.

I took a big breath and gently rested my hands, just barely, on her bare shoulders. Then, I leaned over and looked more closely at the tattoo under her neck. It was dark inside the tent, but the flickering campfire light helped a little. I could see what appeared to be a pattern of luminescent blue-green dots that made a sort of cross shape. It was nestled between her two shoulder blades and surrounded by an explosion of freckles that swept everywhere across her upper back from shoulder to shoulder.

"Yeah, I see it," I whispered, squeezing her shoulders gently.

"What do you reckon it is?" she asked.

"I don't know, the Southern Cross?" I guessed, trying to connect the dots that looked like a giant letter X or maybe a diamond.

"Nice try, but nah," she said. "Guess again."

"I have no idea. You'll have to tell me," I replied.

"It's Cygnus the Swan," she said, reaching back and pulling her hair off to the side. "I got it two years ago after taking my first astronomy class back in Auckland."

I leaned in closer to examine the cluster of dots. Sure enough, they were the same pattern of stars we'd seen the night before, exactly like the constellation Cygnus high above. They looked like a little cross flying through the pretty freckles on her upper back.

"Wow, it's really cool-looking," I said quietly.

"Thanks, bro!" she cheerfully replied, clearly pleased that I'd made the surprise discovery. I just didn't want her to wake up Aria, and it seemed as if she didn't mind one way or the other.

I resumed Esther's backrub again, working my way down the ridges of her spine. The freckles seemed to fade away and disappear on her lower back. I rolled my knuckles back up to her shoulder blades, making her flinch once or twice on purpose.

"Hey there," she said. "What do you think you're doing?"

I had no idea. I couldn't believe Esther was there with me—a girl from New Zealand with so many experiences I knew nothing about. She was like uncharted waters to me, like the untamed wilderness of the North Woods, like countless lakes and waterfalls and cliffs and campsites just waiting to be discovered and explored.

As I ran my fingertips over her body, I wondered what else I might discover about her that night. I didn't want it to end. I pressed my cold fingers into her warm, soft skin and stared at her beautiful body, her delicate neck, her long flowing hair, the freckles that ran across her tattoo and everywhere else, all the way down to her waist where I was kneeling like a holy man in prayer.

Then, I remembered something I'd noticed earlier in the day but had been too timid to ask about. I moved my fingers down the right side of her body just below her ribs and gently poked her there.

"Hey, you," she said as she flinched to the side.

"What is this right here?" I inquired. "Another tattoo?"

"You found it," Esther said happily. "I was wondering if you would. So, what do you think it is?"

It was another constellation; I was sure of it, but most of it was hidden underneath her body. As I tried to take a closer look, Esther turned completely over and leaned back on her elbows.

"What do you think, Leo?" she asked.

"Hold still, don't move," I said. "I'm still trying to figure it out."

"Yeah, mate, I know," she said softly.

Esther grinned excitedly as I leaned down closer to examine the tattoo. It was another cluster of blue-green dots, which clearly made up a constellation of some kind, but it was hard to see in the flickering firelight. It felt odd to be hunched over her body, staring down at her naked belly, trying to make out a tattoo in the dark.

"I don't know," I finally said. "You'll have to help me out.

"Yeah, mate," she replied. "I suppose I will, but I'd rather have you figure it out all on your own."

"Sorry, Esther," I said, still staring blankly at the mysterious tattoo. "I'm really totally clueless here."

"It's you," she said quietly.

"Me? What do you mean by that?" I asked.

"It's Leo the lion," Esther said, chuckling softly. "I got it just before I came up here to Northern Lights."

I looked more closely. Sure enough, it was the constellation, Leo, placed in the soft crescent of her lower abdomen on the right side just below her ribs. It appeared to be pouncing on her belly button, with its paws disappearing beneath the edge of her cutoffs.

"It's beautiful," I said, unable to think of anything better to say.

At that point, I knew I was totally in over my head. I was crossing uncharted waters without any map to show me which way to go next. Nervousness and excitement washed over me like a waterfall. I felt helplessly frozen in disbelief at the situation in which I found myself. There I was, sitting next to a gorgeous redheaded girl in a tent in the middle of the Boundary Waters, and she was lying there in her bikini in the flickering firelight, showing me the tattoos on her naked body like points of interest on a treasure map.

"So, Leo, do you like it?" Esther asked softly.

"Like it?" I said, drifting back to consciousness from somewhere far, far away. "Oh, yeah," I replied. "It's really cool."

In my feeble mind, however, I was screaming at the top of my lungs, "Holy cow! What is going on? What is she going to say next? What am I supposed to do now?" I had no idea!

"So, where exactly is Leo going down there?" I asked, pinching her in the side down by the tattoo.

Esther gave a muffled shriek and twisted back onto her stomach. She bumped Aria, who stopped breathing and then smacked her lips a couple of times. Esther and I dropped onto our sleeping bags and stared at each other, wide-eyed and motionless as we listened for Aria to start breathing again. We held our breath and waited silently. A few seconds later, Aria let out a long deep sigh. Then, she curled up next to the side of the tent again and went back to sleep.

As Esther and I lay there, I could see a wild joyfulness and a fierce determination in her eyes. She seemed so alive and free, lying there in the darkness of the tent—her beautiful body just inches away from mine. I shook with dazed excitement as things continued to spin wildly out of control. It took my breath away to be caught so off-guard like that. I wasn't prepared for it at all, but at that point, I didn't really care! I just wondered what would happen next.

"Leo is setting in the west," Esther whispered softly.

"What?" I whispered back.

"Leo, the lion," she said. "He's going down in the west. Each night just after sunset, he sets on the western horizon just like the sun."

"Why does he do that?" I whispered.

"To hide from Hercules who's chasing him across the sky," Esther said quietly. "He's going down to hide beneath the horizon and sleep until the morning light."

"I don't want to sleep," I confessed.

"I don't either," she whispered.

Esther grinned sweetly as she propped herself back up on her elbows and gazed out the screen door of the tent. Her blue eyes sparkled in the fading campfire light. We didn't say anything for a long time. I watched her as she gazed at the fire. I wondered what she was thinking about, but I was too afraid to ask.

Esther finally spoke, but more seriously than before. "Leo, in the water when we were swimming and you were chasing Aria; did you want to catch her?"

I thought about the question for a few seconds. Then, I grinned helplessly and replied, "I wanted to catch you."

"Ha!" she said with a laugh. "I wouldn't have let you!" She nudged me in the ribs, then turned serious again. "Do you like Aria?"

"Yeah, I like her a lot," I said. "Why do you want to know that?"

"Well, it's pretty obvious, isn't it?" she replied. "Aria really fancies you, mate."

"We're good friends, that's all," I explained. "I think that's how it's always going to be, at least for the summer."

"And in the future?" Esther asked.

"I don't know," I whispered. "I'm open to the possibility of—"

I suddenly cut myself off. "What am I saying?" I thought. "I'm falling in love with Esther, not Aria!" I felt so stupid and angry at myself. In frustration, I shut up and went completely silent.

"That's good," Esther said calmly in the silence. "Yeah, mate, that's a good way to live."

"What do you mean?" I asked, still furious with myself. I looked down at Esther's pretty toes at the bottom of her sleeping bag. They were almost touching mine.

"To be open and honest with others," Esther replied. "To live and love freely, and to share your feelings as you've done so openly with me. It's so nice and refreshing." She thought for a moment, then continued. "But the truth—sometimes it hurts, eh? It can totally hurt, but it's still the truth. And to say it, to speak it . . . can be so freeing. Do you understand what I mean?"

"What?" I asked, still wallowing in despair over my stupidity.

"To speak the truth," she said plainly.

"About what?" I asked.

Esther chuckled. "Well, about you and me, of course."

I glanced at Esther. Her eyes came to life in a flash of light from the fire, then fell back into darkness as the light flickered and went out again. In the dark, I could see her smiling sweetly back at me. The erratic flames of the dying firelight flashed now and then on her face. She kept looking at me until I had to look away.

She was right. The truth hurt, and for some reason, I was terrified of it. I was hesitant to even speak it. I was afraid of what Esther might think of me. I was afraid of what might happen—of being loved and left again, of being exposed and then rejected, of being hurt again just like before.

The silence lingered . . . a little too long, and I could tell the moment had passed. Her comment about the two of us was left unanswered, and my stupidity stubbornly remained in place. Esther waited in the silence. Then, finally, she settled back down on her sleeping bag and gazed at me in the darkness.

"Hey, Leo," she whispered. "Give me your hands."

Esther reached out to me across her sleeping bag. She stretched out her fingers and waited for me. Slowly, I pushed my hands out toward her. I wondered what she was planning to do with them. I had no idea what was going to happen, but at that moment, I would do just about anything for Esther.

Yeah, I would do just about anything.

chapter 45
the northern lights

"It takes time and patience and a willingness to wait."

Esther took my hands and pulled them close to her body. She wrapped her warm fingers around my left hand, and then she began to pinch and squeeze the muscles. Her fingers moved slowly up around my wrist to my forearm—pressing and releasing, pressing and releasing. Then, she worked her way back down to my palm and found a hard knot there. Esther pressed firmly on the knot and rubbed all around it, pressing again and again. It hurt so much it was almost unbearable, but I was not about to cry out.

Her hands moved patiently from one finger to the next, massaging each individual joint and muscle, moving methodically up one finger, then down the next, pressing firmly, then releasing, pressing and releasing. It was a heavenly experience that I didn't deserve. I savored every second of it, and I didn't want it to end.

After a while, it became evident that Esther was not just giving me a hand massage. Every so often, in the darkness of the tent, I could see her eyes flickering in the firelight, gazing directly at me. I looked down at our feet again, lying so close together. I had no idea how to respond to her tender care. "She must think I'm a complete idiot," I thought. "I really blew it."

Fears and frustrations poured over me as we both lay there in the darkness. But as Esther continued to rub my hands, my doubts and worries slowly faded away. I closed my eyes, content to fall asleep in that heavenly moment—in the hands of Esther as she gave me her complete and undivided attention. I drifted back and forth, into and out of sleep, wondering if I was dreaming or still lying there in the tent next to her. I wondered if something else was coming—if something even more amazing was about to happen.

"No, it's over," I thought. "I should just get some sleep."

But as Esther continued to rub my hands and gaze at me in the darkness, I realized that she wasn't about to stop anytime soon. Her warm fingers just kept on rubbing my cold hands. There was a purpose and a determination to what she was doing. I could feel it in her hands and in her eyes, which were fixed on me. Suddenly, I was wide awake again. Something *was* about to happen.

"Leo," she whispered. "I have to ask you something."

"What?" I whispered back.

"Well, mate," she said quietly. "It's kind of hard to say."

"Why?" I asked.

"Leo," she replied, somewhat exasperated. "You're not making this very easy, are you, bro?"

"What do you mean?" I asked, still not getting it.

"What do *you* think I mean?" she countered.

"I don't know," I replied, playing dumb again. "But you can ask me anything you like."

"All right," she said. "I'll just spit it out then." She paused for a second and then continued. "Leo, I think you are a strong person, and good, on the outside. Everyone can see that. You're a good canoe guide too. You know how to find your way in the wilderness and keep us safe. But Leo, I want to know what you're like on the inside."

She left the request hanging there in the darkness as she continued to rub my hands. I thought about it and wondered what she was getting at. What was I like on the inside? I suddenly realized that Esther wanted to know what I'd been thinking about her.

"Really?" I thought to myself. "I can't tell her that!"

It was such a simple request, but my fears overwhelmed me once again. I had no idea how to give her an honest answer. I lay there, trying to come up with a response—anything at all, but nothing came. In frustration, I had to look away. Esther waited for me to say something, but when I didn't, she began to speak again.

"I think, on the inside, you are a good man, caring and respectful of others," she said. "You always treat people with kindness, but you are cautious too. Maybe you're afraid to let some people get too close to you—too friendly or too intimate. Maybe you're afraid of what they might think of you or what they might do or say. Maybe you're afraid of being hurt by them."

I listened, frozen in silence. I felt entirely exposed by her words as she lay there next to me, reading my mind in the darkness of the tent. She kept rubbing my hands with her warm fingers as she looked intently into my eyes.

Her words were hypnotic, and the steady, gentle rubbing of her hands over mine was so comforting and reassuring. I slowly and cautiously looked up again into her beautiful eyes, still gazing intently into mine. The dying firelight somehow made it a bit more tolerable and safe. I waited in silence, wanting more, hoping and wishing she would say more, and thankfully, she did.

"Leo," she said softly. "Do you want to know what I really think of you?"

"Yeah," I replied desperately. I waited—quiet and still—wondering what she would say next.

"With most people," she said, "I'm pretty reserved, cold, even rude sometimes. It's what I do, I guess, to protect myself, to keep people away that I don't trust. But when I find someone who is kind and gentle, someone who is strong and respectful, someone I admire and care for, it's so attractive to me. When I find someone like that, I set my fears aside and open up my heart, and then I simply love . . . freely. When I find someone like that, I don't hold back. I give myself openly, generously, and extravagantly."

Esther paused for a few fragile seconds. Then, she said, "Leo, that's how I feel for you right now."

She fell silent again, as if waiting for me to respond. Her eyes remained fixed on me—tender, intense, and penetrating. It was clear that Esther was being completely open and honest with me. Her eyes seemed to glow in the darkness, confirming the truth she had just spoken from the heart.

My fingers rested in the palms of her hands. She was still holding on to them firmly, but her warm fingers had stopped rubbing mine and were completely still. She was waiting patiently, waiting for me to respond. Her heart was laid bare, and mine was broken wide open. I felt as if I were completely at her mercy, but I didn't know what to say. Her words pierced my heart and pressed into me like a waterfall crashing down all around me. I was overwhelmed, and to be honest, it was so much more than I could take.

Her tender hands loosened the grip I had on my emotions, my stubborn pride, and my need for self-control. Her words softened me, warmed me, and melted me. She must have realized how utterly paralyzed I was. She must have known, because she said a few more sweet and wonderful words that, by then, I had guessed were coming, words I desperately desired for her to say. They came as an added blessing, even before I could utter any kind of feeble reply.

"Leo, you are that person," Esther said quietly. "I have found such kindness and strength in you, and such great love and respect for me, that I find myself wanting to love you freely. I don't want to worry about it or hold myself back. I want to show you what I feel inside. Leo, I want you to let me love you."

She gave a nervous sigh and a quick grin; then she looked down. I realized that it wasn't as easy for her as it first seemed. She was risking something, and suddenly, there was a nervous tension in the darkness between us. In the silence, I was still reeling from the fact that Esther had laid bare her heart and soul . . . with me, of all people. It felt amazing, yet terrifying. As the silence lingered, I realized that I needed to say something, anything at all, to respond to her. The silence became louder and louder in my head as I frantically grasped for the right words to say.

Finally, I attempted a response. "Esther, I feel so completely blown away by your words and by you . . . here . . . now. I'm amazed by your openness and honesty and the way you live life so freely. I'm trying to live like that too. I'm trying to be all those things you said about me, but sometimes I fail so miserably. I'm just afraid that when you get to know me, you won't like what you find."

"I'm not asking you to be perfect," she replied earnestly. "I just want to know you better. I see something beautiful inside you. There's a diamond hidden in there somewhere, and I want to find it . . . if you'll just let me in."

"I want that too," I said. "It's just difficult for me to let people inside . . . and to love freely, as you said."

"It doesn't have to be so difficult," she replied. "If life brings you something beautiful, if fate gives you a chance to love someone, you just open your heart and love them freely with all that you have. It can be so simple, Leo. It can be so easy."

"I'm afraid my heart is too closely guarded," I confessed, perhaps being a bit too honest. "I've been hurt before, so it's not easy for me to open myself up completely to other people."

"Then, open it up just a little bit," Esther said fervently. "I'm only asking for what you are willing to give. Just give what you can, and it will be enough for me. To love freely is a risk, yes, but it can be so sweet too. I'm just asking for a little bit, that's all."

I didn't know why I was hesitating. I wanted Esther desperately, but when it came down to it, I shrunk back, terrified . . . why? How could I trust Esther with my heart? What would happen if she broke it just like every other woman I had known?

The way she talked about loving freely was mystifying to me. I didn't understand what she was talking about. She wanted to get closer, to get to know me better. She wanted me to let her love me. I had to admit, that was exactly what I wanted too. It was a big step for me, a huge risk, but I knew I had to take it.

"Esther," I said quietly. "I want that more than anything."

I looked up again at Esther lying there next to me in the darkness. I could see her smiling. Her eyes sparkled in the faint glow of the dying campfire outside. She propped herself up on one elbow; then ever so slowly, she leaned in close to me.

"I knew you'd say that," she whispered excitedly.

"You did?" I replied.

"It's so dark outside, Leo, so very dark," she whispered. "But right now, you are shining like a sunrise."

She brushed a few strands of her hair aside, then leaned forward and kissed me on my cheek. She moved over closer to me in the darkness and gently placed her hand on my chest.

"You're like the North Star, Leo," she whispered. "I'll follow you anywhere you want to take me."

She moved slowly across, just inches away from my face, and kissed my other cheek. Her hair brushed against my eyes as she slid over and leaned her body up against my side.

"Our love will be like the Milky Way," she whispered. "Dazzling, mysterious, infinite . . . and spinning totally out of control."

She moved in closer, very close, and gently kissed my lips. Her eyes glowed like fiery embers in the fading firelight. To me, they seemed like the living waters of a deep blue stream, like sparkling diamonds discovered in the dry sands of a desert. I could feel the warmth of her soft breath so close to me and taste the tangy sweetness of her kiss still lingering on my lips. Her long hair fell around her shoulders, down over her face, and onto us both lying there.

"Esther," I whispered, "I think you're shining more brightly than the northern lights right now."

She grinned, then softly chuckled. Then, I did too. We both laughed at my feeble attempt to wax poetic in response. I pulled her close to me and kissed her soft red lips. I ran my hands up the sides of her body, feeling the smooth softness of her skin as she melted into my chest and kissed me again.

She moved in closer and pulled herself up a bit. Resting on her elbows, she looked down on me as her eyes glowed brightly in the darkness. She traced her fingertips slowly across my eyebrows, then down my nose and over my lips.

"I really like you," she whispered as she giggled softly and felt the stubble on my chin. "But you're kind of hairy."

I just looked up at her in awe. I was completely captured by her tender love, her gentle touch, and her sweet kisses, which she kept on giving so freely. A faint glow gradually came over us. It slowly filled the tent and gave it a greenish hue that appeared to grow brighter, then weaker, then brighter again—rising and falling over and over again as we kissed. The light continued to grow brighter and brighter until we both had to stop and look out the screen door of the tent. There in the far north, across the glassy lake and just above the tree line, the northern lights glowed in the night sky.

Greens and blues and some yellow streaks too, fell like a soft misty curtain out of the evening sky. They moved slowly down like a gentle river of light, flowing west in the atmosphere, then down and west again. We watched in silence for a long time, holding on to each other in the tent, overwhelmed and amazed by the magnificent light show in the far northern sky.

"Hey, Esther," I said softly. "Happy birthday."

"Thanks, Leo," she replied. Esther drew in a big breath, and her face was filled with wonder.

"You got a nice birthday surprise, didn't you?" I said. "I couldn't have planned it any better than this."

"Are you talking about the northern lights or about us?" she asked.

"I don't know," I replied. "Both, I suppose."

"Yeah, I'll take 'em both," she said with a smile. "I couldn't ask for any better gifts than these."

"This is pretty special," I said. "I've only seen the northern lights a few times this summer."

"They're so beautiful," Esther said. "I've seen the southern lights in my country a couple of times, but they were nothing like this."

"Why not?" I asked.

"It's too bright there. Auckland is almost two million people and very bright all the time," she said.

"What stars can you see in your city?" I asked.

"Only the bright ones," she replied. "Sirius is the brightest star, and the Southern Cross is so beautiful. Lyra and Leo are hard to see. In New Zealand, they lie low on the horizon in the far north."

"How do you know so much about the stars?" I asked.

"I told you, Leo," she replied. "I've always thought the stars were so fascinating and amazing to learn about."

"Like you," I said.

"Like me? What do you mean?" she asked.

"The stars," I said. "They're fascinating and amazing like you. You're like the northern lights, Esther. It sounds funny, but it's true. You can't just walk outside and see them anytime you wish. The northern lights are a rare sight, even up here in the Boundary Waters. They're unpredictable, elusive, and mysterious. It takes time and patience and a willingness to wait, sometimes all night, to get to see them. Then, at the most unexpected times, they show up, usually in the middle of the night. Out of nowhere, they appear, falling like silvery rain in the night sky, swirling and dancing across the northern horizon in complete silence—graceful, delicate, and peaceful. They're like a beautiful surprise. When you experience them, you realize how lucky you are to get to witness such incredible beauty. They shine and glow for a while, and then they're gone. The memory is all you have left, but it stays with you—amazing, special, and unique."

Esther grinned brightly at me. "And I'm like that to you, eh?"

"Yeah," I said.

Esther kissed me again and said, "You're beautiful too. There's so much more hidden inside you. I just know it."

"Well, if you say so," I replied, chuckling at her unwavering optimism and affection for me.

"Yeah, bro, I'm sure of it," she said. "You just need the right time and place to let others to see it. You need someone patient enough to help you find it inside yourself and let it out."

"Like you?" I asked.

"Yeah, mate, like me." She grinned innocently, then looked away, embarrassed, and said, "I pushed myself on you, didn't I?"

"You sure did," I joked and then turned serious again. "No, Esther, it's what I wanted too. I just didn't know how to respond. But when you said those things about me, it was like you were reading my mind. How did you do that?"

"Do what?" she asked.

"Know what I was thinking," I replied. "How did you know how I felt about you?"

"I could feel it in your hands," she said softly. "I could see it in your eyes too. From the start, I knew we were so much alike—when I first came to camp, and then as I got to know you better. I just didn't think it would lead to this . . . here . . . now. This is quite a surprise for me. I never thought we'd end up being . . ." She paused.

"Lovers?" I asked, risking a little more.

"Yeah, okay," she said with a chuckle. "We're star-crossed lovers, just like in the movies." She leaned in and gave me another kiss.

"I like kissing you," I whispered.

"I love kissing you," she whispered back. Esther pounced on me again and gave me another sweet kiss.

As the northern lights drifted across the sky and slowly began to fade away, Esther and I held on to each other in the darkness of the tent. It was a moment I'd never forget. It was an amazing night that we would always have, just the two of us. Aria was there as well, but she never knew what had taken place, not until later.

Esther and I talked in whispers for a long time about all sorts of things: our memories from the day on the lakes, how we'd first met back at camp, quiet words, and simple thoughts. She pulled her sleeping bag over next to mine and snuggled up close. I wrapped my arm around her and pulled her closer as she laid her head down on my chest. After a while, we realized how tired we were.

"Goodnight, Leo," Esther whispered as she squeezed my hand and held it tightly in hers.

"Goodnight, Esther," I whispered back.

I slid my other hand around to Esther's side near the place where Leo was crouching just above the horizon in the west. As I closed my eyes and slowly drifted off to sleep, I could feel her warm body lying there next to mine, stretched out like the earth, blue and green, sweet and lovely. Her soft belly gently rose and fell just like the rolling hills of the tallgrass prairie. Her breath came smooth and steady like a quiet breeze across a glassy lake. I could see the hills and valleys and the secret places far away in the distance. It was all laid out before me as far as my eyes could see, resting there patiently in the dark of night, but I was so tired. Quietly, I slipped away like a sleepy lion crouching in the west, content to dream of the beautiful land that lay waiting to be discovered and explored one day.

Together, Esther and I drifted off to sleep as the northern lights silently faded away in the far north. In the distance, I could hear the faint rumble of thunder. It was still far away and off to the southwest. I listened to Esther breathing peacefully with her head tucked under my chin. The thunder came closer but stayed to the south. Raindrops began to fall, and the wind picked up. It didn't bother me. After all, I was in heaven, drifting off to sleep with the girl of my dreams as the rain came down gently on the roof of the tent.

A little later, I woke up and listened to the rain again. It was coming down harder, and there was a steady roll of distant thunder. Flashes of lightning lit up the inside of the tent. I guessed that the storm was five or six miles away to the southeast but moving away from us. I pulled Esther's sleeping bag over her pretty toes that were curled up next to mine. She snuggled in closer and slid her leg over on top of me as she slept. I was completely trapped and thrilled to be so. I just hoped Aria wouldn't wake up and discover the two of us lying there intertwined like two ropes tangled up together.

The rain gradually tapered off to a light mist that made a gentle hissing noise on the roof of the tent. It was a steady, comforting sound that carried me off to sleep again. I held on to Esther as she breathed quietly next to me. We slept for the rest of the night and on into the early morning hours.

It was the most amazing night of my life.

chapter 46

morning visitors

"Staff training didn't prepare me for this!"

As usual, the morning light woke me up before anyone else, but it was well past sunrise. I lay there in the tent, still dreaming of the previous night. I glanced over at Esther, lying next to me. She was still curled up close but buried inside her sleeping bag. Her cute freckled nose and sunburned lips were just barely showing.

"Had I actually been kissing those pretty red rosy lips last night?" I wondered to myself as I blinked my eyes awake. I studied the pattern of freckles that crossed her nose and ran up under the edge of the sleeping bag. I wondered what the new day would bring. What would our relationship look like since we had shared so much together? How would she treat me after that? What should I say to her when she woke up? Should I give her a kiss?

The call of a loon echoed far away across the lake. I could tell two chipmunks were running around and squeaking at each other near the fire grate. But then, the sound of loud scraping on the bark of a tree suddenly forced my eyes wide open. I listened. There it was again, followed by more scraping on the other side of the tent.

"Another tree?" I thought. I lifted my head slightly to try to get a better handle on the strange noise, when suddenly, the sound of a branch crashing to the ground jolted me straight up out of bed. Esther woke up in a daze as I scrambled over the top of her and unzipped the screen door of the tent.

"Hello? Something wrong?" she mumbled, rubbing her sleepy eyes. "What's going on?"

"I don't know," I replied, poking my head outside the tent. I had a pretty good idea, though, and it made my heart begin to race. On the other side of the campfire ring about twenty feet away, a rope angled down into some bushes where a large tree branch had fallen. The branch jerked and moved unnaturally on the ground. Something was pulling at it or maybe tangled up in it somehow. I unzipped the tent quickly and scrambled outside on my knees.

"You guys, get up!" I whispered hoarsely. "We've got a bear!"

I ran across the campfire ring toward the branch on the ground. It was the one we had hung our food pack on the night before, and it was moving back and forth violently. Suddenly, the furry face of a large brown bear popped up over the branch and stared back at me. It was only a few feet away.

"Hey!" I yelled as I waved my arms around wildly. The startled bear grunted and jumped back away from the downed branch, but it still had the food pack in its mouth. I yelled even louder, "Hey, you! Get out of here!"

The bear just ignored me and kept pawing at the pack as it tried to rip it open to get at the food. I raced back to the fire ring as Esther stumbled out of the tent, holding her camera in one hand and a can of mosquito spray in the other.

When Esther spotted the bear, her eyes suddenly bugged out, and she yelled, "Aria! It's a bear!"

I grabbed a couple of big rocks from the fire ring and raced back into the woods, launching them at the bear as it gnawed at the pack. The bear grunted loudly as one of the rocks struck it in the behind. Startled, it jumped up and galloped away into the woods.

As I ran back to get more rocks, I noticed Esther hopping around near the tent with her camera, trying to get a picture of the bear.

"Look, Leo!" she cried, pointing excitedly up into the pine trees above our tent. She was gripping the bug spray so hard, it was spraying out in the air above her head. "Oh, crikey!" she exclaimed.

"What in the world is she doing?" I thought. "I don't have time to stop and look around."

"Esther!" I cried frantically. "Get Aria up!"

Esther immediately spun around and raced back to the open tent and yelled, "Aria, this ain't no bloody holiday! Rattle ya dags and get your lazy arse out here!"

As I grabbed two more rocks by the fireplace, Aria tumbled out of the tent and fell over on the ground. I ran back in the direction of our pack and was met by the tenacious bear, which had returned and was trying to simply drag the pack off into the woods.

"Aah!" I yelled. "That's our food!"

I heaved the rocks at the bear, but they missed the mark. I watched as the bear scrambled away into the woods again. "It'll be back in no time!" I thought.

"Aria, bang some pots together!" I yelled, racing through the campsite on my way down to the lake to find more rocks. She hopped over the campfire logs, grabbed a couple of pots, and started bashing them together.

As I ran back up the hill with three more rocks, I was horrified to see the angry bear galloping directly at me! I skidded to a stop just a few feet away from the bear as it did the exact same thing. Wide-eyed and terrified, we both stared desperately into each other's eyes for a split second. It was sheer terror! I chucked the rocks up in the air and tore off back toward the beach in fear of being attacked. Just as I did that, the crazy bear did the same thing, galloping away in the other direction back into the woods.

"It's going after the pack again!" Aria shouted as she beat the pots together like a maniac.

I ran back and picked up the discarded rocks. Then, I raced off toward the branch again. It was being pulled into the woods, still attached to the rope, which was still attached to the pack, which was still attached to the bear's teeth.

Esther was still jumping around, snapping photos of the crazy three-ring circus: the ornery bear, Aria banging on the pots, me chucking rocks, and for some reason, the trees overhead. I couldn't figure out what she was doing with the camera. I wondered why she wasn't helping us fight off the bear. Aria was still banging away on the pots, but it didn't seem to be helping much.

I threw my fresh load of rocks fiercely in the bear's direction, but by then, it was so far back in the woods, I couldn't tell if anything hit it or not. Then, to my shock and surprise, the bear appeared out of the woods again, and it looked angry! I turned and ran for my life as it chased me back down toward the lake.

"Esther!" I yelped as I raced through the campsite with the bear hot on my heels. "Help!"

The bear chased me halfway to the water, but then suddenly, it turned and ran off back into the woods again. I hobbled back up, completely worn out, and halfheartedly threw a couple more rocks into the woods, but by then, I'd lost all hope of regaining the pack. It was finally over.

"Staff training didn't prepare me for this!" I thought. The bear had easily won the fight, and it was three against one! I looked over at Esther, still holding the camera and looking excitedly up into the trees. "What is she doing with that camera anyway?" I wondered. "Why on earth won't she help me?"

Suddenly, I heard the sound of paddles banging on a canoe out in the lake. As I turned to look, two park rangers pulled up to shore in a yellow fiberglass canoe. They looked far too serious and somber to me. "They're a little late," I thought.

"You've got some trouble?" the ranger in the front asked.

"Yeah," I gasped. "A bear dragged our food off into the woods. I'm afraid it got away with the pack."

"Was it a male or a female?" the ranger asked.

"I have no idea," I replied, still trying to catch my breath.

The two rangers didn't move. They just sat there eyeing me. One of them pulled out a little brown notebook and a pen. He opened it and began to write something down. I felt as if I were about to get a traffic ticket or something. "Are they both stupid or just amused?" I wondered. "Why won't they get out and help?" They seemed utterly clueless and unconcerned about our predicament. Meanwhile, that bear was getting away with our food!

"All right, let's go have a look," the one in the front finally said. Slowly, the rangers stepped out of their canoe and pulled it up onto the shore. As we walked up to the campfire ring, Esther ran down excitedly and greeted us.

"Did you see them, Leo? Did you see them?" she cried.

"What, the bear?" I asked. "Yeah, I almost got eaten by it."

"No, not the big one!" she shouted. "The little ones up in the trees? Did you see them?"

"What?" the ranger with the notebook broke in. "How many bears did you see?"

"Three cubs!" Esther exclaimed, pointing up into the pine trees. "There were two in that tree, and another one up there, and the mama bear on the ground too! I've got pictures of them all."

"Holy cow," I mumbled under my breath. "I could have been eaten alive by that she-bear!"

Apparently, the female bear was in a fighting mood, not because she was hungry, but because her cubs were up in the pine trees. Esther clicked through the pictures on her camera. Sure enough, there they were, but they just looked like little brown specks clinging to the sides of the tree trunks. Esther only had one picture of the female bear's brown butt as she ran off into the woods. To me, that bear had been as gigantic and terrifying as a five-hundred-pound grizzly!

The rangers said I never realized the danger I was in the entire time. It could have ended much worse, but thankfully, the little ones scurried down and scampered away to safety just in time. If I had paid more attention to Esther prancing around with her camera, I would have noticed the cubs up in the trees. It was the best bear encounter I had all summer and the most dangerous one too.

The rangers and I walked back into the woods to examine the crime scene. To my surprise, we came upon the food pack, still attached to the rope. The bear had tried to gnaw it off but couldn't chew through it in time. When her cubs got down out of the trees, they all probably scampered away together. I carried the pack back to the campsite as the rangers wrote up a report in their notebook.

"Check these out!" Aria said, holding up the two aluminum pots. She had beaten them together so hard that the bottoms were completely concave and useless.

"We're gonna get busted big time for that," I said.

"It's all your fault, Farm Boy," she replied. "You're the one who told me to do it."

"I told you to bang the pots together, Hunter, not destroy them," I complained, staring at the damaged pots in disbelief. The larger one was so badly dented; I could see a crack through the bottom of it. "Chuck's not going to like this one bit."

"Whatever, Leo! It's still your fault," she said.

"Yeah, I suppose so, but it was totally worth it, don't you think?" I said with a grin of satisfaction.

"Yeah, totally!" she said, smiling back at me.

"That was sweet!" Esther cried as she bounded around, still wildly excited. "We saw bears, mates! Bears! And little cubs too!"

Esther was still coming down off her high. As she bounced around the campsite, showing off the photos, I grinned back at her and nodded in agreement. She was still wearing her white bikini top and blue jean shorts. She looked so adorable and cute.

"What a goofy girl," I thought to myself. "I was kissing that pretty girl just a few hours ago."

I was still coming down off my high too.

chapter 47

waking nightmares

"Keep paddling, just keep paddling."

Before they left, the rangers called me down to the lakeshore and told me that there was another reason they were checking campsites. During the night, a lightning strike had started a forest fire off to the southeast near Jasper Lake. They recommended that we head back to Northern Lights as soon as possible. They said we would be fine as long as we kept moving and didn't stop along the way.

The rangers also gave me some instructions on what to do in case the situation got worse. They said the fire was already spreading east toward Diamond Lake, and the wind was expected to pick up that afternoon. We had to pass through Jasper Lake only a few miles north of where the fire had started. They said we would be okay if the wind didn't change direction, but if it did, we'd have to go back the way we came. Once they left, I told Aria and Esther.

We decided to get out on the water as quickly as possible. We packed up our gear in a hurry; then we set off. We moved steadily east, portaging into Annie Lake, then Ogishkemuncie, but the wind, which had picked up considerably, was nerve-racking. As we paddled out onto Ogish, we could see the smoke rising above the tree line in the distance. It was billowing high up into the sky, churning in the atmosphere, and drifting slowly off to the east as one enormous ugly gray mass overhead.

Out in the middle of Ogish, the sky grew dark, and it began to lightly sprinkle. It wasn't too bad at first, so we just kept on moving. But then, it started to rain, and after a few minutes, we were soaked to the skin. Thinking back on it, we should have stopped, even out in the middle of the lake so that we could dig out our rain ponchos, but we were so focused on getting out, we didn't want to take the time to stop for anything.

As we paddled across the lake, Esther sat, quiet and still, in the middle of the canoe. Aria was pulling us fiercely ahead with each stroke of her paddle. I kept silent in the back, deep in thought. I wondered what would happen if the fire beat us to Jasper Lake. There wasn't a lot of wiggle room there, especially on the far side just before the portage into Alpine Lake.

I began to dream up nightmare scenarios of paddling into the narrow channel on the east end of Jasper and getting caught in the forest fire. What would we do if we couldn't make it through? We'd have to turn around and go all the way back to Knife Lake and then head north to Saganaga. That would take an entire day of paddling, even if we didn't stop, and we were almost out of food.

I shook my head free of the waking nightmares and kept paddling. We pulled harder and harder, moving steadily northeast up through Ogishkemuncie. Every few seconds, I'd glance off to the east at the smoke rising steadily into the sky. I paddled myself into a sort of frenzied trance, stroke after stroke, as we raced across the lake. Every once in a while, I'd have to shake myself awake and get back to the work of paddling. I'd pull harder for a while, but then worries would build up and wash over me again.

The rain kept up for the rest of the way across Ogishkemuncie. I was sopping wet, but the work of paddling kept me warm. Esther had settled down quietly in the middle of the canoe, where she seemed deep in thought. Aria just kept paddling like a workhorse up in the front. I was glad to have her up there, pulling us across the lake. It was a long stretch across Ogish—too long, I thought. I tried to focus on the task at hand, but my mind kept drifting off to thoughts of what might happen up ahead on Jasper.

"Keep paddling," I thought. "Just keep paddling."

chapter 48

dance party on the trail

"That's disgusting, and in the sixth grade, people!"

As we pulled into the portage at the end of Ogishkemuncie, we stopped paddling and took a short break. My arms and back ached from the long trek across the lake. Aria and I were beat, so we decided to shoot the rapids instead of doing the portage. It saved us time, but it probably wasn't the best decision in the world.

As we entered the rapids, it became clear that the water was too shallow for us to paddle straight through. That meant hopping out into the water and getting even wetter than we already were. We did it anyway. We worked our way down the rapids and then jumped back into the canoe at the bottom. Then, we paddled out into Kingfisher Lake and headed for the next portage not far ahead.

As we crossed the lake, I studied the sky above, looking for any signs of an actual fire, but still, the only thing I could see was the smoke rising overhead. I started to wonder how serious the rangers' warning had actually been. Perhaps they were mistaken, or maybe they had exaggerated the danger on purpose, simply to scare us into getting out of there as quickly as possible.

The rain hadn't let up. In fact, it seemed to be coming down even harder. To make matters worse, Esther didn't look well. She'd been duffing in the middle of the canoe all morning, and she was sopping wet. By the time we had crossed Kingfisher, Esther was shivering uncontrollably. Her cheeks had turned pale white, and her lips looked almost blue. As Aria and I pulled the packs out at the next portage, Esther just stood there, shaking by the canoe.

"Get the rain ponchos out," Aria said as she snapped open one of the Duluth packs.

"I don't feel quite right," Esther mumbled.

"What have you had to eat today?" I asked.

"Not much," she said. "A bit of water, I think."

After the rangers stopped by that morning, we had skipped breakfast in a rush to get going. It seemed more important at the time, but we were paying the price for that decision. We hadn't eaten anything all morning, and Esther was beginning to show the initial signs of hypothermia: a condition that could shut her entire system down. If we didn't stop and do something immediately, she could be in serious trouble. I got Aria's attention and then pointed to Esther. She had recognized it too.

"Come here, girlfriend," Aria said, giving her friend a hug. "Let's get you warmed up. Okay?"

Esther stood shivering in the middle of the trail as Aria removed her wet clothes. She started with Esther's T-shirt and the cutoffs she'd been wearing. Then, she slipped off her undergarments as well. I dug out my beach towel and handed it off to Aria. Then, I went fishing for Esther's dry clothes in her pack, finding a sweater, dry pants, socks, and underwear. Aria wrapped Esther in the towel. Then, she helped her get dressed again.

Meanwhile, I kept myself busy. I snapped open the Whisperlite stove and put a small pot of water on to boil. Esther shivered uncontrollably as Aria worked to get her into the dry clothes. Esther couldn't seem to control her clumsy fingers and limbs, but Aria kept at it diligently until she was dressed again. Aria wrapped her up in my towel too. Then, she took her own rain poncho off and slipped it down on top of Esther, who, at that point, looked like a chubby penguin shivering in the cold.

The water heated up quickly. When it was warm, I dumped the last of our Russian tea mix into it and gave it to Esther to drink. Her hands shook as she quickly sipped the warm liquid down. When she asked for more, I refilled the cup.

"Drink it slowly," I said. "You don't want to warm up too fast."

"But it feels so good," she said. "Besides, I'm freezing."

"Slowly," I repeated, giving her a stern but reassuring look.

I watched her closely and made sure she took little sips the second time around. Meanwhile, Aria dug out the last bit of the GORP trail mix from our bear-bitten food pack.

"Here you go, Esther," she said with a concerned look. "Eat some of this in between sips."

Aria handfed the trail mix to Esther, bit by bit, as she sipped on the hot tea. Aria was shivering as well, but I wasn't worried about her. She had been paddling all morning. She seemed shocked, not from the cold, but from the sight of her best friend standing there, shivering in the freezing rain.

"Here, cuz," Esther finally said. "Just give me the bag."

She snatched it out of Aria's hand and helped herself to a handful of the trail mix. She grinned at me as she sipped the tea and nibbled away on the raisins, peanuts, and little bits of chocolate. After a few minutes, Esther was looking much better.

"Thanks for taking such proper care of me, mates," she said, grinning at us both.

"How do you feel?" Aria asked, still a bit shell-shocked.

"Peachy keen," Esther said, managing a weak grin and a nod.

"You look a lot better," I said with relief.

I gave her a hug; then I felt her fingers and cheeks. They were still ice-cold, but the color had returned to her face and lips. To me, she seemed fine, but Aria wasn't entirely convinced.

"We should get her moving again," said Aria.

"No, just let her be," I suggested. "She needs to warm up slowly."

"No, Farm Boy," she insisted. "We're gonna get her moving before we get back in that canoe."

"Okay, Hunter, have it your way," I replied.

I knew better than to argue with Aria when she was upset. I felt like Esther had already snapped out of it anyway. In fact, she probably wasn't as bad off as we'd first thought, so I let Aria take over.

"Esther," she said. "We've gotta get you moving again, so here's what we're gonna do."

"Why? I'm feeling fine now," Esther replied weakly.

"No, no," Aria insisted. "We're gonna have a little dance party."

"A what?" Esther asked.

"You heard me," Aria said firmly, as she massaged Esther's shoulders. "We're gonna have a dance party, just like that night in Chicago a few months back, but this time we're gonna do it right here on the trail."

"All right, cuz," Esther replied as she grinned helplessly at me.

"Okay, girlfriend! Let's go!" Aria shouted as she grabbed Esther and began to jump up and down in place.

"Come on, Aria, stop it!" Esther complained, trying desperately to escape. "We don't need to do this."

"Yes, we do!" Aria shouted back. She grabbed Esther again and kept working on her. "Now, I want you to think about all your favorite things. Remember that game from the other night? Ask Me Anything! You're gonna tell me all your favorite things again, right now! Come on, girlfriend, shout 'em all out to me!" At that point, Aria was hopping around and huffing up a storm.

"Good grief! You want me to do what?" Esther replied as she reluctantly began to hop in place.

"Tell me all the favorite things you like," Aria insisted. "Come on, cuzzy! Start shouting 'em out! We're not stopping this dance party until you do! So, what's your favorite color?"

"I like forest green, you crack up!" she said as Aria hopped up and down like a crazy rabbit.

"That's right, girlfriend!" Aria shouted. "You like frosty green Christmas trees! Keep it coming!"

"I like Kiwi burgers and Jaffas too," Esther said.

"Kiwi boogers and candy!" Aria shouted. "That sounds delicious! Tell me more!"

"I like Hokey Pokey ice cream!" Esther said with a chuckle as she began to get into the game. "I like Foxton Fizz too, and raspberry is my favorite fizzy drink of all time!"

"She likes raspberry fizzies, everybody!" Aria yelled. "Did you hear that, world?"

"I like the Soul Shine Café in Auckland!" exclaimed Esther with a smile. "It's the absolute best! I like Hello Beasty too. They have the best potstickers in the world!"

"The best potstickers in the world?" Aria cried. "Did you all just hear that? The best potstickers in the world!"

"I love the stars!" Esther shouted as she jumped around with Aria. "I'm gonna write a book about them too!"

"She's gonna write a book about the stars people! Everybody better watch out! Her book's coming out soon!" Aria yelled.

"I like horseback riding!" Esther shouted as she began to jump around wildly with Aria. "I had my first boyfriend in the sixth grade! Stanley Buttons! And I kissed him too!"

"Aah!" Aria exclaimed wildly. "She kissed Sandy Bottoms! That's disgusting, and in the sixth grade, people!"

I stood nearby and watched as the two girls hopped wildly up and down. They were spinning around, stomping on the ground, and knocking over anything and everything in their way.

"Come on, Leo!" Aria shouted as she grabbed my arm. "Get on in here! Esther kissed somebody's bottom in the sixth grade!"

I jumped in with them, and together, we hopped and jumped and danced up and down the trail. Esther wasn't shivering anymore. She was smiling and laughing and having a great time. I hoped someone would come strolling by on the portage, just so that they could see us acting like the crazy fools we knew we were.

Our canoe was floating in the water. The packs were wide open. Our clothes were strewn all over the place. We had a pot of water boiling on a stove. And we were jumping around like fudge-pop crazies in the middle of a rainstorm. When the girls finally broke apart, laughing, Esther pulled Aria and me in close and hugged us.

"Hey, mates!" she shouted. "This has been totally weird!"

"Did you hear that world!" Aria shouted to the trees all around. "This has been totally weird! Aah!"

Aria grinned and began to jump around again. A couple of times, she tried to head-butt me, but I was onto her shenanigans by then, and I really didn't want another bloody nose. At the end of the dance party,

Aria and I gave Esther a big bear hug that included a few more hops up and down. Her bright eyes and warm hands were proof that she was back to normal again.

"Are you feeling better?" I asked.

"Yeah," she said with a reassuring grin.

"Because, if you're not, we'll just have to strip you down, stuff you in my sleeping bag, and have another dance party!" I exclaimed.

"Nah, I'm all right now," she said with a chuckle.

"Are you sure?" I asked. "Because I'd really like to get you naked again. I'll go and get the sleeping bag out right now."

"Cut it out, goofball!" she said, punching me softly in the stomach. "You didn't actually steal a squiz of me all nuddy, did you?"

"Just your backside," I admitted sheepishly.

"You dirty little fudge-pop!" she said with a grin as she gave me a couple of friendly slaps across the face.

"You looked mighty fine too!" I blurted out, grinning back at her as I waited for a few more friendly slaps.

"Leo! You dipstick!" she said, slugging me softly. "You're such a big weasel sometimes!"

"All right," Aria broke in. "It's time to break up the lovefest or whatever it is you two got going on there. We probably should keep moving, right, Leo?"

"Yeah, let's get going," I said, drifting back to reality.

We packed up our camping gear, tucked away Esther's wet clothes, and then finished out the rest of the portage. As we set out on Jasper Lake, we made sure Esther was paddling up in front. Aria took the stern while I duffed in the middle. It was good to be on the water again, but I hated duffing. There was nothing for me to do except sit there, watch helplessly, and worry.

I knew worrying was useless, but I couldn't help it.

chapter 43

race to jasper falls

"We better get a move on!"

As we paddled out onto the choppy waters of Jasper Lake, my nightmarish daydreams returned in full force. By that point, a huge plume of smoke was rising up into the sky almost directly in front of us. There were no visible flames or any sounds of fire, but gusts of wind were swirling all around us. The cold air was rushing eerily across the lake directly into the enormous column of smoke, as if it were being drawn forward by the forest fire itself.

"We better step it up, Aria!" I said nervously, not used to being a helpless passenger in the middle of a canoe.

"Yeah, I'm on it!" she replied. "I'm paddling as hard as I can!"

Up in front, Esther was definitely pulling her own weight. I wished I'd brought along a spare paddle so I could've pitched in.

Even so, we were moving quickly across the water. The strange wind was helping too as it pushed us along. It was unnerving to feel as if we were being sucked in ever closer to the forest fire along with everything else. The entire day seemed surreal to me. It was odd in all sorts of strange ways, as if reality itself were being twisted out of shape right before my very eyes.

Thick smoke rose into the atmosphere high above, but oddly enough, behind us and to the north, the sky was clearing, and the sun was shining. The choppy waters of Jasper Lake were ashen and unnaturally green, reflecting the strange color of the smoke cloud looming overhead. Rather than trying to escape it, we were heading straight into it, as if we were looking for trouble.

The girls kept paddling furiously as we moved steadily east into the narrow channel of the lake. It was where all of my nightmares had taken place, in that thin stretch of water just above the portage. It was no more than a wide river, where the water flowed around a bend and down over Jasper Falls into Alpine Lake below.

I held my breath as we navigated down the center of the long narrow passageway. The forest fire was just over the top of the ridge to the south. Dark smoke was billowing upwards as it sucked in all the air from down below. The unsettled water seemed to tremble and turn deep green as we paddled frantically ahead.

As Aria swung our canoe left just above the waterfalls, the fire breached the ridge and began racing down the hill. Suddenly, I could feel the intense heat of the flames and hear the loud crackling of dry pines in the forest nearby. The light of the burning trees began to reflect on the water all around us. The trees on both sides of the channel began to shake as air rushed through their branches and up toward the fire that was bearing down on us.

"Aria, paddle harder!" I shouted as we neared Jasper Falls and the rough rocky portage on the right side.

"I'm paddling, Leo!" she shouted back. "We're almost there!"

As we approached the shore, Esther jumped out and pulled the front of the canoe forward into a shallow wedge of the rocks. I hopped out too, as did Aria. The girls grabbed the packs like pros as I swung the canoe up onto my shoulders. As Aria and Esther raced off down the rocky trail, I stopped to look back at the fire that was engulfing the forest all around the lake.

The narrow channel of water that we had just plowed our way through appeared strangely calm and unaware of the approaching doom. The majestic spruce, fir, and pine trees stood tall and beautiful, exactly as they had for a hundred years or more. The waters of Jasper Falls rolled over the smooth granite boulders as they always had, roaring, foaming, and plummeting down through the trees, making their way to Alpine Lake below. The forest seemed to be as content and peaceful as it had always been. "Isn't it aware of what is about to happen here?" I thought. "Doesn't it even care?"

I took one final look at that beautiful place tucked away in a little corner of the North Woods of Minnesota. It had become one of my favorite spots in all the Boundary Waters, and I realized I would be the last person to see it like that, probably for better than a hundred years or more. As the fire engulfed everything around me in flames, I turned and galloped down the trail with the heavy canoe on my back, heading for the safety of Alpine Lake.

As I huffed along the trail, I could hear the fire roaring behind me. I moved more quickly, tiptoeing over the uneven rocky terrain, finding the smooth stones and level parts of the trail to keep from twisting an ankle and falling. I thought of that beautiful spot, Jasper Falls, and how it was being engulfed in a fiery inferno so devastatingly hot and furious, it would burn nearly everything to the ground. I felt like crying, but I was too terrified to do anything but run. I had to keep moving to reach the girls at the bottom of the steep trail. When I finally got there, Aria was standing out in the water with Esther, looking frantic and sick to her stomach.

"What the hell, Leo!" she shouted. "Where have you been?"

"I had to have one last look!" I shouted back.

"We thought you fell or got lost or something!" she yelled.

"No, I'm fine," I replied.

"Look over there!" she cried, pointing to a line of trees along the lakeshore that was bursting into flames. The trees were lit up like massive torches. Huge pieces of burning ash were swirling up into the air and floating out over the water in front of us.

"It's gonna jump the lake!" I shouted.

"Get in!" Aria yelled. "We have to go now!"

We threw our packs into the canoe, leaped in, and started paddling like mad, but the fire, smoke, and burning ash had already engulfed the lake. Within seconds, it jumped across to an island directly in front of us. Then, it jumped again to the mainland to the north. There was no other way around, and we couldn't go back. The only option was to go straight through the blazing inferno.

As we curved to the north, we had to pass so near to the fire, it felt like the flames were searing my skin. Ancient pines on both sides of the channel hissed loudly as flames shot up through their branches and lit the tops on fire. All around us, branches were burning and falling into the water. Gusts of thick black smoke and fiery sparks shot straight into our faces from the north side of the channel.

"Look out!" Esther cried as a hail of burning ash swept over us. The smoke was so thick, I could barely see Aria up in the front.

"We're not going to make it!" I heard her yell desperately from somewhere in the smoky haze.

"Yes, we are!" I shouted as I grabbed both sides of the canoe and rocked it back and forth.

"What are you doing?" Aria cried.

"Hang on!" I yelled as I threw my body to the left, bringing the canoe along with me.

I heard the girls screaming as we tipped all the way over in one swift motion. Under the water, I reached up and grabbed on to the canoe rails and pulled myself back up inside it. Aria popped up inside the overturned canoe as well.

"Where's Esther?" I shouted.

"I don't know!" she replied.

"Hold on to the canoe," I said. "I'll go and find her."

I ducked under the canoe and came back up outside. I looked all around, but I couldn't see Esther anywhere. In a mad rush, I swam around the canoe and finally found her treading water on the other side, looking confused and terrified.

"Come on, Esther!" I shouted, trying not to appear too frantic. "Grab my hand and come with me!"

Together, we plunged under the murky water and came back up inside the canoe.

"Thank God!" Aria cried. "Are you guys all right?"

"Aria!" Esther shouted.

"Hang on to the canoe!" I exclaimed. "We're gonna have to stay under here for a while."

"No kidding!" Aria replied.

"Hey, wait!" I said desperately. "I'm going back out again!"

"What for?" Aria cried.

I ducked under the canoe and came up outside once more. I swam around the canoe again, frantically searching for the paddles. When I found one floating nearby, I shot it back toward the canoe and kept looking for the other one. I made another sweep around the canoe farther out, but still found nothing. Finally, I spotted the missing paddle floating off to the south.

As I swam over to it, I couldn't help but stop to take one last look at the forest near the portage we had just come through. It was completely engulfed in flames. The fire had jumped across the stream that was flowing down from Jasper Lake. All around, the trees were burning and smoking and crumbling. The fire was sweeping north along the western edge of Alpine Lake, burning everything that stood in its path.

I heard a crack overhead, and then right in front of me, a burning branch crashed down into the lake, hissing loudly as it sank into the churning water. I moved away as quickly as possible. Then, I turned and swam back to the overturned canoe. I grabbed both of the paddles, ducked underneath, and came back up inside.

"Leo! Where did you go?" Aria asked.

"I had to get the paddles before they floated away," I replied as I jammed them up over the seats of the canoe. "We'll need them if we ever get out of this alive."

"What are we going to do?" Esther asked.

"Stay put for a while," I said. "That's our only option."

"But the fire?" she said.

"It'll pass," I replied. "There's no other choice anyway, so just hang on. We're gonna have to wait it out."

As we held on tightly to the sides of the canoe, we listened to the unnatural sounds of the raging inferno outside. The water below us glowed dark red and blood orange as it reflected the flames of the firestorm burning all around us. With loud terrifying booms, more trees came crashing down into the lake. The water slowly turned dark, but we could still see the light from the flames in the water underneath us. We listened in silence, breathing heavily in the cold water for at least an hour, maybe more.

Finally, I said, "I'm going back out to have a look around."

"Be careful, Leo," Esther said.

"Yeah, don't do anything stupid," Aria added.

I ducked under the canoe and popped back up outside. The fire had taken out the entire southern shore near the portage. It was burning away to the north as the wind drove it wildly on. The air was black with burning ash and smoke swirling all around. Suddenly, Aria surfaced in the water right next to me.

"What's going on?" she asked.

"Look," I replied.

"Yeah, I know," she said in dismay. "Esther and I were just getting worried about you."

"Thanks, Hunter, but I'm all right," I said.

"If you can call this all right," she replied sadly.

"Yeah, this is pretty bad," I agreed.

"Well, that's an understatement," she said dryly. "Way to look at the bright side of things, Leo."

"Yeah, but we're all right," I reminded her. "I think we can make it through the channel now. In fact, I think we could've made it without flipping the canoe over."

"No, Leo, I think it was a good call," she replied. "We almost got burned alive back there."

I looked south across the lake. We had drifted north almost a hundred yards from where we'd flipped the canoe back near the portage. Through the smoke, I could see blackened trees still smoldering all along the steep ridge above the water's edge. Several of them had tumbled into the lake near the shore. Ash and debris were floating everywhere.

"Yeah, you're probably right," I said sadly.

"Come on," Aria said. "Let's get back to Esther. She's probably worried sick about us."

We ducked under the canoe and returned to Esther underneath. Together, we flipped the canoe back over and climbed inside. It was full of water, but we used our hands to paddle over to a large submerged rock just under the surface of the lake. We flipped the canoe over and drained it out. Thankfully, our waterlogged packs were still attached to the canoe. As we rolled them back in, they felt like hundred-pound rocks.

"Good thing you tied the packs to the rails," Aria said.

"No kidding," I replied. "We wouldn't want to lose our packs on the last day out."

"Yeah, right," Aria said sarcastically. "Chuck would've thrown a big hairy fit if we lost one of his Duluth packs."

We climbed into the canoe and set off into Alpine Lake. Aria traded places with me in the canoe, but we kept Esther at work up in the front. Esther threw me a confident smile; then she turned and dug in heavily with her paddle. Despite all that had happened that day, Esther somehow found a way to encourage me.

The two of us paddled in sync, moving the canoe swiftly out into the safety of the big lake. I paddled as hard as I could, not only to escape the fire, but to let Esther feel me in the back of the canoe. I wanted her to know that I was there with her, moving us forward through the water together.

The fire hadn't moved to the east as much as I had expected. It was still burning along the southern shore of Alpine Lake, but not as quickly as before. After our narrow escape back at the portage, it seemed as if we were finally in the clear.

But then, up ahead in the distance, a canoe came racing around the edge of an island. There were two people in it, and they were paddling like mad, heading straight for us. As they drew near, I could tell that it was a canoe from Northern Lights. Then, I realized it was Chuck and Percy, moving so fast that the canoe was creating a wake behind it. Within seconds, they pulled up alongside us. I grabbed on to their boat and held it there as they caught their breath.

"Leo!" Chuck shouted. "Dude, it's so good to see you!"

"You too!" I replied. "What are you guys doing out here?"

"Finn sent us to look for you!" Chuck said, still breathing heavily. "This is a bad one!"

"Yeah, we just barely made it through," I said. "We had to flip our canoe back by the portage and wait it out for a while."

"It's moving fast!" Percy shouted. "The wind is pushing the fire northeast. It'll be on Diamond Lake within the hour."

"Are we okay portaging into Diamond? Or should we go around through Sag?" I asked.

"You should be okay," Chuck said. "Just keep moving and stay along the north shore."

"Aren't you coming back with us?" I asked.

"Nope," Chuck replied. "We're going farther west to look for other groups. Finn went north on Alpine to look for you guys. He's probably already up in Red Rock by now."

"Who's still out?" I asked.

"Anne is probably up on Saganaga—Finn will find her—and then there's Nancy." Chuck looked sick to his stomach. "She's been out for five days," he said. "She could be just about anywhere, so we're heading west to look for her group."

I pointed to the burning trees and black smoke to the southwest. "You're gonna go through that?"

"Yeah, we're going for it," Chuck said with a weak smile. "I've got Percy here, so we'll be okay."

Percy grinned confidently, but I could tell he was exhausted too.

"We better get a move on," Chuck said. "We'll see you back at camp later, maybe tonight or tomorrow."

"Okay, but just don't do anything too heroic!" I exclaimed.

"What? Me and Percy . . . heroes?" Chuck replied with a laugh. "That'll be the day!"

"Take care, Chuck!" I shouted. "See you soon!"

"Sure thing, dude! We'll see you guys back at camp!" he replied as he pulled away.

As we paddled east away from the fire, they raced off to the west, straight into a wall of smoke that was beginning to engulf the entire lake. I hoped they'd make it through Jasper and not have to deal with anything as bad as what we'd encountered. I knew Chuck would do whatever it took to find Nancy before the day was out. Actually, he'd probably do that for just about anyone. That's just the kind of guy he was. I had a feeling Percy would too.

I glanced over my shoulder one last time, just before they rounded the point and turned toward Jasper Falls. They were still paddling like madmen, straight into the smoky black mass that towered overhead. I felt a sudden swell of pride to be counted as one of them. I said a quick prayer as I fell back in sync with Esther, who was straining on her paddle up in front.

We continued to race east across Alpine. It didn't take long to do the portage into Diamond Lake. It was a long one—about a hundred rods—but I was happy to be back on my feet again. The pain of the canoe on my shoulders seemed to rejuvenate me. I was still sopping wet, but the adrenalin in my system was making me sweat. On the other side, the three of us grabbed another quick bite to eat—granola bars and water—the only edible things left in our soggy food pack. Then, we headed out onto Diamond Lake and the safety of base camp, which was still several miles away.

As we paddled into the big lake, we froze in shock at what we saw. Coming down off the high slopes above the southern shoreline, we could see several fires burning and spreading to the east. Even from a distance—over two miles away—we could hear the immense fires burning through the dry forest, crackling and snapping, furiously devouring every living thing. Huge tongues of fire rose high above the trees, eerily swaying back and forth, burning bright yellow and deep smoky orange. It looked as if the flames were rising over one hundred feet into the air at times. The fire was spreading along the entire southern shoreline, consuming everything in its path, all the way down to the water's edge.

The whole of Diamond Lake seemed to be churning like a boiling pot of purple stew. The water was unsettled and choppy, with gusts of wind rushing out of the northwest, shooting across the lake toward the fires, creating white caps farther out in the middle. Smoke was rising along the entire southern shore, slowly and relentlessly, as high as we could see. The enormous plume of smoke looked as if an atomic bomb had just gone off somewhere to the south.

Vast swaths of beautiful boreal forest were going up in smoke like mere kindling in the enormous flames. I understood why Chuck and

Percy looked so deathly sick when they'd met us back on Alpine Lake. It was a horrible sight.

"Oh my God," I heard Aria gasp in shock as she stared sadly at the destruction happening on the southern shoreline.

Other than that, we were completely dumbstruck. My heart sank as I watched the disaster unfold, knowing there was little anyone could do to stop the devastation. I wondered what was happening back at camp. They were probably preparing for the worst, but the main concern would be for the groups that were still unaccounted for. I'm sure they were worried sick about us too.

Without a doubt, the Forest Service was hoping the firebreaks that had been put in place after the Big Blowdown would hold. Their greatest fear had always been that a fire would ignite the millions of downed trees and set everything ablaze like a box of dry matches, and it had finally happened.

Without saying another word, we began to paddle east again, staying close to the north shore, just as Chuck had advised. I could see four other canoes moving east as well, coming up off the portage from Paulsen Lake, dangerously close to the fire. Just like us, they were racing east to safety.

Thankfully, we were out of danger. We weaved our way through a few small islands. Then, we veered southeast into an open part of the lake. As we drew up to Miles Island, we rested on the south side away from the wind. We watched helplessly as the entire southern shoreline of Diamond Lake went up in flames.

My nightmares had come true before my very eyes.

chapter 50
the palisades

"Let's hike to the top."

In the calm water, Aria and Esther switched places in the canoe, and then we took off again. We made a bee-line for the Palisades: a wall of enormous red-streaked granite cliffs that rose majestically out of the lake about a mile away to the east. As we drew near, the huge landmass of ancient volcanic rock loomed higher and higher. We could see a couple of canoes sheltering beneath the sheer drop-off on the south side. The cliffs towered up before us like a fortress standing defiantly against the raging firestorm that burned along the southern slopes of the lake.

"Hey, Leo," Aria called from the front of the canoe. "Let's stop and take a little break."

We coasted into the rocky landing on the western tip of the Palisades and carefully slid our canoe into a narrow wedge between the jagged rocks. We hopped out and pulled the canoe out of the water to protect it from the gusty winds that were pushing waves into the little rocky cove. After the long paddle across the lake, it was a relief to be standing on solid ground again. I was stiff and sore, and I could tell that the girls felt the same too.

Esther was silent and distant. She looked pale and cold, just as she had on the portage off Kingfisher Lake. She stood shivering in the wind that blew steadily across the lake and into our faces.

"Let's hike to the top," I said. "Come on, follow me."

I started up the narrow overgrown trail that led into the woods. The trail wound back and forth, climbing the steep western edge of the Palisades all the way to the top. The girls followed close behind. We had to wade through low-hanging evergreens on the trail, clamber around huge granite boulders, and sometimes crawl straight up rough rock faces as we made our way higher and higher. We finally came out of the woods into a large open area of bare granite, about a hundred feet above the surface of the lake.

I scrambled over the peak to my favorite spot: a small amphitheater of jagged rocks that jutted out over a sheer drop-off, some eighty feet straight down to the water below. From that spot, we could view the entire lake stretched out far and wide. We could see over a few nearby islands to the big part of the lake from where we had just come. It was about four miles of open water, with several islands scattered here and there, mostly on the northern edge of the lake.

The Palisades were a highlight for nearly every group that came through Diamond Lake. I always stopped there with my groups as we began or ended a trip. The majestic view from the high cliff seemed to compel visitors to stop and rest and quietly gaze out over the vast expanse of open water that stretched to the south and west. Often one could see groups of canoes moving slowly across the water far in the distance. From so high up, it was easy to spot gulls soaring over the lake, sometimes even eagles higher up. The Palisades were the perfect place for inner reflection, solitude, and quiet discussions. But on that day, the view was horrifying.

By the time we got there, it was already late in the afternoon. The sun was sinking lower in the west and turning the smoke-filled sky deep orange. Black billows of smoke rose up all along the southern shore. The fire was spreading eastward and becoming more dangerous than ever before. As enormous flames shot up through the trees in the distance, the whole sky appeared to be going up in smoke, as if the clouds themselves were on fire.

From our vantage point high above, Diamond Lake took on a ghastly appearance. The water was murky, dark brown, and choppy. Great wind gusts moved in wide swaths over the open water, swirling and churning, as if being stirred by a giant hand. Far away across the water, the fire continued to burn like a massive furnace, consuming everything in its path. With the wind blowing so furiously, we couldn't hear the fire; we could only watch in horror. The three of us huddled together in the wind and sadly watched the beautiful forests burning to the ground.

"If it keeps moving east, it won't be long until it's just across the lake from the camp," I said.

"Well, that's a worry, mate," said Esther.

"Yeah," Aria agreed. "I hope Northern Lights is okay."

"If it jumps to Three Mile Island, I'm afraid it's just a hop, skip, and a jump to base camp," I said.

"Let's just hope that doesn't happen," Aria said.

We stood there and watched the fire move slowly east as if in slow motion. Northern Lights was directly in its path. All it would take was one spark to drift across the channel to the islands. I knew everyone at camp would be trying frantically to prevent that from happening, but it seemed inevitable. There was nothing anyone could do but watch, wait, and hope that it would burn itself out.

"I can't believe this is happening," I said mournfully.

"I know," Esther said. "I'm so sorry."

She hugged my side tightly, and so did Aria, but it didn't feel right. I had a sickening feeling that the closeness we'd enjoyed for the past few days was about to end—suddenly, violently, and relentlessly—like the burning of a forest fire that consumes everything in its path and leaves nothing in its wake. Our trip, which had started so peacefully, was coming to a sudden and violent end.

"We better get going," Aria said as she pulled away and began to find her way back down the trail.

Esther pulled away too and walked over near the edge of the cliff. She was shivering in the cold, so I took off my flannel overshirt and wrapped it around her.

"Thanks Leo," she said as she slipped her arms into the sleeves. "You're good at taking care of me."

I wrapped my arms around her and held her close. I never imagined that the fire would be the last thing we'd see in the Boundary Waters, but it was actually happening.

After a while, Esther tugged on my arm to go. We hiked back down to the canoe landing where Aria stood waiting, still looking southwest across the lake at the fire that was glowing orange beneath the smoky skies. Aria jumped in the front of the canoe. Esther climbed into the middle as I steadied it. Then, I stepped into the back and pushed us off into the choppy water.

As we made our way east, we paddled directly below the Palisades and into a narrow channel. We continued on, weaving through a cluster of islands on our way back toward camp. It was a relief to finally be out of the wind and waves of the big lake. In the quiet waters around the islands, we could finally relax.

"Our trip is almost over," Aria said sadly.

"The fire's going to put an end to a lot of things," I replied.

"I don't want to think about that anymore," Aria said.

"Well, let's think about something else then," Esther said. "Aria, what do you think you'll remember the most from our trip?"

"The fire," Aria said sadly.

"What about the good times?" Esther asked. "What good things will you remember?"

Aria sat quietly for a while, thinking to herself. I did too. I was still in shock at the sight of the fire raging behind us. I was paddling, but I was still in a daze. When Aria spoke up, it snapped me back out of somewhere far away. I don't even know where.

"I'll remember our first night on Saganaga, floating across the lake under the stars," Aria said. "I'll never forget dumping Leo in the lake and swimming around in the dark. I'll remember our deep talks and hanging out around the campfire with you guys last night. Our dance party this morning on the portage trail was pretty cool too. Actually, it was a pretty fun trip."

"Yeah, it was pretty sweet," Esther replied. "Hey, Leo, what about you? What will you remember?"

I didn't really feel like talking, but I knew what Esther was up to. As always, she was trying to get us to think about deeper things and then share our thoughts with each other. She was good at that. I thought for a minute or so and then spoke up.

"I'll remember a lot of stuff from our trip," I said. "I'll remember hanging the food pack in the dark, stargazing on Saganaga and learning about all the constellations, paddling around on Jenny Lake last night and listening to the loons calling across the water, and getting a great backrub from Aria in the tent."

"Oh yeah!" Aria exclaimed triumphantly. "I knew you'd remember that one, Farm Boy!"

"It's the best backrub I've ever had," I replied, knowing she'd love the compliment.

"There's more where that came from!" she exulted.

"Yeah, Hunter, I really owe you one," I said foolishly.

"That's right!" she exclaimed. "You owe me big time!"

I enjoyed the banter with Aria. It was a nice distraction from everything we had endured throughout the day. Besides, I didn't want to think about the fire or the fact that our time together was coming to an end. As we paddled along, I realized that Esther hadn't shared any of her memories from the trip, so I asked her.

"How about you, Esther? What are some of the fun things you'll remember?" I asked.

She turned her head and smiled back at me. Clearly, she had a few things on her mind, and I could tell that she wanted to talk. "Oh boy, watch out!" I thought to myself.

"Hmm, what should I say?" Esther replied. "I'll remember the stars, for sure, and stargazing with you guys the first night. I'll never forget Eddy Falls and the bears this morning. I'm going to remember getting to see the northern lights last night too."

"Wait a minute," Aria interrupted. "You guys stayed up last night and watched the northern lights without me?"

Esther glanced back at me and said, "Yeah, we tried to wake you up, Aria, but you were sleeping like a log."

"Actually, you were sleeping like a dead dog," I said with a snicker. "No, it was more like a pregnant hog. Man, you were snoring up something fierce, like a croaking bull—"

"Leo, shut up!" Aria snapped from up in front. "When we get back to camp, I'm gonna beat the bullfrog out of you!"

"And I'm gonna love you for it too!" I replied happily.

"Oh, brother!" Aria exclaimed. "So, what else did you guys do last night without me?"

"Oh, not too much," Esther replied. "We had a bit of a chat. Then, Leo gave me a totally sweet backrub. Then, I took my T-shirt off and gave him a squiz at my tattoos."

"Wait! What?" Aria exclaimed. "You showed him your what?"

Esther grinned excitedly back at me again. "Oh no," I thought. "Here it comes."

"Straight up, girlfriend!" she exclaimed. "I showed him my tattoos, and then . . . we kissed for a while."

"Holy fudge-pops and applesauce!" Aria exclaimed. The words echoed across the lake and bounced back to us.

Esther glanced back at me and grinned. I smiled back and listened to Aria cut loose with every nasty euphemism her poor mother had so unsuspectingly taught her.

"Are you telling me that you two made out in the tent last night?" she cried. "You were making out . . . while I was sleeping right there next to you?"

Esther chuckled and replied, "Uh-huh."

"I knew this would happen!" Aria shouted "Leo, you snake! I look away for a second, and you go and steal my best friend right out from under my nose . . . while I'm sleeping!"

As Aria sat there in shock, I just kept paddling and tried not to laugh. I was pretty shocked myself to hear Esther come right out and say it so casually like that, but I was beaming inside. I'd remember that night too, for a long, long time. Esther reached back with her hand and waited for me to slap it. I gave her a gentle high five and then reached forward and messed up her hair.

Esther flashed her eyes back at me and then settled back down, silently grinning as Aria slowly came back down to earth. It took a while. Aria would stick her paddle into the water and pull once, then set it down on her lap and mutter, "I can't believe it." Then, she would drop the paddle back into water and pull again, only to stop once more and mutter the same thing over and over again.

Esther finally said, "I'm going to remember the lovely talks the three of us had too. I feel like I know so much about you guys now. Even though this trip is coming to an end, I feel like I'm going to take a part of you with me when I leave tomorrow. You've been there for me when I needed you. You've taken care of me. You've put up with my craziness. You guys are the best friends a girl could ever have. It's been such an incredible time out here."

We paddled through a narrow channel and floated by an empty campsite. Suddenly, Eagle Island came into view across the last stretch of open water. We were almost back to camp.

"I'm not the same as I was three weeks ago," Esther said. "I don't know what I expected, but it wasn't anything close to this. I've been changed, and it's not just because of the stars, the sunsets, the trees, or the lakes. It's because of you guys. It's because of what we went through together. When I hit the road tomorrow, I'm taking a part of you with me, and you're taking a part of me with you too. I don't want to lose you guys. We have to stay together somehow. I'm not even sure what that means. I just want us to stay in touch and make more memories together in the future."

Esther's dreamy words hit me like a brick wall. I didn't want our trip to end either. I wanted it to go on forever, just as she said. We paddled across the last stretch of the lake in silence. I wanted to turn the canoe around and head back out again, but that wasn't an option. We slowly cruised into the narrows and coasted ahead into the calm water near base camp.

Our trip was coming to an end.

chapter 51
state of shock

"We were so worried!"

As the bridge and the canoe landing by the beach came into view, we saw people standing around everywhere. There were groups huddled together on the dock. Others stood on the beach, and others lined the bridge across the lake. Everyone was looking west in the direction of the forest fires. As evening approached, the smoke covering the western sky had turned to a deep dark orange as it glowed from the fires burning just a few miles away.

When we pulled up onto the beach, Cassie ran up and greeted us. She gave Aria a big hug first, then Esther, and then even me.

"We were so worried about you!" she exclaimed, almost in tears. "How are you guys doing?"

"We're okay, but just a little bit in shock," I said.

"We'd better get you out of those wet clothes," she said, looking us over like a frightened mother hen.

A small crowd gathered around. As they swarmed us, they asked question after question. "Did you see the fire? Did you see Percy and Chuck? What about Finn? What about Anne's group? What about Nancy's group? How close was the fire to the islands?"

Cassie and the other female guides huddled around Aria and Esther. Some of the guys gathered around me and asked for more details about what I knew. In the chaos, I watched as Esther was escorted away with Aria up the trail to their cabin to get changed. It felt as if she were being ripped out of my arms, and all I could do was helplessly watch.

There were no silly songs or stories around the campfire that night. In fact, there wasn't a campfire at all. Everyone met in Starlight Lodge instead, but there were only huddled conversations here and there. Cassie was busy talking to a group of strangers out on the deck. They looked like park rangers or firefighters. I didn't know, but it appeared as if something was being organized to help prepare the camp for the approaching forest fire.

About an hour later, Finn showed up by himself. He was weary but in good spirits. Word quickly spread that he had located Anne's group and got them safely back to camp. When he spotted Aria, Esther, and me sitting at a table in the dining hall, he came straight up to us, grinning from ear to ear. When I stood up to greet him, he lunged at me and gave me a big bear hug.

"It's so good to see you safe and sound," he said, pulling back and giving the three of us a long look of relief.

"Thanks, Finn," I replied with a sheepish grin. "We're just happy to be back in one piece."

"You've got a good man here," he said, turning to Aria and Esther. "I knew the three of you would make it back all right, but I still said a little prayer for you anyway."

"Thanks, Finn," I replied, taken aback by his emotional display. "We had a pretty nice trip in spite of everything."

"I'm sure you did," he said, grinning at Esther. "Nice to see you too, little lady. I heard you had a bout of hypothermia."

"Thanks, Mister Kriger," she replied. "Aria took care of me, and we were in good hands with Leo there."

Finn leaned in and gave the two girls a big hug. "I'm sure you were," he said, still grinning.

It was the biggest show of emotion I'd seen out of Finn all summer long. As it turned out, he had just missed us when he took off to the north on Alpine Lake. He had searched for us all the way up to Lake Saganaga, then farther west to Ottertrack Lake, where he happened upon Anne's group.

"Good to have you three back," he said. "I'll see you all later at the cabin dedication tonight."

I admired Finn, even though I never got to know him very well. His simple words hit home. As he turned to go, he threw me a smile and a wink. That one little wink went a long way for me.

Not long after that, Cassie rounded up everyone in the dining hall. She gave a report on the status of the fire and what still needed to be done. The rangers were hopeful that the fire would burn itself out before reaching camp. Apparently, the fire breaks that had been put in place over the last few years were working. Everyone breathed a sigh of relief, but we weren't out of the woods yet. There were still two search parties out on the lakes, including Chuck and Percy, who were looking for Nancy's group. It was likely they'd be out all night and wouldn't make it back until the next morning, if they were found at all. We hoped and prayed for the best.

Then, to everyone's surprise, Cassie announced that the dedication for the newly built cabin would proceed as planned immediately after the meeting. The cabin dedication, which was actually an all-camp party, had been in the works for a couple of weeks. No one felt like sleeping anyway, so it seemed like a good idea to go ahead with it. Cassie said it would help everyone calm down a bit and take their minds off the fire.

Not long after the meeting ended in Starlight Lodge, the whole camp proceeded en masse to the south side of the island. Aria and Esther went along with the crowd. I made an excuse to go back to my cabin, but then I bailed on the party. I had no desire to be around anyone else that night . . .

. . . no one, that is, except for Esther.

chapter 52

at the crossroads

"You know what I mean."

At my cabin, I grabbed my guitar and then made my way down to the bridge. Base camp was completely dark and empty. I sat down in the middle of the bridge, content to be alone for a while. I quietly played my guitar and stared blankly at the ominous orange glow in the west. It wasn't how I had imagined the night would end.

About ten minutes later, the bridge began to creak with the sound of footsteps. I glanced over, and sure enough, it was Esther, still wearing my flannel overshirt. I stopped playing the guitar as she quietly walked out to me.

"I was hoping it was you," I said quietly. "What's up?"

"I didn't see you at the party, so I came looking for you." she replied, kneeling down next to me. "I missed you."

"I missed you too," I said.

"You're turning into quite the little piker," she said, poking me gently in the side. "Going bush on me, here, eh?"

"Yeah, well, I'm not feeling too good right now," I admitted, giving the guitar a miserable strum.

"So, you feel like spewin' again?" she asked with a grin.

"No," I replied. "You know what I mean."

"Yeah, I do," she said softly. "You know, Leo, I just want to be with you tonight." Esther slowly wrapped her arms around my shoulders and gave me a soft hug from behind.

"I was worried I wouldn't see you again," I replied, loving the feel of her touch.

"You're my special bro," she whispered. "I couldn't let you slip away on our last night together, now, could I?"

I started strumming the guitar again as Esther held on to me. After a while, she began to hum along. Then, just barely above a whisper, she started singing a simple melody, warm and delicate. In that quiet moment of sadness, her lovely voice made me feel like everything was going to be all right.

Somehow, Esther kept finding ways to love me. It was amazing how she kept right on blessing me with her presence, her words, her actions, and her gentle touch. The past three weeks had brought us close, just as I had hoped, but not in the way I had first imagined. It wasn't only a story of my love for her. It had become a story about her love for me too.

I thought about all the times Esther had reached out to me during her short stay at Northern Lights. When I got sick, she brought soup to my cabin. When we were stargazing, she reached out and held my hand. When we were in the tent on Jenny Lake, she rubbed my sore fingers until I forgot about the pain. When I was at a loss for words, she shared her feelings openly. When I hesitated to return her affection, she waited patiently until I was finally set free, like her, to share my feelings too.

Esther was so full of light, life, grace, and energy. It radiated out from her like sunlight—out of everything she did, everything she said, and everything she was. In spite of all the obstacles, she kept finding joy and light along the way. When I felt defeated, she brought hope. When I was in pain, she offered healing. When I saw destruction, she breathed new life. When I saw nothing, she saw everything. She just kept pouring out her love on me over and over again.

It was embarrassing to think of how I had been so obsessed with her appearance: her physical qualities, her clothes, her makeup, and how she looked in a bikini. I was captivated by her glorious red hair, her blue eyes, her long legs, her sunburned skin, her mysterious tattoos, and her pretty freckles. I had become so fascinated by her outward beauty. I couldn't believe it had taken so long to realize how beautiful she was on the inside.

Over the past three weeks, and especially the past three days, Esther had blessed me in so many ways. I felt as if I had done so little in return, other than to serve as a canoe guide on the trip, but even that was a selfish act on my part. I spent the days watching her, thinking about her, trying to get noticed by her, and desperately hoping for the chance to kiss her. Esther loved me so selflessly, so tenderly, and so freely. She brought everything back into focus. She exposed my shallow, pathetic expectations, and in the light of her brilliant love, I had to face the truth about my feelings for her.

I was finally beginning to wake up and realize how much Esther had come to mean to me. I was going to miss having her in my life. Not only her lovely smile, her pretty freckles, and her beautiful body, but I was going to miss her joyful presence and how she seemed to find the best in life through the good times and the bad. I was going to miss her childlike heart that looked at everything with fascination and innocent idealism. I was going to miss her enthusiasm, her humor, her acts of kindness, her words of grace, her tender touch, and her expressions of love and affection, which she gave so freely. She made me feel good and strong inside, so blessed to be alive, and so joyfully expectant of the future. She made me feel so important, so wanted, so needed, and so loved.

As our time drew to a close, I felt as if I had missed so many opportunities to love her and be a better human being. I felt as if I could have done so much better. I felt as if it were all going to be lost when she left. Still, Esther was there with me on the bridge. She could have stayed at the party, but she was with me.

It seemed as if we were at a crossroads. To the left was Turtle Island, the party at the cabin dedication, and everything else being played out as usual. To the right was Eagle Island and a place where we could be alone together without anything getting in the way. Our future, if it was to be together, was in that direction.

I had a choice to make too. Was I going to continue to pursue Esther at all cost or just let her drift away like all the other girls I'd dated in the past? We were at an important juncture in our relationship, whether we wanted to admit it or not.

Esther sat down quietly on the bridge next to me. She reached up behind her neck with both hands and slowly lifted her collection of silver necklaces over her head. I reached out and helped move some of her long hair out of the way.

"Good grief, Esther," I said. "You have a lot of hair!"

"Isn't that the truth!" she replied. "I reckon I'll have to go and get it all chopped off one of these days."

"No, don't ever do that," I begged. "I love it long like this."

She laughed. "Well, you're one to talk, aren't you Leo, the joker with the longest hair at camp, eh?"

"We were made for each other," I replied.

"Straight up," she said with a soft chuckle. "You and I . . . we were meant to be together."

Her words made my heart jump, but I couldn't tell if she was just joking around or not. Were we meant to be together? That was the hope I was still clinging to on our last night together.

She set the necklaces down on the bridge and began untangling them. There were seven chains in all, each with one or more jewels or charms attached to it. I had wondered about her necklaces. I knew each one must have a story, but in our time together, I'd never been able to get a very good look at them.

Esther slowly untangled the chains and then pulled one out from the others. It was fine and delicate, with a single charm attached to it. It looked like a silver bird, and its wings had tiny little diamonds and blue sapphires set in them.

"This is for you," she said, holding it up between the two of us. "It's a gift . . . for you to remember me by."

"What is it?" I asked.

"It's my favorite trinket," Esther said as she carefully placed it into my hands. "It's a swan. It reminds me of Cygnus in the sky. In New Zealand, it can be seen far away on the northern horizon."

"I can't take your favorite necklace," I said, offering it back to her.

"Leo, I want you to have it," she insisted, pushing it back into my hands. "It's a reminder . . . of my love for you."

"But I don't have anything to give you," I replied.

"No worries," she said with a grin. "I'll just hang on to your shirt for safekeeping, if that's okay with you. It's not exactly my size, but it'll always make me think of you."

"That sounds good to me, but I still wish I had a present to give you before you leave tomorrow," I replied.

"Oh, Leo," she said, gazing out over the lake. "You've already given so much. You gave us this trip. You took care of Aria and me. You saved us from the bears. You led us past the wildfire. You brought us safely home. I feel like I've seen who you really are, but I know there's so much more to you."

I listened to her words falling down on me like rays of sunlight on a cold winter's day. The way she talked gave me a sliver of hope for the future. I didn't know how to respond, so I simply hung on as she continued to pour out her sweet words.

"You blessed me in our times alone, too," Esther said. "You let me share my deepest feelings, and then you opened up your heart. You let me kiss you as we watched the northern lights. We've shared so many perfect moments together."

"But you're leaving tomorrow," I replied, looking down at the swan necklace in my hands. "I'm going to lose you."

"No, Leo, I'll always be with you," she said softly. She lifted my chin and looked into my eyes. She was so sure of herself. It seemed as if she wasn't as terrified about the future as I was. I wanted her to miss me as much as I was going to miss her.

"You won't lose me," she whispered as she reached out and put her hand over my heart. "I'm here," she said. Then, she reached up and gently touched the side of my face. "And I'm here too."

"But Esther, I want more than that," I said desperately.

"I know you do," she replied. "But Leo, I don't think we should try to make this any more than it is right now. There might be more to our story, or there might not."

"How can you say that after everything we've shared together?" I asked in despair.

"Our time together has been wonderful," she said softly. "It might be the beginning of something, but how can we know that now?

I think it's time for us to let go and trust that whatever it is will work itself out in the future."

"That's what I'm afraid of," I replied. "I'm afraid of losing you in the future. I'm afraid you won't love me the same way I love you. I'm afraid everything is going to change once you leave."

"I think that's a chance we have to take," Esther said. "For me, love doesn't hold on tightly; it releases freely. It doesn't fear sadness; it trusts joyfully. It isn't painless or without suffering; it accepts pain and suffering as part of life. It accepts all of life as it comes and goes—trusting, believing, open, and free."

"Will you ever be able to hold on to something?" I asked. "Will you ever be able to hold on to me and not be so free?"

"I'm not ready to do that, not just yet anyway," she replied softly. "Maybe someday in the future, but for now, I think we need to hold each other with open hands."

"Open hands?" I asked, confused.

"Who knows what the future will bring?" she replied. "I know you don't like to hear it, Leo, but we have to trust that if it's meant to be, then it will happen. In fact, I believe that if it's meant to be, then there's nothing in this world that can keep it from happening."

Esther undid the clasp of the necklace and fastened it around my neck. As she leaned in close, I drank up her warm, sweet breath. Her hair brushed softly across my face. Her lips were only inches away from mine. I wanted to kiss her, but she seemed so far away . . . as if she were preparing to fly off to a distant galaxy. I wanted to hold her and never let her go. I didn't want to leave her ever again. I didn't want tomorrow to happen.

As the sky glowed fiery orange in the west, we held on to each other in silence on the bridge. The world we knew seemed to be coming to an end. Reality was slowly sinking in. A feeling of gloom and despair came over me. I'd felt that way before.

That was how our whirlwind love affair was going to end.

chapter 53

standing on the edge

"Well, that right there sounds like a heap of trouble."

As we sat on the bridge, the moon made a brave attempt to break through the smoky sky in the east. After a while, we heard people slowly drifting back to base camp. The lights in Starlight Lodge turned back on, and there were people talking out on the deck. The party on the south side of the island was winding down.

"Come on, Leo," Esther said. "Let's blow out of here."

"Why?" I asked.

"I don't want anyone to find us," she said. "How about we go up to Eagle Bluff one last time before we call it a night, eh?"

"Sure, let's go!" I replied.

We walked across the bridge and took the trail that wound its way up to the bluff. Esther didn't race ahead like before. Instead, she reached back and took my hand. Together, we climbed the steep path that wound back and forth up the hill. It was dark outside, but the moonlight helped us find our way.

When we got to the top, Esther walked straight out to the edge just like before. I went with her, and together, we stood on the very edge of the cliff. Across the narrows, we could see flashlights bouncing along the trails through the woods. The lights in cabins flickered on here and there as people settled down for the night. For some reason, a feeling of dread crept over me again. It was our last night together at Northern Lights.

"I can't help feeling like this is it," I said. "I still feel like I'm going to lose you forever."

"Well, if you like, Leo, we can let this be it, eh?" Esther's words struck me. "Then, tomorrow, we can just go our separate ways."

"Is that what you want?" I asked with dismay.

"No," she said softly. "I don't want this to end, but it's going to anyway. I don't know how it'll all pan out, but there must be something more. I think there's a reason we met this summer."

"I do too," I replied, squeezing her hand. "But the future looks so impossible. What are we going to do?"

"Let's expect the best, whatever that is," she said. "We can find ways to stay in touch. It's just the time and distance that seem so ominous right now."

"That's what I love about you, Esther," I replied. "You always find a way to see the bright side of things. No matter how bleak the future looks, you're still expecting the best."

"Straight up!" she exclaimed. "That's just who I am."

"You're awesome," I gushed openly. "You know that, right?"

"Who me?" Esther said with a laugh. "Nah, I don't think so, mate. You don't know me very well, I guess."

"No, really," I insisted. "I was smitten with you from the first moment I saw you on the dock. You were so beautiful. Then, you started waving at me, or well, at Aria, I guess. I thought you were waving at me. It scared the hell out of me!"

"It did, eh?" she said with a laugh. "Yeah, bro, I have that effect on guys sometimes. It's why I wear dark makeup—you know, the lipstick and sunglasses. I like scaring the hell out of guys."

"Yeah, you're pretty good at it," I said. "But it got you into a bit of trouble here, didn't it?"

"Yeah, I reckon it did," Esther agreed. "But I had this long-haired buck who took care of everything. He really told off those piss-awful roosters, didn't he? He stuck his neck out for me and almost took a beating for it too."

"Hey, I could've taken those guys," I said, slightly offended.

"Yeah, right!" Esther laughed. "You just about passed out when I kissed you on the cheek the next night. You're a real tough chap, eh? Yeah, nah!"

"I'm not feeling very tough right now," I admitted sadly, looking down at the lake below.

Esther chuckled. "You've got the collywobbles, eh?"

"Yeah, I've got the collywobbles!" I exclaimed, then I realized how loudly I'd just spoken. What if someone heard us across the channel? I didn't want anyone to know where we were.

"Well, I'm not letting you sneak off again, not just yet, that is!" Esther said as she squeezed my hand. "We've got all night, and don't forget, you're my special bro. So, what do you want to do now?"

"I can think of a few things," I replied with a grin as I grabbed Esther and pulled her in close. Suddenly, I realized we were standing much too close to the edge of the cliff.

"Easy, Leo!" she exclaimed. "I like you and all, but I'm not ready to fall head over heels to my own death quite yet!"

"You're not gonna make it easy on me, huh?" I replied, backing away from the edge and pulling her with me. "How about we go a little farther down the trail. There's something I want to show you."

Esther pulled back on my hand and smiled. "Well, Leo, that right there sounds like a heap of trouble. Maybe you should just turn around and walk away before I clock you in the kisser! I've heard that line plenty of times before."

"I bet you have," I said. "Sometimes, I think you're way out of my league. Why'd you have to go and be so good-looking?"

"Ha! Who me?" Esther blurted out with a laugh. "You should see me in the morning. I'm quite a sight!"

"I have seen you in the morning, and you're amazing!" I said, pulling her toward me again. "You're the most beautiful girl I've ever seen in my entire life."

"Crikey, mate!" she exclaimed. Esther pushed me away, but she was still grinning. "What you just said was so scary! I just have to say it one more time! Crikey!"

"I love it when you talk sexy like that!" I said, pulling her back to me. "Come on, Esther, there's something I want to show you, for real. It's just a little farther down the trail."

"Okay, stud," she said. "I'm coming with you all the way."

"Holy cow, Esther," I replied. "You've got to stop talking like that. You're gonna drive me crazy."

"Oh, I'm gonna drive you crazy, all right," she whispered in my ear. "You just wait and see!" Esther's blue eyes sparkled in the dark as they reflected the lights of the cabins across the lake.

"Holy cow, girl!" I exclaimed again. "I swear, you're driving me completely nuts right now!"

"Holy cow?" Esther replied. "Is that all you Iowa farm boys know how to say when you get nervous? There must be an awful lot of cows down there in Iowa."

"Esther, you just talk so crazy sometimes," I said.

"Straight up!" she replied emphatically. "I gotta keep everyone rightly entertained, you know."

"Well, you do a pretty good job at it," I said.

"If I didn't," she replied, "I wager you wouldn't pay too much attention to me. No one would."

"I would too," I insisted, giving her hand a squeeze.

"Yeah, I suppose you would," she agreed. "I just like to talk about more important things most of the time."

"Yeah, that's one thing I love about you," I said.

"I don't know, Leo, most people don't really get me," she said softly. "They probably wouldn't like me if they really knew me."

"I think if you let people get to know you, they'd find out how amazing you really are," I replied.

"Nah! I don't think it'd last," Esther said with a shrug of her shoulders. "I reckon they'd find me a wee bit amusing for a little while, but then the fascination would wear off."

"It's probably over already," I said, suddenly egging her on. "Just put the book down and go find something else to do. Who needs to know how it'll all turn out in the end?"

"Hey!" Esther said, giving me a friendly shove. "I'm serious, bro! Most of the chaps I know are just up on themselves. They don't give a stitch about the real me—what I think or who I am on the inside. They only want one thing, it seems."

"What's that?" I asked the obvious.

"You know!" Esther exclaimed. "But it's more than just the bloody bucks. It's nearly everyone. Most people only want what *they* want, and if you don't give it to them, they turn on you or abandon you, and then they go looking for someone else to get it from."

I wondered where that came from. Was there more anger and hurt inside her than she'd been letting on? I wondered what she had been like when she was in high school back in New Zealand. What kind of girl was she really? What about her friends? What was she like around them? There was so much I didn't know about her. Still, I was falling hard for her, and I wasn't about to let her go.

"Hey, there's still someone here for you," I said, pulling her close. "Someone who sees you, all of you . . . inside and out."

"Well, I wonder who that could be?" Esther said with a grin. "Here you are, mate, throwing a freakin' Hollywood on me, so I'll turn it up for you, eh?"

"I have no idea what you just said, but sure . . . yeah," I replied blindly. "Whatever you say."

"Thanks, Leo," she said. "I thought so. It's so nice of you to try and buck me up. You're quite the corker. You're really out there on your own, aren't you?"

"What?" I replied, trying to piece together what she'd just said.

"So, you're looking to perk a friend's discount, eh?" She kept talking nonsense. "Come on then, mate, rattle ya dags!"

"Good grief, Esther! What are you talking about?" I asked.

"You have no idea, do you?" she said softly. "If you're not careful, Leo, it could get you into a heap of trouble."

"I'm fine with that," I replied, still clueless as to what we were actually talking about.

"Crikey, mate! You're such a goofball. You know that, right?" she said, giving me a friendly shove.

"Yeah," I replied with a laugh. "You've told me that a few times already, but I've come to terms with it by now. You seem to like my strange sense of humor, so, yeah!"

Suddenly, I noticed two people running up the hill to Pleiades Village. Their flashlights bounced wildly along the trail in the dark.

Two others were walking out onto the bridge. They were talking together, and they seemed concerned about something.

"That sounds like Aria's voice on the bridge," Esther whispered.

"Yeah, it is," I replied. "Finn is with her too."

The two people with the flashlights went to my cabin, looked inside, and then ran back down the hill in a hurry. Finn and Aria stood in the middle of the bridge talking. Aria had a flashlight too. She was shining it at the beach and then up at the bluff near us.

I grabbed Esther and pulled her away from the edge of the cliff. I didn't want them to know we were there. I didn't want them to see Esther's eyes too. I swore you could see them glowing in the dark from a mile away. In fact, her entire body seemed to be glistening with excitement in the darkness.

"Hey, Leo," Esther whispered, "I was a bit brassed off when I left the party. I reckon when they didn't find me at my cabin, they might have gotten a wee bit worried."

"Yeah, they're looking for us, that's for sure," I said.

"Do you want to go back?" she asked.

"No, not yet," I said. "I still want to show you something farther down the trail. Come with me."

"Awesome," she replied. "I'm all yours."

chapter 54
down into the west

"Just where exactly are we going?"

I grabbed Esther's hand, and we ran down the trail toward the bridge. I was afraid that we'd meet Finn and Aria there, but they were still out in the middle of the bridge, talking. We quietly hung a left and took the trail to the sauna. As we moved along in the dark, we could hear Finn and Aria coming behind us on the trail, so we raced ahead to put some distance between them and us.

Just before we reached the sauna, I cut right across a flat slab of rock and continued into the woods to the northwest. I held on to Esther's hand and carefully waded through the underbrush in the moonlight. As we inched our way up another ridge to the north, we could hear Finn's voice at the sauna. Aria was shining her flashlight down toward the dock and then into the woods near us.

"So, Leo," Esther whispered excitedly, "I know I said I'd follow you anywhere, but just where exactly are we going?"

"Down there," I replied, pointing west into the woods. "But let's wait until they've left."

Aria and Finn, however, didn't leave. They walked out onto the dock and kept talking and looking around. On the dock, at least, they were farther away, so we quietly moved deeper into the forest.

We dropped down off the ridge and slowly worked our way through a grotto of large rocks. Then, we tiptoed out underneath a grove of towering pine trees and finally made it to the spot I'd been aiming for. I had been there a couple of times before, just never in the middle of the night.

As she looked around, Esther's eyes slowly lit up. "Leo, this is quite the sweet little snooker, isn't it!" she exclaimed. "It's like a secret cove with its own sandy beach and everything."

We were standing on the western edge of Eagle Island. The little beach was nestled in between two large jetties of rocks that extended out into the water on either side. Even though the spot was clearly visible from the lake, it was completely hidden from the rest of the island by a ridge to the east.

Throughout the summer, I had passed by the cove several times with canoe groups, heading out onto Diamond Lake or coming back off a trip. Earlier that summer on one of my days off, I hiked around and found it just over the ridge from the sauna.

"This is such a pretty spot," Esther said excitedly. "Why wouldn't Northern Lights build a lodge right here?"

"I think I know why," I said. "This isn't owned by Northern Lights. We crossed the border into the Boundary Waters when we came over the ridge back there, so this is actually part of the BWCA itself, even though it's on Eagle Island and so close to camp."

"You can see the whole lake from here!" Esther exclaimed.

"At least the eastern half of Diamond," I said, sitting down on the sandy beach. "I've come here a couple of times this summer to watch the sunset on the lake."

"I can see why," Esther replied as she settled down in the sand next to me and took hold of my hand.

"The tip of Turtle Island is only about fifty yards away over there," I explained, pointing across the lake. "It's the closest spot in the whole channel between the two islands. They call it Heaven's Gate. Once you pass through here, it opens up to the entire eastern half of Diamond Lake and beyond."

"Oh, I get it, Leo," she said. "So, this is what you wanted to show me, eh? Here we are on our last night together, just the two of us, in your secret spot overlooking Heaven's Gate?" Esther grinned and nudged me in the shoulder. "It's pretty romantic, Leo, you sly dog. I reckon you brought me here to this secluded beach with the intentions of making passionate love to me, right?"

"Well," I replied, "I don't know about that."

The idea had crossed my mind, but not that night. The sky was still glowing deep orange from the massive fires out west. Overhead, dark brown clouds slowly rolled eastward in the night sky. The smell of thick smoke filled the air all around us. Besides, Aria and Finn were still hot on our tails.

"Things just don't seem to be working out the way I expected," I said sorrowfully.

"What did you expect?" Esther replied. "We've only known each other for three weeks. Did you think we were gonna fall madly in love on this little three-day adventure into the wilderness where all our problems in life would be instantly solved, and then you'd ride off with me into the sunset?"

"Well, yeah," I stammered. "I don't know . . . maybe." I suddenly felt on the defensive as I reconsidered what I'd originally intended. Was that what I really wanted?

"Well, why not throw a couple of botched love interests in there along the way, eh?" she said. "Then, I magically show up, the perfect ship-girl for you to rescue from her checkered past. While you're at it, why not toss in a murder mystery and some high-stakes courtroom drama just for good measure?"

"Yeah, that'd be cool," I said with a grin. "That's how it always works out in the movies."

"Oh, come on, Leo," she said seriously. "This isn't a movie."

"Yeah, I know," I replied, trying not to laugh. "I was just hoping for a little more syrupy sentimentality and a few schmaltzy love scenes to spice things up a bit, maybe a little less drama, and yeah, a more happy, satisfying end to our story."

"This isn't a romance novel we're writing here, Leo," Esther replied directly. "This is real life. It doesn't always end up like in the movies. You can't just close the book, and suddenly everything is back to normal again. If you want me . . . if you really want me, it's gonna take some more time."

"Yeah, I get it," I replied, getting serious again. "But tomorrow is coming too soon, and I don't want this to end."

"This doesn't have to be the end of our story," she said. "It can be the beginning. We're not trying to wrap all this up in the last few chapters of a book because we're running out of pages. We're trying to build something more meaningful than that, something that will stand the test of time."

"I want that, but it's all just so terrifying to me," I replied. "All of the past relationships I've been in ended so badly. I just don't want that to happen again."

"Leo, I think you have to break free from those past relationships," she said. "They're old worn-out stories. It's like you're saving them on a shelf somewhere, like a stack of used books. You want to relive them somehow, but you can't. It's like you're paralyzed off in fantasyland, looking for another perfect girl, a perfect story, or a perfect ending. I can't be that for you."

"I know," I replied. "I just don't want this to end,"

"Then, there has to be more, right?" she said indignantly.

"I'm sorry for letting my fears get the best of me," I replied. "I'm just a miserable wreck. I can see how you'd have to be cautious with a guy like me, especially here and now."

"I'm still here, aren't I, mate?" Esther said with a grin.

"Yeah," I replied cautiously.

"Well, I'm not going anywhere if you're not," she said. "I'm just saying, let's be honest with ourselves and let this be whatever it is . . . let it be enough for now, and we'll see what happens in the future."

"In the next chapter?" I asked.

"Yeah, mate," she replied, "but maybe . . . in the next book."

"Okay, I got it," I said.

Suddenly, we heard Finn and Aria calling for us. We heard Cassie too. It sounded like their voices were coming from out on the lake. I wondered if they had taken a canoe out on the water, but no, they wouldn't be that desperate. They were probably still over by the sauna, standing on the dock.

All of a sudden, two small figures immerged out of the woods and raced toward us across the beach. At first, I was startled, but then I realized they were the two camp dogs, Siri and Star. Thankfully, they didn't bark as good hound dogs would have. Instead, they simply ran around us, happily wagging their tails.

"Hi, Siri! Hello, Star!" Esther said, welcoming them. "How did you two blokes find us all the way out here?"

The dogs wagged their tails and panted as they let us pet them. They seemed to think that they had done their job and were getting justly rewarded for it.

"I love dogs!" Esther said as she grabbed little Star and scratched his furry belly. It was apparent they loved her too. They both jumped around her and tried to lick her face. She laughed and played with them as they wagged their tails. I would have enjoyed a good romp in the sand with the dogs, but it wasn't the best time for that.

"If they don't leave," I said nervously, "Finn and Aria are gonna come looking for them."

We heard Aria calling from just over the ridge—not for us, but for the dogs. "Siri! Star! Come!" she cried.

"Go on, you guys," I said softly, trying to shush them away, but the two dogs just kept running around and wagging their tails. They weren't getting it. Finally, I stood up and said, "Siri, Star, git!"

Instantly, both dogs spun around and took off back through the woods, wagging their tails and chasing each other as they went. It had been a successful hunt, and it was time to return to their master who was calling for them.

A moment later, we heard Aria exclaim, "Siri! Star! Where have you two been? You naughty dogs!"

I wondered why she hadn't followed them over the ridge to where we were. I thought Aria would have recognized their excitement, but she didn't. "You naughty, naughty dogs!" I heard her exclaim one more time. It felt like she wasn't scolding the dogs anymore, but instead, was scolding us.

For a while, we could hear Finn and Aria talking back by the sauna. Then, everything became eerily silent. I wondered if they were quietly making their way over the ridge toward us. It felt strangely exciting to realize that they were out there somewhere in the dark, looking for the two of us . . . as if we were being hunted.

I wondered about Finn. What would he do if he found us? Was he concerned for Esther? Was he upset with me? Or was he simply amused by it all? We sat on the beach, quietly awaiting our fate.

Esther grinned at me in the dark. "This is scary!" she whispered.

"Yeah," I whispered back.

We listened in silence for a little while longer, but we didn't hear either of them again. We concluded that they must have finally given up the search and gone back to base camp.

"Do you think we should go back?" I asked.

"Nah, let 'em keep looking for us," Esther said.

"But they're probably worried," I replied.

"Let 'em worry," she said. "It'll be all right in the morning."

"Esther," I said softly, "I wanted tonight to be so special, just the two of us. It's just not turning out the way I'd planned."

"Hey, Leo, we're here together," she replied. "This *is* special . . . and you're still my special bro."

"Thanks," I said sadly. "I'm just thinking about the fire, everyone searching for us, and the fact that you're leaving tomorrow."

"Leo, you've got to stop worrying," she said. "You know, this is the fourth time we've been together, just you and me."

"It's what?" I asked.

"This is our fourth time alone together," Esther repeated as she leaned back in the sand and looked out at the lake. "Remember the first time, when I visited you at your cabin?"

"Yeah," I replied. "I couldn't believe you actually did that."

I felt the significance of Esther's comment. She'd been keeping track of our times together. It made me feel very special and very loved. It reassured me that our times together hadn't been fleeting moments to her. They had been deeply meaningful.

"You just couldn't stay away from me, could you?" I said, poking her playfully in the side.

"That'll be the day!" Esther exclaimed. "Aria was gone, and you were feeling crook. I just brought you some take-aways, and besides, Aria kept yabbering on about some bloke named Leo and ra ra ra! So, I decided to go and have a squiz for myself."

"And?" I asked.

Esther nudged me softly in the shoulder. "And find out if you truly were the sweet little cracker she said you were."

"And?" I asked again.

"And I don't know," she said. "You sort of caught me by surprise. Yeah, I guess I was a wee bit intrigued."

"Just a wee bit?" I asked.

"Aah!" Esther said as she pushed me over in the sand. "I don't know! Maybe! But then the next day, when you stood up to those jokers down at the volleyball court, that really got to me. I have to say; I was fully impressed. I didn't expect you to do that."

"I would've done that for any of my friends," I replied honestly.

"Well, I thought it was pretty sweet," Esther said. "Then, Aria got to yakking about the trip. At first, I didn't think it would work out. But when it did, and you said yes, it really got me to thinking."

"About what?" I asked.

"About you, of course!" Esther gave me another friendly shove.

"That's what I thought!" I replied. "Now I'm wondering who was chasing who this whole time! As I recall, you were the one who kissed me by the cabin. Then, you held my hand up on Saganaga."

"That was our second time alone together," she said quietly.

"But Aria was there too," I pointed out.

"Aria was sleeping," Esther noted. "And don't forget, Leo, that's when you let it slip that you were sweet on me."

"Yeah, you took it pretty well," I joked. "As I recall, you punched me in the gut the next day and almost left me stranded in Canada. Then, you dumped me in Jenny Lake and teased the heck out of me while I tried not to drown!"

"Straight up!" she exclaimed. "A girl's gotta do what a girl's gotta do! Besides, it was my birthday. I was having a grand time, and I have to say, the day ended pretty nicely too."

"Our third time alone together?" I asked.

"That's right, and crikey, mate! I can't believe what I had to go through to get your attention!"

"You do have a flair for the dramatic," I replied.

"Oh, Leo," she said with a chuckle. "That backrub you gave me was a wee bit more than just an ordinary backrub!"

"What?" I asked, confused. "To you?"

"No, to you! You blockhead!" she exclaimed.

"Hey, you're the one who ripped off your T-shirt and started showing me all your tattoos right there in the tent!" I cried in my own defense. "What did you expect?"

"Go on! That was nothing, bro!" she crowed. "I just about had to bare my entire soul to get you to open up!"

"Well, you got what you wanted, didn't you?" I replied.

"Straight up!" Esther said triumphantly. "I had to go in for the kill myself, or we'd have been up all night, thinking about it!"

"It was pretty great," I said quietly.

"Yeah, it was," she replied. "You were so sweet, Leo. You've been adorable this whole time. That's why I'm still here with you, mate. As I said, this is our fourth time alone together."

"So, I can make passionate love to you on the beach now?" I threw the idea out there again, half-jokingly, but also testing the waters to see how Esther would respond to the idea.

"Oh, Leo, there you go again!" Esther said as she laughed and nudged me in the side. "Are you asking me for permission? Or are you telling me that's how it's gonna be?"

"I don't know," I said awkwardly. "I want to, but things just don't seem to be working out for us, do they. I mean, look at everything that's been going on."

I realized that I had absentmindedly confessed something there. Was that what I really wanted? I panicked and wondered what might happen next—either acceptance or rejection. It was a terrifying few seconds that came and went in a flash.

Esther turned toward me, suddenly serious. "I do too," she said earnestly. "But I don't know, Leo. I'm leaving for New Zealand tomorrow. I'm worried that I'll break your heart."

"I don't care," I replied without giving it a second thought. "I just want to be with you now."

"And I with you," she said softly.

Esther's immediate response made my heart begin to race inside my chest. I blinked my eyes and swallowed hard, realizing what her honest confession meant for the two of us. Instinctively, I leaned over and kissed her. It's what I'd been dreaming about for the past few days, and perhaps, the past few weeks, ever since that first day she'd arrived at Northern Lights.

I couldn't believe how Esther had kept track of the times we'd been alone together. She hadn't just been playing around with me after all. Our time together meant a lot more to her.

I leaned back on my elbows and gazed at Esther. She grinned and then lunged at me, pushing me down in the sand underneath her.

"I caught you," she said proudly.

"You sure did, you wild thing," I said with a grin. "Now, what are you going to do with me? Kill me?"

"Yeah, mate," she said, locking her hands in mine. "But I'm gonna love you to death first!"

"Sounds good to me. I'm all yours," I replied.

"But then," she continued, "I'm gonna let you go so that you can run free . . . for a time."

"Wait . . . what?" I asked. "You're gonna let me go?"

"Yeah, mate," she replied. "I'm gonna set you free. I can't keep you. You're a wild thing too, you know."

"Oh, I'm wild, all right!" I agreed, pulling her down to me. "I'm gonna tear you apart."

"Yeah, I know," she whispered. "You're going to break my heart too. I just know it."

"I would never hurt you," I said quietly.

"I know, but it still might happen," she said softly, looking into my eyes for a split second. "But . . . I'll love you, anyway."

"Anyway?" I asked, confused yet again by her strange choice of words. I was still getting used to it.

"Yeah . . . anyway," she said again. "If you want my love, then that's what you'll have to settle for."

"Okay, then I'll love you anyway too," I replied, pulling her in close to me again.

As Esther leaned forward and kissed me, I wondered about her words. She seemed conflicted. Did she really want to make love or not? Why would she even hesitate? As we kissed, I put the thoughts out of my mind, but they wouldn't go away. Esther was such a free spirit, but I still knew so little about her. What would make her hesitate to love me? What was she really thinking?

Was she really going to let me go? I had a feeling, and I didn't like it. But I had her in my arms, and I wanted to make the most of our time together while it lasted. Esther had definitely caught me. She wouldn't let me go, would she? I didn't ever want to be let go again, but at that moment, it seemed sadly inevitable. I had a sinking feeling that the reality of the next day was going to break my heart. In fact, I had a feeling it was going to break both of our hearts.

As we kissed in the sand, it began to mist and then lightly sprinkle. It reminded me of our time together in the tent the night before. But then, suddenly, a gust of wind rushed overhead, and it began to rain in earnest. We laughed about it at first, but when a crack of lightning hit nearby, we realized it was going to be a real thunderstorm. We sat up in disbelief as the rain poured down.

I had wanted our time at the cove to be so special, but even that wasn't ending up the way I had planned. The chaos happening all around us—the forest fire, the people searching for us, and then the thunderstorm—it all seemed to be forcing us apart. It seemed as if every external force imaginable, even nature itself, were insisting that we could never be together.

I looked over at Esther sadly, but she was smiling and staring straight up into the storm.

"Go on! Send her down, Hughie!" she shouted, lifting her arms up toward the storm clouds overhead.

"Come on, Esther! Let's get out of here!" I yelled.

"Go on!" she shouted up into the sky again. "You can't stop us! We're ready for whatever you try to throw at us!"

"Esther, come on!" I cried.

I grabbed her hand, and together we ran back into the woods where we found the trail again. We moved along slowly in the darkness as the rain poured down relentlessly. When we got to the sauna, I tried the door, but it was locked, so we kept walking. By the time we got to the bridge, the thunderstorm had passed, and it was only lightly sprinkling. We were sopping wet and had no place to go, so we walked across the beach and found the trail to Pleiades Village.

As we started up the hill, we saw what looked like a green blob, all lit up, coming down the path toward us. As it came closer, I realized it was Aria in her green rain poncho, still carrying her flashlight. She saw us, and strangely enough, she didn't look surprised. She seemed upset, though, which wasn't an unusual mood for her to be in.

"I've been waiting up for you kids," she said, looking exhausted yet relieved to see us.

"You have?" Esther replied.

"Yeah," she said. "Everyone's been looking for you all over camp, even over on the other island. I'm sure they've all gone to bed by now. Where have you been anyway?"

"To one of Leo's favorite spots," Esther said with a grin. "We were just hanging out and chatting."

"Oh, really," Aria said. "Well, Finn told me I couldn't go to bed until I found you, and look, here you are."

"I'm sorry, Aria," Esther said. "I should've told you where I was going after the party. I really didn't know, myself, but when I found Leo, we decided to go for a walk."

"That's okay, I'm all right," Aria said. "I'm just glad you're back. When I heard you coming across the bridge, I figured my job was done. So, I'm going to bed now."

"Okay," Esther and I said together.

"By the way, Leo," she said, turning to me, "Finn says there's a meeting tomorrow morning at breakfast, and everyone needs to be there, including you. Cassie's gonna send all the guides out, after breakfast, to check on a bunch of campsites. Oh, and just FYI, Chuck and Percy still aren't back yet. They're probably not getting in until tomorrow. Anyway, I just thought you guys would want to know. So, goodnight, lovebirds."

"Thanks," I replied.

I wondered what the reason was for all the extra information. It didn't seem like Aria to remember to relay a detailed message to me in the middle of the night, but whatever. Maybe Finn was more upset than I'd first thought.

"So, it's pretty late," she said, turning to leave. "I'm calling it a night. You guys really should get to bed too."

"Okay," we said together again.

Aria stopped abruptly and pointed her flashlight up at both of us standing there, hand in hand, sopping wet, and grinning at her in the dark. She eyed us both sleepily for a few seconds.

"Oh, good grief," she finally said. "I'll see you in the morning."

Aria slowly turned and trudged down the hill. We watched her walk across the beach by the volleyball court, where not long ago, she had barreled into my life.

"She seems a wee bit upset," Esther said.

"She's just tired," I replied. "She'll be fine. You'll see."

I tugged gently on Esther's hand as I turned to leave, but she kept looking back at the green blob disappearing into the woods on the other side of the beach.

"I really do love her," Esther said with a heavy sigh.

"I know, I do too," I said.

Together, Esther and I slowly counted to three and then shouted, "Goodnight, Bear Bait!"

We listened, then heard her reply, "Whatever!"

chapter 55

after the rain

"I get it. I totally get it."

Esther and I were both completely wet and starting to shiver in the rainy mist. We hiked up the trail to my cabin in the dark. I knew the trail well, but in the woods, I could hardly see my hand in front of my face, especially after looking into Aria's flashlight.

I wondered what Aria had been doing up there. She'd probably been looking for us at the cabin, but I wondered why she hadn't waited for us down at the bridge. There had to be a reason. When Esther and I reached the top of the hill, we saw it. My cabin, the third one on the left, was glowing like it was on fire, but it wasn't burning. Esther grinned at me and ran ahead to the cabin.

When I caught up to her, she opened the cabin door and quietly said, "Look, Leo, it's amazing."

I expected Aria to jump out from a corner and pounce on us, but no one else was there. The cabin was lit up with seven white candles that had been placed around the room—one in each corner and three angled across the middle of the floor like a belt.

"Sweet as," Esther exclaimed, beaming with delight. "Aria did this. It's a gift from her. She's just the sweetest thing, eh?"

Together, we slipped inside. We tiptoed carefully around the candles and climbed up into my top bunk. The candles below made the whole cabin glow with golden light just like a campfire. It felt like we were back on Saganaga, floating on the water and watching the most beautiful sunset we'd ever seen.

"This is so cool," I said, leaning over the side of the bunk bed.

"Yeah, it's beautiful," Esther said as she grinned and looked around the cabin. "I really love that girl. You know, she's trying to tell us something, and I get it. I totally get it."

"What?" I asked.

"Oh, Leo, you're so dense sometimes," she joked.

"Yeah, I know," I replied, but I still didn't get it.

We were both still sopping wet, so I climbed back down and found a pair of flannel pajamas on my shelf. I'd never worn them all summer, but it seemed like the appropriate time.

"Here you go," I said, handing them up to Esther. "These'll warm you up. My mom sent 'em along, but they're really not my style."

"They're perfect," she said happily. "I'd like to meet your mum someday and thank her."

"Um, maybe not for a while," I replied.

"You don't want me to meet her?" she asked.

"No . . . well, I mean, yeah, I want you to meet her," I replied. "Just don't tell her that I gave my pajamas to you, okay?"

"Why not?" she asked.

"She might not understand," I mumbled from below.

"Oh, Leo, you scaredy-cat!" Esther replied. "I'm gonna tell her everything if I get the chance."

"Um, okay," I said, realizing that there was simply no use in arguing the case sometimes.

"She'll be so proud of her big boy for loaning his pj's to his hot tangerine of a girlfriend," she said as she tossed her wet clothes down onto the floor at my feet.

"Okay, if you say so," I replied, carefully lifting her wet underwear up with my toes.

Esther slipped into the pajamas as I changed into a dry shirt and shorts on Chuck's bunk below.

I grabbed my guitar and climbed back up into the bunk, where Esther had scrunched over against the wall to make room for me. She was resting her head in her hands as she leaned back on my pillow. I could tell she was tired. I was worn out too, but I didn't want to sleep. I wanted to be with Esther for as long as possible.

"You know, Leo," she said. "Just twenty-four hours ago, we were way out on Jenny Lake, watching the northern lights together."

"Yeah, that was really special," I said. "I love Jenny. That lake has always been one of my favorite places up here."

"Why?" she asked.

"Oh, I don't know," I replied. "It's a pretty plain lake when you first see it, but there's more to Jenny than meets the eye. Most people are in such a hurry, they pass right through the middle of it. They paddle straight to the next portage without taking the time to explore it or really get to know it."

"Is that what you were doing when we were swimming in the lake last night?" she asked.

"Yeah, probably," I said. "There are pretty spots on Jenny away from the main route that are so beautiful—rocky points, hidden coves, majestic cliffs. They're like hidden jewels and diamonds waiting to be discovered. There's so much more to explore on that lake; I just know it. I was hoping to paddle to the east side this morning, but the bears got in the way, and then the fire too."

"Well, Leo," she said. "We'll always have good memories of Jenny Lake to remember each other by."

"I'm not going to forget anything about the trip," I said.

"Yeah, it was more than I could have ever imagined," she replied. "I learned so much about you along the way too."

"Maybe too much?" I asked.

"Nah, that'll never happen," Esther said softly. "I'd like to learn a little more if there's still time?"

"There's still time," I replied as I leaned over to kiss her.

Esther leaned back suddenly and said, "Leo, about what we talked about earlier on the beach. I know what I said, but I'm not in any rush to do anything . . . you know, if you're not ready for it."

I thought about her words for a split second. Esther always had a way of getting right to the point. I had probably been thinking about it too much, and suddenly it seemed almost absurd to think that we needed to take that step, especially given the fact that she was leaving the next day.

"You know, Esther," I said. "It's never been my goal to get you into bed. I've never had a secret agenda here. I'm not smart enough to pull it off anyway. I just want things to be right."

"I know, Leo, and I love you for it," she replied. "Everything in me is screaming, 'Yes!' I just don't know if this is the right time for us. Making love to you is something that I don't take lightly."

"Yeah, I know," I said. "But I really want this . . . I mean . . . us."

"I know you do, but I'm worried about you," she replied.

"Worried about me? Why?" I asked.

"I'll be leaving tomorrow," she said. "Things are going to be different. Everything will change, and we will too."

"What do you mean by that?" I asked.

As I waited for her to respond, an ominous feeling of dread came over me. Was Esther trying to warn me of something? It seemed as if she was trying to prepare me for her departure, and she wasn't planning on ever coming back.

"Leo, I just don't want to break your heart," she said. "There's so much you don't know about me. I don't think I could live up to everything you've imagined in your mind."

"You don't have to live up to anything," I insisted.

"I don't know, Leo," she continued. "Life has a way of rudely awakening us to the harsh realities of the way things really are, and there's nothing anyone can do to stop it."

"Yeah, I understand," I replied. "I have a ton of friends who've taken the plunge, only to break up later. Not to mention all the guys who only have one thing on their mind, and when they get it, they dump the girl and move on to the next one. I've never wanted to do that to a girl and certainly not to you."

"I've never worried about that with you," Esther said. "You're not like the other fellows I've dated. You mean too much to me. Maybe that's why I'm hesitating to rush into anything. I just don't want us to do anything foolish and then drift apart later."

"It's a pretty big step," I admitted. "Everything seems to be steering us away from getting together—the forest fire, the people searching for us, and the thunderstorm. For a second back there, I thought my cabin was going up in flames. Even now, I'm still worried that it might catch fire before we get around to doing anything."

"Go on!" Esther laughed as she poked me in the side. "You're a pretty pessimistic chap, aren't you, Leo?"

"Yeah," I agreed. "Mostly, I'm worried about tomorrow and having to say goodbye. I might not even get to see you leave. Everything is just so crazy and out of control."

"The signs seem to be telling us to wait," she said plainly. "I think that just might be for the best, after all."

"So, what about all this time we've spent together?" I wondered aloud. "What's the point of it all then?"

"Are you looking for another Hollywood answer or a real one?" she asked, suddenly serious.

"Real," I replied.

"I think that's a question you have to answer for yourself," she said. "Why do you think we're together?"

"Because . . . we love each other," I replied.

"Oh, Leo, lots of people fall in love," she said. "You know, some people seem to be able to do it repeatedly on a regular basis. They fall in and out of love over and over again in their minds like a big stack of cheap dime-store novels, one after the next."

"What are you saying?" I asked.

"I want more than that," she replied.

"More than that?" I asked, confused by her comment.

"Leo, do you want to know what the point is?" she stated emphatically. "Do you want to know why we are together?"

"Yeah," I said softly.

"Isn't it about commitment, dedication, and sacrifice?" she said. "Isn't that what true love is about? Now, here at the end of everything, as you see it, comes the ultimate question for us."

"Yeah?" I said, hanging on to her words by a thread. As usual, she was so far ahead of me, and I was just trying to keep up.

"Will our love stand the test of time?" she said, answering her own question for me. "Will it last or simply fade away? Because there's a test coming, Leo. This chapter has to come to an end sometime.

You're gonna have to close the book pretty soon and wait awhile for the next one to be written."

"That's hard for me to do," I confessed.

"I know, but it's going to happen," she said. "It's the first big test of this story we've got cooking here. Can you close the book and wait awhile? Can you trust that everything will be all right?"

"You mean us, right?" I asked. "That we will be all right?"

"We don't know, do we?" she replied. "But that's what I'm asking you to do, Leo, to let whatever happens in the future just happen. Everything seems so pointless to you right now, but it's not pointless. In fact, it's actually the main point. It's the burning question for you and me right now, and it seems to me that it's very appropriate that it comes now, here at the end of our time together."

"I get it," I said. "When we were in the tent back on Jenny Lake, you asked me to love you freely."

"I'm asking you to do that now too,' she said. "If you want more, then I do too, but it'll take more too . . . more commitment, more dedication, and it seems . . . more sacrifice."

"I understand," I said. "But to be honest, I don't know if I've got it in me to do all those things or not, but I'm willing to try. That's all I can say to you right now."

"That's all I'm asking for," she replied. "As I said, I'm still here. I'm not going anywhere. Let's just see where our love takes us, not just for tonight, but for the long-haul, eh?"

"Okay," I said softly. "I just want to be with you."

"And I with you," she replied with a grin. "You've always treated me with respect, Leo. You've watched out for me, protected me, and stood up for me. You've listened to me go off on all sorts of rants and speeches. You've let me do just about anything to you, and you've taken it all with a smile. You're quite a catch. After all, it's not every day that a girl finds a sucker as big as you."

"Thanks, I appreciate that," I said, amused.

"You know what that means, right?" she asked with a laugh.

"I think so, but tell me anyway," I replied as I grinned and waited for her to gush on me again.

"Leo, do you remember our first date at the campfire?" she asked. "Then, afterward, you walked me back to my cabin?"

"Yeah, and then you kissed me on the cheek," I said softly.

"Yeah, mate," she whispered. "I knew, right then and there, that you were going to be someone very special to me, and Leo, you have come to be so much more than that."

Her words melted into me like the warmth of a sunrise. It was as if she had broken down all the walls I'd put up. Everything had been stripped away. I was completely exposed and totally free.

"I was hoping for the same thing," I admitted. "You're everything to me now, Esther. There's nothing else . . . just you."

"Easy, bro," she said. "Don't go falling too hard, all right?"

"Yeah, I'm trying not to," I replied.

Esther looked into my eyes as one of the candles flickered and went out. She seemed to be falling into me like a shooting star, as if we were becoming one right then and there. She hesitated, deep in thought, as if she were realizing something for the very first time. I'd become used to her doing that over the past few days, and I waited for her to spill it out whenever she was ready.

"You know who you are, right?" she said softly.

"Yeah, I do, and I know who you are too," I replied.

Esther blinked her eyes excitedly and waited for me to say more. I leaned over and dropped my guitar on the bunk below. Then, I returned to her lying there next to me.

"You wouldn't mind sleeping with a lion tonight, would you?" I whispered cautiously.

She grinned happily and whispered back, "Not if you wouldn't mind sleeping with a swan."

I leaned forward and gave her a soft kiss on the cheek. "Oh, Esther, you're so much more than that," I said.

"Oh, really? What else do you think I am?" she asked so softly, I could barely hear it.

"We can talk about it later," I said as I slid down next to her. "Just let me hold you for a little while." We lay quiet and still as another candle mysteriously went out, followed by another one.

“It’s magic,” she whispered in the growing darkness.

“What, this?” I asked. “You mean us?”

“No, the candles,” she said. “They’re a gift from Aria, you know. She’s tough on the outside, but on the inside, she’s magical.”

“I don’t want to talk about Aria right now,” I said, pulling her closer to me. “I just want to be with you.”

“I know,” she replied, “and I with you.”

She leaned forward and gave me a soft kiss. We snuggled under my sleeping bag as the last few candles gradually flickered and went out. When only one remained lit up in the corner by my bed, Esther reached up and put it out with her fingertips.

The cabin suddenly became pitch black. The dim light from outside slowly seeped in through the screen windows. We could see the ghostly tree trunks and the gray cabins nearby. We listened to the soft misty raindrops falling on the leaves and dripping off the sides of the cabin into watery puddles below. They made a tiny chorus of drips and drops that filled the air with delicate sweetness all around the cabin. We held each other and fought off sleep, quietly whispering in the dark as we lay in each other’s arms.

I could feel the steady rhythm of Esther’s heart beating against my chest, her blood pulsing through her soft neck, her strong arms, her warm fingers, and her cold toes. The rain slowly came to an end, and everything became quiet and calm outside. We held on to each other as a sweet stillness filled the air all around us.

I gazed into Esther’s eyes—so deep and beautiful, so alive and free, so peaceful and still. They were like pools of living water, like priceless pearls discovered by surprise on a distant shore. As she gazed back at me, I had an overwhelming feeling of being deeply cared for and passionately loved. Even in the darkness, her eyes seemed to glow with an intense fire from deep within. They focused intently on mine, as if they could see inside me, as if they were looking into the vastness of space itself, searching the deepest parts of my soul.

I didn’t look away that time. Instead, I let Esther’s deep blue eyes completely penetrate and wash over me like cleansing water and healing medicine, like the brilliant stars on high, like the sweet rainy mist of the mysterious northern lights. The light in her eyes looked like eternity itself. It was as if I could see into her body, into her spirit, and into our future forever and ever. I could see the mighty constellations and the distant galaxies far away. I could see the stars and planets. I could see the beautiful blue-green planet earth too, and the two of us lying there, gazing up into the night sky, looking deep into the immeasurable vastness of the universe high above. It was beautiful and terrifying, humbling and exhilarating, peaceful and sobering to be there holding Esther, looking into her eyes and knowing how amazing her love for me had become.

We held on to each other, not wanting to let go, not wanting our time together to end. We quietly kissed and gently loved each other. Eventually, we rested and held on to each other as we had the night before. As we curled up together under the sleeping bag, Esther snuggled in my arms and laid her head on my chest. We whispered quiet words to each other—intimate words meant only for the two of us, secret words that will forever be hidden and remain a mystery, to be shared only between Esther and myself.

I wanted that night to be so full of passion and fire, but it hadn't worked out that way. It had come, all right, but it had come in quiet tenderness, peaceful silence, and gentle rest.

There was fire, just not the kind I'd been hoping for. The fire was far too real, and it came with scorching flames, columns of smoke, and utter destruction. It seemed as if my future with Esther was being destroyed too. I'd wanted to experience so much more with her. But it was as if we were being forced to plunge into the deep again, to ride the choppy waters on the edge of Knife Lake one last time, just trying to make it safely across, to make it last a little longer.

I'd ridden those waves many times in my mind, wave after wave of unhindered passion and blood pounding desire, like bodies of water crashing upon a rocky shore. But the cold reality of life was breaking those fanciful dreams all to pieces. We held on to each other, not in heated passion, but simply for dear life, not wanting our time together to end. Together, we dreamt of another reality that might come true somewhere, sometime in the faraway, distant future.

"Leo," Esther whispered softly in the dark.

"Yeah?" I whispered back.

"Oh, you just looked like you were slipping away with the fairies," she said. "Are you falling asleep, Love?"

"Yeah," I replied as I closed my eyes. I couldn't keep them open any longer. "You seem like a fairy to me," I whispered, slowly drifting off into oblivion.

"Yeah, this is all so magical," she whispered back.

"What is?" I asked mindlessly.

"Everything that's happened to us these past few days," she said. "I just wish I could stay with you for the rest of the summer."

"I wish we had a night-light," I mumbled, desperately trying to keep myself awake.

"Why?" whispered Esther.

"So, I could see your pretty face as I fall asleep."

Esther slowly leaned forward and gave me one last kiss on my forehead. It felt like a kiss my mother would have given me long ago when I was a little boy.

As I drifted helplessly off to sleep, I vaguely remember whispering, "Esther, I don't want to sleep."

"Me neither," she whispered back. Then, quietly, she said, "Leo, give me your hands."

Slowly, I slid my hands out toward her. The last thing I remember of that night was the sight of Esther rubbing my cold hands with her warm, soft fingers. Her blue eyes gazed intently into mine as I drifted off to sleep in the darkness of the cabin. A warm breeze quietly blew off the lake and gently whispered through the white pines overhead. Everything was quiet and still.

Esther and I slept and were finally at peace.

chapter 56

chuck in the morning

"So, you slept with her?"

The next morning, I woke up with a jolt. It was early dawn and not yet light outside. There was a smoky presence in the room, and at first, I thought the cabin was on fire. I blinked, forcing my eyes open. Over by the door, something was scratching or shuffling in the dark. Guessing it to be a rodent, I hastily clicked on my flashlight and directed it at the bottom of the doorway.

I could see what looked like boots or maybe toes attached to hairy legs, half-covered in a pair of raggedy shorts and a once-white T-shirt that appeared to be all black and sooty. Suddenly, I realized it was a human body standing there, just a few feet away. It was attached to a thickly bearded and filthy face with two beady eyes that were peering straight at me in the dark.

"It's not nice to shine your flashlight into other people's eyes," the body's voice spoke calmly but firmly.

"So that's who it is!" I thought to myself. "Chuck!"

All two hundred plus pounds of his stocky frame filled the doorway. He looked like a mess, and he stunk like a forest fire. It was dark, but I thought I could actually see smoke rising off his blackened body, still smoldering and smelling like charred possum flesh on burnt toast. He was covered from head to toe in soot.

"So, Leo, maybe you should tell me what's going on," he said in his monotone voice, which always sounded so soothing to my ears.

"He could hypnotize a herd of wild billy goats if he had the mind to," I thought to myself.

"Maybe you should tell me too," I responded, still in shock at what I was currently seeing and smelling.

"Leo, dude, talk to me," he said a bit more firmly.

His smoldering frame stood solidly in the doorway. It was six or so in the morning. Apparently, he wanted to chat about something important, and he wasn't going anywhere anytime soon. I had a sudden feeling of déjà vu, but I couldn't seem to place it.

"So, you slept with her?" he asked seriously.

"Oh, now I get it," I thought. "But how does he know? And where is Esther?" I felt around my bed. She was gone. "Way to go, Esther!"

"Dude," he said again.

"Um, yeah, I think so," I replied, trying to calm my racing heart.

"Dude, really?" he repeated. "You slept with her?"

I'd already heard that question before, so I tried to answer as politely as possible. "I just slept with her, Chuck, that's all," I said, a little irritated. After all, it was six o'clock in the morning.

"So, you slept with her? Or you slept with her?" he asked again, still standing there like a sleepy security officer at the door.

"Good grief!" I thought. "Which question do I answer? They're both the same!" I was having that déjà vu feeling again too. I suddenly envisioned a big hairy rabbit bounding across the plywood ceiling of my groggy mind.

I answered the question again, totally straight-faced and somber, but not actually trying to do it that way. "Yeah, I slept with her."

Chuck shifted his stance a bit and scratched his crusty mass of hair. A fresh wave of smoke drifted across the ceiling of the small cabin and hit my burning nostrils.

I coughed on the smoke and then offered a personal opinion. "Holy cow, Chuck, you stink."

"This ain't no *Top Gun* moment for you, Leo!" he bellowed loudly, way too loud, I thought, for so early in the morning. "That was not the brightest move on your part, dude!"

I waited for him to wrap up his speech, or shift again, or whatever one does when confronted by a smelly woodchuck scratching at your door in the dark.

"So, you slept with her?" he asked yet again.

"We just slept together, Chuck," I confessed again. "But nothing happened. Well, just sleep, but nothing more. Okay, maybe we kissed a little, or something, and held each other, and then . . ."

A feeling of weird awkwardness suddenly swept over me. "Why am I even verbalizing the intimate details of my love life to this guy?" I thought to myself. "Maybe it's just what you do with your roommate on those brisk summer mornings after sleeping with a girl. Dang it! I have to stop saying it like that!"

"So, you slept with her, but you didn't sleep together?" he asked, still standing in the doorway like a dull professor waiting for the correct answer from a classroom full of wide-eyed freshmen.

I was starting to get confused. Maybe it was because Chuck kept asking the same thing over and over again, or perhaps it was the fact that it had suddenly become a two-part question.

I swallowed hard and then attempted an appropriate response. "Slept, yes," I replied, "but there was no sleeping involved."

"That seemed to come out completely wrong," I thought.

"Oh, my God, Leo!" he exclaimed. Chuck shifted his weight again, and another whiff of smoke floated across the cabin.

"We didn't do anything!" I cried, trying to sound convincing, but I was clearly failing on all counts.

"Dude, I'll talk to you later," he said as he backed out of the doorway and slipped down the wet wooden steps.

"Ouch!" he cried. Then, slowly, he lumbered away down the trail, mumbling to himself under his breath.

"Chuck! Chuck!" I cried after him.

"I'm gonna go take a shower!" he called back. He uttered a few other choice phrases in the dark as he drifted off over the hill and through the woods to the bathhouse.

"Well, that didn't go so well," I mumbled to myself.

I dropped back down on my bed, closed my eyes, and grinned with contentment.

"I slept with her."

chapter 57

early morning dip

"We're in really deep water now."

Outside, it was beginning to get brighter, but it was still very early. I wondered where Esther had gone in the middle of the night. Why did she leave without waking me up? I looked around my bunk for any clues. The candles Aria had placed around the cabin were still there, and my guitar was lying on Chuck's bunk below.

As I leaned over to look at the floor, a piece of paper crinkled under my elbow. It was a page ripped out of my journal. It was folded in half, and my name was written in cursive on the outside. "It's got to be from Esther!" I thought as I unfolded it and looked inside.

"Dear Leo," it read, "Thanks for being my special bro at Northern Lights. You're such an amazing guy! Thanks for the last three weeks and for your patience with me last night too. I think there's a reason we found each other this summer. I'm not sure what the future may bring, but let's hold each other with open hands, and we'll see what happens, eh? Sincerely, Esther." At the bottom and below two hearts, she added, "P.S. When you wake up, meet me at the sauna, and bring your togs and a towel."

I was suddenly alive, awake, alert, and enthusiastic! "How long ago had Esther written that note?" I wondered. "Was she at the sauna now? Why so early in the morning?"

I dropped out of my bunk, whipped on my swimsuit, and grabbed a towel as I lunged out the door. I had to hop back for my sandals and a shirt; then I was off again, running down the trail, across the bridge, and hanging a left at the trail to the sauna.

When I got there, I was out of breath. It was well past dawn, but it still seemed unusually dark outside. The sun was trying to peek through the gray clouds, but the smoke from the wildfires was making it difficult. They would be serving breakfast at Starlight Lodge soon, and I had to be there. I was hoping it wasn't too late to meet up with Esther. I tried the door to the sauna, but it was still locked. Then, as I walked down the long ramp toward the lake, I saw her sitting on the edge of the dock, dangling her bare feet in the water. All she was wearing was a white T-shirt and her bikini bottoms. It looked like she had already taken a swim in the lake.

When I got there, Esther glanced up at me and smiled. She looked incredibly radiant, especially after the night we'd just spent together. I leaned down and gave her a kiss on the cheek.

"Hey there, Sun Sparrow," she said sweetly. "How are you doing this morning?"

"Not bad, Wild Thing," I replied. "You look as pretty as the northern lights right now."

She grinned and laughed softly. "Thanks for coming, mate. Are you ready for a swim?"

"Sure, what's the special occasion?" I asked.

"Oh, nothing really, but it's our last day together," she said, nudging me gently with her shoulder. "We might not have much time today, so I thought we could at least start the day out right."

"Well, I'm all yours," I replied, starting to sit down next to her.

"Good!" she exclaimed.

Suddenly, I felt both of her hands shoving me forward headfirst into the lake. Completely caught off guard by her surprise move, I flailed my arms about wildly, then crashed sideways into the water like a gullible dog in a world full of sneaky cats. I swam back to the ladder, scrambled out, and went right after her.

"Well, stud muffin, that was quite a beaut!" she said triumphantly. "A real belly flopper that was!"

"I'm gonna get you, Esther!" I cried with revenge as I grabbed at her arms and legs.

"Okay, okay, wait, Leo!" she screamed, giggling with delight.

She tried to fend me off with her towel as I lunged at her. She flailed her arms and legs around desperately, slapping and kicking my hands to keep me away.

"You're such a sneak!" I cried. "You're going in, right now!"

"Leo, wait! Let's jump in together!" she yelled as she tried to kick me away. "Leo! Stop! Let's just jump in together!"

She was a good fighter. I was taking a beating as she pranced around and screamed in fright. She kept slapping and kicking me back as I tried to grab on to her.

"There has to be a better way," I thought to myself. I stopped to give her desperate plea a second thought. "Sure, that would work. Yeah, that would be just fine." I calmly backed away from her and moved over to the edge of the dock again.

"All right, Esther," I said, hoping she believed me. "I'm letting you off the hook, since you're so dang cute."

Esther gradually regained her composure and calmed down. She was breathing heavily as she flashed her bright blue eyes and dazzling smile at me again. She looked so cute in that T-shirt. I could see her white bikini top underneath her shirt too. She was so irresistible, even at six o'clock in the morning.

"Here," I said calmly. "Take my hand. We'll count to three, and then we'll jump in together."

I reached out to her in as non-threatening of a way as possible. She moved forward cautiously and took hold of my hand as we both stepped up to the edge of the dock. In the early morning light, the surface of the water looked as if it were a hundred feet down and we were standing on the very edge of the Palisades once again.

"Okay, Esther," I said as calmly as I could. "When you're ready, let's count to three. Okay?"

"Okay," she said nervously.

Slowly, we counted off together, "One, two . . ."

I sprang behind her and with a big shove, I sent her flying out over the water. She flapped her arms and legs frantically and screeched like a crazy loon as she did a backwards belly flop into the lake.

When she came back up, I shouted loud and clear, "Three!"

"Leo, you bloody rooster!" she yelled. "That was piss-awful! I should've known you'd pull a swiftie like that!"

Esther's insults ended abruptly with another bloodcurdling screech, because I'd already launched myself high up into the air and was descending straight down on top of her in perfect cannonball form. She tried to get out of the way; then she quickly ducked under as I hit the lake like an atomic bomb. Kaboom!

As I went in, I could feel Esther's legs kicking wildly as she tried to escape. I opened my eyes down below and watched her scramble back to the surface, but I wasn't done with her yet. From the depths, I slowly ascended like an octopus hunting its prey. Then, I grabbed her feet and yanked her back under the water, where I could hear her screaming bloody murder. Esther had clearly underestimated my water fighting capabilities. I wasn't that good of a swimmer, but I knew how to play dirty like all the other good old Iowa farm boys.

"Oh, Leo, you beast!" she shouted when we came back to the surface. "You are so evil! And to think I trusted you!"

She splashed furiously in the water like a two-year-old throwing a temper tantrum. I just grinned and slowly swam toward her. She was terrified, frantic, and furious. Mission accomplished! I rubbed it in for a while as she ranted about the evils of my masculine nature.

Finally, I called for a truce and tried to calm her back down. It took a while. We ended up treading water out away from the dock. It was cloudy, smoky, and even a bit windy, but we didn't care. We could only see each other. Everything else seemed to be of no importance and completely out of focus.

"Are you ready for this?" she asked.

"For what?" I replied.

"To swim with a swan," she said, lunging at me in the water.

"Yeah," I replied, "if you're ready to swim with a lion."

I swam around Esther and gazed at her gracefully treading water. Her eyes were flashing bright blue as she moved about freely. Her long red hair swirled around like tongues of flaming fire, reaching out on the surface of the lake, as if trying to ensnare me. I felt so alive and so excited to be with her, and I could tell she felt it too.

"I love you," she exclaimed out of the blue, breathing heavily in the water. "You know that, right?"

I smiled and gently took her hand, slowly pulling her closer to me. "Yes, I know, and I love you too."

She flashed her eyes at me brightly. "I've always loved you, Leo, from the very first moment I saw you."

"Is that so?" I replied, acting somewhat surprised. "From the very first moment you saw me?"

"That's right, from the very first moment," she insisted.

"Is that why you were waving at me so dramatically on the beach when you first arrived at camp?" I asked. "You were looking right at me, and then you waved at me."

I slid my hand under the back of her shirt and pinched her side. She let out a screech and flashed those beautiful eyes at me again. "Man, she's sexy!" I thought to myself.

"I was waving at Aria, you goofball," she said, splashing me.

"I could have sworn you were staring straight at me," I replied, splashing her back as I tried to grab her again.

She laughed and poked me in the ribs under the water. "Maybe I was, maybe I wasn't," she hedged.

"You were looking at me, not Aria," I insisted.

"Yeah, you're right," she admitted. "I saw you too, Leo. How could I not see you?"

"So, you were ignoring me on purpose?" I asked, uncovering the terrible truth.

"Totally, bro!" she said with a sneaky grin. "And look, it worked. You're such a ginormous sucker."

"A sucker?" I asked.

"Yeah, bro!" she exclaimed. "I can spot a sucker a mile away."

"Really," I said, laughing half-heartedly. "So, you like suckers?"

I tried to grab her head and dunk her under, but she moved back and looked at me seriously. She didn't smile. She just gazed at me with her big blue eyes and slowly came closer.

"No, Leo," she said softly and tenderly. "I like you . . . just you. You're my special bro . . . remember?"

Esther moved in close, right in front of me. She slipped her warm hands under the front of my T-shirt and ran them up across my chest. She pushed the shirt up as she sank below the water. I let myself go under too; then I pulled my shirt off and let it sink down and away. When I came back up, she was smiling and treading water nearby, as if waiting for me to make the next move.

I touched the side of her waist and pushed her shirt up slightly. Suddenly, she grinned, and like a flash of lightning, she ducked under the water and pulled it all the way up over her head and off her body. Her long beautiful strands of wavy red hair spread out and swirled all around her. They moved on the surface of the lake like flames of fire shooting out from her sunburned face and freckled shoulders. I gazed at her in awe and wonder, floating there in the water just an arms-length away. Her eyes looked deeply into mine, flashing like burning coals—white and hot, penetrating my thinly veiled exterior and exposing my obvious desire for her.

"So, Leo," she said with a grin. "Are you ready for this?"

"Ready for what?" I asked.

"You know," she replied, waiting for me to figure it out.

"You mean . . . skinny dipping?" I replied in disbelief.

"Yup!" she said with a smile. "Come on, let's give it a go."

Esther moved slowly toward me, still looking into my eyes, as if she were reading my mind. Her lips were just inches away. Her sweet breath rushed in and out of her lungs. Her eyes flashed excitedly at me. She moved in closer and kissed my cheek, then my other cheek. Then, her lips moved slowly toward mine, and she gave me a soft kiss on the mouth. I moved my fingers slowly up alongside her body to her shoulders, just barely touching her skin.

"Leo, it's going to be okay," she whispered.

As she kissed me, I could feel the vibrant force of life in her close presence, which seemed to overpower me in that moment. She moved closer, kissing me again, in spite of my timid movements. Then, she pushed her body forward into mine as we sank below the surface. We held on to each other under the water, then rushed back up to the surface, gasping for air.

"Leo!" she said with a laugh. "You sink like a rock!"

"Because I'm all muscle, baby!" I bragged, lifting my right arm out of the water and flexing my biceps.

"Ooh! I'm so impressed," Esther swooned sarcastically.

"That's right!" I declared again, lifting both arms out to flex them. "It's all muscle!" I said as I sank hopelessly under the water and then scrambled back up to the surface.

"Too bad you sink so fast! It's easier to dunk you!" she replied.

"Don't do that!" I cried. "I can barely stay above the water as it is."

"Yeah, I've got other plans for you," she said softly.

Esther moved in close and kissed me again. The water made being close tricky. It wasn't what I'd anticipated. I was just trying not to drown in the deep water, while Esther seemed to float on the surface like a contented loon. I was almost entirely helpless, but she kept swimming around and coming in close to kiss me. When I caught her again, I pulled her next to me and pinched the spot where the tattoo of Cygnus was located between her shoulder blades.

"You found it again, eh?" she said cheerfully.

She laughed and pushed me away, but I grabbed her arm and pulled her back. My hands moved quickly down the side of her body to where Leo was crouching just above her hips. When I pinched her there, she let out a gasp and squirmed helplessly in my arms.

"Hey! What are you doing down there?" she shouted.

"I'm going down in the west to hide from Hercules," I whispered. "Are you coming with me?"

She moved in close, then brought her beautiful red lips up next to my ear and whispered, "Yes, I'm coming, Leo."

We sank under the water and kissed each other for as long as we could hold our breath. Then, we shot back up to the surface. Esther kept grabbing me and pulling me down in the water while I simply worked to stay afloat. It felt as if she were going to kill me out there in the lake, but at least I would die a happy man.

As we played in the water, I noticed something else: another tattoo. I wasn't sure, but it looked like another set of blue-green dots peeking out from underneath the front of her bikini.

I pulled her in close and asked, "Esther, do you have another tattoo?" I pinched her in the ribs on the left side. "Right there?"

"Hey, Farm Boy!" she squealed, trying to wiggle free.

"Do you?" I asked again.

"Maybe I do, maybe I don't," she said, grinning at my discovery.

"You do!" I exclaimed. "What is it?"

"I reckon you'd like to see it, wouldn't you!" Esther exclaimed as she squirmed out of my grasp and moved back in the water.

"Sure, but why haven't I seen it before?" I asked.

"Well, Leo, a chap really has to be looking in the right place to see it," she replied sincerely.

"Yeah, at your chest," I said with a grin.

"No, at my heart," she said softly as she moved back closer to me. "I've gotten pretty good at hiding it from most people."

"For good reason!" I replied, still not getting it.

"Yeah, mate," she said quietly. "I don't show it to just anybody."

"You've shown it to other guys?" I asked.

I knew I shouldn't have asked that, but I was still clueless at that point. Esther was talking on an entirely different level, and I was still just thinking about her body. To be honest, I didn't want her to answer my lame question, but she did anyway.

"No, I've never really shown it to anyone else," she said earnestly. "It's for . . . my special bro, and I know who that is now." She moved in close and grabbed on to my hand.

"How long have you had it?" I asked yet another lame question. As usual, I was still just struggling to keep up.

"Awhile, long enough to know who it belongs to," she said, letting me pull her in close again.

"Who it belongs to?" I asked, suddenly waking up to the deeper meaning she'd been getting at all along.

"You, Leo, it belongs to you," she said plainly.

"What is it?" I asked.

Esther grinned and said, "You don't know?"

I thought about her love of the stars and then took an educated guess. "It's Lyra, isn't it?"

"Too right!" she exclaimed with a cheerful smile. "Would you like to have a squiz at it?"

"Yeah, gizza geez," I said softly, as my fingertips ran lightly over her back and up to her bikini strap.

"Here, mate," she whispered. "Let me help you, eh?"

She took my hand and spun around in the water, guiding me to the strap. I pinched the little buckle, and the bikini came loose, falling off her shoulders into the water. She grabbed it and quickly swam away. Then, she sank below the water and resurfaced a few seconds later, lifting her bikini bottoms in the air with a triumphant smile.

"All right, Leo! Now it's your turn!" she called to me.

"Hey, wait!" I called back to her. "You said you were going to show me your tattoo!"

"If I'm gonna bear my body and soul, then you are too!" she cried from across the water.

"Seriously?" I asked. "Right out here in the open?"

"Yeah, mate!" she said, slowly swimming closer to me. "I want you to experience what it feels like to be free of everything, to be totally vulnerable and open, to let go of whatever it is you're still holding on to and hiding behind."

"I just want to see Lyra," I replied.

"I know you do," she said, moving closer. "But it's about more than that, Leo. I want someone to see me . . . all of me, not just what's on the outside. I need to know if you can do that."

"All right, I'll do it," I replied. "But then, I need to see your tattoo like you promised."

"You don't need to see it, Leo. You just want to," she said. "There's something else you need, but I don't think you know what it is yet. I don't know if I'm ready to give it either."

"What?" I asked, confused again.

"Oh, Leo!" she exclaimed. "I'm not asking you to give up your life or something. Are you with me or not?"

"Yes, I'm with you," I said.

"All right, then rattle ya dags, Leo!" she replied. "If you don't, then I'm putting my togs back on!"

"I don't know," I said, backing away from her.

"Come on, Leo!" she insisted. "I'll stay all the way over here, so you're safe."

"Okay, but then you have to show me the tattoo!" I replied.

"All right, Leo!" she cried. "Whatever!"

I took a big breath. Then, I sank below the water and slipped my shorts off, snagging them with my toes before they sank to the bottom. Then, I swam back to the surface and held them up for Esther to see. I felt completely naked. Well, yeah, of course . . .

"I've got you now, mate," Esther said as she slowly moved closer. "And you said you didn't want to go skinny dipping!"

I suddenly felt like a helpless frog being openly stalked by a hungry water moccasin. She definitely had the upper hand in the water.

"Actually, Esther, I'm pretty nervous right now," I confessed. "Believe it or not, this is my first time."

"Go jump in a lake, Leo! Really?" she said, laughing out loud. "This is my third time in only three days!" She moved in even closer as I tried to back away.

"I knew that's what you were doing back in Esther Lake," I replied. "I always had a funny feeling about that."

"And in Jenny Lake too!" she exclaimed with delight.

"What?" I cried. "No, you guys were just swimming around."

"That's what you thought!" she said, laughing gleefully.

"Good grief! You're such a wild thing!" I replied.

She grinned proudly and declared, "I knew I'd get you naked one way or another. It just took a little longer than expected."

I smiled back, but I was shivering with excitement and a certain degree of fear at the predicament in which I'd so carelessly placed myself. Esther moved steadily closer in the water. Suddenly, I wasn't as brave as I thought I'd be.

"You know, Leo," Esther said softly, drawing up close to me. "We're in *really* deep water now."

"I just want to see Lyra," I replied, still treading water.

"You what?" she asked quietly, staring me straight in the eyes as she came even closer.

“I just want to see Lyra,” I said, letting her move around behind me. For some reason, that felt safer than having her directly in front. After all, I felt more than a little exposed at that point.

Esther came in close behind me and whispered in my ear, “You’re gonna have to catch me first, Farm Boy.”

Suddenly, I felt her two hands on top of my head. She lunged up, and with a shriek, she dunked me under the water. I gasped for air and scrambled back to the surface. As I did, Esther laughed and swam away into an even deeper part of the lake.

“Hey! You little sneak!” I shouted after her. “I thought I already caught you!”

“No way!” she screeched. “Not by a long shot, bro!”

“Well, that sneaky little fudge-pop!” I thought to myself. “That’s it! She’s mine!”

A sudden surge of adrenalin shot through my body. There we were, skinny dipping in broad daylight, and I simply didn’t care. I swam out after Esther, but before I reached her, we both heard the shrill sound of the bell up at Starlight Lodge.

Suddenly, I realized how late it actually was. Smoke filled the air around us again. The sun suddenly sank behind the dark clouds, and we knew we had lingered there a little too long. Already, we were risking a great deal to be swimming around naked in broad daylight, but hopefully, no one had seen us. We quickly slipped our swimsuits back on and swam back to the dock.

I couldn’t help but think, “This is getting ridiculous!”

chapter 58
running conversation

"If you love something, let it go."

We grabbed our towels and rushed down the trail, all sopping wet. It was kind of pathetic, I thought, the way we carried on like that, teasing and enticing each other, but always getting cut off for some reason or another. It seemed absurd, but I was starting to appreciate the tragic humor in it all. As we slipped and dripped along the rocky trail through the woods, stumbling and tumbling our way down to the bridge, I kept thinking about how wildly bizarre it was. Esther sprinted on ahead as I tried to keep up.

"Wait up, Esther! There's something I need to tell you!" I cried out as I chased after her down the trail.

I tried to catch up to her, but she was fast. Suddenly, her bathing suit, or part of it, went flying up and off into the woods. As I watched it go, I stumbled on a rock and went flying myself, crashing head over heels onto the trail with a thud.

Esther walked back and smiled down at me, lying there in a heap. "You hurt yourself a lot, don't you, Leo?" she said.

"Yeah, well, I was a bit distracted by your flying bikini," I replied, looking over in the bushes for it somewhere. I picked it up and handed it back to her.

"So, you got my attention, mate," she said, ignoring the comment about her bikini. "What's up?"

"After you left this morning, Chuck showed up," I replied, picking myself up off the ground. "And we sort of had a conversation about some stuff."

"Some stuff?" she inquired.

"Yeah, Chuck sort of thinks we slept together last night."

"We did sleep together," Esther said with a grin.

"I know, but he thinks we actually slept together," I clarified. "I tried to explain it to him, but he didn't get it. It was pretty early, and I was really tired this morning."

"Yeah, we didn't get much sleep, eh?" Esther replied, grinning at me as she turned and began walking down the trail again.

"You don't care if people find out about us?" I asked.

"Yeah, nah," she replied. "They can think whatever they like."

"Hey, Esther," I said, trying to keep up with her. "Thanks for staying with me last night. It was really nice."

She turned her head slightly as she kept walking. I could see her smiling brightly. "You can say that again!" she exclaimed.

"No, really, it means a lot to me," I said, grabbing her hand. I spun her around and pulled her close. "It was the best night of my life."

"It was for me too, Leo," she said softly as she kissed me on the cheek. "We had a lot of fun these past three weeks, didn't we?"

"Yeah, I'll remember them for the rest of my life," I said.

"Me too," she replied.

Esther pulled away and started walking down the trail again. Then, she stopped suddenly and turned back to me. "Hey, Leo, I'm sorry if it wasn't what you wanted."

"You don't have to apologize for anything," I said.

"I know what you wanted . . . last night and this morning too," she said, kicking at a root in the trail.

"I already have what I want," I replied, but I felt exactly as she had anticipated. I just didn't want her to know that.

"Thanks, bro," she said. "I've got what I want too. No worries, eh? We've got all the time in the world."

"Yeah, all the time in the world," I mumbled sadly.

I could feel my fears gradually coming to the surface again. We stood on the trail for a few seconds, not saying anything, wondering about the past few days, about us, about our future, about what might be, or perhaps . . . not be.

"This thing about us," I said, trying not to break down. "I'm just wondering if it's ever going to work out?"

"I don't know, Leo, maybe sometime in the future," she said quietly. "I'm wondering what'll happen too, just like you."

Esther stood there all dripping wet, holding her sandals and scrunched-up towel in her arms. Her hair was flung all over her shoulders and across her freckled cheeks. She looked so beautiful and amazing, yet still so completely unreachable to me.

"Maybe next summer," she finally said. "You could come and visit me in New Zealand or something."

I stepped back, closed my eyes, and moaned, "Esther, you're killing me here. I'm dying. I'm literally dying right now."

"Leo, if it's meant to be, it will be," she said. "It just might take more time." She moved closer and took my hand in hers.

"Ahh!" I exclaimed in frustration as I pulled my hand away. "A little more time?" I groaned. "Next summer? Really?"

"If you love something, let it go," she said. "If it comes back to you, it's yours forever. If not, then it was never meant to be."

She reached for me again, but I pulled away and kicked the dirt with my bare foot.

"I've heard that line before, and it makes me sick to my stomach," I said in disgust.

"A year isn't that long," Esther replied calmly. She stood there in silence for a few seconds and then said, "Okay, yeah, it's a long time, but Leo, you can write to me."

"A year?" I complained bitterly. "That's like forever! Will you write me back?"

She grinned cheerfully and nodded. "Sure, mate, a lot, and we can chat on the phone too."

"Writing? Talking on the phone?" I said in despair. "I don't want to talk to you on the phone. I want to be with you *now*."

"Leo, you *are* with me now," she said softly. "You're in my heart, and I'm in yours. We'll never lose what we experienced together."

I stood there, staring at the ground, thinking about her words of promise and hope.

"I know it's not easy, Leo, but let's just be thankful for all the good times we had together," she said, standing firmly in the middle of the trail, looking so sure of herself. "Write, Leo, write down all those songs you've been scratching out on your guitar these past few weeks. Send them to me, and I'll write you back letters so long you'll be able to write a whole book with them."

I gazed into her eyes and drank up her words. I wanted to believe her, but everything seemed to be going up in smoke. There was no escaping the fire and destruction that was sweeping over us. I stood silent and still, aching inside, but still holding on to a faint sliver of hope that our love would survive the next year.

Esther's words flickered like the last bit of light from a dying fire just before it goes out. The future seemed so dark and overwhelming. All I could do was look into her eyes and hope that somehow it would turn out all right. She seemed so certain, but I knew myself too, and I wasn't sure if my heart could handle what was coming.

"Leo, we can't hang on to the past," Esther said earnestly. "We have to let go and trust. We both have our entire lives ahead of us. If it's meant to be, it will be. There's no stopping love."

She came in close and kissed me gently on the lips. Her hands reached out slowly and took mine. She held them in hers and smiled graciously up into my watery eyes. I couldn't find any words to say without completely breaking down in tears.

"Come on, Leo," she said, tugging at me to start walking again. "We'd best get to breakfast. There's a big meeting, you know. They'll be looking for us to be there too."

"Yeah, I know," I said, still frozen and embarrassed at my pathetic display of emotions. "You'd better go first. I'll be along in a while."

"Leo, are you okay?" she asked.

"Yeah, I'm okay," I replied. "But Chuck thinks we slept together last night. I just think it'd be best if we didn't walk in there holding hands, if you know what I mean."

Esther slugged me gently in the gut and said, "Got it, stud."

She spun around and ran off down the trail. As she ran away, I noticed that something fell out of her towel.

"So long, Sun Sparrow! I'll see you at brekkie!" she called back to me as she dashed away.

"Yeah, I'll see you soon," I replied sadly as I walked up the trail to see what she had dropped.

It was a plain white envelope with my name written on the outside. I picked it up and flipped it over. It was sealed. I thought about opening it, but then I changed my mind.

"She wanted to give it to me?" I wondered to myself. "Or did she?" I stood on the trail, waiting to hear her footsteps bouncing across the bridge before starting out on my own.

"She called me a stud," I mumbled to myself. "Esther always knows how to cheer me up, doesn't she?"

As I waited on the trail, the sun broke through the clouds and lit up the trees all around. The forest floor glowed with bright green ferns and wildflowers scattered everywhere. Small spruce and pine saplings glistened brightly in the sunlight, dripping wet from the previous night's rain. Beautiful clusters of orange wood lilies and even some dainty wild roses dripped with morning dew. The forest seemed to awaken from its slumber and happily rejoice at the sun's glorious return. The birds noticed it too, and somewhere overhead, a pair of chickadees began chirping to each other with delight. Suddenly, the world didn't seem so gloomy after all.

I heard the bridge creaking cheerfully as Esther ran across. I started walking slowly down the trail, looking at all the beautiful wildflowers springing back to life in the misty morning light.

"What was it that Esther said?" I thought. "If you love something, set it free." I rolled the idea over and over again in my head. It sounded so completely absurd to me.

"How am I supposed to do that?"

chapter 53

rescue operations

"Okay, we're heading out!"

I ran to my cabin and changed in a hurry. Then, I raced up to Starlight Lodge, where everyone was gathered for breakfast and the morning meeting. I got in the food line and took whatever they gave me. The room was buzzing like a beehive, but in a hushed sort of way. I sat down on the far end next to Chuck, who looked surprisingly clean but clearly fatigued.

"Hey, Leo," he greeted me. "Nice to see you."

"You too," I replied, wondering what he was really thinking.

The big news floating around the tables was how Percy and Chuck had paddled all the way to Kekakabic Lake the day before and found Nancy's group. It had been an all-night paddle for them, north through Ottertrack and Saganaga, to make it back to camp that morning. People kept turning to Chuck and congratulating him, but in his tired state of mind, he seemed oblivious to it all.

"Hey, Leo," he mumbled as he munched on a hash brown.

"Yeah, Chuck?" I replied.

"Dude, we're cool," he said. "No need to explain anything."

"Thanks," I replied. "Thanks . . . dude."

As I ate my breakfast, I noticed Esther sitting with Aria in the middle of the dining hall. She looked so cheerful and radiant. I couldn't keep my eyes off her. She was listening to someone at the table, smiling and laughing and talking. Her red hair was bunched up in the back, all wet from the morning swim. The freckles swooped across her sunburned nose right above her cherry-red lips.

"I was kissing those lips just a few minutes ago," I thought to myself. "Shoot, I was swimming in the lake naked with her!"

As I finished off my glass of orange juice, Esther glanced up and noticed me. She lifted her chin slightly. Then, she blinked her pretty blue eyes twice and grinned sweetly at me through the crowded room. I smiled back, but I wanted to do so much more than that. I felt like jumping up on the table and making a public announcement. "Esther and I are together," I'd say, "and there's nothing in the whole world that can keep us apart." The entire room erupted in thunderous applause as I was suddenly jolted back to reality.

It wasn't me they were applauding. It was Percy. He had just walked into the dining room and was standing in the food line. His face lit up with a huge grin as everyone congratulated him on finding Nancy's group. He waved back and then grabbed a tray.

"Andie, my girl, my beautiful princess," I heard him bellowing over the din of the crowd. "I'll take a heap of eggs, and throw a few hash browns on there if you don't mind, darling." He winked at her as she smiled back at him from behind the counter.

"What a hot-fudge sausage biscuit," I mumbled under my breath.

"What's that?" Chuck asked.

"Oh, nothing," I replied. "Hey, Chuck, good job on finding Nancy last night. Is she okay?"

"Oh, yeah," Chuck said. "She didn't need us. She was fine. We met her coming out of the Kek ponds. From there, we went north through Hanson and Esther, then around through Sag and back to camp."

"That's the same route we took," I exclaimed. "We just did it in the opposite direction."

"Did you have a good trip?" Chuck asked.

"You have no idea," I replied with a helpless grin.

He finished off the last bit of his milk. Then, he said, "You and Esther, huh?"

"Yup," I said with a nod, grinning back at him and trying not to appear too lovestruck.

"Cool, dude, I'm happy for you, man," he said, scooping up the last bit of eggs off his plate.

"Thanks," I replied, and then I went back to watching Esther through the crowded room.

After breakfast, Finn stood up and reported on the status of the wildfire. It was still burning out of control, but thankfully, not threatening homes and businesses along the Gunflint Trail. The threat wasn't over yet, with the wind still a big question mark. So, we all had some important jobs to do, and it would take all day.

Cassie stood up next, looking very somber. She said that all future trips had been canceled indefinitely. She proceeded to give out assignments for the day. All base camp staff and volunteers were going to work on the islands, helping to clear away dry brush near vulnerable lodges and cabins. Finn would direct the work crews.

All the canoe guides were being sent out to check the campsites on Diamond Lake and up through Red Rock Bay, all the way north to Lake Saganaga. There were only a few people still unaccounted for in the Boundary Waters, but they needed to be found immediately. It was imperative, she said, that we check every campsite thoroughly and not miss anyone who might still be out there.

Cassie handed out fresh Fisher maps to all the guide teams, each with the specific campsites we were to check circled in black. Chuck and I were assigned to the southern half of Alpine Lake. Even though he had canoed for several miles the day before, and then all through the night, he said that he was ready to go again. He looked wiped out, but I knew he wouldn't have it any other way.

When the meeting broke, everyone swung into action. The room erupted as people headed out the door, or carried their trays back to the dish window, or met up with their work crews.

"Chuck," I said in a rush, "I'll see you down at the beach. I gotta say goodbye to Esther."

"Sure, man, I'll get the canoe ready," he replied.

"I'll be there," I said, turning to look for Esther and Aria in the chaotic mass of people. I could see the top of Esther's red hair bobbing up and down behind a big group of guys as she and Aria tried to make their way through the room to me.

Suddenly, I heard Aria shout, "Hey, freak! Move it!"

The room quieted down slightly, and the big group of guys parted like the Red Sea as both of the girls came strolling straight through the middle to me.

"Man! This is nuts!" Aria exclaimed.

"Nothing you can't handle, Bear Bait!" I exclaimed, grinning back at my fierce little friend.

"Hey, Farm Boy!" she replied, shouting above the noise. "Where are you headed?"

"Alpine Lake," I said. "How about you?"

"The west side of the island," she replied. "We're going out past Pleiades to a couple of lodges over by there."

"Leo!" Esther interrupted. "You'll be back before I leave, right?"

"Yeah, I'll try. When do you take off?" I asked.

"Right after dinner," she replied with a worried look. "Around six o'clock, I think."

"I'll be back," I said, giving her a big hug. She grabbed me and kissed me like it might be the last one we'd ever have together. Aria watched uncomfortably as we held each other close.

Esther grabbed my neck with both of her hands and whispered in my ear, "I love you, Leo."

"I love you too," I whispered back. "I'll be back, I promise!"

"See you later!" she said, clutching my hand as I turned to go.

Suddenly, two big guys pushed their way between us, and I had to move or get trampled underfoot. I waved to the girls as I waded through the crowd toward the front door. Outside, I hopped down the steps and took off for the beach.

Chuck was waiting there with my paddle and life jacket in his hands. We ran the canoe out into the water and hopped in. There were a bunch of other teams already on the lake. Some were paddling east, heading up to Saganaga. Several others were heading out west to check the multiple sites on Diamond Lake. Percy was in a canoe ahead of us. It looked like Anne was with him in his canoe.

We followed behind them and moved through the narrows between the two islands. We paddled past the sauna over the exact spot in the lake where Esther and I had been swimming earlier.

We rounded the point and passed through Heaven's Gate and the hidden beach where I had taken Esther the night before.

All the memories of the previous night came rushing back as I paddled, straining to keep up with the brisk pace Chuck was setting up in front. I was tired and sore, but it wasn't my aching muscles that were bothering me; it was my heart. As we passed the secret spot, my throat began to choke up. I let the tears come freely as we paddled hard into the wind, heading west through the cluster of islands toward the Palisades and the big open part of the lake.

Eventually, I stopped crying. Chuck never knew. The wind on Diamond Lake made our forward progress slow. The wildfires were still burning in various places on the south side of the lake. Water-scooping planes were flying directly into the smoke, dropping thousands of gallons of water on the flames every few minutes. The wind had helped the fire jump across to some islands. Given the right circumstances, it looked as if it might make the jump to the north side. I was hoping that it wouldn't.

"Pray for rain!" Chuck called from up in front.

"Yeah, and for the wind to die down!" I replied.

We didn't say much more than that. As we passed beneath the Palisades, we could see a few people standing on top—probably the U.S. Forest Service, surveying the fires. We worked our way straight across to the portage into Alpine Lake. It took a lot longer than I'd hoped. I guessed at about three hours just to get to the portage, and we still had a dozen or so campsites to check on.

It felt strange to be walking on the same trail I'd been on with Esther and Aria not twenty-four hours earlier. Chuck and I moved quickly along. We had no packs to carry, just the canoe and a small knapsack of food and first aid supplies. We raced across the portage and set out immediately on Alpine Lake. We saw Percy and Anne on the other side, paddling north. We turned south and began checking off the campsites on our map.

The south side of the lake was unrecognizable. The entire shoreline had been burned all the way down to the edge of the lake. The fire had jumped across the water and taken out one of my favorite islands in

Alpine, which had two nice campsites, one on each end. Only a few clusters of trees remained around the once-beautiful sites, and they didn't look in very good shape either. We stopped at three more campsites along the southern shore. They were completely burned to the ground. I couldn't see a single tree there that had survived the fire. Then, we curved around to the portage into Jasper Lake to check on two more sites.

"Did you see anyone on Jasper when you went through there yesterday?" I asked Chuck.

"No, we checked all those campsites. We didn't see anybody up there," he replied.

"That's probably a good thing," I said. "I don't see how anyone could've survived this fire."

"No kidding," he said. "You guys almost didn't."

As we rounded the point, I saw the portage up into Jasper Lake. The south side was totally gone. Fires were still burning along the stream. Tall tree trunks that looked like black smokestacks were sticking up all over the place. I couldn't believe my eyes. Just the day before, as we had rushed through that portage, the forest had been green and lush and beautiful, but not any longer.

The fire had obliterated almost every living thing. Whole hillsides looked scorched and bare, as the fire had consumed the trees, bushes, grass, and even the soil itself. Where there had once been a thick green forest, bare blackened rock was all that was left. The swirling smoke mixed with the gray clouds in the sky above. The water looked muddy and ashen. Everything appeared smoky, dead, and black. It was an ugly, heart-wrenching sight.

"We're not going up into Jasper, are we?" I asked again, beginning to worry about the time.

"No need to," Chuck replied. "Nobody's there. I'm sure the park rangers did a thorough check from there out west."

It was getting on into the afternoon, and we still had a few more campsites to check. Chuck and I paddled around a small bay near the falls and found three more sites burned to the ground. I'd stayed at one of them during staff training. It was totally gone.

We paddled north to find a couple more campsites on the west side of the lake. Then, we turned back east and stopped at one more site located on an island in the middle of the lake. It was the only one we found that had not been burned by the fire.

"I really gotta take a break," Chuck said, as we walked up into the campsite. He looked like he was about ready to fall over.

"Sure, let's stop here for a rest," I replied.

"Here you go," he said, tossing me the knapsack. "There's some trail mix and apples in there. I'm gonna go find the throne."

As I dug out the trail mix, I saw Percy and Anne paddling across the lake. They were heading back to the portage into Diamond. I ran down to the shore and called to them. When they saw me, they swung their canoe around and paddled over to the island.

"It's good to see you guys!" I called out. "Why don't you stop and take a break. We've got some food we'd be happy to share."

"That's great! We're starving!" Percy replied, pulling up to shore. "Go ahead and let Anne have first crack at it, though."

Anne smiled at Percy as she took a handful of trail mix and sat down. She looked worn out, but I could tell she was in heaven.

"We checked all the northern sites," Percy said. "They're all clear and mostly untouched by the fire so far."

Chuck bounded out of the woods and sat down. He looked much better after his visit to the throne. "Hey, Percy, Anne, nice to see you two. How are you holding up?" he asked.

"We're fine," Percy replied. "Anne is amazing! She's been paddling like a trouper all morning."

Anne beamed and gazed into Percy's eyes with longing and admiration. It looked as if his words were going straight to her heart. There was nothing better than receiving a compliment from the man of her dreams.

"It's getting on into the afternoon," I said, still worrying about the time. "We should get going soon."

"Yeah, we're done with all our sites," Chuck said as he cut an apple in half and handed me a piece. "We'll be on our way back to base camp here in a sec."

I bit into the apple, but I wasn't hungry; I was worried. It had to be nearly four o'clock, and it was still a couple of hours of paddling to get back to camp. I'd been fretting all day long about not making it back in time to say goodbye to Esther, and it looked as if we'd be cutting it awful close—too close for comfort.

"Okay, we're heading out," Chuck said. "Leo's got a date to keep, and we don't want him to be late for his last goodbye."

"Sure," Percy said. "Anne and I are heading back too. We can travel together . . . that is, if you can keep up with us."

We jumped back in our canoes and took off across Alpine Lake. Percy was right. He and Anne were fast. For once in my life, I was happy to be chasing after Percy as he raced on ahead of us.

"Come on, Anne!" I heard him shouting in the wind. "Let's beat those two hairballs back to camp!"

Anne smiled back at him. Then, she dug in deeper with her paddle and pulled ahead with all of her might.

"She's gonna win over that big sucker in the end," I thought to myself, "I just know it!"

"Go, Anne, go!" I whispered under my breath as I dug my paddle in deeper too.

They beat us to the portage and raced up the trail. They were already paddling out onto Diamond Lake when we got to the other side. We threw our canoe in the water and sped off after them. Out on the lake, Chuck suddenly kicked it into overdrive and pulled us up next to them. Chuck smiled casually over at Percy and then dug in again. I couldn't believe he still had any energy left. He pulled so hard, it felt like I was hardly doing anything in the back. We inched our canoe ahead of Percy and kept right on going.

"Come on, Anne!" I heard Percy shout behind us. "We can take 'em! Paddle, darling, paddle!"

I was thrilled that it had turned into a race for home. We cruised swiftly across the open stretch of the lake and shot beneath the Palisades. As we sped through the maze of islands west of base camp, I wished I'd brought along a watch. With the smoky haze overhead, I had no idea what time it actually was.

We were completely exhausted. We kept paddling, but we weren't moving as quickly as before. My hands ached from gripping the paddle for the past eight hours. My arms and shoulders felt like they were on fire. My stomach was starting to cramp up from the daylong strain on my abs. Still, we pressed on as fast as possible.

We paddled by the hidden spot, on through Heaven's Gate, and then around the point by the sauna. Suddenly, the beach came into view, and I froze in panic. I could see Esther's group boarding the Voyageur canoes by the dock, getting ready to leave.

Percy suddenly paddled up next to us, grinning like a crazed billy goat. I watched in fright as he tossed his paddle in the water and grabbed on to the back of our canoe. Then, with all of his might, he gave us a massive shove, shooting our canoe forward like a rocket through the last stretch of the lake.

"Get a move on, Leo!" he shouted. "You gotta kiss that foxy redhead goodbye!"

"Damn right!" I called back as I paddled ahead like a madman. "Thanks, Percy!"

"No problem!" he shouted. "Go get that pretty darling!"

"Will do!" I cried. "She's all mine!"

Chuck and I raced ahead as Percy watched us go. As we paddled away, I heard a scream in the lake behind us. I glanced back and was surprised at what I saw. Percy had flipped his canoe, and he was taking off after Anne in the water. I heard Anne scream with delight as he caught her and dunked her in the lake.

Anne had finally caught the man of her dreams!

chapter 60

final goodbyes

"Typical."

When Chuck and I pulled up onto the beach, I was immediately out and running for the dock. My legs felt like jello pudding, and I was breathing like a racehorse. After a few steps, I stumbled helplessly forward and did a header straight into the sand.

"Typical," I muttered to myself.

I picked myself up and walked the rest of the way to the dock. I was covered from head to toe in sand. It was stuck to the sweat on my arms and legs and even my face. Somehow, it felt like the good old days to be back there on the beach.

"Nice one, Farm Boy!" I heard Aria call from somewhere.

I didn't look. I had my eyes on Esther, only Esther. She had climbed back out of the Voyageur canoe to say goodbye. She hopped down off the dock and stood waiting for me in the sand. She was dressed to kill, just like the day she'd first arrived. I blinked my eyes and stared at her. She was barely recognizable.

I couldn't believe it was her: the same girl I'd spent the last three days with, the girl I'd kissed in my cabin last night, the girl I'd gone skinny dipping with that morning . . . the girl who said she loved me. But it was her, Esther, all decked out in her eye shadow, red lipstick, and sunglasses set on top of her head. Underneath her denim jacket, she was wearing another tight top that looked like the color of the sun going down in the west. Her long red hair was flowing down over her shoulders, and her pretty freckles swooped across her nose and cheeks, just like on the first day I'd seen her.

I was suddenly terrified that she wasn't the same person I'd fallen in love with over the past three days. It was as if she'd gone back to being the stranger that I'd met on her first day at Northern Lights. I was worried that she wouldn't even remember me and all the amazing times we'd had together.

I remembered all of them. The memories flashed before my eyes like shooting stars. I remembered seeing Esther for the first time when she arrived at camp, watching her from a distance out of the corner of my eye, listening to her talk at the dinner table, standing by the volleyball court watching the others play—looking so strong, so tough, and so beautiful. I remembered looking away and avoiding her eyes to keep from being noticed by her, to hide my fascination and intense attraction to her. I realized that she'd known all along what I had been trying so hard to hide. Each time I had looked away, she had seen me. She had always known.

I walked up to Esther, standing there smiling at me on the beach. I wrapped my arms around her waist and pulled her in close. Then, I kissed her full on the lips as if we'd just been married or something. I gave her a big long hug and held on, not wanting to let go. I didn't care what people might think of my emotional display. It didn't matter. Esther was all I cared about at that moment.

When I finally let her go, she wiped the sand off her beautiful red lips and calmly said, "You're filthy, Farm Boy."

"I didn't want to miss saying goodbye to you," I replied, gazing at her one last time. Her long red hair was more ravishing and brilliant than ever. She looked absolutely stunning. I couldn't believe I was standing there, holding Esther in front of everyone else. I couldn't believe it was our last goodbye.

She brushed the sand off my cheek and gave me a soft kiss. Then, she whispered in my ear, "You found it, you know."

I looked at her, confused, precisely as I'd done so many times before. "I found it?" I asked.

"Yeah, mate," she replied. Esther took my hand in hers and placed it over her heart. "You found it . . . right here. You found me, and I'm so glad you like what you found."

"I love what I found," I said desperately. My eyes went wet as they began to tear up.

"I know, I do too," she said tenderly. "Maybe someday we'll find each other again. Then, I'll show you even more of who I am."

"There's more?" I asked innocently.

Her warm hands wrapped around my cold fingers just like so many times before—like when we were stargazing up on Lake Saganaga, and falling asleep in the tent on Jenny Lake, and the night before in the darkness of my cabin.

"Oh, Leo!" she replied with a laugh. "You really are such a goofball sometimes. There's always more, mate."

"You're amazing," I said, trying to fight back the tears. "I'm going to miss you so much."

"I'll miss you too," she said gently. "Goodbye, for now, Leo. I hope to see you again someday."

"Goodbye, Esther," I replied. "It's time for you to fly . . . across the Milky Way on high."

"Yeah, straight up," she said with a pretty grin. "And it's time for you to rest awhile down on the western horizon."

Esther traced her fingertips slowly across my eyebrows, then down my nose and over my lips. Then, she came in close and kissed my right cheek and then my left one too. "I'm so glad we found each other this summer," she whispered softly.

"You know, you captured me," I whispered, barely able to utter my final confession as she gazed back at me so tenderly.

"And now, Leo . . . my special bro," she said, just barely above a whisper, "I need to let you go."

Our hands dropped as she pulled away from me and hopped back up onto the boat landing. With her head held high and proud, she walked down the wooden planks of the long dock to the Voyageur canoes, full of people waiting to leave the islands. It felt as if she were walking away to her own death, and there was nothing I could do to stop it. She boarded one of the canoes and sat up near the front, close to the bo'sun, who barked out orders for the paddlers to shove off and turn the canoe to the east.

I watched as the canoes moved out into the open water and across the channel to the mainland on the eastern shore. I could see them at the far dock, climbing out of the canoes, unloading their gear, then walking up into the gravel parking lot. I watched as the cars drove up the hill and out of sight, heading back down the Gunflint Trail to Grand Marais and other places far away.

A beautiful girl, tall and slender, with long red hair stood on the dock—her hair shining as if on fire in the golden sunset. She raised her arm straight up and waved one last time. I raised my hand up high and waved back to her as the light faded and the sun set behind the trees. The far shore suddenly fell into darkness. She was gone.

For a long time, I stood alone on the beach where I'd first met her. The canoes returned to the boat landing. Everyone else on the beach gradually cleared out and went off to their cabins and lodges around camp. I could hear people talking up at Starlight Lodge and others walking on a trail in the woods somewhere.

As evening fell, a gloomy mist formed over the water and slowly veiled everything around me in a shadowless haze. My only comfort was the gentle lapping of the waves on the shore as the lake became completely calm and still. Only a few dim stars were visible through a thin break in the gray clouds above. In the growing darkness, I looked off to the eastern shore one last time.

"But you've already slain me," I whispered sadly.

I walked back up above the beach to where I'd first seen Esther waving at me from the dock down below. I tried to picture her standing there, but all I could see was confused emptiness. I stood there for a while, alone, in frozen silence. Then, I left the beach and went back to . . . I don't know where—maybe the bridge, or the open-air cathedral, or maybe my cabin.

I can't remember anymore. It was over.

chapter 61
afterthoughts

"There's always more."

I didn't get to do any more trips that summer. For the next two weeks after the fire, the whole place shut down—not just Northern Lights, but almost everything on the Gunflint Trail. I didn't hear from Esther, but of course, I did a lot of thinking about her. Meanwhile, the canoe guides and camp staff worked mainly in base camp. Some of us went out on the lakes to observe the fire as it moved north and east, burning everything in its path. The fire continued to spread, and a week later, it finally burned itself out.

The firebreaks that the U.S. Forest Service put in place worked well. The fire stopped short of overrunning the Gunflint Trail and never made it close enough to do any damage to the camp. But there was renewed concern over how such a fire could have started so easily from one lightning strike. There were still thousands of acres of dead trees lying on the ground from the Big Blowdown. Everyone knew that it could happen all over again at any time.

I started to have panic attacks, not about the fire, but about Esther. They usually came early in the morning. I would wake up on my bunk just before dawn in a hot sweat, panicking, reaching for her, but she wasn't there. My dreams were vivid and intense. I would relive the last three days with her, over and over in my mind, but every time I woke up, she would be gone.

I started to wonder about the reality of it all. I began to wonder if it had all just been a dream. Had it actually happened? Would I ever hear from her again? My mind flashed back and forth between reality and fantasy, uncertain which was which, unsure of everything. I started to write it all down in my journal, which turned into two, then three journals full of memories, feelings, stories, and the quiet words we shared in our short time together.

As I wrote, I began to wonder if it were too good to be true. How could it have happened to me? But then, no, I had experienced it. I had seen it, touched it, breathed it, and lived it. It had to be true, but where was she? And why didn't she write? I was probably thinking too much about everything, but honestly, I couldn't help it. Those three days with Esther had been so amazing, so intense, so real, and so wonderful. But the longer I didn't hear from her, the more it all just felt like a fairytale.

Had she left in the same way she first appeared to me? Like a vision from heaven, like a luminescent goddess who crosses over into the physical realm, who simply walks off the boat and stands there shining in the glowing sunset; her hair ablaze, her eyes burning deep sapphire blue; seeing all, knowing all, capturing me instantly, from the very beginning, without even trying; immediately slaying me: Leo, the one who could never be caught or trapped in a cage. I'd always valued and protected my freedom, but she had captured me from the very start without my ever realizing it. She captured my heart, my love, my life, my hopes and dreams, my future . . . everything.

I didn't know if she really was Cygnus the swan or Vega shining down in Lyra from on high. Maybe she was Virgo, placed in the night sky just above Leo, nearby the entire time and so much closer to him than he could have ever imagined. Perhaps, she had been all three combined, or could she have been even greater than that? How could I ever be expected to know or understand?

The past and present began to blur hopelessly together. It got so bad, I couldn't tell the two apart. I began to relive all the memories with Esther and Aria, as if they happened yesterday, or this morning, or today. They haunt my dreams. They're all I think about now. They seem to change and grow by the hour, as if my very existence is tied directly to them. Esther is everything to me. She is my past, my present, and my future. She is everything to me now.

Our time together at Northern Lights seems to make for a pretty good story, but it's humbling to think that it actually happened to me, just as I've said. Maybe that's why it's still so hard for me to believe that it's true. But it is true—all of it, every last word.

I'm just grateful to have been a part of the story. I've told it in my own words as best as I can remember, and I hope it makes some small degree of sense. But even I, who lived it, still don't understand what it all means. I don't know if this is the end of the story or if there is more to come. It's been almost two weeks now, and I wonder about a lot of things. Where is Esther? What is she doing? I need to find her. I need to feel her gentle touch. I need to see her pretty face. I need to feel her eyes gazing intently into mine.

I desperately want all those things, and I want them right now. But as Chuck so wisely said, I need to stay the course. I need to persevere. I need to keep the faith. So, I'll try to do that now and not skip ahead to the end of the story.

After all, there were some other things that happened at the end of the summer that still need to be told. So, I apologize for this slip-up. As I mentioned before, I'm struggling to separate the past from the present, and besides, I tend to ramble on and on, especially when I don't know what to say or exactly how to say it.

So, if you're still reading this . . . that, in and of itself, is a miracle. I'll try to wrap everything up now, if that's even possible. There's just a little bit more . . . I promise.

Yeah, I know, there's always more.

chapter 62
the spanish inquisition

"Well, this has been quite nice, hasn't it?"

A couple of days before camp ended, everyone drove into Grand Marais one evening for pizza. I decided to go along, but I couldn't convince Aria to go. Ever since Esther left, she'd become more and more distant, and I knew enough to let her alone.

Everyone traveled together in a long caravan down the Gunflint Trail late in the afternoon. When we got to Grand Marais, the little town was quietly closing up shop for the night. It was still a bit of a shock for me to see street lights, city traffic, and people everywhere. After all, I hadn't been off the islands and lakes for the entire summer. The sight of "civilization" unsettled me as never before. Everyone walked around town in the fading light as we waited for tables to open up at Sven and Ole's Pizza.

When I showed up, Carly, Anika, and Jim were standing in line outside the restaurant with the rest of our group, waiting to get in. They invited me to join them, so I hopped in line. The wait was worth it. We got a table in the corner of the noisy restaurant and enjoyed some of the best pizza I could remember.

We talked about what each of us was planning to do in the fall. I didn't want to think about it, so I listened to the others do most of the talking. While we were eating, the conversation gravitated back to the summer at Northern Lights. I hadn't seen that much of Carly, Anika, or Jim since staff training.

"Hey, Leo, how was your summer?" Jim asked. He seemed more reserved than he'd been at the beginning of the summer.

"Actually, I loved it," I replied. "The time in base camp was nice, but I enjoyed being out on the lakes most of all."

"Yeah, I did too," Carly chimed in. "The summer sure flew by in a hurry, didn't it?"

"It sure did," I replied. "I didn't see you guys that much, but I made some great friends."

"Yeah, we know," Anika said quietly, "Aria Hunter and her friend, Esther, right? They were always hanging out together at camp."

"Yeah, they were awesome!" I exclaimed. "Hey, you both bunked in the girls' cabin with them, didn't you? Did you get to know them very well?"

Carly and Anika glanced at each other and grinned uncomfortably. They suddenly looked unusually nervous.

"No, not too much," Anika said. "I was kind of scared of them. They didn't talk to me very much."

"Yeah, but *they* both talked a lot," Carly broke in. "I never could understand it, though. It was always like, 'Hey, Hunter, cuzzy bro, gizza geez at this, mate!' and 'Bugger this!' and 'Bugger that!' You know, that weird Aussie talk all the time."

Carly and Anika grinned awkwardly at each other again and then looked back over at me.

"She was from New Zealand, you know, not Australia; Esther was," I said plainly.

"Oh, yeah, I forgot," Carly replied.

"What else did you think of them?" I asked, suddenly curious about their take on my two best friends from the summer.

"Esther kind of intimidated me a little," Anika said cautiously. "And Aria acted so rough and tough all the time, especially around the rest of us girls. I had a difficult time relating to her and Esther, with all that thick makeup, the tough talk, and the foreign words. She was so hard to understand."

"I mean, like, yeah!" Carly chimed in. "I only saw them a few times around the cabin. They were always running off, staying out all night, and then coming in late and waking everyone up."

"Yeah, I hung out with them a little too," I said.

"Oh, yeah! We know all about that!" Carly exclaimed.

"You do?" I asked.

"Come on, Leo!" she replied, rolling her eyes. "I mean, like, you were always hanging out with those two girls, goofing off in the dining hall, running around camp all night long, and carrying on like wild animals. I mean, what were you thinking?"

"Um, I don't know," I said, getting a little defensive. "We were just having fun. I'm sorry if we disturbed your sleep schedule."

Carly was getting worked up; I could tell. My comment about her sleep schedule didn't help either. She huffed back at me and then let into what she was really upset about.

"Nobody could even believe it!" Carly erupted. "Everyone—and I mean everyone—was totally in shock when Cassie went and let you guys go off on that . . . that threesome!"

"That what?" I asked.

"You know!" she replied. "That trip with just the three of you a couple of weeks ago, right before the wildfire destroyed half the Boundary Waters! I mean, like, nobody could believe it!"

"Yeah, that was pretty tragic," I said, referring to the fire, but on second thought, perhaps not.

"You know she's only seventeen, right?" Carly snapped back at me. "Aria, that is."

"What?" I replied, suddenly feeling ambushed by the three stooges sitting across the table from me. "No, she's eighteen. She's going off to Indiana State this fall."

"Yeah, right! Was that what she told you?" Carly shot back.

"Yeah, she did," I replied firmly.

"Good grief, Leo! She really pulled the wool over your eyes, didn't she!" Carly exclaimed harshly. Then, she leaned forward and cut loose with pent-up fury. "Aria's seventeen and still in high school, Leo! And that Esther chick—she was no little princess either! You have no idea what she was like when you weren't around. She wasn't anything like what you think she was."

"What are you talking about?" I exclaimed in complete disgust. "Esther is amazing!"

"You are, like, so totally whipped!" Carly said as she chuckled sarcastically. "Esther was a completely different person around us girls. You don't know anything about her, do you? I bet you don't have any clue about Aria Hunter either. Those two girls were like walking timebombs. We were all terrified of them both, especially when they were together. They just roamed around camp and raised hell wherever they went. They had Finn totally whipped too!"

"What exactly are you saying, Carly?" I asked bitterly, beginning to boil over with anger.

"You heard me," she hissed back with an icy stare.

I stared back at Carly. She looked completely serious, that's for sure. Anika and Jim just sat there too, looking at me with cold, blank stares. They obviously agreed with her. Suddenly, I felt as if I were sitting in front of a panel of judges, or the Spanish Inquisition itself, being sentenced to burn at the stake. A rush of anger shot through me. I wasn't about to sit around and put up with Carly's badmouthing of my best friends from the summer.

"Carly, I think you're the one who has no idea what you're talking about," I said sternly.

"Leo, you're totally clueless!" Carly countered. "You should find out more about Esther and Aria before you—"

I dropped both of my hands down hard on the tabletop and glared across at the three of them.

"We're done," I said harshly. "I've heard enough of your bullshit. It's been a very eye-opening experience."

Carly spoke up again, "Leo, we're just trying to say—"

"Is this what getting into hell is going to be like?" I pondered out loud. "I gotta have a sit-down with you three—Larry, Mo, and Curly—before I get a pass inside to go on all the fun rides?"

"What?" Carly muttered.

The three stooges stared blankly back at me, pathetically unaware of what they were talking about.

"Well, this has been quite nice, hasn't it?" I said, getting up to leave. "Here's ten bucks for the pizza and a couple more for the tip." I threw the cash down on the table and turned to walk away.

"We already paid for the pizza," Jim called to me.

With disdain, I glanced back at them, sitting there looking at each other and the money on the table. I couldn't stand to listen to Carly's stupidity any longer. I stormed out of there and walked down the street as it began to sprinkle outside. I was so mad.

It hadn't been quite nice at all. I only said that because that's what Esther would've said if she'd been there. I had learned so much from her, even that nice little parting shot.

I couldn't believe what had just happened. It was just idiotic, cruel, insensitive, ignorant, mean—the words just kept coming, rolling across my mind like the relentless waves out on Saganaga. Why would they say those things about my friends? Why did they dislike them so much? I didn't even want to know why.

I hit the road and cruised back up the Gunflint Trail in the dark by myself. I couldn't stop thinking about what Carly said about Aria and Esther. Her bitter words kept pounding away at me as it began to sprinkle outside. Could what she said actually be true? Did I really know Esther and Aria like I thought I did? Or was I merely blind to it all as she had insisted?

I couldn't believe that the others agreed with her too. What did they know? They didn't know Esther and Aria like I did. They had no idea what they were really like, did they? The questions and doubts swirled inside my pounding head the entire way back to camp. It was a miserable drive as the sprinkles turned into a downpour.

When I got back to the boat landing, it was still raining. I snatched a canoe off one of the racks and paddled back across to the islands. By the time I got to the beach, I was sopping wet. I wanted to find Aria, but instead, I headed for my cabin. As I walked up the path, I could still hear Carly's harsh words echoing in my head. In two days, it would all be over. My dream job for the summer was finally coming to an end.

Bloody hell.

chapter 63

dreams and visions

"I know, I'm still obsessing."

When I got back to my cabin, there was a letter waiting for me on the desk. A single white candle was there too, glowing in the darkness. Immediately, I thought of Aria. I thought about going to look for her, but I had to read the letter first. It was from Esther.

She said she got home to New Zealand safe and sound. Her parents were glad to see her again. She missed me, of course. She said that she got a new tattoo—Virgo, down on her right side just above Leo. It was the perfect one for her and for us.

She sent some photos along too: one of me standing in the water at Monument Portage and one of the bear cubs. Her letter was a long one. Much of it is too personal to share with anyone, but I'll include a few bits and pieces of it here. Her words mean the world to me.

"Dear Leo, I miss you so much. I hope you'll write to me often. Remember, when you get off the islands, you can always give me a ring!

Please send me the songs that you've been playing on your guitar. I can still hear them, but only as a faint memory now. Send me the words and the melodies too. I want to hear your voice and listen to your heart songs again.

We're far apart now, but know that you're still in my thoughts, near to my heart always, and with me each and every day. Don't forget, we'll never lose the memories of what we experienced this past summer.

Let's keep holding each other with open hands and see what the future brings. Remember, there's no stopping love!

Until we see each other again, I'm sending you all my love." ~ Esther

I decided not to go looking for Aria. By the time I had finished reading the letter for the tenth time, it was too late anyway. She was probably still up, though. Everyone else was. After everyone returned from the trip to Grand Marais, I could hear them talking all around camp. They were out on the bridge, back by the campfire ring, and across the narrows up at Eagle Bluff too.

Someone said it was a full moon that night, but it was too cloudy to see it. Still, it cast an eerie gray light everywhere outside as it tried to break through the clouds. I tossed and turned all night long. It was justifiably fitting, I thought, after so many sleepless nights in that cabin. The next morning, I woke up at daybreak after having another vivid dream of Esther.

I was standing at the bottom of Eddy Falls when I saw her. She was standing up high in one of the pools as the water splashed everywhere. She was alone, but I had the sense that there were people all around her too. I couldn't really see them, though. They were gray and lifeless. They didn't move, but still, they were there, like ghosts, holding hands along a distant shoreline.

All I could see was Esther, so alive and free. It felt as if I were seeing her again for the first time. Just as before, I knew that I'd never witnessed anything so beautiful in all my life. She stood there alone in the crowd, as if from another planet or galaxy, surrounded by the things of this world—the plain, the common, and the mundane.

The late afternoon sun set her red hair ablaze with golden light. Misty rays of glorious light fell down upon her, as if to christen her like a heavenly goddess, glowing and gleaming among a world of mere mortals. She was beauty, in and of itself. I saw nothing else, only her. Everything else faded in the light of her presence, standing there like a holy epiphany dropped straight out of the sky from above.

I was cut to the heart, immediately slain, and stripped of everything I'd once held so dear and so important. Gone were my fears of falling in love and my worries about how I might be hurt again. Instantly, they vanished at her appearance, as darkness vanishes at the striking of a match. All I could see was her radiant light, and I felt myself drawn to her like a helpless moth to a burning flame. I would pursue her at all costs. I would strive to know her, to be close to her, to be loved by her, or I would die trying.

Esther and I played in the waterfalls for a while. We took turns sticking our heads under the water pouring down over the rocks. We sat underneath the falls with our legs sticking straight out into the freezing water. Esther reached out and took my hand in hers. Together we walked through the pools of water as they splashed and sprayed all around us. It was like walking in heaven, like paddling across Jenny Lake again . . . as if God were smiling down on me.

As we stood next to each other, Esther looked off to the west. It was as if she knew she had to leave but didn't want to go. As she looked away, I had what can only be described as a completely new vision of how beautiful she was. It was as if a delicious awakening suddenly poured down all around me—slowly and relentlessly, like the waterfalls splashing and spraying all around us.

It was as if I were seeing her again, but with new eyes. Gone were all the trappings of this world—her rugged appearance, the dark eye shadow, and red lipstick. It was just Esther, plain and simple, a normal person like anyone else. What made her so beautiful wasn't her appearance; it was her presence in the midst of her surroundings—the trees, the waterfalls, the rocks, the sky, and the sounds of the North Woods. It was the whole of the landscape that I discovered to be so amazingly beautiful. She didn't need all the clothes and makeup. They were gone, useless, and only distracted from the truth, the real beauty that she was, surrounded by everything else.

It was as if I were falling in love with her all over again, just like the first time I'd seen her standing in the sunlight back at Northern Lights. But this time, beauty was radiating out from her, out of every part of her being—her dazzling smile, her sparkling eyes, her joyful laugh, her playful attitude, her youthful presence, the simple way she moved, how she stood there surrounded by the natural world, totally at ease with herself, with me, and with everything around her. She was one with the universe. It was in her and all around her. It had created her, and she was destined to return to it. She was content to be simply that, and it was so beautiful to behold . . . all of it.

It was amazing to be there, to be a part of it, to be close to her, to be blessed by her presence, her smile, her laughter, and her life. She made me feel so alive. She made me realize that I was all those things too, just like her, but in my own way.

Suddenly, I was standing on the beach again, looking at her from far away. It was like the first day I saw her standing on the dock surrounded by the crowd of people. She was that same mysterious girl, dressed to kill, standing there boldly with her knapsack flung over her shoulder. She looked tough as nails, intimidating, and even a bit dangerous. Then, the mysterious redheaded girl turned back to me. She smiled as she looked directly into my eyes. She lifted her arm straight up in the air and waved excitedly. I stood paralyzed and frozen in disbelief. Was she waving at me? Yes, she was!

Suddenly, it felt as if I were falling out of the sky or being pulled back into the real world. Desperately, I waved back as she drifted away into the gray evening mist. When I opened my eyes, I was back in the top bunk of my cabin at Northern Lights.

What woke me up was the deep voice of Chuck from down below. "Dude, dude," I heard him whispering. "Are you okay?"

"What?" I asked, rubbing my eyes awake. "Who me? Yeah, I'm okay. What's going on?"

"Leo, dude," he said. "You were . . . crying."

"Oh, hmm," I replied, somewhat embarrassed. I stared at the plywood ceiling for guidance, but nothing came.

"Esther again?" he asked.

"Yeah, probably," I said. "I know, I'm still obsessing about her."

"That's cool, man," he said.

"Thanks," I replied. "I just can't help it."

chapter 64

packing up

"No way!"

The last day at Northern Lights was completely different from the first one. Everyone was somber, quiet, and teary-eyed. Each group gathering included a series of sad hugs, funny memories, and dramatic promises to stay in touch. I let a few people hug me, but I really just wanted to get out of there.

In the morning, I helped Chuck straighten up the trail shack. As we worked, I realized that I was going to miss him. He had taught me so much that summer. I would always remember that first trip with him on the water—his lollygagging around in his canoe, his delicious coffee cake, his desire to go exploring deep into the North Woods, and especially how he let Nancy have her way with him.

I was ready to leave, but still, I felt an overwhelming sadness at the thought of leaving such a beautiful place behind. Memories were lurking everywhere. As I walked quietly around camp, every once in a while, something would come back to me, and I'd get a lump in my throat as I remembered what happened in that spot. Everywhere I looked, the memories came flooding back—at my cabin, down at the beach, out on the bridge, over on Eagle bluff, at the sauna, in the dining hall, and outside Esther's cabin.

Around one o'clock, everyone met in Starlight for a late lunch. When Percy saw me standing in line, he came straight up to me and gave me a big hug and a couple of pats on my back.

"Take care, Leo," he said with a big broad grin. "Don't let that redhead get away, you hear?"

“No way!” I replied. “Take care, Percy. I’ll see you next summer.”

“Probably not,” he said, “I’m off to Switzerland in a few weeks. I’m planning on staying there, maybe for a couple of years.”

“Are you taking Anne with you?” I asked.

“I asked her, but we’ll see,” he replied. “I don’t think her mom is too keen on the idea of her running off with a spoiled prince like me.”

“Yeah, well, have a nice time in Switzerland anyway,” I said.

“Will do,” he replied.

Percy grabbed a tray and turned to Andie, who was waiting behind the counter. As always, he started right in on flirting with her. She smiled back at him helplessly. I’m sure she would’ve jumped at the chance to fly off to Switzerland with him. All he had to do was ask.

“Slap one of those burgers and some fries on my plate, darling,” he said with a confident smile. “I’m starving!”

“Sure thing, Percy, whatever you say,” she replied, swooning over him one last time.

I had to laugh. Percy and I had started out the summer completely at odds with each other, but on the last day of camp, there we were, chatting and hugging each other like long-lost brothers. I was actually going to miss that big arrogant son of a sausage biscuit.

After lunch, everyone gathered in the lounge in Starlight Lodge for a closing ceremony. We sat in a big circle around the edge of the room. One after another, people stood up and shared their highlights from the summer. I didn’t stand up or say anything. I felt like if I’d done that, everyone would just stare at me and wonder what exactly Aria, Esther, and I really did on our three-day trip into the Boundary Waters. So, I just sat and listened as everyone else talked.

After the meeting, I went back to my cabin and packed my things. It didn’t take long. I couldn’t help but remember the times Esther and I had spent in that cabin—when she brought me supper, our first talk together, being surprised by Aria’s candles, and our last night together. Even with the sun shining through the screen windows, the cabin felt so cold and empty.

It was all coming to an end.

chapter 65

sunset on the lake

"Yeah, that would be so sweet."

As the afternoon wore on, the feelings began to overwhelm me. I decided to skip dinner. Instead, I went down to the beach and hung out by myself. I could hear everyone laughing and talking up in Starlight Lodge. I just wanted to be alone, but I felt so lonely too. A few minutes later, it didn't surprise me at all when Aria found me, sitting on the rocks under the bridge.

"Come on, Leo," she said. "Let's go."

"Where?" I asked.

"Out," she answered.

I knew exactly what she meant. I got up and followed her without saying a word. We walked across the bridge and took the path down to the boat landing. We quietly pushed a canoe out into the water. I hopped into the front, and Aria jumped into the back. We paddled around the eastern edge of the island, staying close to shore. Then, we headed north. The sounds of talking and laughter up in Starlight faded away as we turned west and paddled out into the big part of the lake. When we were far away from the shore, we stopped and let the canoe just float on the calm glassy water.

As I crawled back into the middle compartment of the canoe, Aria climbed forward and nestled down behind me. I leaned back into her body as she wrapped her arms tightly around my chest. Together, we watched as the sun sank deep and low on the horizon.

"You know I'm hopelessly in love with you, right?" she said.

"I know," I said quietly. "And I'm hopelessly in love with Esther."

"I know," she whispered. Then, she fell into silence again.

I knew my words hurt her, but it was the truth, and I had to be honest. I didn't know what would happen with Esther so far away. I knew what I wanted, though. Still, anything was possible.

"What are we going to do?" Aria asked.

"I don't know," I said softly, letting the silence surround us again. "This is good."

"Yeah, I guess so," she said sadly.

I hung my arms out over the sides of the canoe and dipped my fingertips into the cool water. Aria let go of my chest and slid her arms slowly out over mine. I turned my hands up and caught hers as she laid them down on top of mine. I wrapped my fingers between hers and gripped them tightly. Together we watched the clouds drift eastward and gradually change colors in the western sky.

The sun grew wider as it dropped into the humid atmosphere above the lake. The mighty star seemed so close, as if we could reach out and touch it. The ball of fire hung over the water, radiantly rich, blazing orange, and enormous. It became bigger and wider than I have ever seen before or since. As the giant star burst forth in all its dazzling glory, golden rays of light spread out far and wide to the north and south. It appeared to dissolve into the glistening lake, setting the water on fire with colors of radiant orange, golden yellow, and luminescent white. Long magnificent pillars of crystal light shot far up into the sky. Sparkling ripples skipped toward us, dancing across the water as we watched in awe.

"Let's go, Leo," Aria said, stirring behind me. "Let's just grab our stuff and go out again."

"Yeah, that would be so sweet," I replied, thinking about what it would entail. It would be a different trip—just the two of us—a quieter, more intimate one. "I'd love to, Aria, but not now."

She shifted her body behind me and then went silent again. I knew it wasn't what she wanted to hear. I had a feeling that Esther would understand it, though. I was just trying to love Aria freely and openly, exactly as Esther had done to me.

"You're gonna go after her, aren't you?" she asked.

"I don't know, maybe," I said quietly. "She's such a free spirit. Anything's possible." I released Aria's hands and spread mine out underneath hers.

"What about us?" she asked as she spread her hands out over my palms and set her fingertips gently down on top of mine.

I let her heartfelt question drift out over the waters of Diamond Lake. It was an honest inquiry full of hopeful possibilities, fanciful dreams, and long-lasting consequences for us both.

"Aria," I said gently. "You know I belong to Esther now."

"I'm sorry, Leo," she replied with a heavy sigh. "I can't help myself. I just can't seem to stop chasing you."

"I'm pretty good at not getting caught," I said with a chuckle.

"You let Esther catch you," she said.

"Yeah, I suppose so. I couldn't help it," I replied.

"And now, as usual, I'm just getting in the way," she said. "If I'm not careful, I'll find some way to hurt you again."

"That won't happen," I replied. "Esther knows we're close. She knows we're good friends."

"Friends?" Aria said quietly.

"Yeah, Bear Bait," I replied. "You know I don't want to lose you."

"That won't happen, right?" she asked.

"Let's not let it happen, okay?" I replied. "We need each other, and we need Esther too."

The words floated out over the silent lake. I wondered how Aria would deal with the uncertainty of our relationship. I had a feeling it would never be the same between us. In fact, I wondered if it might be the last time I would ever see her.

"Yeah, all right," she said quietly. That was the last either of us mentioned it for the rest of the evening.

The sun sank lower as it expanded, wider still, across the horizon. It gently kissed the earth like a lover as the moon rose jealously in the eastern sky. The fading sun seemed to pause and come to rest for one last fleeting moment, smiling above the tall pines on the distant shoreline. We watched in silence as it slowly, slowly sank behind the trees and bid us a fond farewell.

The sky gradually transformed into a deep reddish-purple, then faded further into a dusty blue, and then finally, a deeper, darker blue. The first stars and planets had already begun to shine, then more and more appeared and filled the heavens above. We looked up in reverence and wonder as the constellations took shape and moved slowly across the sky. In the growing darkness, more stars, thousands of them, filled the vast empty space until the entire expanse above the lake was full of shining lights.

Vega sparkled directly above us in Lyra, shining as brilliantly and beautifully as ever, even though it was so far away. The beautiful white swan, Cygnus, flew in the Milky Way on high, racing southwest across the sea to a land far, far away. Hercules stood guard nearby, looking for Leo as he dropped down lower and lower, crouching behind the trees above the western horizon. In the east, the mighty hunter, Orion, not yet visible, would rise later that night, following Pegasus, the winged horse, up into the evening sky.

There was a time and place for everything. Brilliant and beautiful Esther had blessed us for three short weeks that summer, then left us sadly shaken and forever changed. The time for Aria and me had come and gone as well, and it might never come again; only time would tell. I was being hunted, it seemed, not by Aria, but by my old life. I didn't want to return to it ever again. I wanted to be free, just like Esther. I wanted to escape my past and my future somehow, but all I could do was run and hide from it for a while, like Leo the lion, going down in the west, only to rise again the next morning.

We stayed out on that glassy lake for a long, long time—floating on the peaceful water, drifting aimlessly in the canoe, and gazing up at the stars and galaxies far above us in the evening sky. Together, we pointed out the familiar constellations and whispered their mysterious names to each other as we rested quietly on the sleeping water. Somewhere, someplace, far, far away, we hoped and wished and dreamed that Esther would be gazing up into the evening sky as well on that starry, starry night.

Somehow, we knew she would be too.

epilogue

whatever...

"Life goes on."

So, that's it. The story is over . . . or is it really? I feel as if I've been visited by the divine, gods and goddesses, angels, and spirits in the wilderness. Ancient wisdom somehow found its way to me, of all people, and I've been changed . . . for the better, I hope.

I'm not who I used to be, and I'll never be the same again. I see everything and everyone with new eyes. Life is more meaningful and more purposeful. It's more vibrant and colorful in all sorts of ways. It's deeper, richer, wider, and stronger. Now, life is more thought-provoking, more disconcerting, and more spiritual too.

It's because of Esther. She's a part of me now, and so is Aria. They're both in me—all our experiences, all our deep talks, and all that we've been through together. It's all a part of me. It's who I am today, what I am becoming, and what I will be someday.

I feel as if it's time for me to go now, to fly back to my place up in the night sky and rest there for a while. I wish it were so. I wish it could be like that, but it can't, not yet anyway. My life is still here on earth. My time isn't over, not just yet.

Life goes on. It continues for me, and I must live it out as best as I am able. But I see everything differently now, and it's not so easy to live anymore. It's deeper and richer, yes, but it's darker and more difficult too. It's as if my guiding lights have left me. They're far away, and I've been left alone in the dark, surrounded by the common, the mundane, the ordinary everyday stuff, the worldly things of this life, all crowding around me again.

It all seems so meaningless now—everything—the things of this world, my possessions, my appearance, my physical needs, food, water, clothing, my car, my education, my career. It all pales in comparison to what I experienced last summer.

Everyone is racing around, zooming past me, trying to get ahead, looking for their dream job, trying to find happiness, trying to fill the emptiness in their lives. I don't understand why they're in such a rush. Why can't they slow down? Why can't they just take some time to enjoy life and drink up the beauty all around them? Why can't they talk about the important things in life instead of just the weather? Why can't they stop and listen and breathe . . . and be?

I know they can feel it deep down inside, calling to them, but for some reason or another, they've failed to make the simple connection between letting go and finding life. They know something is missing, and they're looking for it like a set of lost keys, a misplaced phone, or a pair of eyeglasses. They set it down somewhere long ago, but their lives have become so full of stuff, so messy, so cluttered; they can't find what they so desperately need.

I feel like they need an intervention. They need to experience a personal crisis or have a "Come to Jesus" moment. They need to be stripped bare of everything and go jump in a lake somewhere. They need to let the whole forest burn down to the ground to allow new life to begin. But who would ever do that? How could it ever happen? Why do I feel like it happened to me?

It's not easy to explain, but it feels like the summer at Northern Lights was all that and more. My life will never be the same again. Everything is different now. I think and feel and see with entirely new eyes, with a whole new perspective on life. I've been changed. I've been freed too, to dream of what my future might be, no longer restricted by the trivial matters of this earthly life, but free to be whatever I want to be. Whatever . . .

Ever since Esther left, I've wondered about her. I've wondered why she let herself fall in love with me. Was it really me? Or was it something else? Was it because she was so far removed from her old life, her friends, and her family? Was it because she was so starstruck with the beauty and perfection of the Boundary Waters? Did she see it as a fleeting fantasy, as a summer romance that came and went in a flash, or as an ideal way to escape from a not-so-perfect life? After thinking it over and over again, I still don't know.

Whatever it was, it was beautiful. It came and went like the mysterious northern lights that appear for a while and then fade away before the dawn of a new day. Everything we shared is still so vivid and intense. I remember all of it, as if it happened yesterday. It's as if I've been staring straight into a thousand suns, and the fiery images were burned into my mind like flames of blinding light.

They're just memories now, but I'm grateful for all of them. The memories of our time together will always be mine to have and to hold, like a mysterious and mystical bride. Esther is gone now, but she will always be a part of me, and no one can take her away.

Now, at the end of the summer, I've come to realize there are deep places in my heart that have been untouched, just like so many beautiful places tucked away in the heart of the North Woods of Minnesota. They're like priceless pearls hidden in a field somewhere, or a seam of diamonds discovered deep within the earth. They're like love letters sent to me by a secret admirer, and all that I can do is simply receive them . . . gratefully.

To be given such a gift is lifechanging. I'm not who I was at the beginning of the summer. I'll never be that person again. I feel as if I've grown so much, and I've given up a lot too, but at my own choosing. I don't know exactly how, but my restless heart has found a place to rest again, a place where it's at peace. Through the events of the summer, it was softened, repaired, renewed, and healed . . . and then it was broken anyway.

Even after the fire, the pain, and the loss, I know the green trees and growing things will come back, as well as the animals, flowers, stars, and even the magical northern lights that will eventually reappear when the clouds clear. It gives me a feeling of hope for the future, even though everything seems so uncertain now. I'll always carry that feeling with me . . . when I close my eyes, when I pick up my guitar, and when I love someone deeply again.

I feel as if I've come back to life, and I'm ready to truly live again. It's because of everything that I experienced last summer. When I go back to my "normal life" at school, I'll carry the gift of knowing this place exists. It's a part of me now. It's all a part of the natural course of life . . . and death . . . of birth and rebirth.

I've come to realize, as painful as this life is, it's still so beautiful. I'll never forget the silent beauty of the Boundary Waters . . . the bright blue sky above, the deep blue waters below, and the green everywhere in between. It's all so simple, yet so incredibly breathtaking. It's all a part of me, and I'm a part of it too.

I never could have anticipated what happened to me this past summer. It's not easy to explain, but I have a sense that it's just the beginning. I feel as if there's so much more to learn about the world and about myself too. There's a narrow path laid out before me. It'll be a beautiful journey, and I must choose to take it wherever it leads. I've been avoiding it for far too long. The time has come, and I feel as if I'm ready to do the difficult work of living again. Whatever happens, whatever is meant to be, I'm ready to accept it with joy and gratefulness . . . and with open hands.

Since the summer's end, I've reconnected with my first love again: time alone in the quiet stillness of nature to think, walk, write, and dream. It's in those times apart, away from normal life, where my spirit is refreshed and renewed. It's in the quiet, solitary, and often silent times that I feel the most connected to life, the most alive, the most at peace, and the closest to the divine. I feel as if my spirit has been renewed, and I've been completely reborn.

It doesn't just happen, though. You have to go looking for it. You have to listen for it, and there might be some waiting involved too. But if you're patient, it will speak to you . . . through a misty sunrise, under a starry sky, out on a glassy lake, along a trail through the forest, or in the faint glow of the mysterious northern lights. In those quiet moments, your spirit will be reborn. Your emptiness will be filled. You will find a renewed perspective on life, a deeper meaning to your existence, and a clearer direction for your future. You will encounter a still, small voice speaking to you . . . in the silence.

The gods and goddesses are up there somewhere, looking down on us and watching with keen interest to see what we will become, to see what we will do with our time on this earth, to see if we will overcome ourselves and rise one day to join them in the sky.

I think it's possible, but I believe it's up to us. I believe it's in us, hidden somewhere deep down inside. We just have to find it. We just have to open our hearts and accept it freely. We just have to learn to love each other, take care of each other, and talk to each other on a deeper, more meaningful level. When we do that, anything is possible in this world . . . and the next.

Anything, absolutely anything, is possible.

thank you!

Dear reader,

Thank you for reading Northern Lights. I hope you enjoyed it. As you probably figured out, there is a lot woven into the story, and it certainly hasn't come to an end quite yet. If you liked the story, rest assured, the sequel is on the way.

I would love to hear what you think of the Northern Lights story. Other people might appreciate what you have to say too. If you like, please feel free to write your own review of it at Amazon or wherever you purchased the book. If you have comments or questions about anything, I can be reached at my Goodreads profile page. I'd love to hear from you.

If you'd like to know more about the creation of Northern Lights, you can check out my website at www.leosolstrom.com. I will post more info about the next book when it is ready. I really do love the Boundary Waters, and I get up there often. I'll be sure to post some photos and highlights from those trips too.

As you know, in the story I hinted at being a songwriter of sorts. Esther asked me to write my songs down and send them to her. Well, I did just that! You can listen to the music from the Northern Lights story at my website or via other streaming services. I'm certain you'll recognize various parts of the story in the music. Hopefully, they capture a bit of what many people find so amazing and beautiful about the Boundary Waters.

Thanks again for spending some time on the lakes with me in the North Woods of Minnesota. I hope you will return to read the next part of the story. I'll try to finish it soon!

Sincerely,
Leo Solstrom

acknowledgements

"Nature and Selected Essays" by Ralph Waldo Emerson. Copyright 1982 Penguin Classics, New York, New York.

"The Sacred Journey: Prayers and Songs of Native America," Watercolors by Claudia Karabaic Sargent. Selected and Edited by Peg Streep. Bulfinch Press, Boston. Copyright 1995 by Peg Streep and Claudia Karabaic Sargent.

"Peter Pan," by James M. Barrie. Copyright 2004 The Modern Library, Random House, Inc., New York, New York.

"The Poetry of Robert Frost: The Collected Poems, Complete and Unabridged," by Robert Frost, Edward Connery Lathem (Editor), First Owl Book Edition, Copyright 1979. Henry Holt and Company, Inc., New York, New York.

"Skyguide: A Field Guide to the Heavens," by Mark R. Chartrand. Golden Press, New York. Copyright 1990 Western Publishing Company, Inc.

"An Instant Guide to the Stars and Planets," Pamela Forey and Oliveria Fitzsimons. Consultant Editor Ian Ridpath. Gramercy Books, New York. Copyright 1988 by Atlantis Publications Ltd.

"The Bible," by various authors, especially Jesus. Yeah, of course. Copyright expired long, long ago.

kiwi slang

Yeah, I know, mate! Esther says some pretty weird stuff sometimes. If you're not sure what she means, have a squiz at some of her sayings here in an abbreviated dictionary of New Zealand slang. I've had fun learning each of them, and I can't help how some have slipped into my everyday life too. Maybe they will for you as well.

A into G: ass into gear (get going)
Ace: excellent, the best
All good: okay, fine
As: used to emphasize an adjective, i.e. "Sweet as!"
Away with the fairies: daydreaming
Awesome: okay, used to begin sentences a lot
Bang on: dead on
Beached as: to be stuck
Beaut: ironic, excellent
Belt up: shut up
Biscuit: cookie, cracker
Bit of a worry: troubling event
Bivvy: tent
Bloody hell: expression of anger, disgust, or surprise
Blow out: to leave
Bogan: a redneck, hick, or unsophisticated person
Box of budgies: cheerful, happy, literally "box of parakeets"
Brassed off: annoyed
Brekkie: breakfast
Bro: a good friend
Buck: man
Buck up: cheer up
Bugger: a New Zealand curse word
Bum: butt
Bush: wilderness

Bush oyster: hard snot
Bush telly: campfire
Bushman: man of the bush
Bust a gut: make an intense effort
Bust it: expression of frustration
Carked it: died
Cheeky: sassy
Cheers: thanks
Chilly bin: ice cooler
Choice: okay, sure, awesome
Chum: friend
Clicks: kilometers
Clock: punch
Collywobbles: upset stomach
Corker: excellent person or event
Crack onto: to hit on someone
Crack up: funny
Cracker: something excellent
Crib: holiday home
Crikey: wow
Crook: ill
Cuz, Cuzzy bro: affectionate term for a good friend
Dipstick: idiot
Dodgy: bad, unreliable
Double-bunk: sleep two to a bunk
Eh: don't you think?
Faaaaaa: wow, far out
Fancy: to like, to be attracted to
Fizzy drink: soda pop
Foxton fizz: New Zealand brand of soda
Friend's discount: a discount or favor given to a friend
Fully: totally, completely
Gawk: stare
Get the willies: become afraid
Give it a buck: give something a try

Give it a go: to try something
Gizza geez: let me have a look
Going bush: leave to be alone
Good as gold: everything is fine
Grotty: disgusting
Hard out: totally, you agree
Heaps: a lot
Holiday: vacation
Hughie: the fancied weather-god of trampers
Hunky dory: everything is fine
Jaffa: orange-chocolate candies
Jandals: flip flops
Jersey: sweater, pullover
Johnny cake: pancake
Joker: bloke, chap, fellow
Jumper: sweater, pullover
Jungle juice: strong liquor
Keen: enthusiastic about something
Kiwi: New Zealander
Knickers: underpants
Lollies: sweets, candy
Long-drop: outhouse
Loose unit: clueless person
Mad: crazy
Mate: you, friend
Mean as cat's piss: extremely mean, angry
Mission: a difficult undertaking
Mozzies: mosquitoes
Mum: mother
No worries: don't worry about it, it's all right
Not even ow: expression of sadness, disappointment
Not even: not true
Nuddy: naked, in the nude
Oldies: parents
Out on one's own: excellent, beyond reproach

Pack a sad: depressed
Paddock: any piece of land marked off by a fence or boundary
Pashing on: making out, kissing
Perk: to get as a gift or by pilfering
Piece of piss: easy to accomplish
Piker: a person who doesn't want to socialize
Piss-awful: extremely awful
Plate: a dish of one's choice brought to a social event
Poofter: a know it all, full of hot wind
Potsticker: dumpling with juicy filling cooked brown on one side
Quite nice: said to mean the opposite
Ra ra ra: etcetera
Rattle ya dags: hurry up
Reckon: think
Rellies: relatives
Right proper: appropriate, correct
Ripper (Ripping): excellent, an exclamation of delight
Rooster: cocky fellow
Scroggin: Trail mix
She'll be right: it'll be okay
Ship-girl: sexually promiscuous woman
Shut your cake-hole: shut your mouth
Sick: awesome
Skux: hot-looking
Skux deluxe: extremely hot-looking
Snarky: sarcastic or snippety
Snooker: a hiding place
Sparrow: referring to the crack of dawn
Spew (Spewin'): to vomit
Spewin': very angry, throwing an angry fit
Spot on: exactly right
Spotcha later: see you later
Squiz: take a look, have a peek at
Star hotel: the outdoors at night
Stoked: very happy, excited about something

Straight up: to agree or say absolutely
Stuffed: tired, exhausted
Sunnies: sunglasses
Suss: suspicious, questionable
Sweet as: that's okay, sounds good
Swiftie: a trick or deception
Ta: thanks
Take-aways: carryout food
Tata: goodbye
Tea (Teatime): the evening meal, between 5-7 p.m.
Thanks: please
Throw a Hollywood: to pretend to be sick or injured
Throw a wobbly: to throw a temper tantrum
Tiki-tour: the long way around
Togs: swimsuit
Too right: exclamation of agreement
Torch: flashlight
Tramping: hiking around
Turn it up: to agree to have sex
Unreal: excellent, awesome
Up on themselves: arrogant, self-centered
Waka: canoe
Wayback: the remote back-country
Willie-waw: a sudden violent gust of wind
Wop-wops: the middle of nowhere
Yabber: talk a lot
Yak: talk
Yarn: story
Yeah, nah: no

www.ingramcontent.com/pod-product-compliance
Lightning Source LLC
Chambersburg PA
CBHW020354310726
48979CB00015B/2590/J

* 9 7 8 1 7 3 5 8 5 0 8 2 5 *